IN TOO DEEP

Simon McCleave is a bestselling crime novelist. His first book, *The Snowdonia Killings*, was released in January 2020 and soon became an Amazon bestseller, reaching No.1 in the UK Chart and selling over 200,000 copies. His eight subsequent novels in the DI Ruth Hunter Snowdonia series have all ranked in the Amazon top 20 and he has sold over a million books worldwide.

Before he was an author, Simon worked as a script editor at the BBC and a producer at Channel 4 before working as a story analyst in Los Angeles. He then became a script writer, writing on series such as *Silent Witness*, *Murder in Suburbia*, *Teachers*, *The Bill*, *EastEnders* and many more. His Channel 4 film *Out of the Game* was critically acclaimed and described as 'an unflinching portrayal of male friendship' by *Time Out*.

Simon lives in North Wales with his wife and two children.

www.simonmccleave.com

IN TOO DEEP

SIMON McCLEAVE

avon.

Published by AVON
A division of HarperCollins*Publishers*
1 London Bridge Street
London SE1 9GF

www.harpercollins.co.uk

HarperCollins*Publishers*
Macken House,
39/40 Mayor Street Upper,
Dublin 1
D01 C9W8
Ireland

A Paperback Original 2023

First published in Great Britain by HarperCollins*Publishers* 2023

A catalogue copy of this book is available from the British Library.

ISBN: 978-0-00-852485-2

This novel is entirely a work of fiction. The names, characters and incidents
portrayed in it are the work of the author's imagination. Any resemblance to
actual persons, living or dead, events or localities is entirely coincidental.

Typeset in Sabon Lt Std by Palimpsest Book Production Limited,
Falkirk, Stirlingshire

Printed and bound in the UK using 100% Renewable Electricity
at CPI Group (UK) Ltd

This book is produced from independently certified FSC™ paper
to ensure responsible forest management.

For more information visit: www.harpercollins.co.uk/green

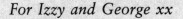

For Izzy and George xx

ANGLESEY

There is a word in Welsh that has no exact translation into English – Hiraeth. It is best defined as the bond you feel with a place – a mixture of pride, homesickness and a determination to return. Most people that have visited Anglesey leave with an understanding of Hiraeth.

PROLOGUE

Castell Aberlleiniog, Isle of Anglesey, North Wales
November 1999

Midnight. A haze of moonlight cast a silvery hue upon the steep grassy hilltop that gazed vigilantly over the Menai Strait to the south-eastern tip of Anglesey. It had once been home to an imposing medieval castle. On the far side of the summit, a freshly dug grave that had just been refilled with earth, patted flat, then hidden with branches and an array of gold, red and lemon-coloured autumnal leaves. A body had been placed into that earth with a suitable degree of care and reverence fifteen minutes earlier. The salty night air was getting icy and the man could feel the cold sweat on his brow and on his back as he put down the spade. Its wooden handle had rubbed the skin on his palms and they were now sore. It had been a long time since he'd done this much manual work. The grave might have been relatively shallow, but digging it was strenuous work.

A woman stood nearby, holding a large torch to illuminate his grisly work. She looked around as her anxiety grew.

The man wiped his brow with his cuff. 'What do you think?'

1

'I think it's done,' she replied hastily. 'I think we should go.'

For a moment, they both gazed at where the body lay and wondered about the repercussions of what they'd done, and the ramifications of its possible discovery. The rhythmic hoot of an owl, high in a nearby tree, broke the silence and added to the tense, ominous atmosphere.

Around them, the broken grey stones of castle battlements were spread out in the darkness where the mighty Castell Aberlleiniog had once stood. On the far side was the base of a broad rampart, fractured parapets, and the crumbled outlines of circular towers. The timber and earth of the original motte-and-bailey Norman castle had vanished centuries ago. But the stone fortifications only dated back to the sixteenth century. The very earth of this place was full of dark stories that went back over a thousand years to the siege of 1094, where over a hundred Norman soldiers had died defending the battlements from the Earl of Chester. These days, the place was overgrown, neglected and forgotten.

Giving the grave a final ceremonial scatter of leaves, the man was satisfied it was now adequately camouflaged. He met the woman's eyes with a look of solemn trepidation that reflected his fear. It didn't matter that this was a crime of necessity, not malice.

'Okay. We should get going,' he said quietly as he leaned down, grabbed the spade from the ground and pointed to the footpath that led down to where they'd parked the car.

'What if no one finds him?' the woman asked.

The man raised an eyebrow. 'Don't worry; they will.'

That was the perverse irony of their crime.

They wanted someone to discover the shallow grave. In fact, they *needed* their malevolence to be uncovered.

And the sooner, the better.

CHAPTER 1

Beaumaris, Anglesey
September 2021

Detective Inspector Laura Hart looked up from where she'd just thrown herself to the ground. The skin on her hands and knees was grazed and bleeding.

What the hell just happened?

Dizzy, trying to piece everything together, she sat up, adjusted her Kevlar bulletproof vest and shook her head to clear it. *Jesus!* She knew it was August 2018. She knew she was part of a police operation at the Brannings Warehouse in West Manchester. But there was something else that was making her feel sick with anxiety. And then it came to her.

Oh my God! Sam!

PC Sam Hart, her husband, was being held captive by a drugs gang inside the disused warehouse that loomed over her.

I've got to get him out of there. The place is rigged with explosives and covered in petrol, she thought as fear overwhelmed her.

A burly-looking firearms officer reached down and helped

3

pull her to her feet. He looked at her with his blackened face. 'Don't worry,' he gasped, his throat raw from the fumes. 'I'm going back in. I'll get him out.'

She looked at the officer and his confident, reassuring expression. She trusted he would do exactly what he'd promised.

Suddenly, without warning, the air shredded with a thunderous noise. The windows along the front of the warehouse exploded in a torrent of bright orange fire and a hail of glass.

For a split second, Laura watched in horror as the entire building erupted and shook, before the force picked her up and hurled her backwards through the air.

Then a terrible long silence.

No! Please, God, no! Sam was in there. He couldn't have survived that.

Blinking open her eyes with a start, Laura fully expected to see the burning shell of the Brannings Warehouse above her.

She gasped a panicky breath. *Where the hell am I?*

Instead she saw a dimly lit bedroom – *her* bedroom. The chrome bedside reading light had been left on and a copy of Richard Osman's *The Thursday Murder Club* was open on top of the smoothed-out duvet that covered her from the waist upwards. With her pulse still racing from her nightmare, she took a long, deep breath. She reached over and took a sip of water.

Jesus, my chest feels tight, she thought as she blew out her cheeks.

It had been over three years since that horrific day in Manchester. The day Sam had been so cruelly taken away from her. Laura had managed to rebuild her life close to the picturesque town of Beaumaris on the Isle of Anglesey, just off the North Wales coast – the place where she was born and grew up. Her children – Rosie, eighteen years old, and

4

Jake, eleven years old – had mixed feelings about the move. If Rosie described Beaumaris as *provincial* and *boring* one more time, Laura thought she'd scream. But Rosie was in her final year at school and was looking at universities. The promise of three years in Leeds, Cardiff or even London had eased some of Rosie's grouchiness.

Like his late father, Jake was an ardent Manchester United fan, so the move away meant trips to Old Trafford were virtually impossible. However, the slower pace of island life – the beach, the sea, the countryside – suited Jake's more introverted, sensitive personality. He was starting to recover from events in June, when he'd been taken hostage by Liverpudlian gangsters who were on the run. After all they'd been through as a family, it was the last thing Jake needed and had done little to build his confidence in the world. He'd received counselling but still had nightmares about what had happened.

Gazing around her bedroom, Laura's mind was momentarily drawn to more mundane things. She noted that there were still a few things to do. The old pine chest of drawers she'd brought with her when she and the kids had relocated was on its last legs. In fact, one of the smaller top drawers wouldn't even close.

It had been Sam's sock drawer.

She remembered so vividly the jumbled mess of socks that used to live in there and Sam's inability to wear a matching pair. His work socks needed to be some shade of black or grey, but the colours of heels or toes or the slogans were never coordinated. For Sam, it was an amusing eccentricity that he took pride in. He was a uniformed police officer, so his mismatching socks were as rebellious and individual as he could get on a work day. A sudden feeling of loss swept over her. What she would give to have him standing here in his pants and socks, giggling at the slogan on the sole: *If you can read this – bring me the remote and a beer.* Laura bit her lip and took a breath. She didn't want to cry. Not today.

Trying to distract herself from her grief, she resolved to buy a new chest of drawers – one that matched her attempt at some kind of fashionable colour scheme. She'd gone for an olive-green accent wall with matching bedding, which she'd seen in some glossy Sunday supplement magazine.

Throwing her legs over the side of the bed, she saw both her swimming kit and her work clothes laid out neatly. Well, when she said work clothes, she hadn't actually worn her new charcoal-grey trouser suit yet.

Feeling a little tremor of nerves, she took another deep breath.

Christ, this feels worse than my first day at secondary school, she thought as her stomach tightened.

After three years away from the police force, Detective Inspector Laura Hart had passed both her physical and psychological North Wales Police tests and was deemed fit enough to return to work.

Putting on her swimming kit, she glanced at the bedside clock: 6.28 a.m. The sun was about to rise and it was time to get to the beach.

After tiptoeing along the soft carpet of their landing, she went downstairs, through the hallway and headed for the back door. Elvis, her beautiful caramel-and-white Bernese mountain dog, looked up with his doleful chestnut eyes and got to his feet.

They went outside and Elvis padded across to a piece of grass, which he sniffed noisily. Then he went for a thirty-second wee, as he did every time they made this early morning trip to Beaumaris beach – three times a week if possible.

Even though autumn had arrived, the morning air was still mild. Smoothing back her blonde hair as she marched down the hill, Laura tied it into a tight ponytail. Elvis trotted by her side in his usual nonchalant manner. Whenever they met other dog walkers, especially those with small, yappy dogs, Elvis would take on an arrogant air of superiority. He never barked back. Instead, he'd give the other dogs a withering look as if to say, *What on earth are you doing? I'm ten times the size of you and could send you flying with a flick of my paw.*

An elderly woman came striding round the corner and gave Laura a friendly wave. She was holding a rubbish bag and a litter-picker stick. Mel Thompson, now in her seventies, had been Laura's English teacher at secondary school. They met at this point on the uneven pathway to the beach at least once or twice a week.

'Morning, Laura,' Mel chirped as she stopped, slightly out of breath.

Her husband, Bob, had died two years ago, so she'd thrown herself into community projects such as keeping Beaumaris beach free from litter.

'Much down there?' Laura asked, pointing to the rubbish bag.

'It's pretty clear now the summer's over,' Mel explained with a smile. 'How are the kids?'

'Jake's much better. And Rosie is looking at universities.'

'Oh, gosh, that does make me feel old,' Mel laughed. 'I remember the day you came to tell me you'd got into Manchester. And that feels like yesterday.'

Laura nodded. It still baffled her how she herself could be heading for fifty. 'Tell me about it.'

'Well, enjoy your swim,' Mel said. 'And pop into the shop if you ever fancy a cup of tea and a natter.'

Mel worked a few days a week at the Cancer Research charity shop in the middle of Beaumaris.

'You know what, that sounds like a great idea,' Laura said. 'See you soon.'

'Bye, Laura,' Mel said as she turned and carried on walking up the hill.

Laura strolled on for a few minutes, reminiscing about Mel's brilliant lessons on *Death of a Salesman* by Arthur Miller for A-level English. She remembered how they'd had to read the play as a class and attempt American accents, much to their amusement.

Above her, the dark sky seemed vast and endless. She called it her *big sky*, which she remembered was a phrase that originated from the inhabitants of Montana to describe the enormity of the sky over the flat Great Plains of that particular state. In her book, it applied as much to Beaumaris as it did to Montana.

Gazing across the Menai Strait towards the Welsh mainland, she saw that the sun had started to flush the thin clouds a deep flamingo pink. The ragged mountainous ridges of Snowdonia were still colourless but would soon be washed with a plum created by the light of early morning. It was a stunning landscape to witness first thing and she reminded herself never to take it for granted. It was the view she'd grown up with and it grounded her.

Laura stopped on the damp sand and stood for a while, just gazing at the view. Recollections of the ghosts of her childhood and those of a more recent past seemed more prevalent than usual. The time her taid – Welsh for grandfather – had taken her and her sister, Emma, to the beach and they'd used a stick to spell out their names in huge letters on the sand. Then they'd sat and watched until the tide came in and washed them away.

Maybe her reassessment of the past was due to the anxiety of returning to the police force. After all, she'd resigned three years ago, realising that the trauma of Sam's death had made it impossible for her to do her job properly anymore.

Just get on with it, Laura, she said to herself as she took off her pink Nike hoodie and black trackies so that she was now just wearing her navy swimsuit. When it got really cold, she'd resort to wearing neoprene swimming gloves and a cap. But the water was still relatively warm – 16 degrees Celsius – as it had retained much of the heat from the summer.

Resting close to where she'd placed her things was a tangle of beautiful driftwood, which had been smoothed by the sea and then blanched to an exquisite pale grey colour by the sun. Maybe she'd take some back with her and she and Jake could make some kind of driftwood sculpture at the weekend.

With a sudden desire to experience that giddy, icy rush once again, she marched down towards the waves, her toes sinking deeper and deeper into the wet sand. The sea looked so inviting and before she knew it, she'd ploughed through the water and dived into an oncoming wave. For a second, she went under the cold water and all sound disappeared. Then she broke the surface as her nerve endings were blasted with the shock of the temperature. Taking a huge breath, she smiled. Her whole body burned with an icy sting. Her head was suddenly clear and the anxiety had evaporated from her whole being.

Cold-water swimming was so addictive. It anchored her and made her feel glad to be alive. Lying on her back, she kicked her legs and swam further out. She gazed up at the sky, enjoying how the sea had numbed her scalp and thoughts. With her arms outstretched, she floated and bobbed gently. She was a minuscule dot on a tiny planet in an endless universe. That's the other thing that open water swimming gave her: a reassuring perspective of her absolute insignificance.

'Christ, it's cold in here,' exclaimed a voice. 'I thought you said it was still warm in September.'

It was Sam.

Righting herself in the water, Laura smiled over at him.

His piercing blue eyes twinkled at her as he used his hands to sweep his wet hair back.

He was so handsome. I forget that sometimes. I got used to his face.

'I thought you'd sworn not to come here again,' Laura laughed.

'Wild swimming makes me feel alive,' he joked darkly.

'Very funny.' Laura rolled her eyes, but she found his black humour made her uneasy this morning. 'I haven't seen you since last week. What's going on?'

'I told you,' Sam shrugged. 'The more you get on with your life, the less I can be around.'

She didn't want to think about that. It was so hard to think about letting him go. It was too painful to contemplate letting the memory of him fade.

'Did you miss me, then?' he asked with a boyish grin.

Laura ignored her sadness and teased, 'You're so needy sometimes.'

'First day at work,' he stated with a raised eyebrow as he swam gently towards her. 'How does that feel?'

'Scary, exciting,' she admitted. 'But you know, it's what I always wanted to do. And having a couple of years on civvy street just clarified that for me.'

'You're going to smash it. And they're lucky to have you. Beaumaris CID is hardly inner-city Manchester though, is it?'

'Yeah, well, I'm not going in with that attitude,' she snorted dryly.

'Ooh, and you'll be working for DI Dickhead, which will be nice for you,' Sam said caustically.

He was referring to Detective Inspector Gareth Williams, who was in charge of Beaumaris Crime Investigation Department (CID). She and Gareth had been having an on-off relationship since they got together in July. Work, kids and

Gareth's messy divorce meant that it had been a series of frustrating false starts.

'Gareth isn't a dickhead,' Laura protested a little too forcefully as she scowled at Sam. 'Needy and jealous. You're not exactly covering yourself in glory this morning, are you?'

'Hey, I'm just looking out for you,' he protested as he turned onto his back and swam a few yards away from her.

As he turned, she saw a playful smile develop on his face. She missed that smile so much that it was painful to remember it. She frowned. She knew he was jealous.

'Yeah, I'm pretty sure that's *not* what you're doing, Sam.'

'Okay,' Sam said in a smug tone. 'Just don't say that I didn't warn you.'

Without waiting for her reply, he turned and dived under the water.

Watching the surface of the sea for few seconds, she soon realised that Sam had gone for now.

Bloody typical! Have the last word and then sod off, Laura bristled angrily.

The irony of cursing a construction of her imagination born from grief and pain wasn't lost on her.

Time to face the day, Detective Inspector.

CHAPTER 2

Wadi Hauran, Western Iraq
Operation Desert Storm, 1991

It had been three hours since the RAF Squadron 7 Chinook helicopter had secretly dropped an eight-man SAS unit into the north-western Iraqi desert under the cover of darkness. Now behind enemy lines, the first part of their mission was to disrupt the three MSRs – main supply routes – that ran west to east from Baghdad into Jordan. The second, to locate and destroy Iraqi Scud missile bases.

At over thirty-five foot in length and weighing 6,000 kilos, the Scud missile had a range of over 200 miles and was deadly. According to US intelligence, the Iraqis had five fixed missile sites. They'd also developed a force of mobile launch units using civilian heavy goods vehicles. And most worrying of all, the Iraqis had both chemical and nuclear warheads that could be attached to a Scud at any location. The unit, codenamed *Charlie Alpha One*, needed to find and disable as many as they could find.

Corporal John 'Paddy' Kelly knew they were now on their own for ten days before resupply. He wasn't complaining.

This is what he'd spent two years of rigorous training for. His stomach flitted with anxiety as they trudged silently up a gorse-strewn dune, boots slipping backwards on the sand.

The freezing desert wind bit into every inch of his exposed skin. He kept his arms tight to his sides, head down, shoulders shrugged to lessen the wind chill. His hands were frozen and numb. He estimated it couldn't be much above zero degrees centigrade as he crooked his thumb over the luminous part of the prismatic compass and checked the unit was heading in the right direction.

Looking good so far, he thought. *Nice and steady.*

The ground had slowly changed to bedrock with shale, which was dangerously noisy underfoot. For once, the howling wind was a blessing, as it covered the sound of their footsteps. Gazing up into the sky, he saw that the half-moon had now disappeared and in the distance the horizon was showing the faintest touches of indigo as dawn approached.

Born in Newry in Northern Ireland, like most of that town, John was brought up as a Catholic. Known as the Gateway to the North, Newry sat on the Irish border, between the Mourne Mountains and the Ring of Gullion. In 1986, John joined the Irish Guards Regiment, affectionately known as 'The Micks', when he was eighteen. To say that becoming a soldier in the British Army wasn't a popular career choice with his staunch republican family was an understatement. He had an uncle and two cousins who refused to speak to him from the moment they heard the news. But John had become sick of the hatred and politics, and joining the army was both his ticket out of Newry and an act of teenage rebellion.

The regiment was immediately posted out to Belize in Central America. When they told him where they were flying into, John hadn't got a clue where it was. He guessed it was in the Middle East and to his delight, Belize had a glorious Caribbean coastline. It was so far removed from Newry and everything he'd ever known that John felt as if he were on a different planet.

From there, the regiment was sent to West Berlin, where John worked undercover with MI5, engaging in forays into East Berlin to deliver documents and communicate with agents. Not only did John find he was physically and mentally strong, but he also had an instinctive feel for working behind enemy lines. He was recruited into the SAS – Special Air Service – at the end of October 1989, a few days before the fall of the Berlin Wall.

An hour later and the temperature of the Iraqi desert was thankfully rising slowly as the tangerine sun burned away the early morning clouds. The sandy limestone ground had cracked in dark, jagged patterns and an upside-down, broken wooden canoe lay to the right. The banks either side were covered in scrubs and grasses that swayed gently in the dusty morning breeze. From somewhere came the tinkling bell of a goat. The unit came up over a ridge and saw a vast, flat, dried-up riverbed stretching out before them for what looked like miles. Wadi Hauran was the longest dry riverbed – or wadi in Arabic – in Iraq. Running for over 350 kilometres, it was situated halfway between Damascus and Baghdad.

Looking out at the endless terrain, John began to worry. The topography was too flat, which made finding any decent cover incredibly difficult. If they were spotted, they'd be sitting ducks. They needed to keep as close to the banks as they could.

Neil 'Sparrow' Roberts, a lithe Welshman with cropped blond hair, looked at John as they squinted at the rising sun. He wiped beads of sweat from his forehead, pulled out his black-and-white cotton shamagh, and wrapped it around his head and mouth.

'This season, I'll be mainly wearing Dolce & Cabanna,' Sparrow joked.

John rolled his eyes. 'It's Gabbana, you dickhead.'

'Whatever,' Sparrow laughed. 'These Arabs have got the right idea. This is a lot more comfortable than a bloody baseball cap.'

The tinkling of the goat bell grew louder and was joined by another bell.

John and Sparrow exchanged looks. They didn't want to run into a local shepherd – they didn't want to run into anyone who might raise an alarm to their presence.

The patrol continued west for another ten minutes, hugged close to the dry riverbanks for cover. Each man kept himself a decent distance from the man in front as a tactic to minimise casualties in the event of an attack.

Stopping for a well-earned break, they took off their huge bergens, drank water and ate chocolate to keep their blood sugar up as they sat silently with their backs to the bank. Then the compass and maps were checked again.

In the distance, they could hear the rumbling sound of explosions from Allied bombing raids that were taking place forty to fifty miles to the north-east. Even from where they were sitting, they could see tracer fire going up from Iraqi positions and flashes of the 2,000-pound penetrator bombs being dropped by F-117A Nighthawks.

God bless the Yanks and their stealth bombers. The Ali Babas didn't stand a bloody chance!

Suddenly, the silence was broken by the deep growl and reverberations of an Iraqi tracked vehicle coming their way.

They froze.

Shit!

It was impossible to know which direction the vehicle was coming from.

John gave the signal. The unit checked their weapons. His

15

adrenaline was pumping and his breathing was shallow. Crouching down, the men fanned out and found what cover they could along the sandy riverbank. If it was just a reconnaissance vehicle, they'd be all right. If it turned out to be an armoured personnel carrier, such as the Panhard VCR, then it was a whole different ball game. The VCR came with a 20mm automatic cannon mounted to its roof plus an anti-tank missile turret.

As John loaded and checked his L110 Minimi machine gun, he could see his hands shaking.

This is it. Come on. You've got this, John.

Once they engaged the enemy, he knew he needed to keep calm, focused, and trust in the repetitive training.

The armoured tracks screeched and the engine's high revs sounded like thunder. It felt like the vehicle was right on top of them.

John held his breath.

Jesus Christ! Here we go.

'Can you see them yet?' Sparrow shouted down the line.

John shook his head grimly. 'I can't see a bloody thing.'

Come on, come on. You can do this.

His heart was hammering and his stomach felt tight and tense.

CRACK! CRACK! CRACK!

There was sudden gunfire from further down the line. One of their unit had engaged the enemy.

BOOM!

The armoured vehicle fired an anti-tank missile in their direction. It exploded with a deafening blast, throwing an enormous plume of sand into the air.

CRACK! CRACK! CRACK!

The air was filled with the sound of gunfire and shouting. They were now in a firefight. It was a question of accuracy, ammunition conservation and firepower. The Iraqis had more troops and far superior firepower with the VCR, but their soldiers lacked training and organisation.

John crawled to the top of the dry riverbank, keeping as low as he could. Spotting two Iraqi soldiers running for cover, he let off three bursts with his Minimi. There was a yell of pain – he must have clipped one of them as they scuttled behind a shrub-covered mound.

John looked at Sparrow, whose eyes were wide as the adrenaline pumped through his veins.

'Covering fire on three,' John hollered to him.

Sparrow gripped his machine gun, readied himself and gave him the nod.

'One, two, three,' John yelled as he hauled himself over the edge of the riverbank and sprinted across the flat ground, heading for the cover of gorse and dips in the earth over to the left.

CRACK! CRACK! CRACK!

Sparrow put down covering fire, forcing the Iraqis to scurry and take cover.

There was sporadic return of fire from Iraqi soldiers who were using the VCR as protection.

Running full pelt, John nearly lost his balance.

Don't fall over here, you twat!

A bullet zipped past his right ear.

Fuck, that was close!

Skidding into a deep depression in the ground, John's chest heaved as he tried to get his breath back. His lungs were burning. Sweat stung his eyes as he blinked and crawled backwards to get maximum cover.

On the far side, two of his comrades, Cleggy and Robbo, were doing the same.

Fire and manoeuvre. Fire and manoeuvre.

John saw the tracer fire whiz past them and hit the ground.

His heart was thumping so hard he thought it was going to come out of his chest.

The babbling of the Iraqi troops became increasingly high-pitched; they were terrified.

WHOOSH!

From out of nowhere, a rocket hurtled low across the ground from where John had left Sparrow. It hit the VCR and exploded, damaging the tracks and wheels.

Brilliant shot!

The VCR tried to move, but the track snapped so that the wheels just spun in the sand. They were going nowhere. Sparrow had used his portable one-shot 66mm anti-tank rocket launcher to devastating effect.

Realising that their armoured vehicle was now unable to move, the Iraqi troops retreated back to where they'd come from, shouting and firing their guns indiscriminately from their hips. This was where their lack of training really showed.

The air exploded as the VCR opened up with its 20mm cannon. John calculated there were probably three or four Iraqi troops still inside.

His Minimi machine gun was going to be useless against its thick armour plating and the cannon would keep them pinned down until reinforcements arrived. If that happened, they'd either be taken prisoner or killed.

What do we do now? His mind was racing.

They could put rounds into the vehicle in an attempt to shatter the gunner's prism, but that was a waste of ammo.

Out of the corner of his eye, he spotted Cleggy making a run from his foxhole as Robbo gave covering fire. The turret spun, the 20mm cannon thundered and Cleggy was hit in the chest. The force of the bullet threw him back over twenty yards. He was dead before he hit the sand.

Jesus! Cleggy!

Someone needed to put the VCR out of action, and fast. For some reason, the soldiers inside hadn't battened down the hatch, which gave John an idea.

Reaching down into his pouch, John pulled out an L2 fragmentation grenade. It was green with a silver top and a large silver ring that pulled the timing pin.

Calculating that the VCR was about fifty yards from where he was hidden, John reckoned he had six or seven seconds to get to the vehicle and get the grenade inside.

Fuck it! Here we go. There's no way I'm sitting in some Baghdad torture cell with my fingernails being pulled out.

'Covering fire!' he roared.

As the rest of the SAS unit opened up, he scrambled to his feet and sprinted towards the VCR, the L2 grenade in one hand and his Blackhawk combat knife in the other.

The turret turned slowly in his direction.

Come on, John. You can do this.

The 20mm cannon was nearly level with him.

Running full pelt, he was only twenty yards from the VCR, when a head popped out of the turret hatch. A young Iraqi soldier locked eyes with him. He looked startled but pulled up a Browning 9mm handgun and aimed it directly at John's head.

Shit! I'm dead.

Swerving to the left, John saw the handgun's muzzle flash.
BANG!

He felt the sharp, burning pain of a bullet hitting the top of his left arm.

BANG! A sharp sting as a bullet ripped through the top of his ear.

He carried on sprinting, dived onto the armoured vehicle and pulled himself up.

I'm still alive!

The Iraqi soldier went to fire again, but John smashed the

gun out of his hand and with a swift move, thrust the knife into the side of his neck.

The terrified soldier looked him in the eye as he gurgled blood from his gaping mouth.

Shoving the dying soldier down into the hatch, John pulled the pin and tossed it after him, hearing it land on the metallic floor of the VCR.

He dived from the side of the vehicle onto the ground below and rolled away.

BOOM!

The grenade exploded with a muffled yet deadly crash, killing everyone inside.

A few seconds later, a figure appeared above him and blocked out the sun.

John squinted up, shielded his eyes and braced himself for the inevitable.

If this is an Iraqi soldier, then I'm dead.

His vision focused on a familiar face. It was Sparrow.

Sparrow reached out his hand to help him to his feet.

'Bloody hell, Kelly, what are you trying to do? Win a sodding VC or something?'

CHAPTER 3

Detective Inspector Gareth Williams sat back on his padded chair in his office in Beaumaris CID, arched his back to stretch and gave an audible groan, which progressed to a loud yawn. The wall clock told him it was 7.10 a.m. He still had two hours before briefing and a mountain of tedious paperwork to get through.

A figure appeared at his open office door and knocked. 'Boss?'

Looking over, Gareth saw it was Detective Sergeant Declan Flaherty, wearing his usual concerned expression. In his early forties, Declan had dark green eyes and a chubby face that was covered with a gingery-blond beard. He'd been at Beaumaris CID for nearly fifteen years – longer than Gareth. Declan's face rarely changed. Whether he was looking at a dead body or ordering a pint of Guinness, he looked permanently wary. But when his face did eventually morph into a smile or even laughter, his whole being lit up.

'What have we got, Declan?' Gareth enquired. There was no expectation for working detectives to be in at seven a.m. The CID team usually worked well into the evening, so the least Gareth could do was give them a start time of nine

21

a.m. Obviously, when there was a major crime, the officers in CID would be in around the clock and catch three to four hours' sleep if and when they could.

'Bit of a strange one, boss. We've had a phone call. Someone reckons there's a body buried up at Castell Aberlleiniog,' Declan said with a frown.

'What?' Gareth asked, wondering if he'd heard Declan correctly.

Declan pointed to the print-out that he was holding. 'Woman didn't say much. She just said that she knew there was someone buried up there by the far flank wall and thought we should know. Then she hung up.'

'No name?'

'No, boss,' Declan replied with a shake of his head. 'Do you want me to send a uniform unit to go and have a look?'

'Yeah, thanks, Declan. Sounds like it might be a crank call, but we'll need to go and check it out,' Gareth said as his phone pinged and then vibrated noisily on his desk.

It was a text from Laura.

See you in a bit. Be gentle – I'm a bit out of practice
x

Detective Inspector Laura Hart was joining Beaumaris CID today. She'd be a major asset to the team as highly experienced officers were thin on the ground in Anglesey. In fact, Laura had far more experience of major crimes than he did. He was concerned that she'd find his leadership of CID wanting and he was still trying his best to impress her with everything he did.

Smoothing his hand over his shaved head, he tried to reassure himself that he ran a tight ship without ever having to resort to being a dick-swinging bully. That was the perfect description of his predecessor, Ian Godfrey, who was now a bloody DCS – Detective Chief Superintendent – in the East Anglia Constabulary. Godfrey was loathed by the majority of the serving officers in Beaumaris CID. Not only was he pompous and judgemental, but he also thrived on sucking the confidence out of any CID officer who showed the slightest hint of weakness. Like all bullies, he had an innate sense of where others were fragile and then picked away at that until they were a shell of their former selves.

As Gareth looked down at his messy desk, his mind was drawn back to Laura.

I'd better tidy it, he thought. *I don't want her to think I'm a slob.*

They'd been in a relationship for nearly three months now. With work commitments, finalising his divorce and Laura's kids all thrown into the mix, it had been a little stop-start to say the least. Spending any meaningful time together had proved problematic, but Gareth knew how he felt about her. They *clicked*, and that was rare. She was beautiful, funny, intelligent and caring. The only real spanner in the works was not letting anyone at work know that they were seeing each other. It wasn't technically against any official regulations. But it was usually frowned upon by senior management for officers who were romantically involved to work together. It could compromise an investigation in all sorts of ways. At best, it was seen as unprofessional. At worst, it could be dangerous. They'd therefore made the decision not to tell anyone.

Trying to put all this out of his mind, he reached over and popped stray pens back in a mug that had the Welsh Rugby crest on it. Grabbing hold of his in-tray, he cleared away a packet of chewing gum, two old USB sticks and a strip of paracetamol.

Detective Constable Ben Corden popped his head in. 'Boss?'

Gareth immediately stopped tidying, as if he'd been caught

doing something he shouldn't, and looked up. 'How can I help, Ben?' he enquired in an excessively cheery tone.

'Reception rang to say they've got a Detective Inspector Hart downstairs,' Ben explained.

Bloody hell, she's early!

'Okay,' Gareth said in an effort to be professional. 'Tell them to give her a day security pass and we can sort out a permanent one later.'

'This is the new DI that you told us was coming to work here?' Ben asked. 'It was her son who was kidnapped in the summer?'

'Yeah, that's right. Jake.' Gareth nodded. 'And today's her first day.'

'She was a DI in Manchester Met, wasn't she?'

'Yes, she was.'

Ben pulled a face. 'She's going to find Beaumaris CID a bit of a let-down after that, isn't she?'

'Thank you, Ben,' Gareth said in a withering tone. 'Just ring reception and get them to send her up, will you?'

Laura looked at her reflection in the mirror of the female locker room and toilets at Beaumaris nick. She made sure her hair was tied back neatly and retouched her lipstick. She'd just been given her day security pass and told that she could make her way up to the CID office.

Christ, I didn't think I'd be this nervous, she thought as she took a long, deep breath.

A couple of female uniformed officers were laughing about something at an open locker on the far side. They hadn't even noticed her come in.

She rinsed her hands and patted them dry with a blue paper towel, then looked at her reflection again. *Come on, Laura, you're just stalling for time. You've got this!*

The door to one cubicle opened and a female detective

came out and headed for the sink next to her. Laura recognised her from the hijacking back in June.

'It's Andrea, isn't it?' she asked.

'Sorry,' Detective Constable Andrea Jones replied with a self-effacing laugh. 'I was miles away, ma'am.'

Laura pulled a face. 'You know what, I'd prefer to be called boss. Ma'am makes me sound like the bloody queen.'

'Right you are.' Andrea laughed as she finished washing her hands. 'I'm heading back to CID if you want me to show you the way.'

'Yeah, that would be great. I was hoping to pick up a coffee along the way.'

'Well, avoid the swill they serve in the canteen,' Andrea joked as they headed for the door, 'DI Williams insists we have a pot on the go in CID. He's a bit of a coffee snob.'

'Oh, so am I,' Laura stated with a smile as they reached the foot of the back staircase and headed up.

'Right, then you two will get along famously,' Andrea said chirpily.

Laura couldn't work out if there had been a hint of irony in the way Andrea had said it. Did CID officers know what was going on between her and Gareth, or was she just being paranoid? They'd agreed not to tell anyone.

'How's your son doing? Jake, isn't it?' Andrea enquired.

'You know what, he's doing all right. He's had a bit of counselling and the school has been brilliant with him. They've got fantastic pastoral care. Thanks for asking, though.'

'Good to hear,' Andrea said supportively. 'I can't imagine how difficult that must have been for all of you.'

Arriving at the door to the CID office, Andrea gestured. 'Here we go, boss.'

Laura couldn't help but feel like the new kid at school arriving at an unfamiliar classroom as butterflies flitted around her stomach.

For a split second, she took a breath as the gnawing sense of trepidation felt overwhelming.

The familiar sound of the CID office – chatter, a phone ringing, a keyboard being tapped – grew louder as Andrea opened the door and indicated for Laura to enter.

Several of the detectives who were sat working at laptops or on the phone did a double-take as she walked in.

She gave them her best smile. *Nice and steady, Laura. Keep it nice and steady.*

Glancing around, she thought that Beaumaris CID looked just the same as the various CID offices she'd worked at in Manchester – only a little smaller. A dozen or so flatscreens and computers lined up on desks that faced each other. Printers and a photocopier on tables on the far side. On the walls, three large red boards were covered in posters and leaflets for various local and national initiatives: *The North Wales Police and Community Trust (PACT) – sponsoring local projects to create a safer environment for everyone.*

In the far right-hand corner, there was a small office that had open Venetian blinds at the window and a water cooler just outside. She assumed that was Gareth's domain.

Before she could make a comment, Gareth appeared at the office door and gave her a half-smile. He was wearing a blue shirt and a navy tie.

I forgot how attractive he is, she thought instantly. It had been nearly a week since she last saw him.

'Laura,' he said, approaching. 'You've met Andrea already?'

'She found me skulking in the toilets,' Laura joked, and then wondered if that was quite the right thing to say on her first morning.

Andrea smiled. 'Can I get you a coffee, boss?'

Laura nodded. 'Yes, Andrea, that would be great, thank you.'

She'd formed a habit of using colleagues' Christian names

as much as she could when she was getting to know them. It put them at ease. And there was nothing more likely to annoy someone than forgetting their name after a week or two of working together.

'You must be doing something right,' Gareth joked with a crooked smile. 'She never offers to get me coffee.'

As Andrea left them, Gareth looked at her and asked under his breath, 'You okay?' in a conspiratorial tone.

'Yeah, fine. Bit nervous,' she whispered and then gestured to the bag she was carrying. 'Where do you want me?'

'Do you want the honest answer to that, or the appropriate, professional one?' he quipped with a cheeky smirk.

'I guess we'll go for the boring answer for the moment.'

'Well, I'm afraid we've only got one DI's office,' Gareth explained almost apologetically.

'That's okay.' Laura grinned. 'I'm happy to share. As long as I get the desk with the window.' It felt strange to be having this kind of stilted, formal work conversation with a man she'd shared a bed with on three occasions.

'Funny.' Gareth smiled and pointed to a large desk and computer in the far right-hand corner. 'Over there okay?' he said.

It looked suitably tucked away from the main hub of the office.

'Looks good to me.'

'I'll let you get settled then, eh?' Gareth said and gave her hand a surreptitious squeeze as he turned to go.

She watched him walking back to his office. *Yep. He really does have a lovely bum.*

CHAPTER 4

SAS Regimental HQ, Stirling Lines,
Herefordshire, UK
October 1998

Sergeant John 'Paddy' Kelly, C Squadron of the 22nd Special Air Service, strolled across the barracks courtyard wondering why he'd been summoned to see Major General Perkins, who was the DSF – the Director of Special Services. John had had little interaction with Perkins, who had been in the role for just over a year. He'd heard he was a belt-and-braces man, which John took to mean that Perkins was controlling, even a little pedantic.

John went into the pre-war office block to the side of A Barracks and strolled down the long, narrow corridor that led down to Perkins' office. There was a series of framed photographs of those SAS soldiers who had died in combat since its inception in 1941. The building smelled musty and old. It had been built in the early thirties and didn't look like they'd touched it much since.

Halfway down the corridor, John spotted a photograph of his friend, Sergeant Gary Cleggs, who had died in an operation with him behind enemy lines during the Gulf War in 1991. With his sandy hair, cleft chin and ruddy cheeks, Cleggy had had a boyish charm that everyone warmed to. A fiercely proud Lancashireman, Cleggy had spent one mundane evening on surveillance explaining to their unit the finer points of the rivalry between his home county and that of Yorkshire. John even remembered a joke Cleggy had told him.

A Yorkshireman takes his cat to the vet and says 'Ayup, lad, I need to talk to thee about me cat.' The vet asks, 'Is it a tom?' The Yorkshireman replied, 'No, lad, I've browt it wi' us.'

John smiled at the memory until his train of thought was broken by a fierce-looking staff sergeant coming the other way. Most of the NCOs – non-commissioned officers – in the SAS had that intense look.

A few seconds later, John arrived at Perkins' office and knocked on the door.

'Enter,' came the deep voice with that Oxbridge public school accent of the higher commissioned officer ranks in the army.

Opening the door, John saw Perkins sitting behind a large oak desk scribbling with a fountain pen. The lit cigarette he was holding in his other hand had a precarious amount of ash at its end that was about to drop.

'You wanted to see me, sir?' John asked.

Perkins was in his forties, balding, with a steely edge to his manner.

'Come and sit down, sergeant.' He tapped the ash from his cigarette into a green glass ashtray.

'Thank you,' John said, walking across the dark wooden floor and sitting down in a chair with burgundy leather upholstery. It was hard and uncomfortable, like most things in the British Army.

29

The office was dark and shadowy, and the bluish cigarette smoke hung like a veil where the soft light came in at the window. It felt incredibly old-fashioned. Shelves were cluttered with folders, box files, and books. There were some photographs of a cricket team up on the wall, along with a picture of the Queen.

Perkins took a final drag from the cigarette, stubbed it out and blew a plume out into the air.

'Do you smoke, sergeant?' he enquired in his plummy voice.

John was used to it. It was rare to find a high-ranking officer in the British Army who didn't have the sound of privilege in his voice. He'd have had a year of officer training at the Royal Military Academy in Sandhurst to perfect it.

'No, sir,' John replied.

'Very wise, very wise,' Perkins stated in a disinterested tone as he looked down at a beige manila folder on the desk. 'Can't seem to quit the bloody things.'

John shifted back on his chair and crossed his legs. The previous afternoon, C Squadron had been for a twenty-mile yomp carrying fifty-pound bergens across the Brecon Beacons over in Wales, so the muscles in his legs were sore. He was no longer in his twenties and he'd noticed that recovery time was getting longer and longer.

'Says here you're originally from Newry,' Perkins muttered, flicking through and then reading from John's personnel record.

'Yes, sir,' John replied, wondering quite what the relevance was.

'Catholic family?'

'Yes, sir.'

Strange question.

'When was the last time you were back in Ireland, sergeant?'

30

John thought for a few seconds. 'It was 1986, sir.'

'You haven't been back since you were twenty-two?'

'No, sir.'

'And why's that?'

'My family didn't approve of me joining the British Army. We don't speak anymore, sir.'

'I take it your family is republican, then?' Perkins asked.

'Yes, sir.'

'But you're not?'

John frowned. How could he think he was? The British Army, especially SAS, had lost men in the fight against the IRA in Northern Ireland for decades.

'No, sir,' he replied. 'I have no sympathy for the republican cause whatsoever. Quite the opposite, actually.'

'Glad to hear that.' Perkins sat back in his leather-backed chair and looked over. 'What do you know about the Real IRA?'

John shrugged. 'Only what I've read in the papers or seen on the news, sir.'

'Which is?'

'Last year, the IRA called a ceasefire and agreed to take part in the peace process,' John replied. 'A splinter group formed who didn't agree with the ceasefire. And they call themselves the Real IRA.'

'Yes.' Perkins nodded and handed him a thick folder. 'Michael McKevitt, former IRA Quartermaster, is their leader. But they have a growing membership from South Armagh, Dublin, County Tyrone and Belfast. They still believe that physical force is the only way to create a united Ireland. And they reject the Good Friday agreement, which was signed by both sides back in the spring.'

'Yes, sir.' John gave him a quizzical look. 'At the risk of being impertinent, I'm wondering where you're going with all this, sir, and why I'm here.'

Perkins gave him a wry smile. 'Of course. As you're probably aware, we have a special undercover unit, the 14 Field Security and Intelligence Detachment, working out of Belfast.'

John knew of the unit, who were known in the army as *The Det*. Its members were trained by officers from the SAS and the SBS – Special Boat Service.

'I know of The Det, sir, yes,' he replied.

'But what we've been struggling to find is an Irish-born officer with a Catholic family,' Perkins explained. 'As you can imagine, it's incredibly rare.'

Which is why I've been called in, John thought as the penny dropped. *They're sending me to Ireland.* The thought of it gave him a jolt of excitement.

'I can imagine it is,' John said. 'And now I know why you've sent for me, sir.'

'Indeed.' Perkins gave him a meaningful look. 'And not to put too fine a point on it, sergeant, we need an undercover operative inside the Real IRA to feed us intelligence.'

John felt his stomach tighten. *Shit, I wasn't expecting any of this when I walked in.*

'Yes, sir,' John said, taking a breath. There were a few seconds of silence. 'When do I leave?'

'Next week,' Perkins stated. 'The feeling is that the Real IRA are going to attempt to sabotage the Good Friday agreement. They've set off bombs in County Down and Portadown. They claimed responsibility for the mortar attack on the police station in Fermanagh. Our concern is that they're planning a major atrocity on the British mainland that will derail the peace agreement.'

'And you want me to find out what that is?' John enquired, knowing the answer already.

'We do.' Perkins nodded, clearly pleased that John was ahead of the game. He pointed to his file. 'I've read your record. Victoria Cross for gallantry in the field of battle. I haven't met many men who would dive on an enemy armoured vehicle and toss in a grenade. That takes some balls, sergeant.'

John shrugged. 'Yes, sir.' He remembered his awkwardness at being presented with the medal by the Duke of Edinburgh at Buckingham Palace six years earlier. As far as he was concerned, he'd just been doing his job.

'Very good, sergeant,' Perkins stated in a tone designed to signal their conversation was over. 'Plane takes you to Belfast next Thursday at 06.00 hours.'

CHAPTER 5

Settling down at her new desk, Laura arranged some of the personal possessions she'd brought with her. Pride of place was a framed photo of Rosie and Jake grinning at the camera. It had been taken at a recent visit to Harry Potter World just north of London. Rosie and Jake had moaned on the way, claiming it was too far and that they'd grown out of Harry Potter. But as soon as they reached the stunning cobblestone set for Diagon Alley, they were transformed. Laura would never forget the joy on their faces as they danced around.

Making sure that everything was neat and tidy, she sat back to admire her handiwork. *A tidy desk, a tidy mind.* She wondered how long that was going to last.

Pulling open her laptop, she powered it up and used her new log-in details to access the in-house database. A bright red and blue badge appeared on the top left of her screen with the words *Heddlu Gogledd Cymru* – North Wales Police.

Here we go again, she thought with a sense of excitement. *I'm back.*

Before she could go any further, her phone buzzed with an email alert. Closing down the homepage, she found her personal server and spotted a new email. It was from Detective

Chief Inspector Pete Marsons from the Manchester Met. Pete was a close friend of Laura and Sam's – they'd trained together. Pete had been at Laura's side during the operation on 12 August 2018 in which Sam had died. He'd been a great support to her and the kids ever since.

On that day in 2018, intelligence from a CHIS – a covert human intelligence source, or informant – had revealed that a powerful Manchester drugs gang, the Fallowfield Hill Gang, were using a disused warehouse on the Central Park Trading Estate in West Manchester as a drug factory, manufacturing crack cocaine and heroin. Laura remembered the tension as the armed raid she was on descended into a gun battle. Then to her horror, Laura learned that her husband, Sam, a uniformed police officer, and his patrol partner, Louise McDonald, had been called earlier to a report of suspicious activity at the warehouse and had subsequently been taken hostage. They were inside. Even though Laura was the top hostage negotiator in the Manchester Met, she just couldn't make any progress in securing Sam and Louise's release. She felt so incredibly guilty and helpless.

Instead, she'd had to watch in total panic as armed units stormed the building to rescue them. However, members of the Fallowfield Hill Gang had rigged explosives and, to Laura's utter horror, the warehouse was blown to pieces. She felt like her insides had been ripped out. Her life had been torn apart that day. She'd had constant nightmares about it – like the one that morning.

Laura swore she'd get to the bottom of why Sam had died that day. She and Pete weren't satisfied with the Independent Office for Police Conduct's inquiry (IOPC). There were too many unanswered questions. How did the gang know the warehouse was going to be raided, for starters? Laura and Pete suspected the gang had someone on the inside in the Manchester Met.

In the months after Sam's death, they conducted their own off-the-record investigation into what had really happened. Their suspicion had grown about the commander of the raid on the Brannings Warehouse, Superintendent Ian Butterfield. By tracing the burner phone used to report the disturbance at Brannings Warehouse early on the morning of the 12th August, they discovered the phone call had been made by someone inside Trafford Police Station. It made no sense unless it was a deliberate attempt to ensure Sam and Louise went to the warehouse immediately.

In July, they found a more shocking revelation. Not only did they realise the burner phone belonged to Butterfield, but also that Sam's partner, Louise McDonald, whom everyone assumed had perished by his side, was very much alive and well. The next focus of their investigation was to track down Louise, but so far they'd made little progress in the past few months. She seemed to have vanished since.

Laura opened the email from Pete with some sense of trepidation.

Hi Laura,

I know we spoke at the weekend, but I just wanted to wish you luck on your first day back in the force. You're going to be brilliant! Hope the kids are okay?

Think I've had a mini-breakthrough with LM. I did some checking and someone tried to access the PNC database with her force identification number. It must have been her.

The date of the attempt was made at 10.11 p.m. on 2 August from a bar in Llandudno.

I know it's a big ask, but I think it might be worth taking a quick trip over there.

Let me know.

Pete x

Before she had time to process Pete's email, Gareth arrived with various forms, which he placed in front of her. At this stage, Laura hadn't revealed to Gareth what she and Pete were investigating. With a new job and a new relationship, she wanted to keep things as simple as possible.

For a moment, Gareth's arm brushed against hers and it gave her a little tingle. She wondered if they'd ever make their topsy-turvy relationship work. Was working together a terrible idea? Probably. Maybe she should have chosen one of the other police stations on the island. But life was short. And she and Gareth had made a connection. And in the moments when they managed to be alone and away from the chaos of their everyday lives, they had something that was beginning to be very special. She didn't want to give that up.

'Sorry. Usual boring stuff to fill in for HR,' Gareth explained. He gave her a warm smile and asked under his breath, 'You okay?'

'Yeah.' Laura nodded. 'Fine. Just getting my bearings, that's all.'

'Must be a bit weird to be back.'

'It is a bit.' She shrugged. 'But I know by the end of the week, it'll be like I've been here forever.'

Gareth nodded. 'At least it's quiet. It's not usually like this.'

Laura pulled a face of mock horror. 'I can't believe you just said that!'

'Sorry, I'm not with you?'

'We had a thing in the Manchester Met. We called it the Q-word.'

'Quiet?'

He clearly had no idea what she was talking about.

'Yeah. It was banned. You couldn't use the word,' Laura replied. 'You know? Like actors aren't supposed to say *Macbeth* because it's bad luck, so they call it *The Scottish Play*.'

Gareth raised an eyebrow. 'And why is the Q-word unlucky?'

'Because every time someone said *thank God it's quiet today*, something terrible happened. There would be a mass shooting or a serial killer would rock up.'

'Do serial killers *rock up*?'

'You know what I mean,' she laughed. 'And I promise that's the last time I mention Manchester. There's nothing worse than someone who spends their life banging on about how great the place where they used to work was. When I was in the London Met, I worked with someone who was forever saying *When I was in the Met, we used to . . .*'

'That's cockneys for you. And I'll be on the lookout for a crime wave today, too.' Gareth turned to go. 'If you can scribble on those, I'll get them over to HR today.'

'What are you doing Saturday?' Laura asked under her breath, glancing around to see if anyone could overhear her.

Gareth smiled at her. 'That's a bit of a handbrake turn.'

'I could text you, if that's better?'

Gareth snorted. 'It's fine. I think I'm free Saturday. Is this work or pleasure?'

Laura pulled a face. 'If I say the word *pleasure*, it sounds creepy. But if Rosie isn't going to yet another house party, we could go for some food or a drink.'

'Sounds perfect. I thought Rosie was taking her driving test?'

'She failed. For the third time.' Laura groaned. 'So, it's still mum's taxi until she takes it again.'

Before they could continue, Detective Constable Ben Corden approached. He was walking with a pronounced limp. 'Boss, something just came in.'

Ben was young and handsome, in a clean-cut boy band way. His blond hair was cut short and Laura could see that he worked out.

Laura smirked at Gareth. 'I told you. You said the Q-word.'

Ben frowned – he didn't get the joke.

'Ben, have you met DI Laura Hart before?' Gareth enquired.

Laura gave Ben a warm smile. 'On the pier back in June. When *The Anglesey Princess* was hijacked.'

Ben smiled back at her. 'That's right. The boss has been singing your praises ever since we found out you were joining us.'

Gareth looked embarrassed.

'Oh, that's really kind, *Gareth*,' Laura stated, looking at him with a teasing smirk. 'I'm very rusty. I'm going to need as much help as I can get.'

Gareth narrowed his eyes. 'I doubt that.'

'What happened to you?' Laura asked, gesturing to the blue plastic cast Ben was wearing around the calf and ankle of his right foot.

'Yet another rugby injury,' Gareth groaned before Ben could answer. 'And if there's one more, I'm going to ban him from playing.'

Ben gave Laura an awkward smile. She got the feeling that Gareth was a bit of a father figure to Ben within CID.

Gareth gestured to the print-out. 'What have we got, Hopalong?'

'Hopalong?' Laura laughed. 'I haven't heard that for years. Hopalong Cassidy. It's what my dad always said.'

'And mine,' Gareth joined in, meeting her eye for a second. 'He was a cowboy, wasn't he?'

'Yeah. It was an American TV series, I think,' she replied.

Ben gave a half-smile. 'I'm going to pretend I know what you two are talking about.'

Gareth pointed to the print-out again. 'What's this, then?'

'Uniform patrol have just called something in,' Ben explained. 'They're up at Castell Aberlleiniog.'

Laura remembered that this was the site of an old motte-and-bailey fortress on top of a steep hill which, if memory served her right, dated back to the eleventh century.

'Yeah, I sent them up there earlier. Have they found something?' Gareth enquired, jumping ahead.

'They think they've found parts of a human skeleton,' Ben explained.

Laura frowned. 'That site's a thousand years old, isn't it?'

Ben shrugged. 'Uniform thought that the skeleton was in a condition that suggested it wasn't a thousand years old, but they're not sure. They thought we should go and have a look.'

'I'll put the Scene of Crimes unit on alert.' Gareth looked at Laura. 'Fancy a trip out?'

'Definitely,' Laura replied without hesitating and got up from her desk. She was keen to get stuck into some proper police work rather than arranging her desk.

Gareth gestured to Ben. 'And as *laughing boy* here can't walk properly, take Andrea. You can be Anglesey's answer to *Cagney & Lacey*.'

Ben frowned. 'Cagney and who?'

'Bloody hell, Ben.' Gareth looked at Laura and rolled his eyes. 'We're working with children.'

CHAPTER 6

Laura and Andrea took the B5109 out of Beaumaris and headed along the coastline towards Castell Aberlleiniog. Even though it was the beginning of autumn, it was mild outside, even warm.

Laura buzzed down the window and let the air blow against her face. This was what she'd missed. That heady mixture of anticipation and uneasiness as she headed towards a possible crime scene. What would it bring? What was awaiting her? It made her feel alive.

A change in direction of the battering, salty wind brought the faintest sound of waves breaking, like a distant shattering of glass. Looking out at the landscape to their right, she saw that the early morning mist was lifting to reveal the gentle contours of the low hills, curving away above the shoreline to the east. The sea stretched out with a smooth, colourless luminosity, so that it was difficult to spot where the sea ended and the sky began.

For a moment, she remembered a long bike ride she and Emma had taken along this part of the island. They couldn't have been more than eleven or twelve at the time. They'd eventually cycled all the way over to their nain's – Welsh for grandmother – house in Llanfaes, a small village right on the shore at the eastern entrance to the Menai Strait. She'd made them ham and pickle sandwiches with thick white bread. Their nain didn't have a television but, as it was a Sunday afternoon, she allowed them to listen to the top forty chart run-down on BBC Radio 1. Simon Bates was the presenter and the number-one single was 'Frankie' by Sister Sledge, which they sang at the top of their voices while their nain laughed. Laura missed her sister. Even though they bickered when they were young, they also had a telepathic ability to read what the other was thinking before they said it. She wished they lived closer to each other.

'We take this for granted, don't we?' Andrea said of the view, breaking Laura's innocent recollection of her past.

'I know I do,' Laura agreed as she took a deep breath in through her nostrils and then buzzed up the window.

'How long is it since you moved back here from Manchester?' Andrea asked in a tentative tone, as though uncertain about asking Laura personal questions.

'Just over three years,' she replied.

'Good to be back?'

'The good thing is that I know loads of people and I grew up here.' Laura then gave Andrea a wry smile. 'And the bad thing is that I know loads of people and I grew up here.'

Andrea laughed. 'Oh, I see. Like that, is it?'

'It can be sometimes. But on good days, I think Anglesey is the best place to live in the world.'

'*Cymru – gwlad Duw ei hun*,' Andrea said. It meant Wales – God's own country.

'Amen to that.' Laura smiled, feeling a patriotic pride in the place she called home. 'How long have you been at Beaumaris nick?'

'Five years.' Andrea gave her a self-effacing smile. 'One year probation, three years as a PC and now a year as a DC.'

42

Laura recognised the suppressed pride in Andrea's voice. It reminded her of when she was a young DC – full of energy, zeal and determination.

'What made you want to be a copper?' Laura enquired.

Andrea thought for a few seconds. 'I usually say something corny like I want to make a difference.'

Laura raised an eyebrow. 'But . . .'

Andrea looked at her. 'I had a really shitty childhood. Kids' homes, foster care. I met a few female coppers along the way who were amazing. They really looked out for me. I just wanted to be like them, I suppose.'

Laura smiled, noting Andrea's refreshingly honest answer. 'That seems like the perfect reason.'

As the sun broke lazily through a cloud, the car filled with light. Laura looked over at Andrea. With her broad jaw, small, pretty nose and dark, globed eyes, she looked like a film actress whose name Laura couldn't remember. Some black-and-white romcom from the 1940s that Sam had condescendingly told her were actually called screwball comedies. It had Clark Gable or Errol Flynn as the leading man.

'If I'm honest, I'm a little in awe of you,' Andrea admitted with a wince.

'Oh, God. Really?' Laura gave a self-conscious cringe. She found praise made her feel very uncomfortable. 'If you knew what my home life was like and the state of the inside of my head, I think you'd actually pity me.'

'No way,' Andrea protested. 'Ever since the hijacking, you've become a total ledge among some of the female officers at Beaumaris. The way you handled that gang, especially on Menai Bridge. I've never seen anything like it.'

'Right.' Laura laughed awkwardly. 'Well, I've definitely never been a *ledge* before.'

They looked up and saw they were entering the tiny village of Llangoed.

'Here we go.' Andrea slowed down and pulled into a small car park.

Llangoed was the nearest place to park, but it was still a mile's walk along the coastal path to get to the castle ruins. Llangoed meant religious enclosure in the wood in Welsh, and the village stood on the banks of the Afon Lleiniog brook, which flowed all the way past the eleventh-century castle.

Andrea parked the black two-litre Astra next to a marked patrol car.

'I guess plod are still up at the castle,' Laura observed as she took off her seatbelt and opened the car door.

'Plod?'

Laura frowned. 'God, I've only been away for three years. We always called uniformed officers plod.'

Andrea shrugged. 'Okay.'

Bloody hell, that makes me feel old and out of touch.

'Here we go.' Andrea pointed to a brown sign that read CASTLE WALK. 'I haven't been out here for years.'

'We came here on a school trip. I was travel sick on the bus.' Laura chortled as they walked through the trees. 'The teacher gave me a bag to be sick in, only to discover that it had a hole in the bottom.'

They came to a clear pathway through the countryside with a new wooden gate.

'Lovely,' Andrea laughed. 'I'm guessing your stomach's a bit stronger these days.'

'Oh yeah,' she replied. 'I've done my fair share of murder scenes and postmortems.'

The temperature dropped as the clouds became hooded in greys and blacks. The faintest hint of drizzle misted Laura's face. The air was fresh with the scent of tall grasses and the nearby ocean. The deep cawing of crows perched high in the trees to their left broke the light chatter of birdsong.

As they turned the bend, an old wooden sign read CASTELL CASTLE 600 M.

'This is going to be a nightmare if we have to get the SOCOs up here with all their equipment,' Laura thought out loud.

SOCOs were scene-of-crime officers, essentially the forensic unit of the police force – and they used a lot of equipment.

As they crossed a narrow wooden footbridge over a noisy brook, the undergrowth became thicker and the trees formed a shadowy canopy over the pathway. Then there was a long set of wooden steps that led up the steep mound to the ruins at the top.

'You're not wrong about the SOCOs,' Andrea agreed, breathing hard with the exertion.

Laura gestured. 'I guess we'd better get up there and see what they've found.'

They climbed the steps and the drizzle graduated to full raindrops, which pattered noisily on the wooden handrails and stairs.

'Oh good,' Laura quipped sarcastically. 'Human remains and rain. Perfect combo.'

They reached the top and surveyed the site in front of them and the view beyond. The distant headlands of the coast lay couchant in a haze cast by the falling rain. The vastness of the Irish Sea glowed a dark and murky green with black mirages and streaks of inky blue. It was views like this that gave Anglesey a timeless, enduring quality. There were several megalithic monuments Laura had seen as a child that dated back to prehistoric times.

To the left of where they stood, a low and uneven rectangular stone wall encircled the entire summit and there were crumbled towers made from grey stone in all four corners. In between, the ground was overgrown with tall grasses, weeds, and fragrant flowers.

Laura spotted two uniformed officers. Getting out her temporary warrant card, she approached them. The nearest officer looked boyish, with a thick neck and short mousy hair. He had narrow dark brown eyes and shiny nose with flaring nostrils. His broad shoulders made him look powerful.

'DI Hart and DC Jones, Beaumaris CID,' she stated. 'What have we got, Constable?'

God, I haven't done that in a while, she thought.

'There's a small patch of ground over here, ma'am,' he explained. 'It looks like someone has cleared some of the leaves. It's hard to tell. And there are parts of a human skeleton in the earth.'

'Can you show me?' Laura asked, signalling to Andrea to follow her.

'Of course, ma'am,' he replied.

They traipsed through the thick grass towards an area by the far stone wall. The grass had thinned out to reveal the earth below.

At the top of the plot was a human skull that was twisted to one side. Below that lay a couple of ribs.

Yep, that's a human skeleton, all right.

'Right,' Laura said, deep in thought.

'I wonder how old it might be,' Andrea said, almost to herself.

'Yeah. Is this someone who died a thousand years ago or five years ago?'

Laura crouched to get a better look at the remains. 'We're going to need to know if this is a medieval peasant or baby-boomer.'

Out of the corner of her eye, she spotted something in the earth that seemed out of place. After scooping away the earth, she pulled a rectangular square of plastic from under a small bone. She wiped it clean with the cuff of her coat and peered at it.

It was some kind of bank card. Actually, it was only half a bank card, as if someone had cut it in half. It had the MasterCard logo on it.

Laura looked up at them. 'I'm pretty sure medieval peasants didn't carry credit cards.'

CHAPTER 7

Belfast 1998

Looking out at the dark rain-swept streets of Belfast, John checked his watch: 3.30 a.m. It had been forty minutes since his plane from RAF Northolt had touched down in Belfast. They'd passed the Falls Road – the Catholic artery out of West Belfast and the main route south to Dublin and the Republic. The streets were strangely devoid of light. No house lights, no shop windows illuminated, and most of the street-lamps had been smashed to allow the IRA to come and go under the cover of darkness.

As they headed south, they passed the Grosvenor Road Police Station, which looked more like a fortress in a war zone. Corrugated iron, chicken wire and sandbags protected those inside from attack. There were two armed sentries, dressed in helmets and body armour, stood beside the heavy wooden and barbed-wire barricades. The Good Friday agreement might have been signed and an IRA ceasefire agreed, but it was going to take a long time for anyone to drop their guard after decades of murder and mayhem. Belfast still looked like it was on a war footing.

John's driver, a podgy local man with the nasal accent of West Belfast, attempted to strike up conversations about politics and football. By the time they'd passed the playing fields over by the Crumlin Road, the man was in full tour guide mode, as if John was an American tourist who had never visited Ireland before. Spotting a snub-nosed Walther PPK pistol in a tan leather shoulder holster, John deduced the man worked for Special Branch.

The man pointed. 'Down there on the left. You see that small alleyway? Couple of paratroopers were shot dead there about five years ago. And you see the Crown pub there? The second battalion of the Belfast Brigade used to meet in there until the UVF bombed it. It's been quieter since the ceasefire, but there's a lot of bad blood in this city just waiting to boil over.'

John wondered if one day, Japanese tourists would come down the Falls Road by the busload on sightseeing tours, taking in the main locations of the Troubles and photographing the gigantic murals on both sides of the conflict. He gazed out at the jagged lines of the city. The schoolyards and church steeples. And in the distance, the shipyards, where nearly a hundred years ago the *Titanic* had been built.

It felt strange to be back in Belfast and Northern Ireland. It had been just over twelve years since he left. Strangely familiar and yet from a different lifetime. Like a dream.

It was another twenty minutes before they arrived at Thiepval Barracks in Lisburn, County Antrim, the headquarters of the British Army in Northern Ireland. Security was noticeably tight. A couple of years earlier, the IRA had used forged ID cards to access the barracks and detonate two enormous car bombs. Dozens had been injured and a young warrant officer killed.

'Here we go, sir,' the driver stated as he pulled into a parking space.

'Thank you,' John replied as he got out and felt the drizzle on his face. He could see where some buildings had been rebuilt in new red brick after the bombing. It was a relief to be out of the car so that the driver's incessant prattle could stop.

The driver said, 'If you'd like to follow me, sir.'

Under the watchful eye of two armed soldiers from the 3rd Battalion of the Parachute Regiment, John followed the driver across the shadowy car park. He could hear an army truck rattling in the distance. A chimney from one of the barrack blocks puffed out blue-grey smoke into the woollen dark grey sky. Somewhere, one of the German shepherd guard dogs barked loudly, its deep, thunderous snarl an unending chorus as John made his way into the main building.

He was shown through to a large meeting room furnished with heavy oak furniture and a couple of oil paintings on the wood-panelled walls. A huge, impressive painting at the far end of the room showed Field Marshal Montgomery accepting the unconditional surrender of the German forces at Lunebürg Heath, just south of Hamburg in May 1945. A dejected-looking Eberhard Kinzel, Chief of the General Staff of the German army, dressed in a leather coat and gloves, looked on as Montgomery handed him a pen to sign.

As with all such places in the British Army, it had the musty smell of an old library and stale cigar smoke.

'Sergeant Kelly?' enquired a thin, reedy-looking man in his fifties, dressed in formal SAS uniform.

He approached and gestured to a chair at the table. His dark eyes gave him a detached look and his lips were pale and cold.

'I'm Captain Stephen Palmer. Please, take a seat.'

John nodded. 'I recognise you from Hereford, sir.'

Another man in plain clothes sat at the far end of the table. He was short, plump, with a clipped moustache and beady blue eyes.

'And this is Detective Chief Inspector Wood from Special Branch.'

Special Branch was a separate unit of the British police force who worked on counterterrorism with MI5.

John nodded a hello and spotted a brown folder on the desk in front of Wood that had the word SECRET stamped across the top. It was his personnel file. He rubbed his hand over his face – he needed a shave.

Wood looked over at him. 'It says here that you were born and brought up in Newry?' Wood had a West Country accent.

'Yes, sir.'

'And your mother and father are both dead?' Palmer enquired in a flat, formal tone.

'That's right.'

Wood flicked over a page of his personnel file. 'Any family left in Newry, sergeant?'

'I'm assuming I have an uncle and cousins,' John replied uncertainly. 'My family completely ostracised me once I joined the army, sir. I've had no contact with anyone in Newry since I left.'

Wood gave a slow nod as he continued to read from the file. 'Good.'

'Clearly, I don't need to remind you the Official Secrets Act covers everything we talk about in this room,' Palmer stated gravely.

'Of course, sir.'

'Ever worked any surveillance, sergeant?' Wood asked. 'It doesn't mention anything in your file.'

'In Guatemala and Belize. Our unit frequently crossed the border to gather intelligence on the Guatemalan rebels during the civil war there. We also ran several informants inside the

51

GNRU,' John explained. The GNRU stood for the Guatemalan National Revolutionary Unity – an amalgamation of all the rebel forces during the 36-year civil war. 'Also, some work in West Berlin for MI5.'

'Bit different to Ireland, though,' Wood mumbled with a frown.

John picked up on his uncertain tone and wondered what the subtext was.

Palmer raised an eyebrow and looked at Wood. 'Same principles, though.'

Reading between the lines, John guessed Palmer was certain that John was up to the surveillance work, whereas Wood had his doubts.

'Possibly,' Wood muttered under his breath.

Palmer looked over at John. 'Your name was put forward when it was mooted that we needed a man to infiltrate the Real IRA. And it's something that has now been sanctioned by Mr Straw, the Home Secretary. We need someone who is experienced in covert work, who looks and sounds the part but has virtually no history in Ireland. And we want to put that person smack bang in the middle of the Falls area of Belfast.'

'Yes, sir,' John said, though the thought of that made him uneasy.

'And you'd be on your own, sergeant,' Wood clarified as he shifted uncomfortably in his chair.

John wasn't surprised. The chairs were narrow and Wood was carrying a lot of extra timber.

'We don't want to take the risk of you being handled by any of the existing intelligence or undercover units,' Wood continued. 'This is a one-man operation.'

'And we need an answer from you this morning,' Palmer stated.

Even though John knew this was incredibly dangerous, he

wasn't about to decline any request from his commanding officer.

'Then it's a yes, sir,' John responded immediately.

'Marvellous,' Palmer said, offering a grateful smile as if John had just agreed to play cricket for the regimental team.

Looking over at Wood, John could see that he still wasn't convinced.

'Your identity will be kept from the RUC, as they're totally against any kind of operation like this,' Wood stated. 'And if I'm honest, Special Branch needed to be convinced.'

You don't say.

Palmer took a folder from the centre of the table, opened it and pulled out a photograph. He pointed to the first one – a man in his forties with coal-black hair and piercing blue eyes. 'Joe Magan. Chief of Staff of the Real IRA. Born in Cork. His uncle Michael was a founding member of the 1st Cork Brigade of the IRA in the 1930s. Imprisoned in 1970 for membership of the IRA, Joe took part in the hunger strike at the Maze Prison in 1981.' Palmer patted the folder. 'In here is everything you'll need to know. Familiarise yourself with the faces and names.'

'What's my cover?' John asked.

'Fifteen years in the merchant navy and time spent mining ore over in Canada. It's hard for anyone to check the records for that. However, there are documents in that folder that will give you background to your cover story. You need to know it inside out.'

John nodded. 'Of course, sir.'

Wood looked over and gave him a grim look. 'I'm not going to try to play down how dangerous this is. The last informant the IRA caught was hooded, tortured and left crucified to a wall in a disused warehouse, where he died three days later.'

CHAPTER 8

Laura sat in Gareth's office, feeding back on her and Andrea's trip to Castell Aberlleiniog. Gareth's office was larger than it looked from the main CID office. It was also tidier. Laura's experience of middle-aged men was that they were generally messy, but she was pleasantly surprised. Either that, or Gareth had attempted to clear up before she'd arrived.

'SOCOs have had to take the remains to Glan Clwyd Hospital on the mainland for a preliminary postmortem,' Laura stated.

'Hopefully they can give us some idea how old the remains are,' he said.

'Either that, or we try carbon dating,' Laura suggested.

'Possibly, but I don't even know where we can get access to carbon dating.' Gareth smoothed his hand over his shaved head.

Laura looked at him. The top button of his neatly pressed white shirt was undone and his charcoal-coloured tie hung away from his chest as he leaned forwards. She noted again that he wasn't her usual type. Normally, she was attracted to softer, more sensitive types. That was Sam. He'd worn his heart on his sleeve and was emotionally literate.

Gareth was rugged, in the old-fashioned sense of the word. He looked like he sweated testosterone and shaved twice a day.

'What about the bank card?'

'I thought it was a credit card, but there's a sort code on it, so it's actually a debit card. Which means we can track down the bank that issued it. And we have the first seven digits of the card itself. I'm hoping that we can trace who it belonged to.'

'And that might give us an identity to our remains.'

'It's hard to know if the two are linked,' Laura admitted with a shrug. 'But until we get the remains dated, it's the best we've got.'

'Talk to forensics. If they can extract DNA from the bones, we can run a match and see if we get a hit on the national database. Long shot, but worth a try.'

Laura nodded and spotted Andrea approaching. She stuck her head through the door and looked at her.

'Boss, I've traced that sort code. It actually belonged to the Midland Bank, which is now an HSBC in Llangefni.'

'Great,' Laura said. 'Any way they can trace the card number?'

'Possibly,' Andrea said with a knowing look. 'The old records belonging to the Midland Bank are in the basement. They said we can have a dig around. *And* the Midland Bank became HSBC in June 1999.'

They all shared a look.

'So, that card expired at the latest in 1999,' Laura stated. 'And if the card was in the pocket of any clothing from the remains we found, then that body has probably been there since then.'

'Looks like it,' Gareth agreed. 'I can't see why they'd be walking around with an obsolete card in their pocket.'

Laura looked up at Andrea. She was impressed by her

work already. 'Thanks, Andrea. We'll get over to Llangefni in about an hour.'

'Yes, boss,' Andrea said as she turned and went.

'She's good, isn't she?' Laura commented, gesturing to Andrea.

'Yeah, she's brilliant,' Gareth replied. 'And given her background, it's even more impressive.'

Laura gave him a look. 'She did mention a difficult childhood to me earlier.'

'Her parents were killed in a car crash when she was six,' Gareth explained quietly. 'They put her in care and then some terrible foster families. Not a great start in life.'

'Good for her,' Laura said, hoping she didn't sound patronising as she got up to go. Then she spotted a photo of two teenagers, a boy and a girl. 'Is that Charlie and Fran?'

Gareth had talked a couple of times about his brother, Rob, who did some high-powered banking job and lived out in Hong Kong. Charlie and Fran were his children.

She peered closely at the photograph, wondering why Gareth had never had children and how he felt about it. He'd make a great dad.

'Charlie looks like you,' she commented, looking at the same hooded dark eyes.

Gareth pulled a face. 'Poor Charlie.'

'You said you and your brother are close,' Laura enquired. 'Must be difficult with him in Hong Kong.'

'I guess so. It'd be nice to have him round the corner,' Gareth admitted with a shrug. 'But it has allowed me three trips to Hong Kong in the past decade. Plus we're always texting each other about the rugby or some obscure, pretentious eighties band we used to love.'

'I love obscure, pretentious eighties bands,' Laura said with a half-smile.

Gareth raised an eyebrow. 'Really?'

'Oh my God,' she remarked with a playful scowl. 'You think I'm referring to someone really obvious like the Thompson Twins, don't you?'

'I think *Quick Step & Side Kick* was a decent album,' Gareth stated with a smirk.

'Go on then, try me.' Laura snorted confrontationally.

'The Associates?'

'Scottish. I loved their single "Club Country".'

'The Teardrop Explodes?'

'Formed by Julian Cope. Best known for their single "Reward".'

Gareth frowned and then asked uncertainly, 'The The?'

Laura gave him a sarcastic smile. 'I had the album *Soul Mining* on vinyl.'

Gareth's eyes widened. 'Okay, you just became the most attractive woman I've ever met.'

'Erm, I thought I was already,' she laughed, giving him a playful hit. 'Unfortunately, you just proved yourself to be smug and a bit patronising.'

Before Gareth had time to respond, Ben stuck his head in and looked at Laura.

'Boss, call from the pathologist in Glan Clwyd. Professor Lovell. He says he's found something significant and needs you to go down there.'

'Thanks, Ben.' Laura turned to Gareth. 'I'd better go. We can resume our conversation later when you tell me what you know about the band We've Got a Fuzzbox and We're Gonna Use It.'

Gareth rolled his eyes. 'Now you're just being silly.'

'Wanna bet?' Laura joked. 'Google it.'

It had been several years since Laura had been to a post-mortem. She and Andrea got into the ageing lift on the ground floor of Glan Clywd Hospital and headed down to the basement. Their descent was slow and noisy as the pulleys and rails clunked.

Andrea looked at her reflection in the mirrored surface, took her bobble out, pulled back her hair and tried to retie it. 'I'd give anything to have hair like yours.'

Laura frowned. 'Thin, lank and greasy?'

'No.' Andrea laughed. 'Straight and manageable. Mine is like bloody dry string this morning, courtesy of my maternal grandmother.'

Laura gave her a quizzical look.

'She was Afro-Caribbean. Trinidad,' she explained as she finally finished retying her hair.

'What was she like?'

Andrea's face changed as she became pensive. 'I don't remember. I met her as a baby, but she went back to Trinidad and died a few years later.'

'I'm sorry to hear that.'

The lift jolted to a stop and the doors clattered open.

Andrea gestured left. 'This way, boss.'

'What's Professor Lovell like?' Laura enquired as they strolled down the stark windowless corridor towards the mortuary.

'Bit of a housewives' favourite,' she said as their shoes clacked noisily on the hard flooring. 'Not my type, though.'

'Good to know.' Laura gave her a wry smile. 'I was actually thinking more in a professional capacity.'

'Oh, God! Sorry.' Andrea snorted in an embarrassed tone. 'He's very professional, doesn't suffer fools. Bit sarcastic, but he knows his stuff.'

'As long as he knows what he's doing.' Laura reached the large black double doors to the mortuary, opened the right-hand one and went inside.

The drop in temperature was marked, as was the instant waft of disinfectants and other chemicals. The mortuary was much like others she'd been in before. There were two large mortuary examination tables nearby, with a third on the far side of the room. The walls were tiled to about head height in pale blue tiles, and workbenches and an assortment of luminous coloured chemicals ran the full length of the room.

Good to be back, she thought dryly.

Looking around, she spotted a man in his late fifties working over at the third mortuary table. He was taking photographs of the remains, using a small white plastic ruler to give an indication of scale, while he mumbled his findings into a small microphone attached to his scrubs.

She saw that all the major bones of the skeleton had now been found by the SOCOs and were laid out like some dark jigsaw puzzle on the metallic gurney.

'That's Lovell,' Andrea commented under her breath as they approached.

Professor William Lovell was one of the foremost forensic pathologists in Wales. His mind was as sharp as his dress sense. He was respected by everyone and he showed a genuine passion for his profession.

The underlying buzz of fans and the air conditioning added to the unnatural atmosphere. The pungent smell of cleaning fluids masked the odour of the gases and the beginnings of rot and decay.

Lovell, who was dressed in pastel green scrubs and a rubber apron, turned off his microphone and looked at them. Pulling down his mask, he revealed a boyish smile on his clean-shaven face.

'Are you the detectives from Beaumaris?' he asked in a friendly tone. His voice was deep and sounded like a mixture of public school and North Wales.

He might not be Andrea's type, but I can see the attraction, Laura thought.

'DI Laura Hart,' she stated, returning his smile. 'I believe you already know DC Jones?'

'Of course,' Lovell replied, raising an eyebrow. 'Although I don't believe she's brought me a skeleton before. Very thoughtful.'

'Thanks,' Andrea laughed. 'Thought I'd keep you on your toes, Professor.'

'What can you tell us?' Laura enquired.

Lovell flicked the wall-mounted light box on, backlighting an X-ray of the skull. 'So, meet Dai.'

Laura pulled a face. 'Dai?'

'In the USA, they use the name John Doe. In England, it tends to be Joe Bloggs,' Lovell explained with a grin. 'We're in Wales, so he's called Dai.'

Laura gave him a wry smile. She liked his sense of humour already. 'Of course he is. So, the remains are a man?'

'Yes.' Lovell went over to the skull and pointed with his gloved hand. 'There is severe damage just here, which is consistent with a heavy blow to the back of the head. A blunt force trauma. I'm pretty certain that's what killed him. The fracture itself is extensive and this darkened patch directly beneath the fracture is the resulting intracranial haemorrhage. He'd have died very quickly.'

Andrea looked over at him. 'So, he was murdered?'

'Yes.' Lovell nodded.

'What we really need is some kind of timescale,' Laura said. 'Are these remains 500 years old or five years old?'

Lovell rubbed his face and then took off the mask. 'Not five years. But it's going to be incredibly difficult to narrow it down to any specific date. The ground you found these remains in is damp and sandy. It's perfect for the preservation of bones.'

'Yes, we heard.' Laura sighed, frustrated. 'I wondered if carbon dating might work.'

Lovell nodded. 'Yes. That was going to be my next suggestion. There was a case over in Oswestry in Shropshire last year. A shooting party came across a skull and some bones. Carbon dating put the remains at AD 600.'

'And I assume we can try DNA and dental records?' Laura enquired.

'I can attempt to get a DNA sample from his bone marrow, which you can then compare to the national database. Dental records are out, I'm afraid,' Lovell said. 'There's significant damage to the teeth.'

'Could that be the result of an attack?' Andrea asked.

'That would be my guess,' he replied. 'A couple of front teeth have been broken in half, so they're too damaged for a match.'

'Anything else that might help us identify him?' Laura enquired.

'I can tell you he's late thirties to mid-forties. Dai is also about five foot nine. Average build.'

'Okay. That narrows it down a tiny bit,' Laura said, thinking out loud.

Lovell gestured to a microscope. 'Your SOCO team found some blowfly pupal casings in the earth around the bones.'

'What does that tell us?' Andrea enquired.

'It tells us that death occurred about three days before the body was disposed of,' Lovell explained.

That doesn't really help us identify him, does it? Laura thought, discouraged.

'Thanks, Professor,' she said with a forced smile. 'If you find anything else, please let me know.'

As Laura and Andrea turned to go, Lovell gave them a quizzical look. 'There is something else.'

Lovell disappeared off and returned with a plastic evidence bag. Inside was a tiny pin badge with some kind of crest on it. It was no bigger than the tip of a little finger.

'This was discovered in the earth beneath the remains,' he said.

'What is it?' Laura asked.

'At a guess, I think it's a regimental pin badge,' he stated and then gave a wry smile. 'This writing here is Latin and my Latin is a little on the rusty side.'

'So is mine,' Laura joked. 'I assume by regimental you mean a regiment in the British Army.'

'Exactly,' Lovell replied and looked at her. 'I think your victim was once a soldier.'

CHAPTER 9

By the time Laura and Andrea were shown down into the basement of the HSBC branch at Llangefni, it was one p.m. Kevin Evans, the deputy manager, led them down a wide staircase and along a windowless corridor that was dimly lit by old-fashioned strip lights.

I'm getting a déjà vu, Laura thought as she remembered her journey to the mortuary a few hours earlier.

Evans stopped and gestured to an enormous room filled with floor-to-ceiling shelving units stacked with folders and files.

'Here we go, ladies. Knock yourself out.' He grinned annoyingly.

Ladies!

Laura sighed. 'Great. Looks like we've got our afternoon sorted, then.'

'Actually, you're lucky they're still here,' Evans chortled. 'Head office told us to start shredding anything that was over fifteen years old. We just hadn't got round to it.' He looked at the two of them as though this were amusingly ironic.

Andrea gave Laura a look as if to indicate he was grating on her. 'Lucky us then, eh?'

'Should be date order,' Evans explained. 'New accounts. Transactions. Accounts. Mortgages and loans.'

'Brilliant.' Laura groaned under her breath.

'What have you got to go on?' he asked.

Laura took out her phone and brought up a photo of the broken Midland debit card and showed it to him. 'Someone told us that this card was only issued in 1996 and HSBC took over Midland in 1999. We're hoping that means we can narrow down the issue of that card to three years.'

Evans raised an eyebrow smugly. His breath smelled of stale coffee and cigarettes.

'I can narrow it down even more for you, if you like.'

'That would be great,' Andrea said.

Evans pointed at the photograph. 'That card's silver-coloured. Which means the holder had a platinum account with the Midland.' He gestured to the shelves. 'There should be a folder over there with records of all the platinum account holders at that time . . . I'll leave you to it.'

Laura gave Kevin a smile. He'd actually proved to be very useful. 'Thanks for your help.'

Gareth pushed himself back in his high-backed chair but resisted putting his feet on the desk. He'd seen Superintendent Warlow – or Partridge, as CID officers called him behind his back, after the incompetent television character – prowling around earlier. Gareth did some of his most effective thinking sitting with his feet on the desk, but to a humourless dickhead like Warlow, it would come across as idle and unprofessional. He didn't want Warlow paying them a surprise visit and him getting the wrong idea about how busy they were or how seriously he took running the CID team.

Glancing up at the shelves to his left, he spotted a space where there had once been a photograph of him and his ex-wife, Nell. He hadn't thought about her for a while, which was a relief. She'd done a real number on him – but he'd facilitated her toxic behaviour, so he wasn't entirely blameless.

Gareth had discovered at the beginning of the year that she was having an affair with the new headteacher at her school, Andrew Leith, and Nell had moved out during the summer. Their divorce had been finalised just over two weeks ago and it still felt a little raw. Being left for another man was devastating for Gareth's sense of self-worth and confirmed all the gnawing doubts he'd ever had about himself.

There had been a night back in the summer where Gareth had driven up to Leith's home and just sat outside, staring up at his house. He'd remembered the opening scene to one of his favourite films, *The Shawshank Redemption*. The main character, a mild-mannered accountant called Andy Dufresne – played impeccably by the actor Tim Robbins – is sitting in a car outside a house with a revolver. Inside, he knows his wife is with her lover. He wants to go inside and shoot them but can't bring himself to do it. For a few seconds that night, Gareth understood with alarming clarity and empathy how Dufresne had wrestled with such a violent act. There had been part of him that wanted to grab a hammer or a baseball bat, break into Leith's home and attack them. He was fully aware that his desire for such bloody revenge was born out of his crushed ego and damaged male pride.

Taking a breath, Gareth felt uneasy at the memory. For a few seconds that night, he'd stared into the darkness of his very soul. For a moment, he'd stood on that jumping-off place where some men leaped and committed terrible acts of violence – and others took a moment to regain their judgement and sense, and walked away. But he'd seen that the line between those two places was much finer than many would have you believe.

'Brought you a coffee, boss,' said a voice with an Irish accent, breaking his train of thought. It was Declan.

Gareth frowned. 'What's this in aid of, Declan?' he asked suspiciously, studying Declan's face for signs of guilt.

Declan looked offended. 'This job's making you cynical, boss. Can't a lowly DS bring his DI a coffee without them assuming there's an ulterior motive?'

'How long have we worked together, Declan?' Gareth enquired.

'A long time now.'

'And how many times have you brought me a coffee?'

Declan looked lost. 'It's just a coffee, boss. I won't do it again after all this kerfuffle.'

Gareth laughed and watched as Declan turned and headed for the door. There was no way that Declan didn't have some kind of hidden agenda or something delicate that he wanted to broach with him.

'I'll see you later then, Declan,' Gareth said, watching him like a hawk. 'And thanks for the coffee.'

Dragging his feet as he headed for the open door, Declan stopped and turned round. 'Oh, just one thing before I go, boss.'

'Ah, got you!' Gareth exclaimed in a victorious tone.

'What?'

'Bloody hell, you're so transparent.' He gave Declan a mocking smile. 'What is it, Declan? This thing you wanted to ask me.'

'Just a couple of the lads were talking,' he stated awkwardly. 'It's DI Hart's first day and before she's been here two seconds, you've effectively made her Senior Investigating Officer on these remains that were found up at Castell Aberlleiniog.'

'So what?' Gareth asked, getting irritated.

Declan shrugged. 'Given that she's been off the job for three years, I just wondered if we should have let her settle in a bit first. You know, find her feet.'

'We?' Gareth frowned and blinked angrily. 'Are you questioning my judgement, Declan?'

'No, boss,' he replied mildly. 'Just an observation.'

'Hey, if you don't like the way I run CID here, there's a vacancy for a detective sergeant over on the mainland in Rhyl.'

There were a few seconds of awkward silence.

Declan nodded. 'Sorry to have brought it up, boss.'

As Declan turned to go, Gareth could see that he was deflated. Gareth had made his point about who was in charge, but it was time to get Declan back on side.

'Declan?'

Declan turned and raised an eyebrow. 'Boss?'

'Next time you bring me a coffee as a horribly transparent attempt to soften me up before questioning one of my decisions . . .' Gareth said with a growing smirk, 'make sure you bring me a packet of bloody biscuits too, eh?'

Declan's face broke into a relieved smile. 'Right you are, boss.'

As Declan left, Ben passed him coming the other way.

'Benjamin, what can I do you for?' Gareth asked, still trying to process Declan's comment about Laura. Of course, their relationship had had no bearing on his decision to give her the case – he did that because she was a bloody good copper – but they'd have to tread carefully if their relationship continued to develop while they were working together.

'I've spoken to the guy who ran the excavation and restoration of Castell Aberlleiniog back in 1995,' Ben explained. 'He said if it's useful, he could meet us down there.'

'Yes, I think that would be useful. Who is he?'

'Alan Clyne from the Anglesey Enterprise and Rural Development Agency.'

'Hopefully, he can shed some light on whether or not those remains could have been there when the work took place,'

Gareth stated. 'Or if they've definitely been buried there since then.'

'Yes, boss.'

Gareth looked at him. 'Any thoughts about why someone decided to tip us off about the remains?'

Ben shrugged. 'No, boss. Guilty conscience?'

'Maybe. Have we got anything else?'

'I've checked the Misper database.'

Misper was short for the UK Missing Persons Unit, which was part of the National Crime Agency, the NCA. It carried out enquiries on behalf of local forces as well as keeping a database of missing and found people in the UK. They also managed the forensic database comprising DNA profiles and fingerprints of those still missing.

Gareth scratched his chin and felt the scab from where he'd cut himself shaving earlier in the half-light of dawn. 'I'm guessing we're looking for the proverbial needle in a haystack.'

'Not as bad as you think. I'm going on the theory that the remains have been there for twenty-five years or less, since the last major excavation at Castell Aberlleiniog. If we then assume that the bank card found with the remains was connected to the victim, then that would give us a timeframe of 1996, when the first card of that type was issued by the Midland Bank, to 1999 when they became HSBC.'

'Assuming that he wasn't carrying it after that because he hadn't thrown it away . . .' Gareth added, but he was impressed with Ben's hypothesis.

'Yeah, there are so many ifs and buts with this at the moment,' Ben admitted. 'Even so, only forty-one adult males were reported missing between 1996 and 1999 on Anglesey. Five are now dead, so we have a list of thirty-six.'

'I'll take those odds,' Gareth commented positively. 'Any forensics for them?'

'I'm still waiting for the MPU to come back to me with that information. But even so, that narrows it down.'

'I've just spoken to DI Hart. According to Professor Lovell, our victim is male, mid-thirties to forty, five foot nine and possibly an ex-soldier.'

Ben nodded. 'I'll do some ringing around and see if I can find anyone who comes close to that description, boss. Hopefully, it'll rule a few others out.'

Gareth gave him a dark look. 'Of course, this could be a wild goose chase if that bank card isn't connected to our victim. Otherwise, those remains could be a bloody Norman soldier from the siege in the eleventh century.'

CHAPTER 10

Laura and Andrea were slogging their way through the Midland Bank account files from the late nineties. There had been over 500 platinum personal accounts held with the branch between 1996 and 1999, and they only had the first five digits of the card number to go on.

Picking up a thick wad of old-fashioned, continuous-feed computer print-out paper with light green bars across, Laura went over to a rickety old table and sat down.

'Bet you've never even seen this kind of paper before?' Laura asked Andrea, who was now sitting on a stool.

'Nope,' Andrea snorted. 'I thought having paper copies of anything was old-fashioned until I saw this stuff.'

Laura ran her finger down the account numbers, looking for any that started with the numbers 4231 . . . 'Yeah, well, I never saw Cagney and Lacey sitting in a cold, dusty basement wading through boxes of paperwork. And they're the reason I'm a copper.'

Andrea gave her an uncertain nod.

'Tell me you know who Cagney and Lacey are?' Laura asked in a mock horrified tone. She could believe it of Ben, who looked like he was twelve, but surely not Andrea, too?

Andrea pulled a face. 'I've sort of heard of them. But I've never seen an episode and I wouldn't know what they looked like.'

'Oh my God, Andrea,' Laura said in disbelief. 'They were incredible. Mary Beth Lacey was this working-class mother with kids. She was always knackered. Christine Cagney was my favourite, though. I had a proper girl crush on her. She had this fantastic blonde flicked haircut. And she drank too much and she was very flirty.'

'And *she* was your childhood feminine heroine and role model?' Andrea enquired incredulously.

'Well, yes. But she was real, and flawed, and took no shit from men.' Laura laughed, getting carried away. 'And you know the best thing? When they were in danger, there was no bloody man coming in to rescue them at the last minute.'

'Sounds like I'm ditching *Love Island* and downloading the full box set.'

Laura looked at Andrea and frowned. 'I know I'm going to regret this, but when were you born?'

'Nineteen ninety-three.'

'Wow.' Laura's eyes widened. 'I was at university in 1993. Now I feel truly ancient.'

'Sorry.' Andrea shrugged, looking embarrassed.

'Hey, I asked you. And I can't blame you for when you were born, can I?'

But Andrea wasn't listening. Instead, she was staring at the page in her hand. Then she turned to look at Laura. 'I've got it. Or *her*, to be more exact.'

'How do you mean?'

'The name on that account is Jenny Maldini.'

Striding along the wooden walkway, Gareth and Declan made their way up the steps towards the Castell Aberlleiniog site. Gareth had insisted that Declan come with him as he needed a metaphorical arm around the shoulder and a pat on the back. Declan had proved invaluable since Gareth had taken the reins at Beaumaris CID and he wanted to keep him on side.

A restless swirl of wind came in from the sea with a noisy hum. The trees on either side were wind-shrunken and formed a continuous grey-green mass, obscuring their view of the nearby beach. Dusk was still another hour away, but the moon was a smoky presence in the sky to the right. The sound of distant waves collapsing on the shingled shore formed an unremitting rhythmic background noise.

As they reached the top of the wooden stairs, the fading glow of daylight hung along the shore. Gareth spotted a large area of recently dug earth that had been cordoned off by blue police evidence tape. The SOCO team had finished their work now, so the lone figure in the distance had to be Alan Clyne from the Anglesey Development Agency.

They headed across the site, navigating a fallen tree whose wood had been hardened and smoothed by the salty wind that whipped in from the sea.

'Mr Clyne?' Gareth enquired, raising his voice against the noise of the wind and taking out his warrant card. 'DI Williams and DS Flaherty, Beaumaris CID. Thanks for meeting us up here.'

Clyne was a tall, imposing man, dressed in full outdoor pursuits gear. He had a bushy grey beard, rounded glasses and steel-blue eyes.

'Not a problem. I haven't been up here in a while. It's good to see it's being kept in such good condition.'

Gareth gestured to the area that had been excavated extensively by the SOCO team. 'As my colleague explained, we found some remains up here and we're keen to establish how long they've been here.'

'We understand that this whole site was excavated and renovated in 1995,' Declan said.

Clyne nodded. 'That's right. Although it wasn't opened to the public until 1996.'

'Our SOCO team reported that the remains we found were only a few inches below the surface of the ground up here,' Gareth explained.

'Okay.' Clyne was deep in thought as he looked around. 'When we came up here in 1995, this entire area was covered with undergrowth and small trees. None of these ruins that you can see here now were visible. We had a team of volunteers up here for months who cleared everything, including digging, weeding and turning over the soil.'

'And what was your role in all that, sir?' Declan enquired.

'I coordinated all the work.' Clyne turned to look at the excavated ground. 'All I can tell you is that if the remains had been here in 1995, they'd have been found. They must have been buried after that date.'

Gareth looked over at Declan – they'd now narrowed the timeframe from 1,000 years to only twenty-six.

CHAPTER 11

Antrim, Northern Ireland 1998

It had been three weeks since John had been taken up to the British Army barracks at Antrim, which were about twenty miles north-west of Belfast. He'd spent his days training for his undercover operation.

Despite still having his Northern Irish accent, he'd been given several tapes to study the specific phonetics of the West Belfast accent. He'd listened to the seemingly innocuous interviews with Belfast locals talking about their daily lives, locking into their slang: '*houl yer whisht*' which meant shut up, or describing something as '*ogeous handlin*'', which meant a situation that was tricky or even dangerous.

The walls of the small apartment he lived in on the army base were covered in maps that he'd learned by heart. Even though he'd spent time in Belfast when he was a child and a teenager, he was surprised how much he'd forgotten. He'd spotted the Ulster Hall on Bedford Street where he had seen Simple Minds and China Crisis in concert in 1982 with two mates from school. They'd bunked off, telling their parents they had rugby practice and were then heading to the local cinema to see *Rocky III*.

John had marked up a large aerial photograph of Belfast with the two major dividing lines – the Falls and Shankill. Other photographs showed street scenes of the major roads where sheets of graffitied corrugated iron kept the Catholics and Protestants apart. As a trained soldier, it was clear where the problem came in mounting any operation in Belfast.

The British Army was an ultra-modern fighting machine trained to be ready for huge conflicts either during the Cold War or in the Middle East. They were taught to fight in deserts or open plains, with tanks and artillery support. What they weren't trained in was the kind of guerrilla warfare they'd encounter in a city that was built in the nineteenth century, where workers' houses were built in narrow streets and back-to-back terraces. The battlegrounds of Belfast were these streets. The cramped housing estates or tower blocks, offered a bewildering maze of blind corners, cul-de-sacs, and back entries for either escape or deadly ambush. At their height, there were 20,000 British soldiers in Northern Ireland who had been unable to overcome a republican army of less than 1,000 men.

Checking his watch, John realised he had weapon training in just under half an hour.

He strolled across the Massereene Barracks, which had been home to the Royal Marines since 1993. It was a base for the Grey Wolf and Grey Fox vessels, which carried out operations along inland waterways. Watching a couple of marines laughing and play-fighting, he realised that's what he'd missed about the last month. The sense of camaraderie you got when you were in a regiment with the same men day in, day out. He quickly put his feelings of envy to one side as he arrived at the shooting range. If he were honest, he'd been using weapons for over a decade and he wasn't sure what else there was for him to learn.

The firearms instructor was Sergeant Harris, a short, muscular Geordie wearing a black boiler suit.

'Forget everything you've ever learned about using a handgun up to this point,' Harris advised him. 'The back-streets of Belfast are very different from anywhere else.'

Maybe he's got a point, John thought as he followed him into a long, cold shed that housed the firing range.

'I'm assuming you've used the Browning before?' Harris enquired, picking up the black handgun with a dark brown handle from a waist-level trestle table beside him.

John knew all about the Browning High-Power L9A1 9mm handgun. With a magazine capacity of thirteen rounds, it had been the SAS standard-issue pistol for decades.

'Oh yeah. A few times over the years.' John nodded as he took the gun from Harris and felt the weight of it in his hand. It was thirty-two ounces, which a previous instructor had told him was the same weight as the human brain. Although, he doubted that particular instructor's brain had weighed the full thirty-two ounces after hearing his facile thoughts on race, religion and politics.

'We don't get many in here with that accent, sir,' Harris stated. 'Not Belfast though, is it?'

'Newry.'

'The hometown of the great Pat Jennings,' Harris commented, referring to the legendary goalkeeper of the 1970s.

'That's right,' John replied with a smile. 'My uncle was his PE teacher and claims it was he who persuaded Pat to go in goal when he was ten years old. I never believed him, mind.'

Harris laughed. 'It's a good story, though.'

'My uncle has plenty of those. The gift of the Blarney, all right.'

'Right you are. Let's see what you've got then, sir,' Harris said brightly as he handed John the dark blue ear defenders and gestured to the 100-metre range with the target of a crouched man at the far end. 'In a combat situation, my advice is to fire off the first round or two as quickly as possible. Put them on the back foot. Then, with the third or fourth, go for accuracy. And whatever you do, keep count. This gun is a bastard to load and you don't want to be trying to do that while you're under fire.'

'I'll bear that in mind,' John said as he clamped on his ear defenders.

He moved his legs apart to steady himself. His arms were outstretched, body slightly hunched, the gun gripped with both hands.

Harris gave him a tap on the shoulder. 'Off you go, sir.'

Squeezing the trigger slowly, John closed his right eye and tried to keep his hands steady.

CRACK! CRACK! The sound of the gun thundered around the range.

He fired off two more rounds before taking a breath.

Steadying himself again, he drew in a breath and fired again.

CRACK! CRACK! CRACK!

Harris tapped him on the shoulder. 'Seven rounds should give us an idea of how you're doing. Your firing stance is spot-on, sir.'

'Thanks,' John said as he rested the gun on green baize on the table. 'I spent a lot of time on the range in West Germany.'

Pressing the button that sent the target down the range towards them, John wondered how he'd fared. He'd always prided himself on being a decent shot.

As the paper target of the crouched man hoved into view, John gave a smile of satisfaction. There were six holes in a small grouping in the man's chest area and one in his stomach.

'Don't know what happened to that one.' Harris joked about the rogue bullet and then gave him a smile. 'That's pretty impressive, sir. There's not much I can teach you. When are you off to Belfast?'

'Tomorrow at dawn.'

CHAPTER 12

Now armed with an address, Laura and Andrea headed out of Llangefni and drove south. The sky unfurled a dark metallic grey canvas. On either side, the land was flat. A mosaic of grassland and heath containing rarities such as the pale heath violet and the spotted rock-rose. Further on, bryophytes and buckler ferns lay in thick patches. Once in a while a tiny house, smoke drifting from its chimney, appeared out of nowhere set back from the road. One or two even had clothes on lines that flapped optimistically in the wind, even though the ever-darkening skies indicated a certain storm.

As they approached the village, the fields had become rocky and the roads narrow and windy. A soft mist of rain fell on the windscreen. The roads zig-zagged towards the top of the village, where a fourteenth-century limestone church stood proudly over its parishioners.

They turned left and found the row of workers' cottages they'd been looking for. The address they'd found at the bank had been for a cottage called Appleyard.

Getting out of the car, Laura felt the salty wind bite at her cheeks and ears. Curlews and gulls glided on the streams of air coming from the sea, cawing loudly. The air was full of the smell of burning wood and coal from open fires.

Appleyard stood out from others as being a little run-down and neglected. The red paint of the front door had faded to a dark pink and the grass in the front garden was overgrown and strewn with weeds.

Laura knocked at the door and took a step back as Andrea joined her.

A moment later, the door opened and a woman looked out at them with a quizzical expression. 'Hello?'

She was in her eighties and had a thick West Wales accent. Laura guessed Welsh was probably her native tongue. The woman's eyes were blue and milky, her face lined and sallow.

'DI Hart and DC Jones, Beaumaris CID,' Laura explained with a comforting smile. The woman was old and she didn't want to startle her.

'Oh, yes.' The woman frowned nervously. 'Is there something wrong?'

'No, no,' Laura replied. 'Nothing like that. We're looking for a Jenny Maldini. We have this down as her address.'

The woman took a few seconds to think. 'I'm not sure. My husband and I bought this house about twenty years ago.'

Sod it.

'Do you know who you bought it from?' Andrea enquired.

'No, I'm sorry,' the woman replied, shaking her head. 'But it was a woman we bought it from.'

Laura gave her a patient smile. 'Would your husband know who sold you the house?'

'I'm afraid he died a few years ago, dear,' she replied. 'Did you say her name was Jenny?'

'Yes, that's right.'

The woman frowned and stared into space for a moment. 'Yes, I think that was her name. She was living on her own here.'

'Do you have a forwarding address?' Laura enquired hopefully.

The woman gave them a wry smile. 'Oh no. She didn't leave us her new address.'

Why did she say it like that? Laura wondered. There was a subtext to her response, and Laura gave her a questioning look.

'My husband and I got the feeling that she didn't want to be found,' the woman explained.

It was nearly dark by the time Gareth and Declan arrived at the Anglesey Arms pub in the sleepy village of Llanddona, four miles north of Beaumaris. The last touches of vanilla light tinted the dark clouds that lay over the Great Orme, Snowdonia and the Llŷn Peninsula on the Welsh mainland. On clear days, it was said that the Isle of Man and even the southern reaches of Cumbria were visible.

As Gareth parked in the pub car park, he remembered something his taid had told him. It was an old fable about the Witches of Llanddona. They'd been cast out of England and set adrift in a boat with no oars. Eventually, they landed on the beach close to Llanddona but were met by a hostile crowd of locals. However, when they commanded a spring of pure water to appear from the sandy beach, the locals allowed them to come ashore and live in the village. As time went on, the Witches of Llanddona became a term used to describe any female from the village and implied a fierce temper.

Getting out of the car, Gareth looked over at Declan. 'What was this guy's name again?'

'Aled Pearce, boss,' Declan reminded him.

Ben had narrowed down some of the men on the MisPer database. He'd found an Aled Pearce, who would have been thirty-seven-years old when he went missing in 1997. His wife,

Michelle Pearce, had made the report. The database recorded that Aled had gone out one night and never came home.

The inside of the Anglesey Arms was old-fashioned, with low ceilings, oak beams and a log fire. Gareth could see from the pumps and the various logos behind the bar that this was a pub that prided itself on real ale. It definitely wasn't his sort of thing.

'DS Flaherty and DI Williams,' Declan stated as the young barman approached.

He pulled a face when he realised they were coppers.

'We're looking for Michelle Pearce,' Declan continued.

According to their intel, Michelle Pearce was the landlady.

The barman's eyes widened and he nodded. 'I'll just go and get her, shall I?'

'Thanks,' Declan said as the barman left.

'Not my sort of thing. Real cask ale,' Gareth commented under his breath as he gestured to the pumps. 'Tastes like warm mud to me.'

Declan laughed. 'And me. I'll have a cold lager in the summer.'

'What about a drop of the black stuff?' Gareth asked. He was referring to Guinness.

'I don't like Guinness, if you can believe that?' Declan chortled ironically.

'Yeah, I'm not sure I like Guinness, either,' Gareth admitted. 'It looks great in the glass. But then I taste it and I think it's a bit like stale coffee.'

'Red wine is my poison, if I'm honest, boss,' Declan admitted.

'Now you're talking.'

'Can I help?' enquired a friendly voice.

It was a woman in her early sixties, plump, with coiffured hair and a huge smile. She had a southern accent, maybe Essex, Gareth thought.

'We're looking for Michelle Pearce,' Declan explained.

'That's me. How can I help, gentlemen?' she enquired in a cheery voice.

'We're looking into a missing persons case, possibly in the nineties,' Gareth explained. 'We understand you reported your husband missing back in 1997. Is that correct?'

The colour visibly drained from her face as she took a sharp intake of breath. 'Have you found him?' she whispered.

'We're not sure,' Gareth said gently. 'All I can tell you is that we have found some remains. Do you think it would be okay for us to ask you a few questions?'

Michelle pursed her lips as her eyes filled with tears. She looked shaken. 'Yeah, of course.'

'Can you confirm how old your husband was when he went missing?' Declan pulled out his notepad and pen.

'Thirty-seven. He went missing three days before his thirty-eighth birthday,' she replied sadly.

'How tall was he?' Gareth enquired.

'He was big. Six foot two.'

'Was your husband ever in the British Army?'

'No, never.'

Bollocks. It's not him, then.

Gareth looked over at Declan. It looked like Aled Pearce wasn't their man. Gareth took a breath. He knew it was going to be a huge let-down to have raised Michelle's hopes, only to dash them.

'Thank you Mrs Pearce,' Gareth said quietly.

Michelle looked at them desperately. 'Is it him, then?'

'We can't be certain.' Gareth gave her a compassionate look as he said gently, 'But from what you've told us, I'm sorry to say that I don't believe the remains we've found are your husband's. And again, I'm so sorry to have got your hopes up.'

'It's okay.' Michelle nodded and looked back at them, utterly lost.

Gareth knew that she'd have spent twenty-five years wondering what had happened to her husband. And for the briefest of moments, it must have seemed as if she might get some kind of closure to that pain.

As Gareth turned and headed out of the pub, he felt the weight of her loss. And he felt the guilt of having offered hope, only to have taken it away.

Jesus, this job never gets any easier, he thought sadly.

CHAPTER 13

The darkening clouds began to toss up an icy southerly wind as Laura and Andrea made their way back towards Beaumaris nick. Outside, the air looked biting and raw. Andrea clicked on the windscreen wipers as the rain, which had been light and intermittent, fell in spiky barbs.

Laura's mobile phone buzzed. It was Ben. She'd tasked him with doing a thorough search on Jenny Maldini, using both the PNC – the Police National Computer – and HOLMES – the Home Office Large Major Enquiry System. Its title was also a humorous nod to Arthur Conan Doyle's famous detective character.

'Ben?' Laura said, answering her phone. 'Did you find anything?'

'Nothing on the PNC or HOLMES, so this Jenny Maldini doesn't have any form of criminal record.'

Laura felt deflated. That was the problem with anything historic. Tracking down anyone twenty or thirty years after the event was time-consuming and expensive, especially if they didn't want to be found.

'I checked the council tax records,' Ben explained. 'No Jenny Maldini, but there is a Rose Maldini living in

Llansadwrn. I've got the address as Pebble Cottage on Pentraeth Road.'

'It's an unusual surname, especially in Anglesey,' Laura said positively. 'And it's only ten minutes from here, so we'll check it out. Thanks, Ben.' Laura ended the call and looked over at Andrea. 'You know where Llansadwrn is?'

Andrea nodded. 'Yes, boss.' She slowed the car and did a U-turn on the country lane.

Llansadwrn was a small village in Cwm Cadnant. It lay between Pentraeth, Menai Bridge and Beaumaris and was named after its church, which was originally founded by Saint Saturninus in the sixth century.

The village appeared to be no more than a collection of thirty or forty houses and a village pub, The Sexton Arms. The rain had eased and pattered intermittently on the windscreen.

Andrea pointed. 'It should be up here.'

They pulled up outside a small white bungalow with a matching dark green front door and garage gates. The front garden was full of potted plants that had been neatly arranged around the paving stones and on the stone wall that flanked the road. A hanging basket beside the front door overflowed with yellow begonias and rocked back and forth in the wind.

Getting out of the car, Laura pulled up her collar against the rain as she and Andrea marched up the garden path and knocked at the door.

The front door opened and a cheery woman in her seventies faced her. She had a ruddy face and thinning silver hair. She wore an old-fashioned twinset and a long tartan skirt.

'Hello?' she asked with a confused smile. She had a Scottish accent.

'Hi there.' Taking out her warrant card, Laura said, 'DI Hart and DC Jones from Beaumaris CID. I wonder if you can help us. Can you tell us if a Rose Maldini lives here?'

'Yes, that's me.' The woman nodded, sounding worried.

'Do you know a Jenny Maldini?'

'Yes. Oh dear,' the woman replied, as her eyes widened. 'Is something the matter?'

'Does Jenny live here?' Andrea enquired.

'No,' the woman said. 'Is she all right? She's my daughter.'

'As far as we know, she's fine,' Laura explained reassuringly. 'We just need to ask her a few questions to help with an ongoing investigation.'

'Oh, right.' Rose blinked nervously. 'But Jenny won't be at home at the moment. Do you want me to tell her you called for her?'

'Can you tell us where Jenny is?' Andrea asked.

'She's at work,' Rose explained, getting increasingly flustered.

Laura gave her a kind smile. 'And where does she work?'

'The Anglesey Lakeside Lodges,' Rose explained. 'Down by Llandegfan.'

Andrea nodded and looked at Laura. 'Yeah, I know it.'

'Do . . . Do you want me to phone her?' Rose asked.

'Don't worry, Mrs Maldini,' Laura assured gently. 'Please don't. We'll go down there and find her. Sorry to have troubled you. Thanks for your help.'

It was now dark and Gareth sat on a thick stone wall that overlooked the beach close to Penryn Safnas. He and Declan had been trying to track down another address on their list of missing Anglesey men from the late nineties. They knew the missing man's father lived in Penryn Safnas, but so far they couldn't find where he lived. Thankfully, the rain had stopped, but it was getting colder by the minute.

'Maybe this would be better in the daylight,' Gareth moaned. They'd been searching for the exact location of the house for twenty minutes, but to no avail.

Spotting an old man walking his dog, Declan looked at Gareth brightly. 'I've had an idea. Back in a second, boss.'

As Declan scampered away, no doubt to ask for the local man's help, Gareth looked out at the noisy sea that was now only fifty yards away as the tide came in. It was an ugly black and greenish colour. Each resounding roar would culminate in a loud whoosh and then a surge of water up the beach towards him. In the darkness, he found the power of the tide frightening. It was a very different sea from the one that he swam in along the coast at Beaumaris.

He and Laura had shared their love of wild swimming several times. In fact, it had been on Gareth's recommendation that she join the local wild swimming club, The Bluetits. In his mind's eye, he saw Laura's face, and he felt a mixture of excitement and optimism that lifted his spirits. Maybe he'd give her a call when he got back home. If he were honest, he just wanted to fall into bed with her, but school and work nights were complicated.

Gareth's phone rang, breaking his train of thought. It was Ben.

'Ben?'

'Boss, we've identified that pin badge forensics found with the remains. It's a pin badge for the Irish Guards Regiment.'

'Okay.' Gareth nodded. 'That might help narrow it down. Thanks, Ben.' Gareth ended the call.

'I've found it, boss,' said a voice.

It was Declan and he was wearing a curious smile.

'What's the matter?'

Declan pointed. 'It's up there.'

Peering in the direction that Declan had indicated, Gareth spotted a dim apricot light. There was an old cottage dug into the cliffs.

'How the bloody hell are we getting up there?' Gareth growled.

'That old fella reckons there's a pathway all the way up to it. Not as dangerous as it looks.'

Getting to his feet, Gareth rolled his eyes. 'We'd better get up there, then.'

The pathway up through the cliffside was uneven and Gareth could see the lights of Beaumaris twinkling in the distance. As the old man with the dog had informed Declan, it was a relatively comfortable uphill walk through brambles and undergrowth. Gareth was grateful; he wasn't wearing the right footwear to go scrambling up cliffs today.

As they approached, Declan shone his torch towards the house. The powerful beam hit the grey slate roof and then the weather-beaten windows where translucent cloth hung as makeshift curtains. On one side of the ramshackle porch was a pile of peat slices that were clearly the occupant's source of heat. Gareth could smell the pungent smoke coming out of the chimney. The paint on the porch door rose in scabs over bare wood. The walls were covered in lichen and moss.

Declan gave the door an authoritative knock and stood back. A dog barked and snarled from inside.

Gareth gave Declan a sarcastic smile. 'That doesn't sound like a puppy, does it?'

'Not really, boss.'

After a minute or two, a dark silhouette moved across the makeshift curtain, peered out and then disappeared.

They waited again as the salty wind whipped around them. Gareth felt the material of his trousers flapping hard in the violent currents of air.

He looked over at Declan and raised an eyebrow. 'Today would be good, eh?'

And with that, the door opened slowly and a dishevelled man stared out at them. He was in his sixties with an untidy beard, bloodshot eyes and broken blood vessels around the end of his nose.

Christ, it's like coming face to face with a troll!

89

He had stumpy legs, a short, thick body, slightly hunch-backed and a lop-sided mouth with teeth that were jumbled and yellow. Even from where he was standing, Gareth got a waft of something other than the burning peat.

Ah, a whisky-drinking troll, he deduced immediately.

'Evening, sir,' he said politely as he took out his warrant card. 'DI Williams and DS Flaherty, Beaumaris CID. We wondered if we could ask you a couple of questions.'

The man nodded and gave a low grunt.

Uncertain whether or not the man had understood anything he'd said, Gareth peered at him. 'We're looking for an Elis Hughes.'

The man nodded and said in a slurred voice, 'Aye, that's right.'

Declan looked at him. 'We understand you reported a Martin Hughes missing in 1999?'

'My son,' Elis said, nodding slowly. His eyelids drooped, as if he were having a hard time keeping them open.

'Can I just confirm that you've had no contact with your son since the day you reported him missing?' Gareth asked.

'No, of course not.' Elis scowled at them both and then asked, 'Have you found him or something?'

'I'm afraid that we've found some remains,' Declan explained. 'And we'd like to ask you a few questions to establish if those remains could be Martin.'

'All right, then,' Elis said without the faintest glimmer of emotion.

'Can you tell us how tall your son was?' Gareth enquired.

Elis shrugged. 'Tall. Five eleven, six foot, I think.'

Not the same height as the skeleton we found, then.

'Did Martin ever serve in the military? Possibly the Irish Guards.'

'No.' Elis shook his head. 'No chance. They wouldn't have had him.'

'Would you have described him as being average build?' Declan enquired.

'Martin?' Elis snorted. 'Joking, aren't you? He looked like the fucking Michelin man. Lazy little prick, he was.'

Gareth looked over at Declan – it didn't sound as if Martin Hughes was their man.

'I'm afraid that I don't think the remains we've found are Martin, Mr Hughes,' Gareth said quietly, 'I'm sorry to have troubled you, and thank you for your help.'

Bollocks! What a waste of time!

Gareth and Declan turned and headed away from the cottage.

'Bloke you're describing sounds like John Finn,' Elis stated.

What did he say?

Turning back, Gareth gave him a quizzical look. 'Sorry, who's John Finn?'

'Friend of Martin's,' Elis explained. 'They drank together sometimes in pubs round here.'

Declan frowned. 'Why do you think it sounds like John Finn?'

'Was he a soldier?' Gareth asked.

'Aye,' Elis replied. 'I think this John said he was in the Irish Guards.'

CHAPTER 14

Belfast 1998

John smiled at Mrs Houlihan as he looked around the small bedroom of her two-storey boarding house, which backed onto the Falls Road. She was in her late fifties, with dark hair, bright eyes, a warm smile but more lines than one might expect for a woman of her age. Her complexion told of someone who smoked and drank too much.

Jesus. What a shithole!

'This will be grand, Mrs Houlihan,' John said politely.

Mrs Houlihan laughed as if John had said something bordering on flirtatious.

'It's nothing fancy, Mr Doyle. But it's clean, and the mattress is firm.' She gave him a *look* and turned to go.

Oh, God, he thought. *I do not want her creeping in here during the night for 'a bit of company'.*

'Tea is at five thirty sharp in the big room,' she informed him. 'We'll have the television on until nine. And no female companions in the rooms in the evening.'

John gave her a forced smile. 'That won't be a problem, Mrs Houlihan.'

'Right you are, Mr Doyle,' she chirped. 'If you'll wash up, I'll make you a brew when you come down, then.'

'Thank you,' John said as he went over to the grubby windows, which were framed by curtains that were heavily stained with tobacco smoke.

Looking down into the back alleyway, he spotted a group of boys running home from the park, kicking a football between them and shouting as the rain sheeted down. Two of them had red Manchester United shirts on. It was the English football team of choice if you were Irish Catholic. Both of them had the name KEANE and the number 16 printed on the back. Roy Keane was a fierce Irishman from Cork who was now United's captain.

A rumbling noise distracted him and he glanced left to see a British Army Saracen – a six-wheeled armoured personnel carrier – trundling past the boys, who didn't give it a second glance as they ran down a nearby alleyway and disappeared.

John went over to the sink and washed his face and hands. Looking at his reflection in the mirror, he felt an element of satisfaction, even pride, in what he was doing. He took a silver crucifix and chain from the small dressing table and fastened it around his neck, adjusting it so that it could be seen at his throat under his shirt. Traditionally, Catholics wore a crucifix depicting Christ on the cross, whereas Protestants wore just a plain one. John had heard Protestants criticising the crucifix, claiming that Catholics implied that Jesus had never risen from the dead. That was typical Proddy bullshit. John understood that the Catholics' preference for showing the corpus was that it was a more vivid reminder of the crucifixion and what Jesus had suffered for the sins of mankind.

Making his way downstairs, John saw four other men sitting at the table. They were all in their twenties and thirties, except for an older man with a moustache who was

93

probably around fifty years old. There was the obligatory pot of tea and plate piled high with thick slices of bread and butter. Mrs Houlihan busied herself bringing them plates of sausages and beans, and most of them ate in virtual silence except for the odd mumble to ask for salt or another slice of bread. A television was on in the corner showing the news with the sound turned low.

Once the meal was completed, three of the men thanked Mrs Houlihan for 'a grand tea' and went outside to smoke on the patio. John took a swig of his tea, aware that the man with the moustache was sizing him up.

'Not a smoker, then?' the man enquired after a while.

John shook his head. 'I had asthma as a kid, so I never really started like the others.'

'I smoked forty a day for twenty-five years until they took one of my lungs away,' the man explained, pointing to his chest.

John nodded. 'I guess that's a decent incentive to stop.'

'Aye, that it is.' The man gave a wry laugh. 'That it is. I'm Bobby.'

'John,' he said.

'Mrs Houlihan tells me you used to be in the navy?' Bobby asked as he mopped up the last of his beans with a slice of bread.

'Merchant navy,' John stated, keen to play the part of someone who would find it an anathema to be in the British Royal Navy.

'Girl in every port, then?' Bobby asked, clearly trying to get the measure of him.

'I wish,' John grinned, but his attention had been drawn to the television and a local news story featuring British soldiers on patrol somewhere in Belfast.

'Still here after all this time,' Bobby groaned as he indicated the news story.

'Maybe they should spend some time going after the UVF,' John growled. 'They never found whoever shot that taxi driver in Lurgan, did they?'

Bobby gave him a curious look. 'No, they didn't.'

John shrugged. 'He was a Catholic, so they weren't interested. Mate of mine reckons it was the feckin' army that tipped the UVF off. Bastards.'

There were a few seconds of silence. John wondered if he'd gone too far by expressing his political opinions so openly. He didn't have time to spend weeks ingratiating himself with everyone he met.

Bobby took the teapot, leaned over and refilled John's cup. 'So, how long were you in the merchant navy, John?'

'Fifteen years,' John replied. 'Then I worked over in Canada for a while.'

'What were you doing?'

'Working in the iron ore mines,' John explained, sticking to the brief he'd learned until it had become second nature.

'Where was that?' Bobby enquired, as if he had some knowledge on the subject.

It made John feel uneasy, as he only knew what the MOD had given him.

'The Mary River iron ore site on Baffin Island,' John explained.

Bobby smiled and shrugged. 'And where the hell is that, then?'

'Way up in the north,' he said, relieved that Bobby wasn't suddenly an expert on Baffin Island. 'Close to the Arctic Circle. Bloody cold, I can tell you.'

'Aye. And that must have been hard work.'

'Not really. I was on the explosives team. We'd blast the rock underground so it could be mined.'

'What explosives did you use?'

It was a strange question.

'These days it's ammonium nitrate-based. Basically, a mixture of ammonium nitrate and fuel oil,' John replied, trying to sound as matter-of-fact as he could. 'They call it ANFO. They should have really used Semtex, but it's exorbitant.'

Bobby gave him a serious look and asked quietly, 'You know your stuff when it comes to explosives, then?'

For a moment, John took in his question. *Why is he asking me that? Is it an innocent question or something darker?*

John nodded confidently. 'Oh yeah. But if they needed us to break up the big benches of rock, they'd have to shell out for Semtex or C4. The ANFO wasn't powerful enough.'

'Interesting stuff,' Bobby commented. 'You'll have to come with me for a few scoops at McEnaneys on the weekend.'

'Sure. I'd like that,' John replied, wondering if there was any subtext to the invitation or not. Whatever was behind it, Bobby seemed to be strangely fascinated by John's work in Canada.

CHAPTER 15

Laura and Andrea weaved their way through the Anglesey Lakeside Lodges. Essentially, they were luxury log cabins that could have been plucked directly from Scandinavia. The stunning nine-acre lakeside site was lit up with amber lights that gave it an almost magical, unworldly atmosphere.

The young girl at reception told them that Jenny was busy cleaning Tryfan Lodge, which was at the far end of the site.

'This place is amazing,' Laura stated, making a mental note that she should bring the kids here at some point.

Having spotted that a few of the lodges had hot tubs outside, she wondered if she and Gareth could sneak away for a romantic weekend.

Chance would be a fine thing, she thought frustratedly.

'I used to deliver eggs and milk and stuff here for a local farm,' Andrea explained. 'I was always really jealous because my foster parents' idea of a summer holiday was camping in a tiny tent up at Maes Tywyn.' She gave a little laugh, but Laura could see a touch of sadness in her expression.

'Yeah, me and my sister would have killed for a holiday in a place like this,' Laura said. 'And we'd have definitely ended up diving into the lake no matter what.'

'Are you close?' Andrea enquired as they turned left down at the main footpath through the site. 'You and your sister?'

'Emma?' Laura asked rhetorically. 'Yeah, we're close. She lives with her family down in Kent, so we don't get to see her as much as we'd like. And she was diagnosed with MS last year, so she's got all that to deal with.'

Andrea frowned. 'God, that must be difficult.'

As a PE teacher at a prestigious girls' grammar school, Emma's diagnosis had been a terrible blow. All she'd ever wanted to do was be a PE teacher and doctors had told her that her MS would eventually stop her from being able to do that.

'She never mentions it,' Laura explained. 'When Sam died, she was there for me every step of the way. I don't know what I'd have done without her. Have you got siblings?'

Andrea's expression changed. 'No,' she said quietly as she shook her head.

There was a second of awkward silence, and Laura wished she hadn't asked.

Laura's phone buzzed. It was a voicemail from Ben.

'Boss, we've identified that regimental pin badge forensics found with the remains. It's for the Irish Guards. I thought you'd want to know straight away. See you later.'

Laura ended the message and looked at Andrea. 'Seems our victim might have once been in the Irish Guards.'

Andrea nodded. 'Okay, well that would certainly narrow it down . . . Here we go, boss,' she said, pointing to a sign that read TRYFAN LODGE.

The lodge was built from a dark, ruddy-coloured cedar-wood with a sloping slate roof. The garden was neat and the outside lights cast shadows from the plants and small trees across the grass.

Approaching the main door, Laura peered through the glass pane. A woman in her fifties was hoovering. She was wearing a blue pinafore apron over her own clothes and she had flat white pumps on.

Laura knocked hard on the glass so that the woman would hear her over the sound of the hoover.

Nothing. The woman continued to hoover obliviously.

Laura rapped her ringed finger against the glass loudly.

This time the woman looked up, saw her and turned off the hoover. She approached the door, opened it and gave them a quizzical look. Her blonde highlighted hair had been pulled back into a tight ponytail. Her nose was pointed and her face gaunt.

Laura smiled and took out her warrant card as she got a waft of stale cigarette smoke from the woman's clothes. 'Hi there. DI Hart and DC Jones from Beaumaris CID. We're looking for a Jenny Maldini.'

The woman's face dropped. 'Yes. That's me.'

'Okay if we come in?' Laura asked, gesturing to the lodge.

'Yes,' Jenny replied uncertainly. 'Is everything okay? Is it my mum?'

'No, no. We just spoke to her and she's fine,' Andrea reassured.

'We just need to ask you a few questions about an investigation,' Laura explained gently. 'I'm afraid we found some remains up at Castell Aberlleiniog.'

'Okay.' Jenny obviously didn't know what that had to do with her.

'And with those remains, we found a Midland Bank platinum debit card that belongs to you. We're guessing from the late nineties.'

Jenny's eyes roamed nervously about the lodge's living area as she put her hand to her face. Her colour drained and she looked unsteady on her feet.

Andrea gestured to a nearby sofa. 'Do you want to sit down for a minute?'

99

Jenny, whose face had now twisted into an alarmed frown, nodded and sat down slowly.

There were a few seconds of silence.

'You've found him, then,' she whispered, as if talking to herself.

'Do you know whose those remains are, Jenny?' Laura enquired gently as she sat down in an armchair opposite the sofa.

Jenny nodded as she stared into space. 'It's John.'

'John?' Andrea asked quietly.

'Yes. It's John.' Jenny nodded slowly as her eyes then moved around the room. 'He's been gone for so long, you see.'

'Do you think you could tell us what happened, Jenny? And who John is,' Laura asked quietly, with an empathetic expression.

'John was my partner. John Finn. We lived together just outside Pentraeth. John went out to the pub one night. The Panton Arms,' Jenny explained.

Laura looked at her. 'Could you tell us when this was?'

'Twelfth of October 1999.'

'Do you know who John was with that night?'

'He was in a pub quiz team with his friend Rhys Hughes. And then he just disappeared . . . He never came home.'

'Can I ask if you reported it?' Andrea enquired.

Jenny nodded. The reality of what they'd told her was sinking in. She took a deep breath as her eyes filled. 'Sorry . . .' she whispered. 'I just never knew what happened to him.'

'It's okay,' Laura assured as she took a tissue from her pocket, leaned forwards and handed it to her. 'Here you go.'

'Thank you.' Jenny sniffed as she dabbed her face. 'God, I can't believe it.'

Laura asked gently, 'Do you think you're up to answering a couple of questions that might help us establish that the remains we found are John?'

Jenny nodded as she bit her lip. 'Yeah, okay.'

Laura looked over at her and asked quietly, 'Can you tell us how tall John was?'

'Five ten, five nine,' Jenny replied.

Andrea took out her notepad and pen. 'Would you say he was average build?'

'Yeah, I suppose so.'

'Was John ever in the British Army?' Laura enquired.

'Oh yeah,' Jenny replied with a sniff. 'He was very proud of that.'

'Can I ask what regiment he was in?'

'Irish Guards,' Jenny stated, and then her face brightened. 'John was Irish. And then he was recruited into the SAS. He was in Desert Storm. He told me he was in an SAS unit that was dropped behind enemy lines. I think he won a medal for bravery.'

There was little doubt that the remains they'd found were John Finn.

'Can you remember his date of birth?' Laura asked, knowing that might be useful when checking records.

'Second of July 1964,' she said. 'Are you sure it's him?'

Laura looked at Jenny for a moment. 'I'm really sorry, Jenny, but from what you've told us, I do think the remains we've found are John.'

Jenny nodded as her eyes welled again. 'Yeah. I knew when you said it. Part of me is relieved, you know?'

Laura gave her a compassionate smile. 'It must have been incredibly hard for you, not knowing where he was.'

'I thought he might have run off with another woman,' Jenny snorted with an ironic smile. 'But John wasn't that sort of bloke. I knew there must have been trouble of some sort.' Jenny's eyes narrowed. 'Do you know what happened to him?'

Laura hesitated. 'I'm really sorry, but I'm afraid we think that John was murdered.'

CHAPTER 16

It was gone eight p.m. by the time CID officers started the scene boards that had been erected at the far end of the office. Gareth put his hands in his pockets, took two paces back and looked at what they'd written on the left-hand side.

Name: John Finn TBC
Date of birth: 2 July 1964
Date of death: 12 October 1999?
Location: Castell Aberlleiniog
Cause of death: Murder – blunt force trauma

Irish Guards/SAS/Gulf War??

It wasn't a lot to go on yet and until they had DNA or forensic confirmation, they were only going on supposition that the remains they'd found were indeed John Finn.

Looking around, Gareth saw Ben was approaching – he seemed confused.

Gareth tapped his watch. 'You need to go home. I want you sharp and fresh tomorrow.'

'Okay, boss,' Ben said with a reluctant nod. 'Something very strange has come up when I ran a check on John Finn.'

'What do you mean, strange?'

'He's not on the PNC or HOLMES, but if he hasn't committed a crime, that's not a surprise,' Ben explained. 'So, I checked the Armed Forces Service Records, which are all online now. He's not on there. There's no record of him ever serving in the British Army.'

'That is weird.' Gareth frowned. 'Why would Jenny Maldini lie about that?'

'Unless John Finn wasn't his actual name?' Ben said with a knowing expression.

'Why do you say that?' Gareth asked. Ben had obviously found something else.

'Because I checked UK council tax records. John Finn has never paid council tax on Anglesey or claimed any benefit. Nor has he ever been on the electoral roll here.'

Gareth raised an eyebrow. 'What?' *How is that possible?*

'It gets even weirder, boss,' Ben explained. 'I then spoke to HMRC and then the Passport Office . . . A John Finn, with that date of birth, has never paid taxes anywhere in Britain, and has never held a UK passport. In fact, so far, there's no evidence I can find that anyone called John Finn, with that date of birth, ever actually existed.'

'That makes no sense, does it?' Gareth frowned as he took in this information.

'No, it doesn't, boss.'

'Okay. We need to talk to Jenny Maldini tomorrow. Then we need to pull the missing persons file and report. I don't know if they do those sorts of checks when someone goes missing, but I doubt it.'

'Yes, boss.'

'Good work, Ben.'

'Thanks.'

'And, Ben?'

'Yes?'

'Go home.' Gareth smiled. 'That's an order.'

Ben nodded and went over to his desk to collect his stuff. As he glanced around, Gareth realised he was the only person left in the CID office.

Where did Laura get to? he wondered. He didn't even see her leave or get to ask her how her first day had been. He didn't blame her. She was a single mother with two kids, after all. He wondered if there would ever be a time when they went home to the same house. He hoped so.

Rubbing his hand over his shaved scalp, Gareth wandered casually through the CID office towards his office. He planned the rest of his evening. He owed his brother, Rob, a phone call. It was his nephew Charlie's eighteenth birthday in a few weeks and Gareth wanted to get him something special. He just needed to run a few ideas past Rob. Charlie had somehow ended up as a Chelsea fan – the rest of the family were firmly Manchester United. He supposed that's what happened if you went off and lived in Hong Kong.

Maybe I'll stop and get something decent for dinner, he thought as he walked into his office.

'Took your time, didn't you, buster?' said a voice.

It was Laura.

For a moment, he was startled. 'Bloody hell!'

'Sorry, I didn't mean to scare you,' she laughed.

Gareth pulled a mock macho face. 'You didn't scare me. I just didn't know you were there, that's all.'

Laura chortled. 'Erm, you *were* scared because you jumped and your voice went up an octave.' She was sitting back in his chair, feet up on his desk and grinning at him.

Their eyes met for a moment and he felt his insides spark.

'Never mind all that. How long have you been sitting there?' he laughed. It was so good to be in a room on their own.

'Too long,' Laura said with a raised eyebrow.

'You do know it's a disciplinary offence to sit in a superior officer's chair,' he stated, trying to sound sexy.

'Except we're both DIs, you melon.'

'Yeah, well, that's a moot point.' Gareth shrugged. 'Do you make a habit of hiding in dark offices?'

'I was hoping to seduce you, but Ben wouldn't fuck off home.'

Gareth gave her a sexy grin. 'He's fucked off home now.'

'Has he indeed?' Laura asked, getting up from where she was sitting and looking at her watch. 'I think the moment might have gone now.'

No, it hasn't.

Gareth moved forwards and looked directly at her. He knew she was just playing. Without breaking eye contact, he kicked his office door shut with the back of his heel.

'Nice move,' she observed flirtily.

'I've been practising that for weeks.'

He put his hands on her hips and pulled her towards him a little.

'I'm pretty sure this is sexual harassment,' Laura joked.

'Ask me to stop, then.' Gareth smirked.

Without warning, he leaned in and kissed her hard on the mouth.

'Oh, okay,' she laughed. 'Now I'm going to have to report you for that.'

Her eyes sparkled as she looked at him.

Putting his hand around her waist, he gently pulled her further towards him until their bodies touched. He felt her back arch and she took a breath.

He reached over, put his hand to her face and kissed her again, softly at first and then with a growing urgency. Their tongues played lightly.

Moving her head, she nuzzled and kissed his neck before biting his earlobe.

Their eyes locked again.

He felt her hand move around to his crotch.

'Evening,' she said with a suggestive smile.

'Evening,' he whispered as he kissed her hard and pushed her gently towards the desk.

She fumbled for the button on his trousers as he tugged off her jacket and began to unbutton her blouse. He wanted her so much.

Out of nowhere came a noise. A low, rhythmic humming, which came from somewhere in his office.

They frowned at each other.

'What the hell is that?' Laura asked, her hand frozen on Gareth's waistband.

Then Gareth realised with a sinking feeling. 'It's my phone.'

'Ignore it.'

He looked over at the phone on his desk. 'It's Control. I have to take it.'

'Are you joking?' Laura rolled her eyes.

'I really wish I was.' Gareth sighed as he straightened his clothes in mild panic and took the call. After a few seconds, he said gravely, 'Okay, thanks for letting me know.'

Laura frowned. 'Everything all right?'

Gareth gave her a dark look. 'Someone's witnessed a fight up at Gallows Point. Uniform have found a body, so it looks like murder.'

CHAPTER 17

Ten minutes later, Laura and Gareth were racing along the A545 at speed. The blue LED lights of CID's navy Astra CDTi were flickering and the siren shrieking – 'blues and twos' – to clear what little rural traffic there was.

Laura looked up at the sky, which was full of rain. Getting evidence in the 'golden hour' after a crime had been committed was vital. A scene was fresh, less likely to have been contaminated, and if a body was present it might not have been there for long. It was imperative that things were done quickly – she didn't want vital evidence to be washed away by the rain.

'I've heard of hitting the ground running, but this is something else,' Laura joked darkly.

'Yeah, well, I'm starting to believe the curse of the Q-word,' Gareth said, rolling his eyes.

She gave him a half-smile.

The rain had stopped its incessant drumming by the time they arrived at Gallows Point – *Penrhyn Safnas* in Welsh – a stretch of beach just to the south of Beaumaris. A half-hearted drizzle hung in the air, as if the energy of the storm had been drained by the darker events of the evening.

The beachfront was a luminous tapestry of yellow, white and blue lights, where emergency signs had already been set up. An ambulance, two police cars, uniformed officers and two SOCO vehicles with the *heddlu* – police – marking had already arrived.

Reaching the uniformed officer who was manning the police cordon and crime scene, they showed their warrant cards.

'DI Williams and DI Hart. Are you the FOA, Constable?' Gareth asked, immediately taking the lead. The FOA was the First Officer in Attendance at the scene of a crime.

The slim, dark-haired female constable who was holding her notebook nodded. 'Yes, sir. I was first on the scene,' she said, looking pale and shocked.

Laura wondered if she'd ever encountered a murder victim before.

'Are you okay?' Laura asked.

'Bit shaken, ma'am, but yeah, I'm fine, thanks.'

'If you're sure?' Laura gave her a kind smile to reassure her.

'I'm sure.'

Gareth nodded. 'So, what have we got?'

The officer looked down at her notepad. 'Eyewitness saw two people fighting on the beach. She saw the victim fall over there and the assailant came up the beach, got onto a motorbike and drove off.'

'Did she get a decent look at the attacker?' Laura asked.

'Not really, ma'am. It was dark and raining,' the officer explained, shaking her head. 'Eyewitness is a Patricia Wells. She was walking her dog. She's over there.'

Laura spotted a woman in her sixties sitting on the beach wall, nursing a cup of tea. A border collie sat at her feet.

'Okay, thank you, Constable,' Gareth said as they moved on, ducked under the tape and made their way over to the white scene-of-crime tent that had already been erected over the victim's body.

Laura could see that SOCOs had just arrived. A noisy generator juddered nearby and two forensic halogen arc lamps on stands burst into life, dazzling her for a moment. Other SOCOs were taking crime scene photographs and a video. Having attended murder scenes in Manchester on a regular basis, she was reassured that, even though they were on Anglesey, everything was in hand. She knew that was patronising, but 'local yokel' officers were often a source of amusement to big city cops, whether it was fair or not.

Gareth and Laura pulled on a set of white SOCO overalls, purple latex gloves, paper shoes, and a face mask. Inhaling the unpleasant smell of rubber and chemicals for the first time in years, she felt strangely at home.

Laura walked over to the body. The victim was a man in his early sixties. He had a shaved head and was thick-set. His feet were splayed at an unnatural angle and his shirt was a dark, sticky mess of blood. She could feel it in the pit of her stomach. Death.

Gareth took a pen, crouched and moved the bomber jacket back to get a better look. 'Looks like he's been stabbed twice. Once in the chest and once in the stomach.'

'From the amount of blood, the attacker either hit an artery or his heart,' Laura stated.

She squinted in the harshness of the SOCO lights, moving her gaze up the body to the pallid skin of the man's face. His eyes were open, glassy and dark. For a second, she felt sucked in, compelled to look into them. Into that emptiness where death lay.

Gareth looked at his watch. 'We're going to need everyone in CID for a briefing at six.'

'Yes.' Laura came out of her trance and gestured to the

woman sitting on the beach wall. 'I'll go and see what Mrs Wells has to say.'

As Laura walked back along the sandy footpath, she looked up at the inky blackness and the stars that glistened above. She'd been back in the force for less than twenty-four hours and was dealing with two murder cases.

Welcome back, Laura, she thought wryly.

Pulling into his driveway, Gareth turned off his ignition and sat for a moment in icy silence. However hard he tried, he couldn't seem to get Laura out of his head – like that bloody Kylie Minogue song. Yet, they couldn't find time to be together where they could hit some kind of even keel. Laura had warned him when they first started dating that she had very little time and that her kids were her priority. He completely respected that. He knew what they'd been through, especially Jake. But logic didn't come into it. He had an overwhelming desire to be with her and possibly build a new life together. However, they couldn't possibly do that now. Not without laying down some foundations for that type of relationship. He didn't know how Rosie and Jake would react to him being in their mum's life, either.

Gareth gave an audible sigh of frustration as he opened the car door and got out. He'd put those thoughts to one side and tackle them later. The frozen wind caught his face, stinging his nose and ears. He jangled his keys in his hand as he strolled up the neat garden path to his home.

A figure moved out of the darkness a few feet away from the wooden porch.

Who the hell is that? he wondered as he stopped in his tracks and clenched his fist. He was a police officer. He'd dealt with criminals all his life, so someone waiting in the shadows by his front door made him instantly on his guard.

110

'Gareth?' asked a woman's voice that he recognised. She sounded upset.

It was his ex-wife, Nell.

'Nell?' Gareth frowned. 'What are you doing here?'

As she moved a step closer, the amber glow from a nearby streetlight washed over her face, which was streaked with tears. He peered closely at her. Her right eye was swollen and dark. Someone had hit her.

'I don't know,' she whispered.

Gareth gestured to the front door. 'Do you want to come in?' He could feel himself getting both concerned and angry.

She pursed her lips and nodded slowly.

Ushering her inside, he closed the front door and snapped on the hall lights.

Then he looked at her. 'What the hell happened?'

For a few seconds, she didn't say anything. Then her eyes moved down towards the floor. 'It was Andrew.'

Andrew? Mr Perfect? The man of her dreams? he thought. Then a sense of vindication, which he knew wasn't appropriate, but he couldn't help it. He knew that Andrew Leith had been too good to be true. *What an utter prick!*

'Are you okay?' Gareth asked and then pointed in the direction of the kitchen. 'Come on, I'll put the kettle on.'

He wasn't about to gloat, but the man she'd left him for had hit her and now she was here looking for Gareth's help.

'I could do with something stronger,' Nell admitted as she followed him down the hallway.

'I've got that smoked Highland malt your dad bought me last Christmas,' Gareth said as he entered the kitchen. It was both strange and comforting to slip into the ease of the type of conversation they'd had for so many years.

'Yes,' Nell mumbled quietly. 'Please.'

Grabbing two tumblers from the cupboard, Gareth watched as Nell went over to the freezer and grabbed the tray of ice. For a second, it was like she'd never left. This was the kitchen she'd designed and been so proud of.

'Is this the first time?' Gareth asked.

Twisting ice cubes from the tray, she shook her head but didn't say anything.

'Jesus Christ, Nell,' he said, shaking his head as he poured an inch of whisky into the glasses.

She looked up at him. 'I know I've got no right to come here. And I wouldn't blame you if you told me to go away and leave you alone.'

'I'm surprised you didn't go to your parents',' Gareth stated. His ex-in-laws lived over in Cheshire and represented everything he hated about small-minded middle-class England.

'They're at the villa in Spain.'

Right, so I wasn't actually the first choice.

'You've got a key to their house,' he pointed out.

'Yeah, I know,' Nell said, her eyes welling. She looked at him and sighed. 'I just didn't want to be alone, that's all. I was scared.'

He looked at her face. Her mascara had smeared and she looked incredibly vulnerable. He'd forgotten how needy and childlike she could be. Her parents, Nigel and Linda, had been emotionally cold and unavailable. Nigel was one of those men who seemed actively terrified of physical contact and liked to have a security zone of at least ten feet of personal space. Linda wasn't far behind in the lack of affection and indifference stakes. On good days, she'd air-kiss when greeting her daughter, leaving a good twelve inches between them, just to be on the safe side.

'Do you want me to go?' she asked.

'No,' he said quietly. 'Where would you go?'

'I could go to Harriot's,' Nell suggested unconvincingly. Her best friend was married with five children and two dogs. She lived over on the Welsh mainland and her house was utter chaos.

Gareth gave her a sarcastic smirk. 'Oh, that would be nice and relaxing for you.'

'Yeah.' She laughed.

'Are you going to press charges?' He pointed to her swollen eye.

She shrugged. 'I don't know.'

'How long has he been doing this?'

'Ever since our divorce was finalised. I can't seem to do anything right, and then he loses his temper. He doesn't mean it.'

Christ, how many times had Gareth heard phrases like that during his time as a copper when dealing with domestic violence issues. He also knew that at least twice, those cases had ended in murder.

'You can't go back there. It's not going to change and it'll just get worse. And, as you know, we deal with this stuff all the time, so I know what I'm talking about.'

Nell took a large swig of whisky and pulled a face. 'I know the Scots like to smoke most things, but I'm not sure smoking whisky is the right thing.'

That was a handbrake turn of a conversation change.

She clearly didn't want to face up to the long-term consequences of what had happened. He didn't blame her.

Gareth laughed. 'Yeah, it tastes like an old bonfire.'

She looked at him and pulled an embarrassed face. 'Can I stay tonight?'

He nodded. 'The spare bed's made up.'

Am I being made a mug of here? he wondered.

'Why are you being so nice?' Nell asked. 'If it was the other way round, I'd have told you to fuck off.'

He shrugged. 'I'm a soft touch.' Throwing her out wasn't an option. And being this nice allowed him to show her what she'd thrown away to be with that twat, Leith. He was of

113

course completely over her and very happy with Laura now, but his ego couldn't resist it.

'You're not a soft touch,' she whispered. 'You're just a decent human being. You always have been.' Nell moved forwards, wrapped her arms around him and buried her head in his chest. 'I just need to be held for a moment,' she sighed.

Okay, I think we might be overstepping boundaries here, he thought. It would be way too easy for something they both regretted to happen in this moment. Releasing his arms, Gareth moved away from her.

'I'll get you a couple of clean towels, shall I?' He wandered out of the kitchen and away from temptation.

Laura opened the front door and struggled down the hallway towards the kitchen with two heavy bags of shopping. Elvis trotted over, his tail wagging at full speed as he sniffed her excitedly.

'Hello, mate,' she said as she plonked the shopping on the kitchen worktop with a sigh.

Rosie's music was blasting from the floor above. It was Fleetwood Mac's album *Rumours*.

Very retro, she thought. *Better than Stormzy.*

Jake came running in with his mobile phone in hand and they hugged.

'Hello, buster. Sorry I'm so late.'

He wasn't really listening to her as he waved the phone at her.

'My Steph Curry video got a hundred views on YouTube,' he stated excitedly.

'And Steph Curry is?' Laura asked with a wry smile.

Jake had recently become obsessed with basketball, so she assumed he had something to do with that. Jake pulled a face as though it were an utterly ridiculous question.

'How can you not know who Steph Curry is?'

'I know. I'm sorry,' Laura laughed as she began to put the shopping away. 'Fish fingers or meatballs?'

'Fish fingers and waffles,' Jake replied. 'Steph Curry is the greatest shooter in NBA history. He plays for the Golden State Warriors.'

'Oh, right, that's great,' Laura said as she put the oven on.

'He's scored the most three-pointers in the history of the NBA,' he said, wide-eyed. 'Guess how many?'

'About a hundred,' Laura shrugged.

'Mum!' Jake put his hand to his head. 'Over three thousand.'

'Gosh, well, that's very good,' she commented, retrieving the fish fingers and waffles from the freezer.

Given that Rosie was now eighteen, she wondered why she hadn't managed to make herself and Jake tea, but she didn't have the energy to go down that road. Maybe they could have *that* discussion at the weekend.

'How long will it be?' Jake enquired as he wandered towards the door, gazing at his phone.

'Twenty minutes, *sire*,' Laura replied as she unscrewed the top of the cold Sauvignon Blanc. It might have been Monday, but she needed at least one enormous glass to unwind. 'Can you ask your sister if she wants anything for tea?'

'She had some weird salad thing earlier,' Jake explained as he left.

Some weird salad thing? That doesn't sound good. Laura was still worried about her daughter's troubled relationship with food and her weight. It hadn't developed into a full-blown eating disorder, but Laura was anxious that it wouldn't take much for that to happen.

Taking a large gulp of wine, Laura leaned back on the worktop and took a breath. *First day out of the way,* she thought. It had gone well, and she certainly thought she'd hit the ground running. She'd spent enough of her working life as a detective for it to have become instinctive.

'What are we doing on May 15th?' Rosie enquired as she came in, looking at the screen of her phone.

Is there any danger of anyone making eye contact with me this evening?

'Hi, Mum,' Laura said sarcastically. 'How was your first day at work? It was okay, Rosie. Thanks so much for asking.'

Why did you say that? It's inflammatory.

For a few seconds, Rosie didn't even register what Laura had said and then she glared at her.

'Are you really going to be like that when you haven't got home until 8.30 p.m. and I've had to look after Jake?'

'When you say *look after Jake*, do you mean sit in your room listening to Fleetwood Mac and being on your phone?' Laura asked.

There were a few seconds of silence.

'Anyway, why are you asking me about May next year?' Laura enquired, attempting to defuse the tension.

'Sam Fender is playing Liverpool on May 15th and me and Katie want to go. Are we doing anything?'

'Sam Fender? Remind me?'

'Geordie. Really fit. Sings that "Hypersonic Missiles" song,' Rosie explained.

Laura tried her best to keep up with the latest bands and music but often resorted to listening to the music of her teens – Madonna, Janet Jackson or, if she was attempting to impress, U2 and The Smiths.

'Oh, is he the one who's a bit like Jake Bugg?'

Rosie rolled her eyes. 'Not really, Laura.'

Oh, God, please grow out of calling me Laura soon!

Laura only liked Jake Bugg because he sounded like a blend of The Everly Brothers, The Beatles (circa 1963) and Oasis.

'When did you say again?' she asked Rosie.

'Next May.'

Laura frowned. 'That's nine months away, so I've no idea. Aren't your A levels in May?'

'Jesus, Mum!' Rosie snorted. 'They start at the beginning of June.'

'Right.'

'So, can I get tickets?'

'Have you got any money?'

Rosie looked at her with a forced smile. 'Can I borrow some?'

'And by *borrow*, do you actually mean *have*?'

'No, I'll definitely pay you back. Please?'

Going to her handbag, Laura found her purse, pulled out her Visa debit card and waved it. 'How much are the tickets?'

'Seventy-five pounds if I buy it now,' Rosie said excitedly.

'And that's for one ticket?' Laura enquired rhetorically as she handed Rosie the card.

'Oh my God, you're the best mum in the world.' Rosie hugged and kissed her.

'What did you have for tea?' Laura asked her.

'I just had a salad and some fruit.' Rosie shrugged as she headed out of the kitchen.

'I could make you some pasta.'

Rosie gave her a quizzical look. 'Carbs? Erm, no, thank you.' And with that, Rosie thundered upstairs.

Best mum in the world? Or a mug who feels guilty about working late?

Laura popped the fish fingers and waffles in the oven. She'd tried to encourage Jake to have a less *beige* diet, but he just didn't like anything that wasn't plain and devoid of most nutrients. She consoled herself that he'd grow out of it.

Taking her glass of wine through to the living room, she grabbed her laptop and flopped onto the sofa. Elvis jumped up beside her and licked her ear.

'Jesus, Elvis,' she groaned as she pushed him away. 'Just lie down there for a minute. I'll take you out in a bit.'

The laptop screen burst into life and she navigated her way over to her emails. She wanted to check the one that Pete had sent her earlier. Then she noticed that he'd sent her another half an hour ago with a Jpeg attachment.

Her phone rang. It was Pete. He must have been reading her thoughts.

'Pete,' she said as she opened his latest email so it was in front of her. 'I'm just opening it now.'

'Okay. At the moment, all I can get is this still from the CCTV at Seymours Bar in Llandudno,' Pete explained.

'Right, I'll have a look.'

The image that came onto her screen was blurred, but it clearly showed a figure nearest the camera with a black baseball cap behind the bar. It looked like all the staff were wearing caps. Laura peered at the figure. It was definitely a woman. She'd kept her head low to cover her face with the peak of the cap. It looked deliberate and, therefore, slightly awkward. Why would you work in a bar with your head bowed like that unless you actually wanted to avoid being seen on CCTV? It was certainly suspicious. And it could be Louise, but it definitely wasn't clear-cut.

'What do you think?' Pete asked.

'I think the woman in shot is avoiding looking up because she knows there's a CCTV camera looking down at her.'

'That's what I thought. Do you think it's Louise?'

'If I'm honest, I don't know, Pete.'

'That's fine,' he said calmly. 'I've pulled some council CCTV for the street outside. We might get something from that.'

'Okay, thanks.'

'Hey, how was your first day at work?'

Laura hesitated. 'It was good. Once I got into the swing of things, it was like I'd never been away.'

'Great,' Pete said enthusiastically. 'I've forgotten – who's your guvnor down there?'

'DI Gareth Williams,' Laura said, making sure she gave nothing away.

'And he's all right, is he?'

'Yeah, he's fine. He's a good bloke. You know, no ego. Fair. It's going to be good to work with him.'

There were a few seconds of silence.

'Right,' Pete said in a curious tone that she couldn't read. 'Sounds too good to be true.'

'What's that mean?' Laura asked with a nervous laugh.

'Your voice went all funny when you talked about him,' Pete teased her. 'Anything you want to tell me?'

'No.'

'Laura?'

'What?'

'Come on. We've known each other for twenty-five years. What's going on between you and DI Williams?'

'Nothing,' Laura protested. And then, 'Yet.'

'You're thinking about it?'

'Well, there might have been a couple of dalliances,' she giggled.

'*Dalliances*?' Pete snorted. 'Right. Right, well tread carefully, eh? He's your boss. But if you really like him . . .'

Laura paused for a second and then said, 'I do like him. I really like him, Pete.'

CHAPTER 18

Gareth stirred, rolled over and felt the flesh of his right arm. It was freezing cold where it had been resting outside the duvet. That's how Gareth needed to sleep. Naked and in a cold room. BBC Radio 5 Live burbled from the bedside table. It had been nearly two decades since he'd slept without the background chatter of the radio, an audiobook or a podcast. And now when he tried to sleep in silence, it was virtually impossible.

He needed something to focus his mind on. Absorbing enough to hold his interest but not so dramatic that it would keep him awake. Music didn't work and nor did live sport. Silence meant that his brain was left to its own devices and it would cruise the dark alleys of his mind and subconscious. It would soon latch onto something bleak or anxiety-inducing and then whirl the event around on a continuous loop until he was wide awake. He guessed a restless mind went hand in hand with the job, and listening to the radio was a lot healthier than booze or sleeping pills, which he knew some police officers used to turn off their brains.

Rolling over again, he saw it was only 4.23 a.m. and he needed a pee.

What happened to those halcyon days where I could sleep for eight hours without waking to go for a wee?

If he'd drunk too much Coke Zero or beer, he could get up twice or even three times during the night. Was that a sign of a weak prostate, or was there a tumour growing down there?

As he padded over to the en-suite bathroom, he caught sight of himself in the wardrobe mirror.

Hey, early fifties and I still don't have some terrible middle-aged paunch. I'll take that.

He peed for about twenty seconds with his hand flat against the wall behind, as if he needed to support himself. He didn't. *What was that about?* Then he returned to bed, folded the edge of the pillow and faced the opposite way to the bedside table. An in-depth discussion of American politics was rambling away from the radio. A senior Republican was unhappy about the latest nominee for the Supreme Court. It was the perfect stuff to drift off to sleep to.

From somewhere in the room, there was a metallic click. *What was that? It sounded like the door.*

Gareth didn't know if he was dreaming or not. Then he heard a movement by the door. Someone was coming in.

Nell?

Rolling over, he looked over and saw her padding quietly over the carpet. She was wearing a long sky-blue T-shirt that stopped just above her knees.

'Nell?' His voice was croaky.

'Sorry,' she whispered. 'I didn't mean to wake you.'

'What are you doing?' he whispered back.

She shrugged and whispered with a sad expression, 'I just didn't want to sleep alone. I thought I'd just slip in next to you and not wake you up.'

Gareth nodded and then said in a normal voice, 'Why are we whispering? There's no one else in the house.'

'I don't know.' Nell laughed, turned and then padded back towards the door. 'It's fine. Sorry to have woken you.'

Let her go, said a voice in his head. *Let her go*.

She hesitated by the door.

'Where are you going?' Gareth enquired. He knew the sensible thing was to let her go back to the spare room.

She turned and looked at him.

Pulling the duvet back, he gestured. 'Just get in. It's fine.'

'Really?' She took an uncertain step back the way she'd come.

'We've shared a bed hundreds of times,' he pointed out.

'Isn't it weird?' she asked with a frown.

He shook his head. 'Nell, we slept in the same bed on and off for three years, didn't have sex and didn't much like each other. I think it's going to be fine tonight.'

She gave him a wry smile. 'Okay. I'm sorry.'

'Stop apologising.'

He was aware there was a part of him that really wanted her in the bed next to him. She'd rejected him for another man. It had been incredibly painful. Now, she wanted to get into bed and allow him to comfort her. It felt like some kind of victory.

For a second, Laura came into his mind's eye.

Nell came over and slid into bed beside him as he pulled the duvet over her. She rested on her side and looked at him. He held her gaze for a few seconds.

'Is this okay?' she asked.

Silence.

'What happened to us, Nell?' he whispered.

She blinked. There were tears in her eyes. 'I don't know. You weren't here. And when you were here . . .'

'I wasn't here either,' he said, finishing her sentence.

Gareth put his hand to her face and looked at where her eye was swollen. She looked so small and vulnerable. He was looking at a very different woman to the cold banshee who had waltzed out of their marital home several months ago.

Pushing his fingers through her hair, he moved forwards and kissed her gently on the mouth. Without hesitation, she responded and moved her body towards his.

What the hell are you doing? said an irritating voice inside his head. *She treated you like shit. And now she's come crawling back to you. What about Laura?*

He ignored it. He wanted to be held, to be wanted and to be desired by the woman who had rejected him so cruelly.

Nell pushed him onto his back, slid on top of him and pulled off her T-shirt.

CHAPTER 19

Belfast 1998

John had spent the best part of six weeks trying to integrate himself into the Catholic population. He was a stranger in a community where everyone knew everyone and that was hypervigilant and on their guard against informants. The more time he spent at work, in pubs or in the boarding house, the more he could see that this was a population haunted by the murderous UFF – Real Ulster Freedom Fighters – and UVF, trigger-happy British soldiers and an army of spies. He also realised from snippets of conversations that they had an extraordinary ability to smell an outsider and close ranks.

The paranoia was made worse by accusations that the British Army and the RUC – Royal Ulster Constabulary – were operating a shoot-to-kill policy, where suspected terrorists were deliberately killed with no attempt to arrest them. By the early nineties, this policy seemed to be out of control. Petty thieves and local joyriders had been shot at and even killed under the defence that they were possible terrorists.

John tried to strike a balance between saying things such as 'The English don't understand us and they never will,' and avoiding the more controversial or aggressive statements that could potentially sound bogus. He'd spent the time using his search for work as an excuse for detailed reconnaissance. He needed to know the roads, backstreets and alleys where he lived until they were imprinted on his memory. It might one day save his life. He knew that Fallswater Drive, with a funeral director's on the corner, was a dead-end street with a playground and youth centre at the bottom. On the other hand, Iveagh Drive – derived from the Gaelic for 'descendants of Echu' – provided a better escape route with a series of roads and side streets on either side.

The roads he studied all showed signs of the conflict. Properties had been sealed or boarded up. Barbed wire and graffitied corrugated iron surrounded other areas.

As John strolled down the Falls Road, he pulled his collar up against the biting wind. Reaching a pub called O'Hare's, he pushed open the black doors and headed for the bar. It was one p.m. and he'd made sitting at the bar for a lunchtime pint part of his daily routine. According to his intel, members of the West Belfast Brigade of the Real IRA used the pub for meetings. There was a plaque on one of the dark walls to say that the pub had been on the site since 1905. It had been known locally as The Gravedigger's Arms because it was so close to the local cemetery.

Inside, the pub was dark and shadowy. On the far side, there were wooden cubicles and booths that dated back to the 1920s. Photographs on the walls were of republican heroes as far back as the Easter Rising – James Connolly, Patrick Pearse and John MacBride.

'Pint of black,' John said to the young barman, Cormac, as he pulled a stool up to the dark wooden bar.

Black was the local slang for Guinness. Unfortunately,

John couldn't stand the taste of the treacly beer, but what else was he going to drink in a Catholic bar in West Belfast. And he was starting to get used to it.

John and Cormac had chatted at various times over the past weeks. Cormac was in his twenties. Red hair and lanky. He'd told John that he was an engineering student over at Queen's University, Belfast.

'I can tell you've been away all right, John,' Cormac said as he watched the pint glass fill slowly with what the brewery had labelled Black Gold.

'How's that, then?' John asked, resting his forearm casually on the bar.

'Your accent,' Cormac explained as he turned off the tap and waited patiently for the pint to settle. 'Sometimes it's strong and sometimes not so much. It must be all that time you've spent abroad. If it'd been me, I'd have stayed away from this bloody place.'

'Yeah, well, I count myself as an Irishman. And as an Irishman, I can't stay away forever. A lot of brave boys have died in this city since I left.'

'I try not to get too involved in all that stuff, if I'm honest,' Cormac said, bringing over John's pint. He then gestured to a couple of men in the corner and whispered, 'They've been asking about you.'

John was smart enough not to glance immediately in their direction. 'Oh yeah. And who are *they*?'

Cormac gave him a dark look. 'I think you know who they are.'

West Belfast Brigade, John thought to himself. He had no intention of speaking to them or even making eye contact. He just wanted them to be aware of his presence inside the pub before finishing his pint and leaving.

Out of the corner of his eye, he saw one of the men arrive further down the bar. He was in his forties, short black hair, piercing blue eyes and a scar over his left eyebrow. He was wearing a leather bomber jacket with a cobalt-blue shirt underneath.

John drank an inch from his pint, making sure he kept looking in the opposite direction.

'Large Jamesons and a pint,' the man said in a deep Belfast drawl.

There was a long mirror behind the bar and John glanced at it to observe the man. The man clocked John's eyes in the mirror and stared back at him.

Shit!

'Do I know you, pal?' the man asked.

It sounded like a genuine question rather than an aggressive challenge.

John felt his pulse quicken as he turned to look at him. 'I don't think so.'

The man approached, smiled and put out his hand, 'Frank.' His hand was icy, bony, with a powerful grip.

'John,' he replied.

Frank looked at him quizzically. 'You're not from round here?'

'No.' John shook his head.

'Where you from, then, if you don't mind me asking?' Frank said as Cormac handed him the pint of Guinness and a whiskey.

'Newry.'

'Newry?' Frank nodded slowly for a moment. 'I've got a cousin in Newry. Neil Harrison.'

John gave a half-smile. He needed to seem polite but disinterested. 'I haven't been to Newry in a long time, I'm afraid.'

'No?' Frank gestured to Cormac. 'This young fella tells me you're a merchant seaman? Is that right?'

'Yeah,' John said. His heart was thumping. 'Mainly across the North Atlantic.'

'And working the mines in Canada, is that right?'

Should I be worried about how much interest he's taken in my background?

'Yeah.'

'Explosives expert, Cormac tells me,' Frank said in a tone that bordered on scepticism.

John didn't like the way the conversation was going. Something about Frank's questions and manner made him uneasy. Out of the corner of his eye, he spotted the other man, who had been drinking with Frank, get up from the table, head for the door and leave.

There was something about Frank's questions and the man's exit from the pub that was making John edgy.

'No, no. Expert? I wouldn't go that far,' John said, trying to sound as humble as he could.

'Hey, no need to be modest, fella.' Frank smiled at him. 'And if you're an explosives expert, then you're in the right feckin' city, am I right?'

John laughed dryly. 'I suppose so.'

Moving closer, Frank indicated his right hand, which was inside the pocket of his leather jacket.

John's stomach lurched. He could see the outline of the barrel of a gun.

Fuck! Do they know who I am? Has my cover been blown?

Leaning forwards, Frank smirked and hissed, 'I think you should come for a little journey with me and my pal, don't you?'

John took a breath and looked at him. If they knew he was undercover, then he was a dead man. However, if they were suspicious because he was a stranger, then they might be trying to establish who he actually was and if they could trust him.

'I don't . . . u-understand,' John stammered nervously.

Even though he was actually scared, he needed Frank to

think that he was terrified. He needed to act like an innocent civilian who had walked into a pub for a pint and now had a gun pointing at him, not an SAS officer undercover.

Frank pointed to a black door to the rear of the pub. 'Come on. We won't be long.'

'I haven't done anything,' John protested nervously.

'Well, boyo, you have a wee choice to make,' Frank said through gritted teeth. 'You either come with me quietly, or I blow a feckin' hole in your stomach the size of a bowling ball.'

John nodded anxiously as he got meekly down from the stool.

Well, when you put it like that . . .

Frank walked slowly behind him as they made their way past the empty tables and chairs to the back of the pub, past the unlit pool table and out through the black door that was marked with a green fire exit sign. John didn't know if he was going to take a few steps outside and then get a bullet in the head.

Squinting at the daylight, he saw they were now walking across a flat piece of weed-strewn concrete with enormous iron gates that led out onto one of the side roads that ran down from the Falls Road.

Where the hell are we going now?

The man who had been drinking with Frank stood by an old blue Astra with its doors open. He was in his fifties, stout, with pitiless dark eyes and bloodless lips.

'Davie here is going to drive us,' Frank said, giving John a shove in the back and pushing him into the rear of the car.

Before John knew it, Davie had bound his hands behind his back with wire. Then a black cloth hood was pulled over his head and he was shoved down into the space between the front and back seats of the car.

Shit! This is not good. What the hell is going on?

A few seconds later, he heard the car doors slam and the engine start, and the car pulled away.

Even though part of John's SAS training involved being hooded and then interrogated, he still found it claustrophobic. Every time he took a breath, the material was sucked into his mouth until he blew it out. It was hard work just breathing.

The car was now travelling at speed, turning left and right through the backstreets. John's shoulder and back pressed against something hard and metallic every time the car changed direction.

After about ten minutes, the car stopped with a jolt. He heard Frank and Davie get out and the muffled sound of conversation. Was this the moment they pulled him out, shot him and left him in the gutter? His stomach tightened with anxiety.

Then there were a few seconds of excruciating silence.

He tried to use his arms to lever himself up from the footwell, but the wire cut into the skin on his wrists. It was agony.

The back door opened and someone pulled him up.

'Where the feck do you think you're going, sunshine?' growled a voice.

It was Frank.

Still with the hood over his head, John was taken from the car and marched down what felt like a pathway. Then into what he assumed was a house. He was dragged into a room, pushed hard down onto a wooden chair. The wires were cut from his wrists and the hood was snatched off his head. John blinked for a few seconds as his eyes adjusted to the daylight.

Davie went over and drew the frail orange curtains closed, cutting out a slice of the sunlight, and took a position over by the door. The room was empty apart from the rickety chair that John was sitting on. Bare, paint-splattered floorboards, grimy walls and a ceiling with a series of damp patches and mildew.

Frank came over. Deep down, John's stomach reeled. He had no idea what they knew or why he was here. They hadn't said anything that would give him a clue. He looked at Frank's hands – big with long fingers and two gold sovereign rings. His shoes were smart and polished.

Frank came close to John's face. His breath smelled of whiskey and stale cigarettes. 'What are you doing in Belfast, Johnny-boy?'

'W-why are you doing this to me?' John stammered nervously.

'I asked you a question, sunshine.'

John frowned and took a nervous breath. 'I'd had enough of being away from home, that's all. I don't know what you mean.'

Frank moved away and clenched his fist and then stretched out his fingers menacingly. 'You told us you're from Newry.'

'I am from Newry,' John replied adamantly, but he was anxious that they'd been checking up on him.

'We've asked around,' Frank growled. 'No one's ever heard of a John Doyle.'

John looked at him, remembering to keep acting and sounding like a civilian and not a trained member of the SAS. 'They . . . wouldn't. I don't come from Newry.'

Frank looked over at Davie and then took an aggressive step towards where John was sitting. John flinched.

'What the feck are you talkin' about?' Frank snapped. 'You've told everyone you're a lad from Newry.'

'Yeah, I-I . . .' John stammered. 'I come from Ravensdale.'

'Where?' Frank thundered.

'It's the middle of nowhere. Just by the Cooley Mountains, County Louth,' John explained. 'The nearest town is actually

Dundalk, but no one's ever heard of that, either. So I tell everyone I'm from Newry so I don't have to explain all that.'

Frank snorted and paced away with short steps before twisting back towards John. 'We know why you're here, John. We just need to hear it.'

Do *they know or is this a bluff?*

He knew that if they had suspected him of being in the UDR – the Ulster Defence Regiment – or any other Protestant paramilitary, he'd be dead by now. They weren't known for interrogations like this. Just a quick assassination and that was it.

John shook his head. 'I just told you.'

'You take us for feckin' eejits,' Frank sighed angrily. Then he made a sudden lunge for John, putting his hand hard around his jawbone and applying increasing pressure until it felt like the bone might break.

If they knew who he was, wouldn't he be lying in a ditch somewhere? And why haven't they just come out with what they do know?

'Worked explosives in some Canadian iron mine,' Frank continued. He virtually spat out the words. 'Did you think we'd welcome you with open arms and say "Hey, Johnny, would you build a wee bomb, seeing how you're the professional explosives man?"' Frank shook his head and then looked over at Davie with a disparaging look. 'Can you believe this fella, Davie?'

'I don't know why we're doing this, Frank,' Davie said in a withering tone. 'I'd have put a bullet in the back of his skull and buried him in a hole in County Down.'

Frank kicked the chair hard. 'Tell us why you're here and we'll let you away with shooting your kneecaps.'

John was now convinced that they didn't know who he was and they were on a fishing trip. Essentially, they were going to terrify him to see if he had any kind of hidden agenda.

John made sure that he looked and sounded like he was at breaking point. 'I-I don't know what you want me to say. I came back home. That's it. Please, I haven't done anything.' He looked at Frank and blinked to convince him that he was on the verge of tears.

Frank shrugged, scratched his chin and then pulled out a revolver – an old .455 Webley. 'I think we're just going to have to shoot him, don't you, Davie?'

'Yeah, Frank,' Davie said with a nod. 'This is a feckin' waste of time. Let's shoot this gobshite and have done with it.'

Ramming the barrel of the pistol into John's temple, Frank looked at him. 'Last chance, boyo. Tell us who you are and what you're doing in Belfast, or I'm decorating that wall in *hint of brain*.'

Davie gave a nasty deep laugh.

John's eyes widened and he shook violently all over. 'Please, please. I d-don't know anything. I swear. I . . . I just came home. That's it.'

There were a few seconds of silence. He was terrified that he was about to have his brains blown out.

Frank slowly took the barrel away from his temple, looked over at Davie and began to laugh. Davie was laughing, too.

What the fuck? Why are they laughing?

Frank came over and smiled at him as he patted his face. 'You're all right, fella. Sorry about that. We had to find out what you knew and who you were.'

Thank God for that! John felt the tension flow from his body in utter relief.

'We call that *the colonic*.' Davie roared with laughter. 'Youse must be one tough bastard there, John, because most fellas piss or shit themselves by the end of all that.'

133

Yeah, well, thank God for my SAS interrogation training then, eh.

'No hard feelings then, John?' Frank reached out and shook his hand. 'If you was a Prod or a snout, we'd know by now.'

'Yeah, and you'd be dead,' Davie snorted with more laughter.

'Come on.' Frank clapped him on the back. 'We'll go back to the Falls and buy you a pint, eh?'

John nodded, swallowed and let out a slow sigh.

CHAPTER 20

Sitting up in bed, Laura pulled up her laptop and opened it. She glanced at her bedside table – the clock read 5.18 a.m. This morning she wouldn't go swimming. The discovery of the body at Gallows Point meant that it was all hands on deck in CID and a six a.m. start.

Laura clicked on her inbox. Her eyes went immediately to a new email from Pete from 1.22 a.m. Something was attached – it was an MP4 file, which she knew meant it was a moving image file.

Opening Pete's email, she scanned it:

Hiya
CCTV footage came in from the council. Watch the woman leaving the bar about halfway through the clip. I think it's LM. Let me know what you think.
For what it's worth, I know that Sam would have wanted you to move on with your life – in all aspects. Just take it slowly.
Pete x

She'd ignore his final comments until she'd taken a look at the CCTV. She clicked the thumbnail. The file opened and the clip played. The camera had been positioned high up on a main road. On the right of the screen, it was clear to see a bar called Seymours. Watching as the time code moved on, she peered closely as a woman came out of the bar. The time code read 02.11 a.m. Laura pressed Pause as the woman turned and headed towards where the camera was mounted.

Scrutinising the screen, Laura looked at the face that was lit by a nearby streetlight. She recognised her immediately.

Louise McDonald! Got you, you fucking bitch!

She took a second look as she played more footage. There was no doubt in her mind. The woman walking along that street was Sam's ex-partner, who was supposed to have died in the warehouse three years ago. The woman whose funeral she and Pete had stood side by side at and for whom she'd shed a tear.

Laura let out a breath. *Right, I know where you work and I'm coming to get you.*

An hour later, Laura was trying to put all thoughts of Louise McDonald to one side as she sat at her desk in CID drinking strong coffee, having refocused her mind to the man they'd found at Gallows Point the night before. The doors to CID opened and Gareth marched in, holding several files. They'd both been in since six a.m. but had barely said a word. Maybe it was because they were now working on two murder cases, with all the extra pressure and workload that brings. However, she got the distinct impression that Gareth was avoiding her. She wondered if he was tiring of her hectic life and inability to find time for him.

'Right, guys, early start,' Gareth boomed, energised. 'Lots to get through this morning, so listen up.' He strode to the front of the room, put his files down on an empty desk and went over to the scene board. 'Okay, for those of you who don't already know, a man was found stabbed to death on Gallows Point last night. At the moment, we haven't managed to identify our victim. My guess is that he's early sixties, medium height and build.'

Ben looked over. 'Forensics are working on getting finger-prints through the database and taking a DNA sample.'

'What about a PM?' Gareth asked.

'Later today,' Declan replied.

'We spoke to an eyewitness – a Patricia Wells,' Laura explained as she looked at her notes. She hadn't addressed a CID room for several years. It was also only her second day and she was still keen to make a good impression on the team that she would now be working with. 'She was walking her dog. She spotted two figures fighting on the beach. Once the assailant stabbed our victim, they drove off on a motorbike.'

'Any details?' Ben asked.

Laura nodded. 'Patricia said that her late husband had a Harley Davidson and she was convinced that was the make of motorbike our killer left on. As they rode past, she said she saw the person wearing a blacked-out motorcycle helmet with an American Confederate flag on the back.'

Gareth nodded and looked at the team. 'It's a really good lead. Ben, talk to the DVLA and see how many Harley Davidsons are registered on the island. Dec, see if you can track down that helmet. It sounds distinctive.'

Declan nodded. 'I've got a couple of mates who ride bikes. I'll ask around.'

'Great. Let's check if anyone on the island has been reported missing in the past twenty-four hours,' Gareth said. 'Anything on the remains up at Castell Aberlleiniog? I believe we have an identity. Laura?'

'Andrea and I managed to track down the owner of the

Midland Bank Visa card. Jenny Maldini. She told us that her then partner, John Finn, went for a drink with his friend Rhys Hughes at The Panton Arms on Tuesday, 12 October 1999. They were in a pub quiz team together.' Laura explained. 'John arrived at the pub but by the time the quiz started he had vanished. He was never seen again.'

'Have we got any more than just the bank card?' Declan asked.

Laura nodded. 'Yes. The preliminary examination that Professor Lovell carried out on the remains gave us several indications as to our victim's identity. In terms of height and build, John Finn fits the bill.'

Ben looked over. 'We also have a pin badge discovered close to the remains that's worn by veterans of the Irish Guards. And both Elis Hughes and Jenny Maldini have told us that John Finn was in the Irish Guards regiment.'

'Okay, sounds like he's our man,' Gareth said. 'At the moment, we're going to go on the assumption that the remains we found are John Finn. I'm hoping that forensics can extract a DNA sample from his bone marrow. Either that, or we wait to have the bones carbon dated, but that's going to take five to six days.'

'And the PM established our victim was murdered?' Ben asked.

Laura nodded. 'Yes. Blunt force trauma to the back of the head, which caused an internal haemorrhage.'

'What about Jenny Maldini?' Gareth asked. 'It's her card found with the remains. Maybe she killed and buried him.'

Laura shook her head. 'She was devastated when we told her we'd found the remains. My instinct was that she had no idea what happened to John. Andrea, what did you think?'

Andrea nodded. 'I agree. She was in complete shock. I don't think she had anything to do with the remains being up there.'

'Okay. I'd like us to have a look at Jenny Maldini before we completely rule her out of our investigation. Thanks, guys.' Gareth moved back to the scene board. 'We have another issue that Ben came up against last night. Ben?'

'Boss.' Ben looked around the room. 'I've checked the name John Finn, with that date of birth, against the PNC, HOLMES, Anglesey council tax records, HMRC records and the UK passport office. They all came up blank.'

'That doesn't make sense,' Declan muttered with a deep frown.

Gareth ran his hand over his scalp. 'We know he was in the Irish Guards. Ben, can you contact the regiment and see if someone by that name ever served with the regiment?'

'Boss,' Ben replied with a nod as he scribbled on a notepad.

Laura looked over. 'Whether or not Jenny was right that he was in an SAS unit, I don't suppose they're liable to give information like that out.'

Gareth raised an eyebrow. 'Anything on the phone call to tip us off?'

Ben shook his head. 'Call came from an unregistered number.'

Laura frowned. 'Why did someone want us to find John Finn's remains now, over twenty years after we think he was buried there?'

'Do we think the two cases are linked?' Andrea asked.

'I can't see a link, but I'm never comfortable with coincidences.' Gareth perched on a table and took a few seconds to think. 'Okay, what we do know is that a man calling himself John Finn went out for a drink in 1999, disappeared and was probably murdered. Anyone spoken to anyone at The Panton Arms yet? I know it's a long shot, but maybe someone remembers John or Rhys from back then. Laura, can you and Andrea go back to Jenny Maldini. Does she have an alibi for that night? Do we think she had any motive to kill John? Plus, we need her to think carefully about who might want to have harmed John.'

Declan looked over. 'Unless it was a random attack?'

'I don't see how it could have been,' Laura said, thinking out loud. 'I can't see someone randomly attacking a man in his thirties and then going to the trouble of keeping the body for two days before burying it up at Castell Aberlleiniog.'

'Let's not rule that out completely,' Gareth said. 'But I think we go on the assumption that John Finn was deliberately targeted by someone who knew him.'

Laura saw Declan bristle. Maybe he was annoyed that his theory of a random attacker had been put on the back burner. She didn't care. In her experience, in briefings like this, there was no such thing as a bad idea or theory. Everyone threw in every hypothesis they could think of and allowed others to use logic and evidence to rule it out. That was good detective work and if Declan's ego was going to impede that, then that made him an idiot.

'Anyone had any luck tracking down this Rhys Hughes?' Gareth enquired.

'Nothing for him on the PNC or HOLMES, boss,' Ben explained. 'But I haven't got any further than that.'

'Let's see what we can find.'

'Tell a lie, boss.' Ben pointed to his computer screen at something that had just appeared. 'Rhys Hughes was a named owner and occupant of a house close to Lleiniog Beach on the last electoral register.'

Andrea frowned. 'That's a stone's throw from where the body was found.'

Gareth looked at the CID team with a determined expression. 'Right, I'm going to split you guys up. Laura will now be acting SIO on the John Finn investigation with Andrea. Declan and I'll take our victim from last night. Let's do our best work today, okay? Back here at six p.m. sharp.'

CHAPTER 21

Laura and Andrea stood outside the neat bungalow that over-looked Lleiniog Beach, which was three miles north of Beaumaris. It was the address Ben had found for Rhys Hughes. For a moment, they stood with the sea air whipping against their backs and tousling their hair. Laura pulled up her collar.

The door opened about six inches and a neat, bright-eyed man in his late forties looked out at them. 'Hello?'

'DI Hart and DC Jones, Beaumaris CID,' Laura stated, showing him her warrant card. 'We're looking for a Rhys Hughes.' Her voice was almost lost in the noise of the wind.

'Yes?' Rhys said, baffled.

'Can we come in for a minute?' Andrea asked, gesturing inside.

'Erm . . . yes.' Rhys opened the door and beckoned them inside nervously. He was wearing a salmon-coloured sweater and smelled of aftershave. A small poodle jogged around his feet. 'Go on, Cookie, go to your bed,' he commanded.

He led them into a living room, which was more colourful than the hallway. A white piano stood in one corner and the walls were covered with books. He beckoned them to sit down on a huge blue sofa.

'We're currently working on an investigation,' Laura explained politely as she sat down, 'and we're tracking down anyone who knew a man named John Finn. We understand you knew him?'

'Yes, that's right,' Rhys replied as he placed his hands in his lap.

Andrea took out her notebook and clicked her pen. 'You were friends. Is that correct?'

Rhys nodded slowly. His eyes roamed the room nervously. 'Yes. Have you found him or something?'

'We're not sure.'

Rhys' face brightened as he looked directly at them. 'Is he alive?'

'I'm sorry to say that we have found some remains that we believe might be John,' Laura said quietly.

'Oh, God.' Rhys sighed as his face fell. He took a breath as if the news had really got to him. 'What happened to him?'

Laura looked at him. 'We can't discuss that with you. It's part of our investigation, I'm afraid.'

'Did you find him on Anglesey?'

Laura nodded. 'Yes.'

'I didn't think I'd ever find out what happened to him,' Rhys explained as he shook his head sadly and looked away. 'There was a part of me that wondered if he was still alive and living in some far-flung country . . . In fact, I hoped he was, you know? He'd have liked that. Sun, sand, sangria, all that.'

Laura gave Rhys a kind look. 'It sounds like you knew John very well, then?'

'Yeah. He was a lovely man. I had a lot of time for him.'

'What was he like?' Laura asked after a few seconds.

'John?' Rhys scratched his arm. 'Erm, he was . . . a nice person, you know? Generous, kind. And good company.'

Andrea looked up from her notepad. 'Does the date Tuesday, 12 October 1999 mean anything to you?'

'Yeah. It was the day that John went missing,' he stated without hesitation. It was a date that was clearly etched on his mind.

'Can you tell us what happened that day?'

'I . . .' Rhys stopped mid-sentence and looked upset. 'They . . . they had a pub quiz at The Panton Arms every Tuesday night. But there was also this charity thing. Me, John and a few others had raised some money for the local hospice. And John had one of those big cheques he was going to hand over to the manager of the hospice.'

'So, John was definitely in the pub that night?' Andrea asked.

'Oh yeah. At the beginning,' Rhys explained. 'This thing with the cheque was about seven p.m. John was there for that. Then the pub quiz usually started at eight p.m. That's when we couldn't find him anywhere. It was like he'd vanished or something.'

Laura frowned. If John had been attacked, it hadn't happened on the way to the pub or on his way home. Instead, he'd vanished from the pub, which made his disappearance more puzzling.

'Did he tell you he was going somewhere else?' she asked.

Rhys sat forwards. 'No. He didn't say anything to anyone.'

'Were you surprised that you couldn't find him?' Andrea enquired.

Rhys pulled a face as if to indicate Andrea had asked a silly question. 'Yeah, of course. That wasn't like John. He was the team captain and he loved the quiz. He was very good at the history and geography questions.'

Laura looked at him. 'And you never heard from or saw him again after that point?'

'No, nothing,' he said sadly.

143

He clearly felt emotional about John's disappearance even now.

'I spent a day or two looking for John,' he continued. 'When I couldn't find any trace of him, I hitched a ride up to Holyhead. I got a job up there and just stayed.'

'You said that you spent two days looking for John. Did you find anything?'

'No.' He shook his head. 'It was like he'd just vanished off the face of the earth. I went to see Jenny, and she was in a hell of a state by then.'

Laura looked over at him. 'Did you have any idea what might have happened to him?'

'No. No idea, if I'm honest,' Rhys explained as he fumbled around, trying to get a cigarette from a packet on the table in front of him.

Laura moved forwards, took the cigarette and handed it to him. His hands were shaking. 'Here you go.'

'Thanks.'

'Do you want me to light that for you?' she asked.

'Please,' he nodded, embarrassed.

Taking the lighter from the table, she lit the cigarette.

Rhys smiled at her as he took a long drag. 'Thank you.'

Laura took her phone from her pocket and found a photo of the Irish Guards lapel pin they'd found with the remains. 'Did you ever see John wearing this?'

Rhys blew out a long plume of bluish smoke and peered at the camera. He nodded. 'Yeah.'

'Do you know what it is?' Laura enquired.

'Yeah. It's an Irish Guards badge, isn't it?' he said.

'John told you about his time in the army?'

'Not really.' Rhys tapped ash into an old mug. 'He only really talked about it when he was pissed. I got the feeling he'd seen things he didn't really want to talk about.' Rhys pointed to the top of his own right ear. 'He had a chunk of his ear missing from a bullet. You could tell he wasn't bullshitting, because he didn't want to talk about it. It's the ones who go on about their time in the army or whatever who are full of shit.'

There were a few seconds of silence as Rhys blew smoke into the air.

'Rhys, we believe that John may have been murdered,' Laura said quietly.

'What?' Rhys' face twisted in anguish. 'Oh, God, that's horrible.'

Andrea stopped writing and glanced over at him. 'Can you think of anyone who might want to harm him?'

Rhys shook his head, but then stopped, frowning. 'He told me he thought that someone was following him a few weeks before he disappeared.'

'Did he know who it was?'

'No. Then he said he thought someone had been in the house he shared with Jenny. Been through all his stuff.'

'Did he have any ideas about who might be following him?'

'No. He said he was probably being paranoid,' Rhys explained. 'The only person I could think of was Mark Weller.'

'Who's Mark Weller?'

'Mark spent all his time in The Panton Arms. And he seemed to have it in for John. They'd had a few rows and one night, when they were drunk, they'd thrown a few punches at each other.'

'Do you know why Mark Weller had it in for John?'

'No, no idea.' Rhys shrugged. 'He just seemed to take a huge dislike to him. Mark had short man's disease, if you know what I mean. Overcompensating.'

Laura looked over at Andrea. Mark Weller was certainly a person of interest whom they needed to speak to.

'Did you see Mark Weller at The Panton Arms the night John disappeared?' Andrea enquired.

'Oh, yeah,' Rhys replied. 'Mark was always there. He virtually lived in there.'

'Did you see him and John talking, or anything that you now think in hindsight might have been suspicious?' Laura asked.

Rhys shook his head. 'I wish I could be of more help, but I didn't see anything like that.'

Sitting back in his chair, Gareth stretched out his legs. He'd sent three texts to Nell to ask if she was okay, but she hadn't replied. He had no idea why. Maybe she was regretting what had happened the night before. In the cold light of day, he knew it had been a huge mistake. A sudden dry panic overtook him. He'd spent the last few months falling in love with Laura. And yet in a moment of pathetic neediness, he'd slept with his ex-wife, a woman who had rejected him for another man.

A revenge fuck? Jesus! You're a bloody idiot, Gareth, he thought angrily.

In recent months, he'd even convinced himself that if Nell ever came back grovelling, telling him she was wrong and wanted to come home, he wouldn't be interested. Instead, in the space of a few hours, he'd slept with her with no resistance and no thought. Pathetic.

'Boss, I need to run something past you,' a voice said, breaking his thoughts and saving him from more self-loathing, guilt and regret.

It was Ben.

'How can I help?' Gareth asked, trying to get his head back into the investigation.

'The Irish Guards have an online archive where you can search for veterans of the regiment,' Ben explained. 'Nothing for a John Finn. So I rang the Army Service Records, but they'll only release information to next of kin. Then I contacted the Irish Guards barracks in West London. The woman basically told me she couldn't confirm whether or not a John Finn had ever served with the Irish Guards, because the personnel file in question was marked SECRET and therefore couldn't be discussed or released due to the Official Secrets Act of 1989.'

Gareth narrowed his eyes. 'What the hell does that mean?'

Ben shook his head. 'It means that she can't tell me if a John Finn served with the Irish Guards. But even if he did, she can't tell me about it, anyway.'

'Jesus,' Gareth snorted an ironic laugh as he tried to decipher what Ben had just told him. 'Although, if John Finn didn't have a personnel record at the Irish Guards, she couldn't have told us that it was protected by the Official Secrets Act, could she?'

'Good point,' Ben agreed. 'Effectively, she told us he did serve, but we can't have access to his file.'

'I wonder why,' Gareth asked, thinking out loud. 'Did you tell them this was a murder investigation?'

'Yes, boss,' Ben said. 'She implied I'd need to be of a far higher rank to gain the correct security clearance.'

Gareth rolled his eyes. He knew that even as a DI, he wouldn't have the clearance for a military personnel file with a SECRET level of security. 'Shit! That means I'm going to have to talk to Warlow, doesn't it?'

Ben looked over at him. 'I suppose it explains why we couldn't find him on any official records.'

Gareth looked at Ben and frowned. 'I wonder what the hell he was doing on Anglesey.'

Declan gave the open door a knock to attract Gareth's attention.

'Boss, Professor Lovell's assistant rang. There's a few things he'd like us to go and see that have cropped up in the PM.'

CHAPTER 22

Laura and Andrea arrived at The Panton Arms, showed their IDs and waited as the barman scuttled away to see if anyone had been working at the pub back in October 1999.

The pub was old-fashioned with dark burgundy carpets, stools, patterned wallpaper and a scattering of regulars who sat supping beer in a daze at the bar all day. Whereas some of the pubs on Anglesey had gone gastro years ago, The Panton Arms had maintained its authentic, if slightly dingy and tatty, charm. It was pork scratchings, wet sandwiches toasted in bags and fish fingers for the kiddies.

'It's like we've been in a time machine,' Andrea muttered.

She clearly didn't warm to the pub's old-fashioned décor.

Laura smiled. 'The problem is when pubs go the other way. I walked into a "pub" the other day that was serving cod's roe with a duck egg, rabbit lasagne and deep-fried Anglesey anchovies. Jesus. It was so pretentious, I insisted we leave.'

A man in his sixties with a long greying beard, bald head and wearing a stained apron approached.

'Can I help?' he asked helpfully in a thick Welsh accent as he wiped his right hand on the apron.

'Bit of a long shot, but we're looking for anyone who

might have been working here back in October 1999,' Laura explained.

'Right.' The man nodded. 'Yeah, I was. Only a KP back in those days, mind.'

'A KP?' Andrea asked.

'Sorry. Kitchen porter,' the man explained. 'Now I'm the chef, for my sins.'

Laura wondered how skilled a chef needed to be in a pub like The Panton Arms.

'Sorry,' Laura said with a friendly smile. 'We didn't get your name.'

'Jimmy Rose,' he stated with a wry smile. 'Although, everyone round here just calls me Rosie.'

'Thanks.' Laura looked at him. 'I wonder if you remember someone who used to drink here back then called John Finn?'

'John Finn?' Rose thought for a moment and then nodded emphatically. 'Oh yes, I know who you mean. Of course. Irish fella. He drank in here for a little while. Long time ago, mind.'

'Do you remember the night he disappeared?' Andrea enquired. 'I know it's unlikely, but it was Tuesday, 12 October.'

'Yeah, I know,' Rose said. 'I do remember it, funnily enough. Although I didn't know the exact date. I know the police talked to me about it.'

Laura raised an eyebrow. 'Why do you remember that day?'

'John, Rhys Hughes and a couple of others had done a sponsored cycle to raise money for a local hospice,' Rose explained. 'Somehow, they'd raised something like five thousand pounds. The manager of the hospice came down and John had this big cheque that he handed over. I think the local newspaper was here.'

'Do you remember talking to John? Or anything out of the ordinary happening?' Laura asked.

149

'That's the thing,' Rose said. 'John handed over the cheque. The pub quiz was due to start about half an hour later and he was one of the team captains. And that's when he disappeared. Just like that.'

'And you never saw him again?' Andrea confirmed.

'No. It was the weirdest thing. He was a nice bloke, John.' Then something seemed to occur to him. 'Actually, if you come with me, I might have something that could help.'

Laura and Andrea exchanged looks and followed Rose across the pub to an area by the toilets. There were several framed photos of various pub darts teams across the years. There was also a large pinboard with a collage of photos.

'Here we go.'

Rose took a small photograph from the board and handed it to them. It showed a man holding an enormous Midland Bank cheque, which he was handing over to another man.

'And this is John?' Laura enquired, pointing to the man holding the cheque.

It was strange to put a face to the remains they'd found. For a moment, she felt a shiver down her spine.

'Yeah,' Rose nodded. 'That's John. Takes me back just looking at that photo.'

'Can we borrow this so we can get a copy?' Laura asked.

'Of course.' Then Rose looked at them quizzically. 'Have you found him or something?'

Laura gave him an empathetic look. 'I'm sorry to say that we have found remains we believe to be John.'

'Oh dear, I'm sorry to hear that.' Rose's face fell. 'I could never work out what happened to him. He was a nice bloke. Never any bother. There were plenty of theories at the time, though.'

'What did people think had happened to him?' Andrea asked.

'He won the lottery and went to live on a Caribbean

island. Stupid stuff like that,' Rose scoffed. 'I didn't pay any attention to it.'

'Did you know Rhys Hughes, as well?' Laura enquired.

'Of course,' Rose said. 'Him and John were like a bloody old married couple. Do you know what happened to John?'

Laura nodded. 'We're treating the discovery of his remains as a murder case.'

'Oh no.' Rose was shocked by the news. 'Who the hell would want to murder John?'

'We were hoping you might help with that,' Andrea stated.

Rose looked perplexed. 'Christ, I can't think of anyone who would want to do that.'

'Would you be able to remember any names of those drinking in the pub that night?' Laura asked.

'Sorry, it was a long time ago.' Rose pulled a face. 'There were a few old regulars who were always in here at the time, but they're either dead, moved away or in old folks' homes now.'

'Anything or anyone you can think of would be really helpful.' Andrea reached into her pocket, took out a card and handed it to him.

'Of course. I'll rack my brains, but my memory isn't what it was back then.'

'We were given a name,' Laura said. 'Mark Weller?'

'Oh, Mark. Bloody hell!' Rose shook his head and then said in a dark tone, 'I've tried to forget all about Mark Weller.'

Laura looked at Rose. 'We understand that John and Mark didn't get along that well.'

'No, they didn't. Mark was a pain in the arse when he'd had a drink. For some reason, he was always getting at John and trying to wind him up.'

Andrea frowned. 'Do you know why?'

'He had a chip on his shoulder about John's military career.

Not that John ever liked to talk about it. I think Mark was jealous.'

'Does Mark still drink in here?' Laura enquired.

Rose pulled a face. 'God, no. He's been in prison for the last five years.'

'What for?'

Rose gestured to the car park. 'He had a fight with some bloke out there one night. The bloke fell, hit his head and died. Mark got convicted of manslaughter.'

Laura had contacted HMP Rhoswen – a new state-of-the-art prison in North Wales that held around 2,000 Category C prisoners. They'd informed her that Mark Weller had been released a month ago and was now living in 'Approved Premises' – the latest jargon for a bail hostel – north of Beaumaris.

It was a ten-minute drive and as Laura looked out of the car window, she could see that the island was covered by low colourless cloud and a dense, relentless drizzle. Everything was muted green and grey. No colours and no hard edges.

'I'm wondering about John Finn and Rhys Hughes, aren't you?' Andrea asked as they headed south back towards Beaumaris.

'You mean they might have been having a relationship?' Laura had wondered about this as soon as Jimmy Rose described them as being 'like an old married couple'.

'Yeah.' Andrea nodded uncertainly.

'Maybe Mark Weller knew that John and Rhys were having some kind of relationship and that's why he took such a dislike to John,' Laura suggested, thinking out loud.

The windscreen had steamed up. Laura took a cloth and wiped a hole in it. The drizzle outside had turned to rain.

'We know that Weller attacked someone in the pub car

park and killed them,' Andrea said. 'Maybe the same thing happened in October 1999. John was in the pub and then he just disappeared.'

Laura nodded. It sounded feasible. 'Let's check Weller's whereabouts that night. It sounds like he was a regular at The Panton Arms.'

'And I guess we could go back and talk to Jenny,' Andrea suggested. 'See if she ever had any suspicions about John's sexuality or his relationship with Rhys.'

'Yeah,' Laura agreed. 'Hopefully, if she did have any doubts at the time, she'd be more likely to talk about them twenty years later.'

They reached a dip on the road and then a long climb up a hill. From the top, they could see Menai Bridge in the distance. Laura had forgotten what an impressive sight Thomas Telford's suspension bridge was. It had opened in 1826 and was roughly 1,200 feet long and stood 100 feet above the swirling water of the Menai Strait below.

As they turned left, she saw a series of signs, one of which read LLIGWY BAY. It reminded her of her taid and one of his stories.

'Ever been to Din Lligwy?' Laura enquired, gesturing to the sign.

Andrea frowned. 'Think we went on a school trip once? Some sort of Iron Age place, isn't it? I wasn't really paying attention.'

'History not your thing?'

'School wasn't my thing.' Andrea laughed. 'I was too busy chasing boys or sneaking off to have a smoke.'

Laura pulled a face. 'Yeah, well, I was a total geek at school. They had all this pottery and mosaics up to Din Lligwy. And then when I got back off the trip, my taid told me that the site was haunted by the ghost of a Roman soldier.'

Andrea rolled her eyes. 'Oh yeah?'

'Apparently, he pops up in the ruins of the chapel every now and then.' Laura pointed to her nose. 'You see this nose?'

Andrea gave her a quizzical look. 'Erm . . . yes.'

'According to my taid, this is a Roman nose,' Laura laughed. 'He reckoned that the Romans and the local tribes on Anglesey got on very well during the Roman occupation. In fact, they got on so well that they started to interbreed. So, my taid reckoned that his side of the family were all descended from Roman soldiers because of our straight noses.'

Andrea grinned. 'That's a great story. Did you inherit anything else from your Roman ancestors?'

'Yeah.' Laura rolled her eyes. 'An unhealthy interest in Pinot Grigio and pizza.'

Andrea laughed.

CHAPTER 23

Belfast 1998

It had been over a week since Frank Daly had taken John for what had been a terrifying interrogation. Since then, John and Daly had spent a bit of time together, bonding over discussions of Celtic Football Club, or the Bhoys, as they were known, referencing the club's links and origins to Ireland. Daly thought Celtic's Swedish striker Henrik Larsson was a selfish player, whereas John felt Larsson had virtually single-handedly won Celtic their first Scottish League Championship in ten years.

It was a cold Sunday morning and Daly picked John up, telling him that he had someone he wanted John to meet. They soon arrived at a small house round the back of St Anne's Cathedral on Donegall Street. Having been ushered inside with a degree of caution and vigilance, John was led down to a back room, which was filled with cigarette smoke. Sitting in a large armchair was a man that he immediately recognised from the intelligence papers he'd been given to study – Joe Magan. Chief of Staff of the Real IRA.

Somehow, John had found his way into the inner circle.

This was it. It was a big step towards where he needed to be. There had been times in recent weeks when John had worried that he wasn't going to get any further than drinking pints of black with Daly and talking football. But being here in this flat was significant progress.

Magan was now in his fifties and the coal-black hair of the photograph John had been given was now greying. His eyes were blue and alert, his face angular and his face covered in black stubble. The room was adorned with photos and posters of Che Guevara.

'This is the fella I was telling you about, Joe,' Daly said as they stood by the door.

Magan leaned forwards, tapped some ash off his cigarette and gestured for them to sit down.

It's like I'm having an audience with the bloody Pope, John thought dryly.

He peered around at the iconic images of the revolutionary leader.

'You know the great Che Guevara?' Magan asked John.

'I don't know a great deal about him,' John admitted. 'Although I think he did say, "I would rather die standing up than to live my life on my knees." I like that.'

Magan laughed loudly. He was impressed as he looked over at Frank. 'Christ, quoting feckin' Guevara at me! Smart man, Frank. I like him.' Then he glanced back at John. 'Che was a lucky man in some ways. He became a revolutionary martyr before he got old. He'll always look like that.'

'Bit like James Dean,' John stated.

'Yeah, a bit like Jimmy Dean,' Magan agreed. 'Che Guevara, the James Dean of revolutionaries. I like that . . .'

Magan opened a packet of cigarettes and offered one to John. He shook his head.

'You know your politics, Johnny-boy?' Magan asked.

John shrugged. 'A little, you know.'

'What did you think when we signed the Good Friday agreement?' Magan enquired.

It was direct and to the point. John took a few seconds to consider his words.

'It's not right that the republican movement has accepted anything less than a united Ireland. I think it's a big mistake,' he stated cautiously. 'Brave men have died for that cause. I can't imagine what their families must think about their sacrifice.'

Magan nodded. 'Yeah, you've hit the nail right on the head there. I call the Good Friday agreement the GFA. Stands for *Got Fuck All*. I was in the Long Kesh with Gerry Adams.'

The Long Kesh was slang for the Maze Prison, which was used to house paramilitary prisoners during the Troubles.

'Mind you, this was the seventies. The whole thing, the way that man has behaved, is disgusting. Adams is more interested in having his photograph taken with Bill Clinton than fighting for the principles young men have died for.'

At that moment, a woman appeared. She was in her early thirties, very attractive with dark red wavy hair around her shoulders.

She's lovely, John thought to himself.

'Bernie,' Magan called to her as he beckoned her over. 'This is John Finn.'

She gave him a wary look and slumped down in a chair. 'How are ya?'

'Bernie might look like a wee slip of a thing,' Magan said. 'But she had a feckin' British Army running for cover over in Germany.'

John smiled at her. 'Impressive. Even Rommel didn't manage that.'

Bernie ignored his comment and looked directly at him. She had beautiful green eyes.

'So, what are you going to do for us, Mr John Finn?' she said.

It was a good question. John didn't know why he was meeting Magan.

'John here is going to build us a bomb,' Magan said, looking over at him. 'A great big bloody bomb to blow up the British Army.'

CHAPTER 24

'What have you got for us, Professor?' Gareth asked as Lovell moved the spotlight over the dead man's body, which lay like a lifeless mannequin on the metal gurney at the centre of the mortuary.

Lovell pointed with his gloved hand to the two deep stab wounds on the man's torso. 'This lower wound was to the stomach and this one up here hit his ribcage.'

'And that's what killed him?' Gareth asked, noticing a scattering of dark tattoos on the man's upper arm.

Lovell raised an eyebrow. 'Actually, no.' He moved round to the other side of the body, lifted up his left arm and pointed to another wound. 'This is what killed him.'

Declan frowned. 'His armpit?'

Lovell nodded. 'The knife would have severed the axilla artery under here, causing huge blood loss and physiological shock. Your victim would have been incapacitated in seconds and dead in under two minutes.'

'Lucky shot, then?' Gareth shrugged.

Lovell shook his head. 'I don't think so. I think it was deliberate.'

Declan narrowed his eyes. 'Deliberate?'

'Your killer might have had medical knowledge,' Lovell explained. 'But my guess is that they had military training. A stab to the left armpit is a well-known technique in hand-to-hand military combat. It's quicker and more reliable than trying to stab someone in the heart.'

Gareth exchanged a look with Declan and saw from his colleague's bemused expression that he hadn't been expecting that, either. He then noticed something at the top of the arm. It was the tricolour Irish flag.

Gareth went over for a closer inspection. 'Tattoo of an Irish flag.'

Lovell nodded and gestured to the body. 'I noticed an interesting tattoo on his right arm, as well. Gaelic, I think.'

Gareth and Declan went to have a look. There was a large fist with the words *Tiocfaidh ár lá* written underneath.

'It means our day will come,' Declan explained.

'Does it mean anything to you?' Gareth asked.

'Yes, boss.' Declan nodded with a dark expression. 'It's an IRA tattoo.'

Laura and Andrea made their way along the long corridor towards a meeting room on the ground floor of the Approved Premises building. Entering the sparse room, Laura saw that Mark Weller was already sitting at the table, which was bolted to the floor. One of the residential workers sat on the other side of the room.

Laura looked at him with a half-smile. 'Thanks. We can take it from here.'

Weller was in his early sixties. His greying hair was short and brushed forwards from the back. He was overweight, with a rounded jaw, and was clean-shaven.

'Mark Weller?' Laura enquired as she and Andrea sat down at the table opposite him.

Weller sat back in his chair with a smirk. 'Yeah. Who are you two, then? Cagney and fucking Lacey?'

Laura ignored him pointedly.

'We want to ask you a few questions about an investigation we're working on,' Andrea explained in a withering tone.

'Oh yeah.' Weller scratched his crotch. 'What's that, then?'

God, he really is revolting, thought Laura.

She forced herself to look at him. 'You remember a man called John Finn?'

'Yeah, of course.' Weller snorted immediately. 'Popped up somewhere after all these years, has he?'

'You remember him, then?' Andrea enquired.

'We drank in the same pub.' Weller shrugged nonchalantly.

Laura frowned. 'You were friends?'

Weller snorted again. 'I wouldn't go that far, love.'

Laura fixed Weller with her best icy stare. 'I'd prefer Detective Inspector, if it's all the same to you,' she growled.

'Sorry.'

Weller had an annoying smirk fixed to his face.

'And you remember that John Finn went missing?' Andrea enquired as she wrote in her notepad.

'Yeah. I remember. Did a runner, more like.'

'What can you tell us about that?' Laura asked.

'It was pretty bloody weird,' Weller explained. 'He was there doing this charity thing. Then *poof*, he'd disappeared.' Weller gave them a knowing look. '*Poof* being the operative word, if you know what I mean.'

Laura shared a look of contempt with Andrea before glaring back at Weller. 'No, I don't think I do know what you mean.'

'John and this bloke called Rhys were, you know . . .' Weller said, raising his eyebrows suggestively.

Laura wasn't about to put words into his mouth. *It's 2021, for God's sake!*

'I don't know,' she said.

'You want me to spell it out for you, then?'

She gave him a sarcastic smile. 'That would be useful, Mark.'

'John and Rhys were gays,' Mark stated.

Andrea looked over at him. 'And you're sure about that, are you?'

'Of course.'

'And they told you that, did they?' Laura asked.

'They didn't have to. You could just tell. You know, the way they were together.'

Andrea stopped writing, frowned, and glanced over at Weller. 'Do I take it you don't like homosexuals, Mark?'

'What?' he said defensively.

'Am I right in thinking that you don't like gay people?' Andrea asked.

Weller pulled a face. 'Look, I'm not gonna pretend it doesn't make me feel a bit sick. But as long as they leave me alone and do whatever behind closed doors, I don't really care.'

Laura narrowed her eyes. 'That's very enlightened of you, Mark.'

'Eh?'

He doesn't know what enlightened means, does he? thought Laura. However, it wasn't their job to educate Weller on the correct attitude to sexual orientation, even if he was thirty years out of date.

'So, what's all this about then, eh?' Weller demanded. 'You still haven't told me why you're asking me about John Finn.' And then a look of realisation came over his face. 'Unless something's happened to him. Has it?'

'Why do you think something might have happened to him?' Laura asked.

'Because you wouldn't have made the effort to come here and see me if you'd found him alive and well, would you?'

Ten points for deduction, genius, Laura thought mockingly.

'We've found some remains that we believe to be John Finn,' she explained.

'What's that got to do with me?' Weller snapped.

He was definitely rattled now.

'We're talking to everyone who knew John at the time he went missing, that's all,' Andrea explained.

'Oh yeah?' he asked with a tone of disbelief. 'What happened to him, then?'

'We believe he was murdered.' Laura studied Weller's face to see how he reacted to the news.

Nothing. He just blinked and looked into space for a few seconds.

'And you think I did it, do you?' he asked with a sneer.

Laura raised an eyebrow. 'Did you?'

'No, I didn't,' he replied with a mocking laugh. 'Wasted journey, I'm afraid, ladies.'

'We understand that you and John didn't get along all that well,' Andrea said.

'Who told you that? You been speaking to that Rhys Hughes?'

Laura fixed him with a stare. 'Why didn't you like John Finn?'

'Was it because you suspected he was gay?' Andrea asked.

'No.' Weller shook his head and then thought for a few seconds. 'I'll tell you why I didn't like him. He made this big song and dance about how he couldn't talk about what he'd done when he was in the army. Then one night, when he was shit-faced, he told someone he'd been in the SAS. Jesus, what a load of crap. I used to take the piss and ask him what he did in the catering corps.'

'What happened between you and John on the night he went missing?' Laura asked.

'Nothing.'

'You didn't decide to see how tough John Finn really was out in the car park?' Andrea asked.

Weller looked furious. 'No, no way. Whatever Rhys told you, he's a lying little prick. You're not pinning this on me.'

Laura gave him a quizzical look. 'You see, we know that you're in here because you decided to sort someone out in the car park of The Panton Arms and they ended up dead. Is that what happened to John?'

Weller took a breath. 'No. You're way off.'

'Are you sure, Mark?'

'Yes.'

Laura raised an eyebrow. 'You know what DNA is?'

Weller's eyes darted around the room. He was feeling the pressure of their questions.

'What?' he said eventually.

Laura frowned. 'You understand what DNA is?'

'Yes.'

'So, you must know that tiny fragments of skin, hair, even something like a molecule of sweat, can remain for thousands of years,' Laura explained as if talking to a child. 'When we test your DNA, which we have on the national database, against the forensics that we've found on those remains, are you certain that we're not going to get a match?'

Weller's eyes widened and he shook his head. 'If you had anything, you'd have arrested or charged me with something. I'm not saying anything more without my solicitor.'

'That's your right, Mark,' Laura stated with a scornful smile. 'But if you get a solicitor, that does make it look like you've got something to hide.'

'I don't give a shit about that. I'm not saying anything.'

Laura looked over at Andrea. Weller was rattled all right.

CHAPTER 25

Gareth sat in Superintendent Warlow's office. His head was still lost in the idea that the unknown victim from Gallows Point had an IRA tattoo and might have been killed by someone with military training. Gareth had been 'summoned' ten minutes earlier and made the developments known to Warlow, who had used his senior rank to access security clearance for their investigation into John Finn.

Warlow was one of those officers whose every move was calculated only in terms of his next promotion. If a new policy or directive would get him noticed by those at the top, then it was all systems go. If there was any chance of failure or anything that might remotely damage his career prospects, then he wasn't interested. Policy, not policing, was his strength. He was a desk jockey – presentable, good in meetings, full of platitudes. As someone once joked, Warlow was far happier dealing with subordinate clauses than he was with actual subordinates.

'I think you've opened a can of worms here, Gareth,' Warlow sighed dourly as he took off his glasses, gave them a wipe and placed them carefully back on the bridge of his pointy nose. His grey-white hair came halfway down over his ears and had been carefully combed that way.

Unlike Gareth's untidy desk, Warlow's was as you'd expect from someone who took pride in having everything at right angles. Gareth wondered how long Warlow spent every day making sure that everything was neat and tidy on his desk.

He's such a prick.

Crossing his legs, Gareth looked over at him, trying to hide his contempt. 'How do you mean, sir?'

Tapping at his computer, Warlow moved the monitor round so that Gareth could see. A man's face stared back. He had ink-black hair, small features and blue eyes. He was wearing the smart green dress uniform of a soldier. The name underneath read Corporal John Kelly, Special Air Service.

Gareth frowned. 'Sorry, sir. I'm not with you. The man whose remains we think we've found is a John Finn.'

Warlow pointed to the screen. 'This is John Finn. Also known as John Doyle, too.'

'Okay?' Gareth gave a quizzical expression.

Warlow looked at him as though he expected him to make some kind of educated guess as to what on earth he was talking about. He wasn't going to venture a guess only for Warlow to give him a withering look and correct him.

Dickhead.

'You'll have to explain it to me, I'm afraid, sir.' Gareth tried to hide his annoyance.

'Corporal John *Kelly* was a decorated member of the SAS. He was awarded the Victoria Cross for gallantry in the field of battle during the first Gulf War. Apparently, he dived onto an Iraqi troop carrier that had pinned down his unit and threw in a grenade.' Gareth pulled a face. 'Impressive stuff.

'Kelly was born in Newry in Northern Ireland,' Warlow continued. 'In 1998, he was sent to work undercover in Belfast within the Real IRA under the name John *Doyle*. The

166

records are pretty sketchy about his work in Ireland. Most of it is protected under the Official Secrets Act. However, after his work in Ireland, he was given another new identity: John *Finn*. The Witness Protection Unit set him up with a new life here on Anglesey.'

The man murdered at Gallows Point! He was Irish with an IRA tattoo.

'According to his records,' Warlow continued, 'John travelled to Anglesey in September 1998. And from what we know, he went missing in the October of 1999.'

'That's what we think.' Gareth nodded and then looked over at Warlow. 'Do we think his murder has anything to do with his work in Ireland?'

'No idea yet.' Warlow shrugged. 'Someone from the Public Prosecution Service is coming over from the mainland. They should be able to shed more light on it. But my guess is that if they went to the trouble and expense of putting him into a Witness Protection Programme, his life was in danger.'

'There has to be some kind of link to our victim from last night then, sir,' Gareth said. 'He's got an IRA tattoo and was possibly stabbed by someone who had some kind of military training.'

'Yes, I can't believe they're not linked.' Warlow nodded. 'I wonder if your victim knew John when he worked in Ireland.'

Gareth frowned. 'The question is, were they murdered by the same person? And who wanted them both dead?'

Laura and Andrea arrived back at the Anglesey Lakeside Lodges to speak with Jenny Maldini again. Having parked, they made their way towards the reception lodge.

Laura looked out over the lake, which glowed rather than sparkled in the benign autumnal sunshine. The weather was still and strangely without wind or even a breeze so that the lake's surface was smooth, unflecked by ripples or movement of any kind. It was as if it were a solid object.

The lawns under their feet were well kept and short, the blades spread out and smooth after the long summer. Pink and white valerian grew around the wooden struts and bases of nearby lodges. Closer inspection would also show purple flowering thyme and tiny white saxifrage.

They entered the reception. It was plastered with posters and information about local trips and sites on Anglesey with joyous nuclear families enjoying castles or beaches.

Laura approached a man in his fifties who was wearing glasses and sitting on a stool behind the reception counter. He had a bushy grey beard and a long mane of silver hair pulled back into a ponytail. He had an array of wristbands and rings, and wore a plaid shirt with a T-shirt underneath, which stretched over a beer belly.

'Can I help?' he asked with the trace of a Celtic accent.

Laura couldn't place it. *Glaswegian, maybe,* she thought.

Laura took out her warrant card. 'DI Hart and DC Jones from Beaumaris CID. We're looking for Jenny Maldini.'

'Oh, yes,' the man said brightly. 'You're in luck. She's just arrived for her shift.'

And with that, Jenny appeared from a door in her uniform, pushing a small trolley of cleaning products.

'Jenny,' the man said cheerily. 'These officers are here to speak to you. I hope you haven't been up to no good again.'

Jenny gave him a withering look as she approached.

Laura gave her a kind smile and asked, 'We've got a couple more questions to ask you. Is there somewhere we can talk in private?'

Jenny nodded and pointed to the door she'd just emerged from. 'There's the staff room. There's no one in there at the moment.'

'Sounds good,' Andrea said with a nod as they followed

her to the door, along a narrow corridor and into a small room that smelled of coffee and body odour.

Jenny, who looked understandably nervous, gestured uncertainly for them to sit on a sofa as she sat down on an orange plastic chair.

'We've just got a few questions to ask you about John and the night he went missing, if that's all right?' Laura explained as Andrea pulled out her notebook.

'Okay,' Jenny said, nodding hesitantly.

'Since we last saw you, we've spoken to several people who knew John,' Andrea explained. 'There's a few things we'd just like to clarify.'

'I'll do my best.' Jenny smiled weakly.

Andrea looked down at her notepad and turned over a few pages. 'We spoke to Rhys Hughes. Did you know him?'

'Yes. A long time ago.'

'Rhys was a close friend of John's, wasn't he?' Andrea asked.

'Oh yes.' Jenny's face softened. 'Rhys was a lovely man. He'd do anything for anyone. So kind. And yeah, him and John used to go out a lot together.'

'Where did they go when they went out?' Andrea enquired.

'The Panton Arms. Darts team, pub quiz. That sort of thing. I'm not really a pub sort of person, so I left them to it.'

'Just for our records,' Laura stated, 'can you tell us where you were the night John disappeared?'

'Oh, I was at home. As I said, it wasn't my sort of thing. I preferred a night in front of the telly with a cup of tea.'

No alibi for the night John vanished, Laura noted to herself.

'Did you ever think there was anything more to John and Rhys' relationship?'

At first, Jenny didn't seem to understand the question, and then her face dropped.

'You mean, were they gay?' she asked. She sounded annoyed.

'Is that a possibility?'

'God, no. Of course not,' Jenny snapped. 'That's ridiculous. John wasn't gay. I'd have known.'

'It's just a line of enquiry that we have to look at,' Laura informed her gently. 'So as far as you know, their friendship was purely platonic?'

'Yes,' Jenny said emphatically.

They'd clearly touched a nerve.

'Of course it was,' Jenny continued.

'Do you remember a man named Mark Weller?' Andrea enquired, reading from her notes.

Jenny's face visibly drained. 'Yes,' she replied in a virtual whisper.

Laura shared a look with Andrea – something was definitely up.

'How well did you know Mark Weller?' Laura asked gently.

Jenny's whole demeanour had changed. Her body language was completely closed off – arms folded, chin dropped, legs crossed.

'Not that well.' Jenny's voice sounded choked.

'It's okay, Jenny,' Laura said with a benign smile. 'Whatever it is, it's probably best that you tell us.'

Jenny looked over at them with a nervous blink. 'Mark attacked me.'

'What?' Laura asked. 'When was this?'

'Back when John was living with me,' Jenny explained, taking a breath. 'We had a party at our house.'

'I knew John and Mark didn't like each other,' Andrea said with a raised eyebrow. 'Was Mark at the party?'

'He wasn't invited but he turned up drunk. And invited himself in.'

'Can you tell us what happened?' Laura asked.

'There were a few of us in the garden,' Jenny recalled. 'And for a moment, I was on my own just by the fence. Mark came over, forced me back and put his hand up my skirt. I told him to stop and when I pushed him, he grabbed my face.' Jenny wiped a tear from her face.

'It's all right,' Laura reassured. 'Take your time.'

'He told me that I needed to know what it was like to be with a real man,' Jenny said, her voice faltering. 'And then he . . . sexually assaulted me.'

Laura looked at her. 'I'm so sorry to hear that. It sounds horrible. Did you tell anyone?'

'Someone came outside, so he let me go. I told John later on, but Mark had gone by then,' Jenny replied. 'John didn't want to involve the police.'

'Did he say why?' Andrea asked.

Jenny shrugged. 'Yeah. That's why I worried when he went missing.'

Laura frowned. 'What do you mean?'

'John said he was going to sort out Mark himself. He said he was going to make sure he never attacked anyone ever again.'

CHAPTER 26

Belfast 1998

Even though it was cold and frosty outside, John was sweating. The safety goggles he was wearing had steamed up. He blinked as a bead of sweat stung his left eye before moving the soldering iron across to the square circuit board. His hand shook a little owing to the intensity of the work.

Dabbing gently at some solder, he saw it melt into a small globule of molten liquid. The familiar metallic waft of burning floated into his nostrils. Using tweezers, John took the stripped end of the blue electrical wire and placed it into the liquid before it cooled. Once attached, it would create an electrical circuit, controlled by the simple clock.

His mind turned to the dark irony of what he was actually doing. He was a British soldier manufacturing a bomb for the IRA. He still didn't know the intended target and despite some gentle probing, no one would give the slightest hint. He had to find out where they were planning to use the bomb without arousing suspicion. It was a difficult balancing act, as the IRA worked on a need-to-know basis. John was making the bomb but, as far as Daly was concerned, that didn't mean he *needed to know.* The more people who knew, the more likely a tip-off.

Moving the goggles up, he wiped his sweaty brow and face with his sleeve, pushing aside his uncomfortable thoughts as he did so. His eyes flitted around the work surface. Electrical circuit boards, wires, pliers and, of course, the trigger button.

The SAS had trained him well in how to use explosives. For a moment, he remembered his training at Hereford. SAS recruits used a specially constructed building to simulate various scenarios. It was known colloquially as The Killing House. CQB – Close Quarter Battle – techniques were perfected through tedious, exhausting repetition. John was shown how to use door- and wall-breaching explosives, tear gas and stun grenades. When their instructors thought they were ready, live ammunition was used in mock sieges. John remembered his overwhelming anxiety as he sat in the darkness of a room in The Killing House, playing a hostage as bullets whistled past him into the life-size dummies that represented the targets. He still didn't know how no one had been shot in these reconstructions.

A voice called up the stairs. 'How's you getting on, fella?'

It was Tom Breslin, the quartermaster of West Belfast's ASU – Active Service Unit.

'Aye, we're getting there,' John replied, looking around at the paraphernalia required to build a 500 lb car bomb.

A small clock was used as the timer that would create the bomb circuit. This was linked to the detonator line and the detonator itself. The 500 lb Semtex explosive had been packed into three huge beer barrels that would then be placed in the boot of the car. John had heard that the Semtex had been supplied by Libya. In fact, every bomb that the IRA had created since the mid-eighties had been made with Libyan Semtex that arrived by boat. Colonel Gaddafi sanctioned the supply of arms and explosives to the IRA in retaliation for the British Government's support of US air strikes against Tripoli and Benghazi in 1986. Prior to that, bombs had been made from stolen commercial explosives such as Frangex, or the cruder ingredients of ANFO.

Breslin appeared at the door and peered in. He had curly ginger hair, a slightly twisted nose and milky, freckled skin.

'You wanna brew, or something stronger?' he asked, gesturing downstairs.

John blew out his cheeks. 'A wee Jamesons would go down a treat.'

'Right you are,' he replied.

Breslin had a jovial, slightly apologetic manner. However, John had seen him lose his temper and pistol-whip a local drug dealer until his face was awash with blood.

Looking around for the electronic tester to check the circuit for the bomb, John saw that it was on a table by the door.

'Tom, would you pass me that ISFE from there?' John asked, pointing to the small electric device with two wires coming from it.

'A what?' Breslin asked. 'ISFE? You mean this tester?'

Shit!

ISFE stood for Igniter, Safety, Fuse, Electric. But it was a term specific to the British military. A civilian would never use it – but it was just force of habit.

'Never heard it called that before.' Breslin frowned.

John took a nervous gulp. Then he shrugged, trying to remain calm. 'Pretty sure that's what we called it in Canada.'

There were a few tense seconds of silence.

Breslin picked up the tester, walked across the room and looked directly at him. There was a nerve-wracking silence.

Breslin then raised an eyebrow. 'Funny. I thought it was just the British Army that referred to these things as ISFEs?'

'I dunno.' John shrugged, his pulse quickening.

Is he on to me?

174

Breslin went to hand it to John but as John took it, he didn't let go. Instead, he fixed John with an icy stare.

'You sure about that, boyo?'

John felt the tension in his stomach. 'Sure about what?'

'Just seems weird that you'd call it that.'

John had a choice. Either passively continue to brush off Breslin's suspicious comments – or do something more dramatic.

Snatching the tester out of Breslin's hand, John glared at him. 'Something you want to say to me, Tom?'

Breslin raised an eyebrow. 'I'm just saying it's weird, that's all.'

John took a deep breath, then jumped up from his seat, grabbed Breslin by his collar and pushed him up against the wall.

'Are you feckin' kiddin' me! I'm sitting here, risking my feckin' life in a room with 500 lb of Semtex. And you're acting like a feckin' eejit.'

'Calm down, John,' Breslin said, shocked at John's outburst. 'I was just messin' with you, fella.'

John let him go and grabbed the tester. He tossed it over and Breslin caught it.

'There you go, Tom,' John growled. 'You make the feckin' bomb. I'm going for a pint.'

John marched over to the door and thundered down the stairs, hoping that his little act had done enough to alleviate any suspicion.

CHAPTER 27

It was six p.m. and Gareth had assembled the CID team for an impromptu briefing at the end of the day. There had been several significant developments in the investigation. He'd already brought the team up to speed with what they'd found out at the postmortem as well as everything Warlow had told him about John Finn and his military background.

As Gareth walked over to the scene boards, he noticed Laura looking at him as if trying to get his attention. Sleeping with Nell the night before was now weighing heavily. He couldn't seem to get a clear or consistent handle on why he'd done it and how he felt about it. It also meant that he now felt uneasy and anxious every time he saw or spoke to Laura. Maybe he should come clean and tell Laura what had happened. The thought of that made his stomach twist.

Laura caught his eye. 'Up until now, we've assumed that John was killed by someone local. If he was in Witness Protection, his life must have been in danger. Does that mean that one of our lines of enquiry is that John was murdered because of something that happened in Ireland?'

'That would tie in with our victim from last night. I've no idea if his tattoos mean he was a member of the IRA or just a sympathiser,' Gareth said as their eyes met for a second longer than normal, and he felt a pang of shame. 'We have someone from the UK PPS coming here tomorrow with details of John's case. I'm hoping that might clarify things for us. My instinct is that they're connected, but let's stick to what do know until we talk to the Witness Protection officer. Laura, what about the night John Finn went missing?'

Laura got up and went over to the scene boards. 'At some point between handing over the cheque at seven p.m. and the start of the pub quiz at eight p.m., John disappeared from the pub.' Laura pointed to a photo of Mark Weller on the scene board. 'This man is Mark Weller. It's clear that Weller didn't like John. We interviewed Weller today. He claims that John and Rhys were in a relationship with each other. Weller has just served five years of a ten-year sentence for manslaughter after killing a man in a fight in the car park of The Panton Arms in 2016.'

'Right, so he's got previous,' Ben said, raising an eyebrow.

'Weller guessed that we'd been speaking to Rhys Hughes,' Andrea said. 'He wasn't happy about it.'

'Did you ask Rhys about Weller's claim that he and John were in a relationship?' Declan asked.

'No. We interviewed Rhys first, so we haven't had a chance to go back and ask him about that.' Laura shook her head. 'But Jenny thought it was ridiculous. She clearly never thought that John and Rhys were anything more than friends.'

'Thanks, Laura.' Gareth ran his hand over his scalp as he tried to process the evidence. 'You spoke to the chef who was at the pub that night, didn't you?'

'Yes, David Rose,' Andrea replied.

'I think we need to see if we can find anyone else who was at The Panton Arms that night.' Gareth looked out at the team. 'Maybe Weller and John had an argument that got out of hand. Maybe it spilled out into the car park.'

'Okay, well that fits in with something else that Jenny told us.' Andrea used her pen to indicate what she'd written down in her notebook. 'She claimed that Mark Weller had sexually assaulted her at a house party that she and John had thrown. It sounds like Weller gatecrashed it and forced himself on her in the garden.'

'Did they report it?' Declan asked.

'No,' Andrea replied. 'John told her that he was going to deal with it himself and make sure that Weller didn't attack anyone ever again.'

Getting to the car, Laura checked her watch and saw that she'd be home in time to cook dinner and help Jake with his homework. It had been one of her promises when she'd decided to make the leap back into the police force: that she'd still be around to do those things. Jake had told her that he had some maths to do. She'd given him a nod and a smile but had been dreading it all day. She couldn't believe how complicated Year 6 maths had become. It was getting to the point where she was struggling to help him. She was pretty sure that he was doing stuff that wasn't far off the maths GCSE she'd sat in 1989.

Jake and Rosie understood that there would be times when there was a major investigation when getting home on time wouldn't be possible, but she'd assured them that would be the exception, not the rule. Rosie had promised that she could always lend a hand around the house or cook them tea. Laura had thanked her but suspected that she'd have to see it to believe it.

As she opened the driver's door, she spotted something out of the corner of her eye. Gareth was standing by his car in the far corner. Maybe it was his body language, but he appeared to be in a rush.

That's weird. Why didn't he say anything to me on the way to his car?

She'd had the feeling all day that he'd been avoiding her, so she slammed the car door shut and marched in his direction.

'Where are you skulking off to?' she asked in a loud but cheery voice. She wanted to know if he was dodging her for any reason, or if he was just preoccupied with the case.

Gareth jumped out of his skin. 'Bloody hell! I didn't see you there.'

Laura looked at him. Something was wrong. His inability to look her properly in the eye, his jerky, awkward movements. 'Are you okay?' she asked in a way that suggested this wasn't just an empty question out of sheer politeness.

'Me? Yes, fine,' he said, taking a breath. 'Long day, that's all.'

She gave him a half-smile and frowned. 'Yeah, the problem with being a detective is that you have this innate sense when someone is lying to you.'

'Seriously, I'm fine.'

He sounded annoyed. She could either accept this, turn and leave – or dig deeper.

'Nope, that's just not convincing.' Laura gave another half-smile. 'And I've done my advanced interview technique training.'

Gareth let the tension go as he gave a chortle. 'You're very funny, aren't you.'

'Don't change the subject, buster.' She raised an eyebrow. 'What's going on?'

He looked at her with an apologetic expression. 'Nell turned up on my doorstep last night with a black eye.'

And with that admission, his face and body seemed to relax.

'Oh dear,' Laura sighed. 'Why didn't you tell me that?'

'I don't know.' Gareth shrugged. 'I suppose I thought it might be weird, my ex-wife turning up at our old marital home.'

'It's only weird if you slept with her.'

He snorted.

'What happened to her?' Laura asked.

'It turns out that Mr Perfect who she lives with is also a violent bully,' Gareth explained.

'Poor her. Did she stay over?'

Gareth pulled a face as he babbled, 'She said she didn't have anywhere else to go. And I couldn't turn her out on the street.'

'It's all right,' Laura said with a half-smile at Gareth's nervousness. 'Nell was an important part of your life for years. If she needs help, then I don't expect you to turn your back on her. I'm not some kind of psychotic bunny-boiler.'

'Sorry,' Gareth muttered.

She wasn't sure how he'd managed to go from the incredibly masculine SIO of a murder case to looking like an awkward eight-year-old boy, but he'd managed it.

'You don't need to be sorry.' Laura sighed. 'But if you'd told me this morning, I wouldn't have spent the day thinking you're being an aloof dickhead.'

'Point taken.' Gareth smiled. 'And I haven't heard anyone use the word aloof in some time.'

'Yeah, I don't know where that came from. But I think I'm going to start using it more.'

'I think you should.' Gareth laughed.

They looked at each other, enjoying the spark of their to and fro.

'I take it you were chivalrous and slept on the sofa?' Laura asked.

'Actually, the spare room was made up,' Gareth said with a nod.

'Oh, the spare room?' Laura said, teasing him. 'I forgot you have a nice modern three-bedroom house.'

'Which is even more extravagant now I live there on my own.'

'How long is she planning on staying?'

'I don't know yet.' He shrugged awkwardly. 'We haven't got that far.'

'Is she going to press charges?'

'I don't know that either. I told her she should.'

'Too right,' Laura said and then she glanced at her watch. It was a relief to know why Gareth had been acting so strangely all day. 'Right, I've got dinner to cook and I need to try to help Jake with his maths homework.'

He smiled at her. 'Lucky you.'

'Yeah, living the dream, eh?'

'See you later, then.' He clicked the automatic locking system of his car.

'Just tell me the truth the next time, Gareth. It'll save all this crap.'

She turned to go but then spun on her heels, marched over to him and grabbed him by the jacket. Pulling him, she then kissed him hard on mouth. Then she pushed against him so her breasts and hips were touching him. Probing her tongue into his mouth, she rubbed against him before biting his neck and earlobe.

They locked eyes for a second. She gave him a sexy grin as she moved her hand down to his crotch.

Then she took two steps back and grinned. 'Okay, I'll see you in the morning then, boss.'

Gareth narrowed his eyes with a smile. 'What was all that about?'

'Oh, just something to remember me by while you're hanging out with your ex-wife.' She winked as she turned and headed back to her car.

CHAPTER 28

Having reversed his car next to Nell's on the drive, Gareth sat watching the rain falling steadily into the dark sea. The terrible grim simplicity of the scene matched his mood. There was a dark line on the horizon, which was the only thing that distinguished the sea from the sky. A muted, faintly radiant grey.

Catching his reflection in the rear-view mirror, Gareth felt a dart of shame. He wasn't particularly enamoured with the man who looked back at him at this precise moment. He mulled over his decision to lie to Laura half an hour earlier. His whole body sank at the thought. Maybe he should have come clean and faced whatever the consequences were. But he was too much of a coward, wasn't he. And he didn't want her to storm out of his life before she'd ever really become part of it. However, now he had to continue with the guilt of what he'd done nagging away at his conscience.

Getting out of the car, he felt the rain on his head and on the back of his neck. It was refreshingly cold. He jogged to the front door and then hesitated for a second. Nell's car was on the drive, so he assumed she was inside. He had no idea what to say to her or if they were just going to pretend that nothing had happened.

He opened the front door and could immediately feel that the house was baking hot. That's the way Nell had always liked it. Heating on full blast until it was unbearable. He was the opposite. He found the heat oppressive, even claustrophobic, and used to walk around the house in a T-shirt and shorts in the depths of winter.

'Hello?' he called in a cheery voice.

His head was a mess of thoughts, resolutions and plans that changed by the minute. They seemed to have a life of their own.

'In here,' she said in a rather monotone voice.

He took off his shoes and shook the rain from his coat – he was stalling for time. Time for what? He had no idea. Actually, if he were honest, he didn't really want to see her.

Padding down the hallway, he made his way to the kitchen where Nell had called from. She had her back to him and the smell of perfume hit him. As she turned to look at him, he could see she was fully made-up and dressed in clothes that implied she was going out. She had a glass of wine in her hand. It was as if she'd never left.

Jesus! What the hell is going on?

'Going somewhere?' he enquired.

'I'm off out to meet a friend for a drink,' she stated in a withering tone.

Oh my God, I've been transported back nine months in time!

'Okay. Are you up to going out?' he asked.

'Yes, of course I am. I've been rattling around here all day, so I need to go out.' She frowned as if it were a stupid question.

He looked at her and could see that she'd done a good

183

job of using make-up to conceal her bruised eye. It was virtually invisible.

'Do you want me to come with you?' he asked and then realised how bizarre the situation had become. 'Sorry, that was a stupid question.'

'That's very sweet of you,' she said in her well-rehearsed off-hand manner, 'but I really do feel the need for a bit of female company.'

Then why did you come running to me last night? Am I being taken for a mug here?

'And are you staying here tonight?' he enquired.

She sipped her wine. 'If that's all right?'

'Yes, I suppose so.'

She looked at him for a few seconds. 'And what happened between us last night was a big mistake. I don't think it should happen again, do you?'

'No, I agree,' he replied, annoyed that he'd allowed her to get in there first.

He wasn't certain that he was going to flag it up, but now she had, he wished he'd said it before her.

'Right, well, don't wait up.' She waltzed out of the kitchen and left.

Gareth waited for a few seconds and then went to the fridge, grabbed a beer and opened it.

How the hell did I allow this to happen? I'm such an idiot!

He realised he needed to do something about it sooner rather than later. He was fed up with Nell treating him like a lapdog.

Sitting with her laptop open, Laura took a long swig of wine. The CCTV footage from the street outside Seymours in Llandudno was on the screen. Clicking Play, Laura watched it for the third time.

There she was. Louise McDonald. The woman who had been Sam's partner in the Manchester Met for four years. Louise had been to their house several times for summer barbecues and Christmas drinks. She remembered sitting on the stairs while Louise had drunkenly told her about her latest boyfriend who had cheated on her. Putting an arm around her, she'd comforted her as she cried. Another time, Louise had arrived at a barbecue with her 'famous' goat's cheese and watermelon salad. Sam used to tease her, saying that it was far too pretentious for his liking. Secretly, Sam admitted it was incredible.

There had been nothing about the woman whom Laura had got to know in that time that suggested she could become involved in any kind of corruption. How had she managed to get herself embroiled with the Fallowfield Hill Gang and Ian Butterfield? Was it money? Or did they have something over her they'd used to blackmail her?

And Laura also wanted to know what had happened when she and Sam had arrived at Brannings Warehouse on that terrible day. Even though it was too painful to think about, part of her wanted to know about Sam's last moments on earth. He must have been scared. What the hell had happened in there before the building exploded? She felt a lump in her throat as she took a breath.

She closed down the file and spotted something in the right-hand corner of her desktop. A MOV file named Sam's Fortieth. She knew what it was but she'd avoided watching it until now.

Clicking the file, she could feel the apprehension build in her body.

Laura had used her phone to film Sam at the end of his fortieth birthday party at their home in Manchester.

Sam there stood in a blue shirt, boxer shorts and socks, grinning at Laura. He looked merry but not hammered.

'Well say something,' Laura laughed.

'Billie Jean' by Michael Jackson began to play on a stereo.

Sam came up to the camera, grinned inanely and giggled. 'Time for my famous moonwalk, honey.'

'Oh, God, really?' Laura groaned.

'Oh yes, you'd better believe it.' Sam whooped with a beaming smile.

Sam danced across the kitchen floor, spun on his heels and performed a very decent moonwalk, going backwards. As he reached the fridge, he spun on his heels again and moonwalked back towards her.

'Yeah, baby, I'm on fire,' Sam yelled. 'This floor is perfect for moonwalking.'

'Sam?' Laura shouted.

'Yes, my darling,' he replied as he stopped and looked at the camera.

'Did you have a great fortieth birthday?'

'Of course I did,' he replied as he came closer and closer to the lens of the phone camera. 'It was a perfect day. And I'm glad I spent it with you.'

'That's a song, isn't it?'

Sam looked into the camera and smiled, his blue eyes twinkling. 'I love you so much, Mrs Laura Hart.'

'I love you, too.'

The camera wobbled as they kissed and then the screen went black.

With her eyes full of tears, Laura wiped her face, blew out her cheeks and then took a long, deep breath. After a few seconds, she heard a noise from downstairs. Given that it was late, it made her uneasy.

She padded down the landing, then stopped and listened.

Nothing but silence.

Her unease increasing, she went down the stairs and then towards the hallway, where she thought the sound had come from. She clicked on the light and saw a white envelope lying on the mat by the front door. There was nothing written on it.

With a mixture of curiosity and anxiety, she opened it. Inside was a printed sheet of A4 that read:

> *STOP SNOOPING AROUND THE*
> *JOHN FINN CASE.*
> *I KNOW WHERE YOU LIVE.*

CHAPTER 29

It was 6.42 a.m. Laura couldn't wait to get into the sea. She hadn't slept well. The threatening note had rattled her. She was an experienced copper and threats towards her and her family had been made before during arrests or interviews. But she'd never had a direct threat at her home before. She needed to make sure the kids were safe. Maybe she needed to tell Rosie to be more vigilant at home without revealing exactly why.

Beaumaris beach stretched out before her and away to her left. Elvis had settled himself on the sand, resting his enormous head on his paws and looking up at her as if to say 'Off you go, then.'

The horizon was lightening with a blue hue and dawn was probably half an hour away. Laura pulled off her navy hoodie, stretched out her arms and gave an audible sigh. Twenty-five years ago, she used to go to bed at six a.m. She, Sam, Pete and others would dance the night away in the mid-nineties at some seedy place like The Swinging Sporran in Eccles, Manchester. She'd seen The Dust Brothers DJ there before they became The Chemical Brothers. It was all acid house, techno and hip-hop breaks. If she'd told herself that decades later she'd be getting up at dawn to go swimming in the freezing sea, she'd have laughed at the idea.

Padding down the cold, wet sand, she got a thrill at the anticipation of the ocean wrapping itself around her whole body and soul. The first wave slapped against her shins, sending an icy spray over her whole body. She'd reached the point where she didn't even flinch anymore.

Here we go. This is my release.

And then a hop, skip and dive into the dark, stinging cold of the sea.

Jesus, that feels good!

She swam under the water and then let herself dissolve into the darkness for a few seconds. The vibrations of sound were louder and thicker under the surface of the sea. And then she floated there in the black. It was a peaceful nothingness. She wondered if it was like this when you died. A suspension in a tranquil void. She'd take that over a dark nothingness.

Her head broke the surface and she took a deep lungful of cold air. She'd never imagined that she could feel this alive, this interlaced with nature. She gazed up at black sky that was still dotted with a glistening display of stars that were a lifetime away. Resting her feet on the sandy seabed, she took her weight on her legs and stood for a moment. The water level was covering her shoulders. The moonlight spilled across the calm surface of the ocean.

Peering back at the beach, she could see a figure heading her way.

Who the hell is that?

For a moment, she thought it might be Sam, but on the two or three occasions he'd joined her for a swim, he'd merely popped up from underwater.

'Laura?' a voice called.

It was Gareth.

Her pulse quickened as she took a few steps on the shifting ground underneath her feet.

'Gareth?' she called, trying not to show her excitement at seeing him.

The moonlight reflected off his chest and arms.

'I saw Elvis, so I knew you must be here,' he called.

'Great minds, eh? Or are you actually stalking me?'

Gareth laughed. 'Yeah, my night-vision goggles and balaclava are in the car.'

'Yeah, well that's a little too close for comfort, actually.'

He gave her a quizzical look. 'How do you mean?'

'Someone posted a threatening letter through my door in the early hours.'

'What?'

'Yeah, it said to leave the John Finn case alone or else.'

'Jesus. Are you all right?'

'I think so.' She shrugged uncertainly. 'It's not the first time I've been threatened. But the kids are there so it feels personal.'

'Of course.' Gareth nodded. 'Do you want a patrol at your house?'

'No. But getting a patrol to drive by once in a while would put my mind at rest.'

'Of course. Leave it with me,' he said as he waded into the water. He stubbed his toe on something, gave a groan and hopped around. 'Christ,' he growled. 'I was trying to make this cool entrance into the sea and now I'm leaping around like a demented idiot.'

The water level was now at Laura's ribs as she moved towards him. Gareth took a couple of steps forwards, dived gracefully into the sea and disappeared under its surface.

I love it when he dives under the water like that. He looks so powerful and manly.

Gareth's head popped up through the surface and he blew the water that dripped from his nose.

'Bloody hell, that's better, isn't it?' he exclaimed, sounding like someone who had had their first drink after a long, stressful week at the office.

'Works every time, doesn't it?' Laura waded towards him.

'Certainly does.'

He stood up and ran his hands over his scalp. His arms looked particularly sculpted in the glow of the moon.

'Sorry about earlier,' he said.

'Hey, no need to apologise. Our lives are complicated.'

'You can say that again.' He lowered himself into the water. 'What is it they say? "Youth is wasted on the young."'

'Who said that, then? Oscar Wilde?' she asked.

He pulled a face. 'Actually, I think it's a Robbie Williams lyric.'

'Wow. Well-known philosopher of our time, Robbie Williams.' Laura gave a loud laugh. 'You're not doing your street cred a lot of good this morning.'

Gareth grinned. '"And as the feeling grows, she breathes flesh to my bones, and when love is dead, I'm loving angels instead." Come on. That's profound stuff, Laura.'

For some reason, she got a tingle from hearing him calling her Laura.

What's that about?

His eyes twinkled as they looked at each other for a moment.

She shrugged. 'I guess anything's better than "You're about as easy as a nuclear war."'

'Duran Duran, "Is There Something I Should Know?"' Gareth smiled as if answering a question in some pub quiz.

'Ten points, no conferring,' Laura chortled.

'Of course, you do have the immortal "I'm as serious as cancer, when I say rhythm is a dancer" by Snap!'

They both laughed and then looked at each other.

'This is what it's come to, isn't it?' Laura gave him a wry

smile. 'Date night has been replaced by a freezing swim in the darkness or a snog in your office. Jesus.'

'Not very romantic.' Gareth moved towards her.

They were about four feet apart now.

'I'm bloody freezing.' Laura felt her teeth chatter.

Taking the initiative, Gareth stepped forwards and wrapped her in his arms. 'How's this?'

She looked up at him. 'Yeah, that's better.'

He leaned in and kissed her. His mouth was salty from the sea, but she really didn't care.

Their bodies entwined and they kissed more passionately. She reached down to his trunks and he gently pulled away.

'Yeah, it's incredibly cold in here.' He smirked. 'And I don't want you to be disappointed.'

She raised an eyebrow. 'I definitely wasn't disappointed the last time I did that.'

'Except we were under a warm duvet.'

'Good point. Shall we get out?'

'Definitely. I've got a flask of tea.'

'Have you now?' Laura raised an eyebrow. 'The last time we did this, you tried to get me drunk and then kissed me.'

'I think you kissed me.' He frowned.

'Okay, I'm happy to let you believe that.'

'I know my life is a bit all over the place, but I haven't quite got to the drinking in the morning stage.'

'Glad to hear it.'

They traipsed up the beach in comfortable silence, reached where Elvis lay in the sand and got dressed.

Gareth crouched and stroked Elvis' head. 'He really is a beauty, isn't he?'

'Yeah. And he's definitely the man of the house.'

Taking the flask, Gareth unscrewed the top, poured hot steaming tea into a tin mug and handed it to her. 'Here you go.'

She took a sip and then looked at him. 'We're pretty good together, aren't we?'

'We are,' he replied with a nod as he leaned over and brushed sand from her cheek. 'Do you fancy going away somewhere? Once this case is over and things settle.'

'Only if you mean a month in the Maldives,' she joked, but she was intrigued.

Even one night away would be just wonderful. And taking the initiative. I like that.

'There is a romantic hotel that overlooks Lake Vyrnwy,' Gareth explained.

Oh my God, could he be any cuter or more thoughtful?

She moved over to him, took the side of his face with her hand. 'Come here.'

She kissed him softly on the mouth and pushed her tongue against his. He looped his arm around her back and pulled her gently so their bodies nestled.

CHAPTER 30

Belfast 1998

John and Bernie had been sitting on dark wooden stools up at the bar in O'Hare's for nearly two hours. It had been a week since John had spotted Bernie at Magan's place. He'd asked around and eventually got her phone number and asked her out for a drink.

He looked at her. 'One for the road?'

'Why not?'

Bernie had her elbow on the bar and her fingers pushed through her wavy red hair. She gave him a smile and her emerald eyes twinkled.

'What?' John asked.

She pointed her finger at him and narrowed her eyes. She was tipsy. 'There's something about you, Jonathan Doyle.'

'Only me ma ever called me *Jonathan*,' he laughed. 'And that was when I'd been in a wee bit of bother.'

'I bet you were always in *a* wee bit of bother when you were younger,' she said flirtily. 'A right ruffian, no?'

John shook his head. 'Nah. I was a mammie's boy really.'

Bernie frowned and then snorted. 'I don't believe that for one feckin' second.'

'What about you? Prim and proper, or a right tomboy?'

'Bit of a slut, if I'm honest,' she chortled. 'I was giving out hand jobs by the time I was twelve. Boys are such idiots. They'll do anything for you if there's the chance of an orgasm. It makes them weak and vulnerable.'

'Is that what happened with that squaddie in Germany?' He'd heard a rumour about Bernie's work for the IRA over there.

'Of course,' she said with a nonchalant raise of her eyebrow. 'The prick thought he was gonna shag me down the alleyway. He fell for all my bullshit. He took down his trousers and then I shot him in the head.'

John couldn't work out if he was shocked or turned on by the callousness with which she recounted the story. A bit of both, he thought.

'Very ladylike,' he joked.

Bernie's expression changed as she frowned. 'Don't feckin' judge me, fella,' she snapped. 'I'd do anything to get those bastards out of Ireland, wouldn't you?'

'Of course I would.'

She moved closer to him so her face was about six inches from his. He could smell the whiskey and cigarettes on her breath.

'I'll tell you what, boyo. It takes a lot more guts to shoot a man in the head while he's looking you in the eye than it does to build a bomb.'

John wondered if he'd pissed her off. She seemed angry, even bitter. Maybe it was the drink talking.

'I'm sorry if I've offended you . . .'

She put her finger to his lips. 'Shush. I'm just messin' wit' you.' Then she took him by the hand and pulled his arm. 'Come on. I want to go now.'

He got down from the bar stool and let her pull him towards the door out onto the Falls Road. She broke into a run, dragging him so he was forced to follow.

The Falls Road was dark and empty. A car slowed on the opposite side of the road and for a second John felt his stomach tighten. The car then sped away into the darkness.

Probably the Dets, he thought to himself. British Intelligence were still all over Belfast, despite the ceasefire.

Bernie pulled him into an alleyway that ran down the back of a row of terraced houses. It was damp and a nearby streetlight threw a tangerine glow over them as they stopped.

'Aren't you gonna kiss me?' she giggled.

'That depends,' John said with a sexy grin as their eyes locked.

'Depends on what?' she said, giving him a playful hit on the arm.

'I've heard it can be pretty dangerous going into an alleyway with you,' he teased. 'I don't want to be found with my kegs around my ankles and a feckin' bullet hole in my head.'

She gave a laugh. 'You're a feckin' eejit, you know that? Come here.'

Moving forwards, she kissed him hard on the mouth.

He put his hands to her face and kissed her passionately.

'You've got big, strong hands.' She smiled. 'I like that. The hands of a bomb builder. They're very grateful to you – they just don't say it.'

'Anything for the cause. If you're going to blow up the British Army, then I'm your man.'

Bernie frowned. 'The British Army? What are you talking about?'

'The car bomb,' John said, wondering why she was confused. 'It's for an army base.'

'No, it's not.' Bernie shook her head. 'Who told you that?'

'Frank Daly.'

'Then I'm afraid Frank was pulling your tackle. From what I heard, that bomb's intended for a soft target. Cause as many civilian casualties as possible.'

John felt his stomach lurch.

'What?' he asked in disbelief. 'No, no. That's not the deal. I didn't sign up for that. I've never believed that killing women and kids is okay.'

'Neither have I,' Bernie agreed. 'But when you make a pact with Frank Daly, it's as good as making it with the Devil himself.'

CHAPTER 31

Laura pulled a chair from under the oval meeting table and sat down slowly. Warlow had summoned her and Gareth for a meeting with someone from the UK PPS who knew John Kelly aka Finn. They were clearly taking the discovery of the remains seriously, as the officer had travelled over from Liverpool.

The door opened. Gareth walked in holding some folders. He smiled at her as he sauntered over and put a reassuring hand on her shoulder. She touched it with her hand for a moment.

'Laura,' Gareth said in his usual work voice.

'Gareth,' she replied.

'I've spoken to the duty sergeant. Uniformed patrols are going to monitor your house throughout the day.'

'Thank you,' she said quietly.

Gareth pulled out a chair and sat down opposite her before taking out a handkerchief and sneezing into it.

She raised an eyebrow. 'Sounds like you've caught a chill.'

'Yeah, I think I have.' He nodded.

She grinned. 'Well, if you will walk around Beaumaris beach in wet, skimpy shorts at dawn, that's what will happen.'

'They're not skimpy,' he protested. 'Are they?'

'No, don't worry,' she laughed. 'I just like the word skimpy.'

Before they could continue flirting, Warlow had walked in accompanied by a man in his early sixties. He had a shock of short grey hair. He was rotund and appeared to carry most of his weight on his rear, making him a pear shape, which was unusual for a man. He was wearing glasses with thick black frames in the old-fashioned style of Buddy Holly or Michael Caine circa Harry Palmer. He wore a dark suit that strained around the middle and an army regimental tie.

'Morning.' Warlow gestured for the man to sit down. 'This is Detective Inspector Amis from the PPS. DI Hart and DI Williams.'

'Nice to meet you,' Laura said with a polite smile.

'Likewise.'

Amis sat without really bothering to make eye contact with her or Gareth. He had the air of a man who, a decade or two ago, would have really been able to handle himself.

Warlow looked over at Amis, who had opened a leather briefcase and pulled out a couple of manila folders, which he then laid down precisely on the table.

Warlow glanced across the table. 'I've brought DI Amis up to speed with our investigation.'

Gareth looked over at Amis. 'Superintendent Warlow accessed John's file, so we're aware that he was in the SAS and was sent to Belfast to infiltrate the Real IRA in 1998. We're trying to establish if this had anything to do with his death.'

'Okay. I'll give you some background on John to start with.' Amis took a few seconds and then sat back in his chair with a supercilious expression. 'He spent nine months working undercover in Belfast. If you're not aware, John was from Newry, which is about forty miles south of Belfast. That made John unique in the British Army. He was Catholic,

Northern Irish, but also a trained SAS officer who had won the Victoria Cross for gallantry in the field of battle in the first Gulf War. It made him the perfect candidate for undercover work in Belfast. Within weeks, he'd made a connection with the West Belfast Brigade of the Real IRA.'

'Why did he leave?' Laura asked.

'For some reason, he felt that his position had been compromised,' Amis explained. 'He didn't give us many details. It was our policy to take him out as soon as he felt unsafe. Plus, there were some serious discrepancies over the intelligence that he was feeding back to us. We felt that there was some kind of trust issue with his work with the Real IRA and the accuracy of what he was being told by them. It became untenable.'

'Did the Real IRA ever realise who he was?' she asked.

'Yes.' Amis nodded. 'John effectively vanished off the streets of Belfast. Then there were a series of arrests. It didn't take them long to put two and two together.'

'So, he was given a new identity as John Finn and sent here?' Gareth asked to clarify.

'That's right,' Amis said. 'I accompanied John to Anglesey in November 1998 and that was the last time I saw him. He was given a new home and a new passport. Once I'd left, we had a conversation once a month on the phone to check that everything was okay.'

'I assume that there were members of the Real IRA who wanted revenge on him?' Gareth asked.

'Yes, of course.'

Gareth opened the folder in front of him, took out a photograph of the unidentified man they'd found at Gallows Point and showed Amis.

'We found this man stabbed to death two nights ago,' Gareth explained, pointing to the photo. 'He has an Irish flag and pro-IRA tattoos on his arms.'

Amis peered at the photograph. His eyes widened in shock. 'Jesus.'

'I take it you know him?' Laura asked.

'Yes.' Amis nodded with a serious expression. 'Frank Daly. He was head of the West Belfast Brigade of the Real IRA and a member of the IRA's Army Council. It was Daly who recruited John in Belfast.'

'What the hell was he doing on Anglesey?' Gareth asked.

Laura shifted forwards in her seat. 'Maybe he found out that John had been relocated here.'

Gareth nodded. 'And until this week, no one knew that John was lying buried up at Castell Aberlleiniog.'

Amis looked at them. 'I think it would be useful for someone to go and talk to Bernadette Maguire. She was in the West Belfast Brigade and knew Daly well. She had some kind of relationship with John.'

'Where is she now?' Warlow asked.

'Dublin,' Amis explained. 'I know that she and Daly were close. She used to visit him in Portlaoise.'

Laura knew that Portlaoise was the high-security prison in Southern Ireland where many IRA prisoners were now kept.

'Do you know when Daly was released?' Gareth asked.

Amis nodded. 'Yes. A month ago. And Daly had sworn it was his life's mission to track John down and kill him.'

Gareth looked over to Laura. 'Looks like you and Andrea are taking a trip to Ireland.'

CHAPTER 32

'Do you want to tell us about the night you sexually assaulted Jenny Maldini, Mark?' Gareth said.

While Laura and Andrea made their way over to Dublin, Gareth and Declan had travelled across Beaumaris to the Approved Parole Premises building to interview Mark Weller after Jenny's allegation about the sexual assault. Despite the conversation with DI Amis about Frank Daly's relationship to John Finn, Gareth still thought Weller was a viable suspect in John's murder. Good policework relied on methodical TIE: trace, interview, eliminate. If Weller wasn't involved in John's murder, they needed to discount him from the investigation.

Weller snorted with laughter. 'Bloody hell! Is that what she told you?'

'Can you just tell us what happened that night?' Declan asked in an aggressive tone.

Weller took a moment as he straightened his shoulders and exhaled.

'I'm not one to brag, but Jenny had been all over me like a rash for months.' He smirked. 'Couldn't keep her hands off me, you know what I mean?'

What a vile little man, Gareth thought.

'That's not what she told us.' Gareth looked at Weller. He was overweight, with a pockmarked face from teenage acne. In Gareth's book, there was no way that Jenny Maldini would have been *all over him like a rash*. And from the photos he'd seen, John Finn had looked like a relatively handsome bloke. Weller was bullshitting, but it was his word against Jenny's.

'She wouldn't admit it to you, would she?' Weller shrugged arrogantly.

'Can you tell us what happened the night that she claims that you assaulted her?' Declan asked, taking out his notebook and pen.

'Is she pressing charges against me or something?' Weller enquired with a twisted frown.

'Just tell us what happened,' Declan snapped.

For a tense second, Weller just glared at Declan before looking back at Gareth.

'Her and John were having a bit of a shindig at their house . . .' Weller started to explain.

'Which you weren't invited to.' Gareth interrupted him.

'Is that what she told you?' Weller smirked. 'That was just a misunderstanding.'

'So, what happened?' Declan growled.

Weller turned to Gareth and indicated Declan. 'You need to tell Mutley here to calm down a bit.'

Gareth gave Weller a withering look. 'Just answer the question.'

'Okay. It was getting late and everyone had had a lot to drink. You know how it is. All the smokers were out in the garden. Jenny and me were left out there on our own. She told me she fancied me, so we started to . . . you know.'

Gareth shook his head. 'No, I don't know.'

Weller rolled his eyes. 'Kiss, you know.'

'Jenny claims you put your hand up her skirt,' Gareth said coldly.

'That's what she wanted.' Weller leered. 'Anyway, someone came out and interrupted us, so that was that. There's nothing else to tell.'

Declan stopped writing and looked up from his notebook. 'Did you know that Jenny told John what had happened?'

Weller frowned. 'Why would she do that?'

Declan raised an eyebrow. 'Because you attacked her.'

'And I've just told you that I didn't,' Weller snorted.

Gareth had met blokes like Weller before. Arrogant misogynists who believed that every woman they spoke to wanted to sleep with them. Once in a relationship, he could guarantee that Weller would be controlling, jealous and violent.

Gareth leaned forwards and fixed Weller with a stare. 'Mark, the problem I've got is that I believe every word that Jenny told us. So, you need to stop lying to us.'

'I'm not lying. And you can't prove it either way.' He folded his arms.

'What time did you arrive at The Panton Arms on the night that John went missing?' Declan enquired.

Weller laughed. 'How am I supposed to remember that? It was over twenty years ago.'

Gareth glowered at him. 'Okay. Did you arrive before or after John presented the cheque to the hospice at seven p.m.?'

'I suppose it must have been just afterwards.'

'Did you see John when you arrived?' Declan said.

'Only across the pub.'

'Did you speak to him?' Gareth enquired.

'No.'

Declan looked up from his notepad. 'And this was the first time you'd seen John since the party at his and Jenny's home?'

'Yes,' Weller said in a withering tone. 'So what?'

'But you weren't worried about seeing John that night?'

'Why would I be?' Weller snorted. 'I told you already. Jenny was into me. There was no way she was going to tell John that anything had happened between us. She'd talked about me and her shacking up together.'

This bloke is so full of shit.

Gareth waited for a few seconds as he looked over at Weller. He didn't look like a man who was going to be fazed by a long, tense silence, but it was worth a try.

'Okay, I'm going to tell you what happened, shall I? You sexually assaulted Jenny in the garden. She told John, who told her not to report it to the police because he was going to sort it out himself and make sure that you never attacked anyone ever again. At some point after seven p.m. on Tuesday, 12 October 1999, John confronted you about what you'd done to Jenny.

'My guess is that it happened outside, as no one remembers any kind of confrontation inside the pub that night. Maybe you had some kind of altercation. It resulted in you hitting John on the back of the head with a heavy object and killing him. You hid his body, possibly in the boot of your car. A few days later, you drove up to Castell Aberlleiniog and buried his body. Maybe you thought someone would think it was some kind of medieval remains.'

Weller sat back and gave Gareth a slow, sarcastic round of applause. 'Well, Sherlock, you've got it all worked out. The problem is that none of that happened. And if you had any proof, you'd be interviewing me under caution.'

Gareth's jaw tensed with frustration. He knew Weller was right, but he'd have bet anything his theory was correct.

'Did John speak to you at any point after you arrived at the pub?' Declan asked.

'How am I supposed to remember that?' Weller barked.

'I don't understand why you're not taking a much harder look at that Rhys Hughes.'

Gareth and Declan looked at each other, puzzled.

'What makes you say that?' Gareth asked. *Apart from deflecting the suspicion onto anyone but you.*

Weller shrugged. 'You know what queers are like.'

Jesus! Sex pest, homophobic, violent thug. This bloke is a real treat, isn't he? Gareth thought.

Declan frowned. 'What do you mean by that?'

'Rhys was very possessive of John. He didn't like him having other friends. Bit of a cling-on, if you know what I mean. When I heard that John had gone missing, I wondered if Rhys had argued with John, killed him and legged it.'

Gareth took a few moments to take in what Weller had said. Was there anything in it or was this just a way of deflecting suspicion and throwing up some kind of smoke-screen? He'd seen criminals who were expert at muddying an investigation by throwing around lots of accusations.

After five more minutes of getting nowhere, Gareth decided to call it a day interviewing Weller.

Gareth and Declan made their way out of the bail hostel as they processed everything that Weller had told them. As they reached the car, Gareth's phone buzzed. He looked at the screen.

'Ben?' he said.

'Boss,' Ben said. 'I've just had a call from a uniformed patrol. A neighbour of Rhys Hughes was suspicious, so she dialled 999. Officers went in and found Hughes dead.'

'Why did they call it in?' Gareth asked.

'Looks like someone hit him across the back of the head,' Ben explained. 'There's blood everywhere.'

'Jesus,' Gareth exclaimed, completely blindsided. 'Okay, thanks, Ben.'

Declan gave Gareth a quizzical look as he ended the call. 'Everything all right, boss?'

Gareth gave him a dark look. 'Yeah, we won't be checking anything with Rhys Hughes.'

'Why not?'

'He's been murdered.'

CHAPTER 33

Laura and Andrea were sitting in traffic on the outskirts of Dublin. The rain was splattering on the windscreen, the brake lights from the car in front bleeding into the droplets.

'If you'd told me when I jumped in the sea at six thirty this morning that I'd be in Dublin by two p.m., I'd have laughed in your face,' Laura joked.

'The sea?' Andrea gave her a horrified look. 'What on earth were you doing going into the sea at 6.30 a.m.? Are you mad?'

'Probably,' Laura laughed. 'I love it, actually. Sets me up for the day.'

Andrea snorted. 'Yeah, well, staying under a warm duvet until 7.45 a.m. and then chugging a very strong coffee sets me up for the day.'

'You'd never have caught me doing my morning swims when I was younger,' Laura admitted. 'But I'm officially hooked now.'

'I think a certain DI Williams likes a morning swim.' Andrea looked at her with an amused smile. 'Imagine if you bumped into each other in the sea! That would be awkward.'

Oh, if only you knew, Andrea, Laura thought with wry amusement.

'Yeah, I wouldn't want him seeing me in my swimsuit with no make-up on,' Laura laughed, playing along, then her phone buzzed.

Saved by the bell! It was an email from Ben. She'd asked him to dig around and see what he could find out about Bernadette Maguire.

Opening the document, Laura looked over at Andrea. 'Background and PNC check into Bernie Maguire. She seems to have spent most of the nineties working for the IRA in Germany.'

'Germany?' Andrea asked, confused.

'There was a bombing at the British Army barracks in Osnabrück in 1989. A British soldier was murdered in Dortmund in 1992. Maguire was implicated in both. She was captured and arrested by Dutch police, extradited to Germany but acquitted of all charges.' Laura read from the document. 'In 2000, she was convicted of the possession of explosives found in a car she was driving in Derry and given a five-year sentence, of which she served three.'

Laura gestured to her phone. 'She runs a boutique shop called Seasons in Temple Bar, Dublin.'

Andrea pointed behind them. 'Which, if memory serves me right, is about five minutes' drive that way.'

'You've been to Dublin before?'

Andrea rolled her eyes. 'My cousin Lily's very tacky hen weekend. Bit of a blur to be honest.'

'As all hen weekends should be.' Laura turned the car round and headed back towards the Temple Bar district of Dublin.

They parked outside Seasons of Ireland on Suffolk Street, close to the statue of Molly Malone. As they walked over to the shop, Laura could see that it stocked tasteful Irish trinkets, china and fashionable slogan wall art. It was a far cry from the tackier shops in Dublin where green T-shirts

209

with 'Irish Chick', or 'Feck it, it'll be grand' printed on them were sold.

The inside of the shop smelled of essential oils like lavender and eucalyptus. There was some ambient music playing.

A woman in her sixties, lots of fiery red curly hair, a brightly coloured kimono and a beaming smile approached.

'I'm so sorry, ladies, but we're just closing up. Unless there's something in particular you came in for?'

Laura pulled out her warrant card. 'DI Hart and DC Jones. We're police officers over from Wales. We're trying to track down a Bernadette Maguire.'

'Bernadette?' The woman laughed and pulled a face. 'The last person who called me Bernadette was me mam, and she's been dead for ten years. I'm Bernie Maguire.'

Laura looked at her, trying to disguise her disbelief. Was the woman standing in front of her really a former IRA terrorist who had roamed Germany trying to blow up British Army bases? She looked more like the singer Janis Joplin.

'Is there somewhere we can talk?' Laura enquired.

Heading for the door, Bernie flipped the sign to read CLOSED, locked the door and then gestured to the back of the shop.

'There's a back office we can go and sit down in. I've been on these feet all day.'

Following her through the shop, Laura met Andrea's surprised expression. She seemed just as bemused at the Bernie Maguire they'd just encountered as she was.

'Here we go.' Bernie opened a door to a small office and stockroom.

There were shelves stacked with various items. To the right was a desk and a computer. To the left, a small sofa and two chairs.

'Sit yourselves down, my Celtic sisters. Would you be wanting any tea?'

210

'We're fine, actually,' Laura said with a kind smile as she and Andrea sat down together on the sofa, which had a patterned candlewick throw over it.

Sitting herself down in the chair opposite them, Bernie gave an audible sigh. 'So, how can I be of help to the Welsh Police Force?'

'We want to talk to you about a man who you would have known as John Doyle,' Laura explained.

The mention of the name seemed to stump Bernie for a moment, but then she nodded slowly. 'Christ, now you're taking me back a bit.'

'I take it that you knew John Doyle?' Andrea enquired.

'That's right,' Bernie replied cautiously. 'I did. Probably twenty years ago, mind.' Then she looked at them with an uneasy expression. 'Did he turn up somewhere, or something?'

'Unfortunately, we found some remains over on Anglesey that we believe to be John,' Laura said gently. 'We're just talking to people who knew him.'

Bernie gazed into space for a few seconds. The news seemed to have shaken her.

She frowned as she pushed her hair back over her ears. 'How did you know I knew John?'

'We've spoken to a few people,' Laura said, remaining vague.

Bernie blinked and played with the plethora of bangles on her wrist. 'Do you think he was murdered?'

'Why do you ask that?'

'Why do you think?' Bernie snorted.

Laura nodded. 'Yes, we're convinced that he was murdered.'

'Jesus,' Bernie sighed. 'Bloody John Doyle, eh?'

'We know that you and John were in the Belfast Brigade of the Real IRA in the late nineties together,' Laura stated. 'And that you were romantically linked.'

'Feck, you have been doing your research, girlie.'

Bernie laughed, but for a moment the façade of the earth mother running a stylish gift shop was gone. Instead, there was a steely gaze and tense silence.

'Romantically linked, eh? We were just feck buddies, you know? It wasn't anything.'

Andrea frowned. 'We heard it was more serious than that.'

'No, you've got that all wrong.' Bernie sounded annoyed. 'Who's been telling you all this shite, anyways?'

'We understand that you became pregnant with John's baby. Then he just vanished,' Laura stated calmly.

Bernie shrugged. 'I lost that baby after a few weeks.'

'How did you feel when you discovered that John had been working undercover for British Intelligence?'

'You've been having a wee chat with Frank Daly, haven't you?' Bernie snapped. 'Don't believe a word that gobshite tells you.'

Laura didn't answer for a second. 'Frank Daly is dead. He was murdered two nights ago on Anglesey.'

'What? I only saw him a few weeks back.' Bernie shook her head slowly, sat back and blew out her cheeks. Her eyes roamed anxiously around the room. 'What the hell was he doing on Anglesey?'

'You don't know?' Andrea asked.

Bernie snorted. 'No. What are you talking about?'

'John was relocated to Anglesey as part of the Witness Protection Programme,' Laura explained.

'Frank went to Anglesey and murdered John?' Bernie asked.

Laura shook her head. 'No. John was murdered over twenty years ago.'

'What?' Bernie looked perplexed. 'I don't understand.'

Laura looked at her. 'You didn't know that John was on Anglesey?'

'No, of course not,' Bernie replied.

'And you didn't know that Frank Daly was going to Anglesey this week?'

'No. This is all news to me,' she said.

'Can you tell us the last time you travelled within the UK?' Andrea enquired.

'I came home to Ireland from Germany in 1993. I haven't left here since. And you can check that if you want.' Bernie shrugged. 'And the last time I saw John Doyle, or whatever his real name is, he was walking away from me down the Falls Road to get a fish supper and go home in 1998. And I never saw him again.'

CHAPTER 34

Gareth and Declan pulled up outside Rhys Hughes' home. Uniformed officers had already cordoned off the area with blue evidence tape and several neighbours were out on the pavement trying to find out what had happened. Directly outside the house was the SOCO van. Its back doors were open and a SOCO, in full nitrile forensic suit, hat and mask, was putting evidence away inside.

Walking towards a young officer who was manning the cordon and keeping the neighbours away, Gareth got out his warrant card. He didn't recognise the young officer.

'DI Williams, Beaumaris CID,' he said. 'What have we got, Constable?'

'A neighbour arranged to have a coffee with the victim this morning. When he didn't answer the door, she thought it was suspicious,' the constable explained. 'She called us.'

'Where exactly did you find the victim?' Declan asked.

'Lying in the middle of the carpet,' the constable replied.

'Any sign of forced entry?' Gareth enquired.

'No, sir.'

Gareth frowned. 'Start running a scene log, please. No one comes onto the crime scene without my say-so.'

'Yes, sir.'

The constable pulled up the police tape and Gareth and Declan headed for the house.

As they arrived, they showed their warrant cards and a SOCO handed them a full forensic suit. It smelled of chemicals and rustled noisily. Gareth could still remember when CID officers just popped on some gloves and trod all over crime scenes.

Snapping on his blue latex gloves, Gareth looked at Declan and gestured for him to go inside. There were already steel stepping plates across the carpets of the hallway and then into the house. Several SOCOs were dusting surfaces and examining the carpet for forensic evidence.

Gareth made his way through to the living room and saw Rhys' body lying on the floor. A SOCO was taking photographs. He recognised the chief pathologist as Professor Helen Lane. She was using a torch and tweezers while examining the body.

'What have we got, Helen?' he asked.

Lane looked up at him. 'Morning, Gareth. It's been a while.'

'Yes, nice to see you.' He found Lane's uber confidence and sharp mind a little intimidating. 'He was definitely attacked?'

'Yes. Blunt force trauma to the back of the head,' Lane explained, pointing to where the hair was matted, sticky and black. 'I'm pretty sure his skull's fractured.'

'Time of death?' Declan asked.

'He's been here quite a while, given the lividity,' she explained. 'At least ten hours, maybe longer.'

That took the time of death back to twelve o'clock the previous evening or earlier.

Lane pointed to the palms. 'Some defensive wounds here and here. A couple of broken bones in the hand.'

'Any idea about a weapon?' Gareth asked.

'Something big and heavy,' she replied. 'Baseball bat. Maybe even a mallet.'

Gareth looked around the room. A table had been turned over and the armchair wasn't straight. 'Looks like there was a struggle.'

'No sign of forced entry though,' Lane remarked.

Gareth looked at her. 'You think Rhys knew his attacker?'

'Possibly,' Lane replied.

As they moved away from the body, Gareth gave Declan a dark look. 'Andrea and Laura spoke to Weller yesterday and told him we'd spoken to Rhys. And twenty-four hours later, Rhys is lying dead in his living room, murdered.'

'Are we thinking that Rhys' murder is also linked to Daly's?' Declan asked as they left the house and began to take off the forensic clothing.

'Two murders in two days,' Gareth said. 'I don't believe in coincidences, do you?'

'No, but what links Weller and Daly?' Declan asked.

As Gareth handed back the last of his gear to a nearby SOCO, he spotted something from the corner of his eye.

A figure stood on the corner of the road, wearing a black motorcycle helmet, looking back at where they were standing.

Declan spotted that Gareth was distracted. 'You okay, boss?'

Under his breath, Gareth said, 'Don't look up the road yet, but there's someone standing beside a large motorbike watching everything that's going on.'

Subtly, Declan cast a glance up the road.

'Yeah, I see them.'

'Let's get in the car,' Gareth said quietly, 'and see what they're doing.'

Suddenly, there was the noise of an engine starting.

'Shit!' Gareth said as he spotted the figure sitting astride the motorbike, revving the engine.

They moved swiftly and jumped into the car.

Gareth glanced up and saw the motorbike pull away. He grabbed the Tetra radio. 'Dispatch from six-three. We are in pursuit of a possible suspect, black motorcycle, black helmet, heading south on the B5019, over.'

'Dispatch received six-three,' the Computer Aided Dispatch (CAD) operator replied. 'Stand by.'

Hitting the accelerator hard, Declan screeched away from where they'd been parked as they set off in pursuit.

'Don't lose him,' Gareth said. He could feel the adrenaline pump as he buckled his seatbelt with a clunk.

'I won't,' Declan reassured as he worked through the gears.

The motorcycle was a long way ahead of them as they thundered south on the road to Beaumaris. Glancing over to the dashboard, Gareth could see that they were up to 70 mph already. He gripped the door handle with one hand and the front of his seat with the other as they screamed around a long curve in the road.

The motorcycle slid into view and as they hit 90 mph, Gareth could see they were gaining ground. As they rounded another bend, their wheels squealed as the car struggled to grip the road. Hitting the straight, the motorbike was now only 200 yards ahead of them.

Gareth squinted. 'Do we think that's a Harley?'

Declan nodded. 'Yeah. You can tell from the fuel tank, boss – 5 gallons, shaped like a teardrop. It's an older model, so it's going to struggle to do much more than a hundred.'

Gareth frowned. 'Know your bikes then, do you, Declan?'

'Misspent youth.'

'There's something on the back of his helmet, isn't there?'

'Yes, boss. I'll see if I can get any closer.'

Dropping down a gear, the Astra's two-litre engine roared and Gareth felt himself pushed back into his seat as they topped 100 mph.

Now only 100 yards away, the emblem on the back was visible. An American Confederate flag. It was also clear there was no licence plate.

'That's our guy,' Gareth said as he grabbed the radio. 'Dispatch from six-three. We are still in pursuit of a black Harley Davidson. Heading south on the B5019, two miles north of Beaumaris, over.'

'Six-three receiving. We have unit Alpha-four-zero heading north on the B5019, over,' the CAD informed him.

'Received. Proceed with caution,' Gareth advised the CAD. He wanted whoever was on the motorbike alive and at the speed they were travelling, it was getting incredibly dangerous.

Gareth felt the Astra's rear tyres losing grip as they cornered another bend. His stomach lurched. They were now around seventy yards behind the motorbike. They came hammering up a hill and pulled out to overtake a caravan. It went past in a blur. Suddenly, a tractor pulled out in front of them and they swerved to avoid it.

'For fuck's sake!' Declan hissed as he straightened the car.

They were gaining fast as the car ate up the road ahead.

Within seconds, they were only fifty yards behind. Gareth watched as Declan pulled closer.

'Careful,' Gareth said. 'I don't want to be scraping him off the road.'

Without warning, the motorbike suddenly slowed and veered across the road. Declan hit the brakes to avoid clipping the back of the bike. Gareth watched in frustration as the motorbike sped into a field.

'Bloody hell!' he said.

Declan spun the steering wheel and the back of the Astra skidded. For a heart-stopping moment, Gareth thought they'd lost control of the car, but Declan spun the steering wheel the other way to straighten it as they drove into the field in pursuit.

The motorbike left a trail of dirt and dust as it zipped diagonally across the freshly ploughed soil. Hitting bumps and dips, Gareth and Declan were thrown around inside the car as they continued the chase.

Looking up, Gareth saw the motorbike reach the other side of the field and head uphill along what looked like a footpath towards a wooded area. There was no way they could continue the pursuit.

'Bollocks!' Gareth growled.

Declan slowed the car to a halt. They'd lost him.

CHAPTER 35

Laura squinted into the darkness of the A55 – the road that ran east to west across the top of North Wales. She'd arranged to meet her former colleague from Manchester Met, Pete, at Seymours Bar at midnight and she was cutting it fine. Her head was spinning with the events of the day.

Laura found a spot to park and headed into town. The high street was busy, with people moving between the bars, pubs and clubs. Most had been drinking, so there were the usual shrieks of laughter, shouting and unsteady walking. It reminded her of when she and Sam were first together in Manchester, when they went out most Saturdays to see live bands or go clubbing. Watching couples or groups in their twenties or thirties made her feel old.

Turning a corner into a side street, she spotted the sign for Seymours Bar on the opposite side of the road. Pete was standing outside in a dark coat, his hands thrust deep into his pockets.

'Evening all,' he said as he rose on the balls of his feet, gave her a nod and then walked towards her.

'Yeah, you might as well wear a sign around your neck saying copper,' she grinned. 'God, I feel so old, don't you?'

'You *are* old,' he teased.

She noticed he was limping. 'What's the matter with you?'

'I've got an arthritic knee, if you can believe it,' Pete moaned.

Laura raised an eyebrow. 'Oh, and I'm old?'

'Yeah, apparently twenty years of playing five-a-side on Astroturf has ruined my knee.'

Laura smiled and gestured to the door of the bar. 'I can get you a wheelchair.'

'Very funny.'

They went inside. Ambient music was playing, but the place was relatively quiet.

As they walked over to the bar, Laura scoured the place for any sign of Louise.

Taking out his warrant card, Pete nodded at the barman. 'We're looking for a Louise McDonald. We think she might work here.'

The barman frowned and shook his head. 'Sorry. I'm the manager and I've never heard of her.'

Laura fished out her phone and scrolled down to where she'd saved various photographs of Louise for an occasion like this. She turned the phone to show the barman.

'This is a photograph of her,' she explained.

The manager peered at the photo and looked confused. 'Yeah, that's Zoe.'

Pete and Laura looked at each other. It wasn't a huge surprise that she was using a fake name.

'Do you know her surname?' Laura enquired.

'Yeah, I'm pretty sure it's Finch,' the manager replied.

'And she works here?' Pete said, to clarify.

'Yeah. Tonight's her night off though,' the manager explained, looking increasingly worried. 'Is she in trouble or something?'

'No, no. Nothing like that,' Laura reassured. She didn't

221

want him contacting her to warn her they were looking for her. 'Just a few routine questions. Nothing to worry about.'

'Oh, right.'

Pete looked at him. 'But we are going to need her address.'

Pete and Laura drove across Llandudno and parked outside the house where the barman said Zoe Finch lived. There were two wheelie bins with the number 34 painted on them in white, indicating that they were hopefully in the right place.

As they got out of the car, the wind picked up and blew around them with a dull moan. Laura walked over to the tatty white front door and knocked loudly. There was a plastic bag full of beer cans on the step next to a pile of pizza boxes.

After thirty seconds, Laura banged on the door again, but there was still no reply. She listened. Nothing from inside – no voices, no movement.

Pete walked over to a ground-floor window to the right, but the dingy-looking curtains were pulled.

'Anything?' Laura asked.

He cupped his hands to get a better look and then shook his head. 'Nope. Can't see a thing.'

Laura sighed. 'I hope this wasn't a wasted journey.'

She leaned down and opened the letterbox to see if she could see or hear anything inside. The pungent smell of weed hit her as soon as she looked through the narrow gap.

Looking up at Pete, she pulled a face. 'It stinks of what my mum always called wacky baccy.'

Pete laughed. 'I haven't heard that for a while. We called it ganja when I was a kid.'

Suddenly, they heard the clattering of a gate slamming. It came from the back of the house. Laura took a few quick steps to the left and glanced down the scruffy side passage and driveway.

A figure wearing a black hoodie and a black baseball cap

was already climbing onto a wheelie bin thirty yards down. They jumped and pulled themselves up onto the flat roof of a single-storey garage in one move.

'Down here,' she shouted to Pete. He was limping and not going to be chasing anyone.

Is that Louise? It looks like a teenager, she thought.

Laura sprinted down the cracked, overgrown driveway. The figure stopped on the roof and looked back at her. It was Louise. Their eyes met for a moment.

Jesus!

'Stop there, Louise! I need to talk to you,' Laura yelled.

Expressionless, Louise turned, headed to the other side of the garage roof and dropped down, out of sight.

'Shit!' Laura growled.

She had no choice but to follow. Her heart was already thudding. Leaping onto the bin, she jumped and pulled herself up. At first, she thought she was never going to make it. It had been a long time since she'd pulled up her own body-weight with just her arms. She shook with the sheer effort as she clambered onto the roof, grazing the skin off her forearm on the mastic asphalt surface. It stung, but she had no time to think about it. Her focus had to be on stopping Louise from getting away.

Laura rushed to the other side of the roof. Below was an open area of concrete, with half a dozen parked cars that backed on to two warehouses. A large black lorry was reversing up to some steel shutters, its siren bleeping. It looked like a builders' merchant.

Louise sprinted out of the yard through an opening in a brick wall and disappeared down a dark street. Laura hesitated. It was high enough for her to break her ankle.

Bollocks! she thought. *I'm not letting her get away.*

She jumped and hit the concrete with flat feet, a white-hot pain shooting up the outside of her right ankle.

Ow, that really bloody hurt!

Laura gritted her teeth, scrambled to her feet and began to run flat out, heading for the street onto which Louise had disappeared. She accelerated into a full sprint, pumping her fists as she went. To her left, she saw a flash of lurid yellow as she passed Ali's Kebabs, Pizzas & Burgers. On the right, the bright blue of a corner shop. An elderly couple gave her a curious look and moved out of the way as she thundered past.

Ahead, Laura could just make out a figure turning left down a side street and out of sight.

Her phone rang. It was Pete.

'Pete,' she gasped as she continued to run.

'Where the bloody hell are you?'

She looked around for road signs and spotted one. 'I'm heading down Latic Avenue.' As she turned left, she saw another. 'And I've just turned left into Princess Drive.'

'Right, I'm in the car,' Pete said. 'I'll be there in a sec. And be careful, Laura.'

She ended the call, gulping for air. Her feet were numb and her back was damp with sweat. She stopped and listened.

Nothing. No sound of footsteps running.

Bloody hell!

Louise had gone.

Maybe she's hiding.

'Louise!' she yelled. 'I just want to talk to you.'

Jogging up Princess Drive, Laura's vision swam and she shook her head to try to stabilise herself.

Between houses were abandoned garages, alleyways and flat pieces of concrete peppered with weeds. It was quiet except for the distant noise of a dog barking. There were various side streets all the way up Princess Drive. It was basically a maze from here on in, and Louise could have gone anywhere.

A noise from the side of an old boarded-up house. Slowing cautiously, Laura walked across the weeds to take a look.

Then a clatter. Metallic, maybe.

Laura moved slowly and put her back against the wall. The brickwork felt rough against her back.

Another click.

Laura took a slow, quiet breath as her pulse thudded in her eardrums. She didn't want to peer down the side of the house only to get a blade shoved in her throat.

The noise stopped.

Laura moved her shoulder round, face touching the brickwork, and inched across to have a look.

Suddenly, out of nowhere, Louise appeared and threw a punch.

'Fucking hell!' Laura exclaimed as she ducked and wrestled Louise to the ground. Pinning her down, Laura glared at her. 'Stop struggling, Louise! For fuck's sake, what's the matter with you?'

'I'm sorry,' Louise stammered. 'I'm sorry.'

'Get up,' Laura snapped, grabbing her and helping her to her feet. 'Don't you dare bloody run again.'

For a few seconds, Laura just looked at Louise. Her face was gaunt, eyes sunken, and she was shaking. She was broken.

'What the hell happened, Lou?' Laura shook her head.

'I'm sorry,' Louise whispered. 'They told me if I didn't do it, they were going to kill my kids.'

'They?' Laura barked. 'Who the hell are *they*?'

Headlights appeared as a car turned into Princess Drive. *About bloody time, mate.*

Laura pointed. 'You're coming with us. We need to talk to you.'

Louise shook her head. 'I can't. I'm too scared.'

Laura grabbed her arm. 'Tough.'

Squinting at the headlights that were now on full beam,

Laura wondered what Pete was doing. If anything, he was speeding up rather than slowing down.

Then her stomach lurched.

That's not Pete's car.

The car was now speeding towards them, its engine roaring.

Bloody hell!

She scuttled to the right but tripped on the pavement and fell to the ground. Glancing up, she saw the car was fifty yards away.

She got back to her feet.

The car mounted the pavement. It was virtually on her now.

Jesus!

With every ounce of her strength, she dived into some bins beside a garage – and waited for the car to plough straight into her.

It missed her by about a foot but instead hit Louise, knocking her into the air.

Oh my God!

As Laura looked up, the car squealed away and thundered up Princess Drive before disappearing.

She got up and raced over to where Louise was lying. She was unconscious.

Shit!

Laura felt for a pulse. It was weak.

Another set of headlights appeared as a car turned and slowly headed her way. To her relief, she saw it was Pete's car.

Thank God for that.

Getting to her feet, she gave him an urgent wave.

Jumping out of the car, Pete went to her. 'Are you okay?'

Laura pointed to Louise. 'She was hit by a car. We need paramedics.'

'Is she breathing?'

'Yes. I've checked her pulse.'
'I'm sorry. I got lost on the side roads.'
'Not your fault.'
'Did you see the driver?'
'No.' Laura grabbed her phone and dialled 999.

CHAPTER 36

Gareth and Declan were in the meeting room at the Approved Premises building in Beaumaris. Weller sat opposite, looking confused.

'I'm pretty sure I told you clowns everything I know about two hours ago.' Weller shook his head.

'Where were you around midnight last night, Mark?' Gareth enquired, giving him an icy stare.

Weller snorted. 'I was asleep in here. Where the hell do you think I was?'

Declan glared at him. 'You sure you were?'

Weller put up his hands defensively. 'Whatever it is, I was here. This place is locked at night, and I'm on a seven o'clock curfew.'

Gareth raised an eyebrow. 'Yeah, well I've checked. You've got a window just above the flat roof at the back here.'

'I didn't go anywhere.' Weller sniffed and rubbed his nose. 'Do you wanna tell me what all this is about?'

'When was the last time you saw Rhys Hughes?' Declan enquired.

'What?' Weller sneered. 'What the hell are you asking me that for?'

228

'Just answer the question,' Gareth growled.

'I haven't seen Rhys Hughes for about twenty years.' Weller leaned forwards and looked at them. 'Why, what's happened to him?'

Gareth waited for a few seconds and then said, 'Last night, someone went round to his house and caved his head in.'

Weller narrowed his eyes. 'He's dead?'

'Yeah, he's definitely dead,' Declan replied darkly.

'The problem we've got here, Mark, is that you were questioned by two of my officers about twenty-four hours ago,' said Gareth. 'You knew it was Rhys who told us that you had a serious problem with John Finn. They said you were furious that Rhys had talked to us and implicated you.'

'What, so I sneaked out of here and went and killed him?' Weller scoffed.

Declan fixed him with a stare. 'He wouldn't be the first person you'd killed, would he?'

Weller gave them a wry smile. 'If you had any evidence, you'd have cuffed me and taken me down the station.'

Gareth shrugged. 'Well, there's a forensic team all over Rhys' house at the moment. And I'd bet a year's salary they're going to find a trace of your DNA somewhere. And then you're going to spend the rest of your life in prison.'

For the first time, Weller looked worried.

'I wasn't there. I told you.'

'Come on, Mark,' Declan snorted. 'Think about it. We tell you that Rhys has effectively grassed you up. Twenty-four hours later, he's dead. You're a convicted murderer. It's not going to take a jury very long to come to the right conclusion.'

'You're going to fit me up?' Weller asked, sounding anxious.

'We don't need to fit you up, Mark, because you did it,' Gareth thundered. 'You killed Rhys. You might as well tell us now and get it over and done with.'

The colour had drained from Weller's face. 'I'm not saying anything else until I have my solicitor with me.'

Weller answered the next two questions with 'no comment'. Realising there was nothing more they could do, Gareth and Declan decided to wrap up the interview and head for the car.

Gareth's phone rang. It was Ben.

'Ben?' he said.

'Boss, we've had a call from a Jimmy Rose. Says he's the chef at The Panton Arms. He spoke to Andrea and DI Hart. He was working the night that John Finn went missing,' Ben explained. 'He's remembered a regular who was in the pub that night. Peter Bishop. He might have seen something, and if he was a regular, he might have known John Finn.'

'Where is he?'

'In the Plas Mona retirement home in Llangefni.'

'Okay, thanks, Ben,' Gareth said. 'I'll swing by in the morning.'

The trauma unit at Llandudno General Hospital wasn't as busy as Laura thought it might be. She and Pete had followed the ambulance but Louise hadn't regained consciousness. They were waiting for an update from the doctors.

'Do you want a coffee?' Pete asked.

'Yeah, good idea,' Laura said quietly. 'Three sugars.'

Pete frowned. 'I didn't think you took sugar in anything?'

'I do tonight.' Laura shook her head. 'I'm thinking of taking up smoking.'

Pete gave her a wry smile, put his hand reassuringly on her arm and gestured to the Intensive Care Unit (ICU). 'I'm just glad it's not you in there.'

Laura looked at him. 'Louise said something just before she was hit. She said they told her if she didn't do it, they were going to kill her kids. When I said that me and you needed to talk to her, she said she was too scared.'

Pete thought for a moment. 'When I first saw the CCTV of Butterfield and Louise coming out of that cemetery, I thought they were just on the take. My instinct now is that the Fallowfield OCG have something on both of them. And clearly they're using intimidation as well.'

'It doesn't sound like it's just about money.'

'No.'

'I don't think we're going to get either of them to go on record,' Laura stated. 'They'd have to go into Witness Protection. And I've seen what that's like in the past few days.'

Pete frowned. 'I'm not so sure. Talking to the PPS would allow Louise to build a new life rather than hiding out here and always looking over her shoulder.'

'I'm not sure that even when you're in Witness Protection, you ever stop looking over your shoulder. I don't know how she's survived not seeing her kids.'

Pete shrugged. 'I guess she knew that if she made contact, their lives would be in danger.'

'Even then, I don't think I could do it,' Laura admitted. 'I'd have to find a way round it.'

A young female doctor approached. 'Are you the police officers who came in with Louise McDonald?'

They nodded.

'How's she doing?' Laura asked.

'She's still unconscious,' the doctor replied. 'Our main concern is the damage to the back of her head. We're waiting for the results of the MRI and CAT scans and then we'll know more.'

Laura gave her a kind smile. 'Thank you.'

'You might be better off coming back in the morning,' the doctor suggested.

'Okay.' Laura nodded and then looked at Pete. 'I need to get home.'

CHAPTER 37

Laura walked into the hallway of her house, snapping on lights as she went. She got the familiar warm smell and feeling of home.

Good to be home.

She could hear noise coming from the living room. It sounded like the television. She glanced at her watch. It was 12.15 a.m.

'Hello?' she called.

'In here,' Rosie replied as Laura stuck her head round the doorway and looked into the living room.

The coffee table was a blitz of crisp packets and sweet wrappers. The TV was blaring and there wasn't a light to be seen. The whole ground floor had been in total darkness.

'What are you doing up?' she asked.

Rosie shrugged. 'It's a Friday, Laura. Relax.'

'Are you two bats or something?'

Jake frowned. 'Bats? What does that mean?'

'The darkness, you melon.' Rosie gave Jake a playful shove.

'Oh.' Jake shrugged. 'Did you know that a bat can eat 1,200 mosquitoes in an hour?'

Laura gave him a quizzical look and then a smile. 'No, I didn't. But I do now.'

Something about the atmosphere in the room felt off. She could feel it.

'What did you guys have for tea?' she asked, praying that it wasn't just the empty packets that were strewn in front of them.

'Nothing,' Rosie said without taking her eyes off the television screen. 'There isn't anything.'

Jesus! Here we go.

'I had a banana when I got in,' Jake piped up.

'Erm, I think you'll find that the fridge and freezer are packed full of food,' Laura said in a withering voice.

Rosie raised an eyebrow and gave her a patronising look. 'I don't think we should be living off microwave meals, do you? Do you know how much carbon dioxide a microwave emits, for starters? And the sugar, salt and preservative content of most microwave meals makes them worse than fried fast food.'

Try to remain calm, Laura.

'Okay.' Laura gave a forced smile. 'I'm guessing that if I buy fresh, natural ingredients, you guys can cook food for yourselves, then?'

Rosie looked at her as if she were mad. 'Mum, I've got my A levels this year! Jesus!'

'And yet you're watching *Love Island*, which also isn't appropriate for Jake to watch anyway,' she said with more than a hint of sarcasm.

'You let him watch *Gogglebox*,' Rosie protested. 'And they say the word *fuck* in that all the time.'

'Yeah, and last week they said the word dickhead,' Jake said, joining in.

'Okay, okay.' Laura held up her hands.

She watched as they went back to watching the television, still aware that all was not right.

'Rosie?' she asked in a serious tone, gesturing to Jake. 'Is everything okay?'

Jake was sometimes emotionally vulnerable. His father's death and the incident on the boat in the summer had taken their toll.

Rosie picked up the remote, pressed Pause and looked at her. 'Jake's worried about something. We both are.'

Rosie's tone was serious, so Laura entered the room and sat down in the armchair opposite. 'Okay, what is it?'

Jake gave an audible huff and avoided eye contact. 'I don't want to talk about it.'

'It's all right.' Rosie put a reassuring hand on her brother's shoulder. 'There's a boy in Jake's class. His parents got divorced a few years ago. And his mum has met someone new who has now moved in with them.'

Laura nodded. The penny dropped.

'Ah, okay . . . And you want to know if that will ever happen here?' Laura asked.

'Yeah,' Rosie said with a touch of sadness in her eyes.

Laura wasn't sure how to answer. She didn't want to lie and tell them it would never happen. And things with Gareth were going well. But Sam had been such a huge part of their lives and his sudden death had been traumatic for all of them.

'At the moment, you don't need to worry about anything like that,' Laura explained gently. 'And in the future, who knows? We just need to keep talking like this.'

Jake scowled. 'I don't want anyone like that ever to come in this house.'

Laura went over to him, kissed his head and put her hand to his face. 'I'm going to make some toast, if anyone wants any?'

Jake stared at the table. He was still trying to process what Laura had said, but he nodded.

'Sounds good, Mum.' Rosie smiled. 'Do you want me to come and help?'

Laura frowned sarcastically. 'What? Can you say that again? I'm pretty sure that phrase has never left your mouth before.'

Rosie laughed. 'Ha ha. You're hilarious, Laura.'

'Please stop calling me Laura! It really freaks me out.'

'That's why I do it.'

'I'll be in the kitchen if you want me,' Laura said, leaving the room and heading down the hallway.

Opening the fridge, she reached for the half-drunk bottle of Sauvignon Blanc, poured herself a large glass, took a big swig and let out a huge sigh.

Jesus! What a day!

Grabbing a loaf of bread, Laura took four slices and popped them in the toaster.

Melted cheese and onion on toast, she thought. *Great idea.*

She took a block of cheese from the fridge, opened a drawer and removed a large kitchen knife.

'You can see their point though, can't you?' said a voice.

It was Sam.

'Oh, good, it's you,' she said acerbically. 'Are you going to lecture me? Because I warn you – I've had a long, stressful day. And I'm holding a very big, sharp knife.'

Sam grinned. 'Yeah, I'm pretty sure you can't stab me.'

'I can give it a go. If you want to run that risk?'

Sam laughed and shook his head, then his expression changed. 'So, what would happen?'

Putting down the knife, Laura reached for the glass, took another swig and looked at him. The lights from under the cabinets threw a shadow across his face.

'What do you mean?' she asked, knowing full well what he meant.

'If you meet someone. What would happen?'

Laura didn't say anything for a moment.

'Oh my God, you have met someone, haven't you?' Sam blurted before she could reply.

'What?'

'Please tell me it's not DI Dickhead!' he groaned. 'That's so obvious. Jesus, Laura!'

'Hold on a second! You haven't even given me a chance to answer your question, you tossbag,' she growled angrily.

'Tossbag? That's a bit harsh, isn't it?' Sam protested.

'Frankly, what I do, who I see and what happens in my personal life is none of your fucking business!'

'Hit a nerve, have I?'

'I can't believe that we're actually having this row.' She turned her back on Sam, reached for the knife and sliced the cheese, hoping that he'd do his usual trick of just disappearing when anything got uncomfortable.

However, as she sliced off the end of the onion, she could still sense his presence.

Sam came towards her, moved behind where she was standing and put his arms around her. He rested his chin on her shoulder. She could actually smell him.

'I'm not going to mind, you know?' he said quietly.

'Not going to mind what, Sam?' She wasn't in the mood for more cryptic comments.

'You're a beautiful, intelligent, funny and caring woman,' he said with a serious expression. 'And you're a widow.'

Laura felt a familiar sadness wash over her. 'Don't say that word.' Her voice broke.

'You're going to have men queuing round the block, Laura.'

Sam gave her a beautiful, gentle smile. It was the smile she'd seen when he'd first held Rosie and Jake as babies.

'Why are you saying this?' Laura asked, a lump in her throat.

'You're going to meet someone and you're going to fall in love with them. And I want you to know that's okay.'

Laura turned round to face him. For a few seconds, she didn't know what to say.

'Jesus, Sam,' Laura eventually said, using the cuff of her sleeve to wipe a tear from her face. 'Bloody onions. Get me every time.'

'I told you.' Sam smiled. 'Put a spoon in your mouth. It stops your eyes watering.'

'Yeah, it might not work this time. And it makes me look utterly moronic.'

'You don't need a spoon for that.'

'Hilarious.'

For a few seconds, they just looked at each other in a sad but comfortable silence.

From somewhere came the sound of footsteps. She could immediately tell it was Jake.

'Can I help?' he said excitedly.

Laura smiled at Sam – she knew that in a few seconds, he'd be gone again.

'Of course you can, darling.' She ruffled Jake's hair.

CRASH!

The sound of breaking glass reverberated from the hallway.

'Stay there!' Laura said to Jake as she ran to see what had happened.

She immediately saw a chunk of brick lying in the middle of the glass that covered the floor. Someone had just thrown it through the hall window.

'Mum!' Rosie shouted as she and Jake raced into the hallway. 'What happened?'

'Bloody bird,' Laura lied as she moved to block their view of the floor. 'Poor thing didn't see the window and flew straight through it.'

Jake frowned. 'Where is it?'

237

Laura looked at Rosie and gestured. 'You guys go back into the living room while I clear this up. I don't want you stepping on any glass.'

As they turned and walked away, Laura let out an anxious breath.

Gareth was sitting in the dimness of his living room, sipping a beer and waiting for Nell's return – and for all hell to break loose. He had no idea where she was. There had been no reply to his two texts. In fact, he'd a growing suspicion that Nell had gone to patch things up with that prick Leith.

Hearing the spare key in the door, he braced himself for what was going to come next and told himself to be both calm and decisive.

He could hear Nell's heels clicking on the hall floor before they reached the carpet and the sound disappeared.

Here we go.

Nell appeared at the door. She was fully made-up and dressed in a low-cut top and tight jeans. He got a waft of her perfume.

She's definitely been to see Leith, he concluded.

'Why are my bags by the front door?' she demanded in a biting tone.

Gareth put down his beer. He needed to stand up if they were going to have it out.

'Because I want you to go, Nell,' he said in a steady voice.

She looked at him as if he were mad. 'What?'

'Don't look at me like that.' Gareth felt agitated. 'We're divorced, Nell. You left me for another man. I can't have you here.'

'What, so you're throwing me out?' Nell's chest visibly swelled.

'I'm not throwing you out. I want you to leave. You staying here isn't good for either of us.'

'You didn't say that the other night,' she sneered.

'That was a mistake. You said it yourself.'

She shook her head and looked at him. 'Well, thanks for the warning.'

'You don't respond to my texts,' he stated in disbelief. 'How am I meant to give you any warning? Where have you been?'

She bristled. 'I've been out with a friend, not that it's any of your business.'

'Well, we both know that *going out with a friend* actually means you've been to see Andrew,' he said quietly. 'And if you have, that's none of my business. But you have to go. Tonight.'

She glared at him for a few seconds. 'What if I don't want to go?' She shrugged defiantly.

He rolled his eyes. 'What does that mean, Nell?'

'What if I refuse to go?'

Gareth could feel his anger rising. 'You left me for someone else. You do understand that, don't you?'

She looked at him but didn't say anything.

'I bought out your equity in this house. It now belongs to me,' he snapped, taking a breath. 'I agreed to everything you wanted to give you the quick divorce that you wanted. And now I want you to leave.'

Nell looked at him with disdain. 'What? This is your house, so now I'm trespassing?'

'Legally, yes. Just go, Nell. I don't want you here. Just go.'

She blinked, took a step towards him and then put her hand to her face to wipe a tear away.

Here we go.

'I can't believe it's come to this,' she whispered as her voice broke.

He wasn't having any of it this time. He'd seen this tactic before. When everything else fails, a few crocodile tears might just work. He'd fallen for it several times before.

'It came to this about two years ago,' he said sadly as he walked past her. 'Come on. I can't have you here.'

He gestured for her to retrace her steps towards the front door, where he'd placed her packed bags.

The tears suddenly stopped and she narrowed her eyes. 'There's someone else, isn't there?'

'Get in your car and go.'

Turning sharply, she marched down the hallway towards the front door. Gareth followed as if to make sure she actually went.

Then she turned, looked directly at him and smirked. 'I bet she doesn't know we fucked the other night, does she?'

He opened the front door and looked at her. He wasn't going to rise to her attempt at intimidation. She picked up her bags and came towards him.

'Goodbye, Nell,' he said coldly.

'This isn't over,' she warned as she marched out.

'Yes.' He slammed the door behind her. 'Yes, it is.'

It was 1.30 a.m. and Laura was still rattled from the incident with the brick. She'd tried to call Gareth. She knew that it was time to get a uniformed patrol to sit outside her home until the killer could be apprehended. It was also time to find somewhere else for Rosie and Jake to stay until she knew their safety could be guaranteed.

Sitting in bed with her laptop, she'd tried to distract herself by laying out all the files that she'd collated to do with her and Pete's investigation into Sam's death. There were maps, photos, stills from CCTV and other documents. She took a sip of water, sat back and cast her eye over the papers and images spread in front of her.

'Why does this mean so much to you?' asked a voice.

It was Sam again. He was sitting on a nearby chair.

'That's a stupid question.' Laura sounded tetchy. 'Don't you want to know why you died?'

Sam frowned and thought for a moment. 'I guess. But it's not going to change anything for me.'

'It's important for me. And for the kids.' Laura frowned. 'I thought you said you *did* want to know?'

'Not if it's going to keep you up at night worrying, I don't.' Sam gestured to the papers. 'How do you think Louise fits into this?'

'She had to be working with Butterfield. And Butterfield is being paid or intimidated, or both, by the Fallowfield Hill Gang to provide intelligence and protection. He made the 999 call about suspicious activity at Brannings Warehouse because he knew that you and Louise would be the first officers on the scene.'

'Why?' Sam asked. 'Butterfield knew that there was going to be a raid on Brannings Warehouse. He'd called the OCG to tip them off because we know they started to clear the place out and dismantle the drug-making machinery from dawn onwards.'

Laura nodded. 'So, why bother making a 999 call at around nine a.m. to report suspicious activity? Why did he want you and Louise to be sent out there? It doesn't make sense.'

Glancing back at the chair, she saw Sam had gone. Not only were his visits becoming less frequent, but he also seemed to stick around for shorter periods of time.

Her phone rang. It was Gareth.

'Are you okay?' he asked.

'Not really. Someone threw a brick through my window at home.'

'What? Jesus, are you all right?'

'Yeah. Just about.'

'Right. We'll put a patrol on your house.'

'I'm going to see if Rosie and Jake can stay elsewhere.'

'That sounds sensible.'

'I heard about Rhys Hughes,' she said. 'Do we think it's connected to Frank Daly and John F?'

'My instinct is that there has to be a connection. I just can't seem to work out what that is.'

'Ireland?' Laura suggested.

'How does Rhys Hughes fit into that?'

'He knew who killed John.'

'Possibly.'

There was a pause in their conversation.

'How are you?' she asked.

'I'm all right but a bit chilly.'

'Why? Where are you?'

'I wanted to see if you were okay, so I'm now standing on your doorstep.'

Now that's excitingly spontaneous, she thought with a thrill of delight.

'And now I can also see your broken window,' he continued. 'Bit of a mess, isn't it?'

'Yes.'

'I didn't ring the bell, as I assumed the kids were asleep.'

'Why didn't you say you were outside as soon as you rang, you loon?' Laura laughed as she jumped off the bed and headed for the door, the phone still to her ear.

She opened the door and he smiled at her.

'Hello,' she said.

He gestured to his mobile, which was also to his ear. 'I guess we can hang up, can't we?'

They looked at each other and laughed.

Indicating for him to come inside, she turned and he followed her down the hallway and into the kitchen.

'Tea?' She pointed to the kettle.

He nodded, but she could see that he was aching to tell her something.

'I threw Nell out tonight,' he said with relief.

'Literally?'

'No. But I did pack her bags. Left them by the door and insisted that she go.'

Laura smiled. 'I like your style.'

'And I just wanted to tell you that.'

For a moment, he looked like a lost boy.

'I'm glad you did.' She moved towards him.

They kissed passionately.

She looked at him and whispered, 'The kids are asleep in bed.'

'Okay,' he shrugged.

She took him by the hand and led him out of the kitchen. She felt his hesitancy.

'Don't worry – my bedroom door has a lock on it,' she said.

'Are you sure this is okay?'

'If we don't do this soon, I'm actually going to explode,' she giggled.

'God, I feel like a teenager,' he said as they crept slowly up the staircase.

CHAPTER 38

Belfast, August 1998

It was six p.m. and it had been twenty hours since Bernie broke the news to John that the car bomb he was constructing was to be used against civilians and not a British Army target. He'd hardly slept that night – he still had no idea where the bomb was going to be used. If the civilian population on the British mainland were indeed the target, he needed to know where and when.

Marching up the Falls Road in the driving rain, John pulled up the collar of his leather jacket against the summer downpour. He'd formulated a plan. If he refused to finish the bomb's construction until he was told the target, that would force the West Belfast Brigade's hand. It had become clear from working on the timing, circuit and detonator that no one else had any genuine knowledge of explosives. They needed him. And he could use that as leverage. As soon as the target was made known to him, he could pass that information to Military Intelligence.

The traffic along the Falls Road was heavy and the air was thick with exhaust fumes. A double-decker bus slowed beside him and its air brakes gave a sudden explosive hiss, startling him. As he looked ahead, he saw the sign for M & D BROTHERS' GARAGE. There was a mechanic waiting for him to arrive and coordinate the fitting of the bomb into the boot of the car. Even though Semtex was a relatively stable plastic explosive, they had no idea how old it was or what conditions it had been stored in at the docks in Tripoli. And that made it dangerous.

Jogging across the garage forecourt, which was now closed, John reached the dark blue office door and knocked loudly. A second later, a man in his thirties dressed in oil-stained overalls opened the door.

'John?' he asked in a low voice as he looked around nervously.

'Yeah.' John nodded. 'Billy?'

Billy ushered him inside and closed the door behind them.

Following him through another door, John emerged into a large garage space. A red Vauxhall Cavalier was sitting up on a large hydraulic car lift so that the bonnet was head height.

'Is this it?' John pointed to the car.

'Yeah.'

From behind a white transit van at the far end of the garage came two figures. John squinted at them – it was Tommy Breslin and Frank Daly.

What the hell are they doing here? he wondered. The plan had been for John and the mechanic to assemble the bomb in the boot on their own.

'Thought I'd come and look at your handiwork, John-boy,' Daly said as he sauntered over and shook John's hand with a firm grip.

Breslin looked at John and grinned. 'I take it that feckin' thing's not gonna go up without a detonator in it?'

John looked at Daly. 'I'm not finishing it, Frank.'

Daly frowned, looked at Breslin and then laughed. 'What are you talkin' about?'

'You've told me all along that this bomb was for a military target,' John said sternly, holding Daly's gaze. 'To blow up the British Army. But I have it on good authority that this is going to be used to kill civilians. And that wasn't the deal.'

Daly took two steps forwards and sneered. 'Where this bomb goes is none of your feckin' business.'

John shrugged. 'If you think blowing innocent women and children to pieces is going to help our cause, that's up to you. But I'm having nothing to do with it.' He pointed to the bomb. 'Finish it yourselves.'

Turning on his heels, John began to stride back towards the door. In a flash, he sensed Daly moving behind him and experienced a dart of satisfaction that his plan was working.

'Where the feck do you think you're going, pal?' Daly growled. 'Whoever's been getting in your ear, they've got this all wrong.'

John turned to look at him. 'I don't believe you.'

'Who have you been talking to?'

'None of your business.'

'You've been misinformed.'

'Have I?' John wondered if Daly was going to lose his temper and shoot him where he stood.

'Yes.' Daly's eyes narrowed and then his face softened. He reached into his pocket and pulled out a map. 'Take a look at this, you wee eejit.'

John frowned and took the map. It was a map of London. He peered carefully at an area that had been marked off in red, recognising it immediately.

'Chelsea Barracks,' John said.

Daly nodded and pointed to the car. 'That car is being taken on a ferry over to Liverpool in three days' time. Then it's being driven down to London. On Saturday, seventy Irish

Guards are boarding two buses and heading for a tour of Germany. As they leave the gates, this bomb goes off. No civilian casualties, just soldiers.'

John had got the information he needed.

Daly gave him a playful smack across the back. 'You know your problem, boyo? You worry too much.' He pointed to the car. 'Shall we get on with this, then?'

John nodded and took off his jacket.

CHAPTER 39

It was just after dawn when Laura marched into the ICU at Llandudno General. She was running on adrenaline and caffeine. The events of the previous evening had spooked her. She looked for the ward sister at the central nurses' station. Spotting a nurse in her fifties with chestnut hair, glasses and a kind face close by, she took out her warrant card.

'Hi there,' Laura said. 'I'm looking for Louise McDonald. She was brought in here last night.'

The nurse smiled and nodded. 'Yes. She's just down here if you'd like to see her?'

'How's she doing?'

'Stable and out of danger,' the nurse explained as they walked past several rooms and down a corridor.

'Is she conscious?'

'Yes. She's a bit groggy. She's having another CAT scan this morning to check for a bleed on the brain.' They arrived at a single room and the nurse opened the door and said quietly, 'Here we go. She needs to rest, so try not to be too long.'

Laura gave her an understanding nod as she closed the door. 'Of course. Thank you.'

Louise was linked up to a bedside cardiac monitor – oscilloscope – which measured her ECG and oxygen saturation. There was a dark purple bruise around her left eye and cheekbone.

Laura looked at her and wondered what had happened to the happy-go-lucky woman she'd known when Sam was alive.

Louise moved her head on the pillow, opened her eyes and squinted.

'Hello, Louise,' Laura whispered. 'How are you feeling?'

For a few seconds, Louise didn't say a word.

'I've felt better,' she said, her voice croaky and raw.

'Yeah.' Laura gave her a half-smile. 'I just wanted to see how you were doing.'

Louise frowned and shook her head. 'Why?'

Pulling over a chair, Laura sat down. 'You and Sam were so close. I don't understand what happened.'

'I'm so sorry,' Louise murmured as she blinked away a tear.

There were a few seconds of silence before Louise's face twisted and she whispered, 'I loved him. You know that. He was the closest thing I had to a brother.'

'Why were you there that morning?'

'Sam was on to Ian Butterfield.' Louise winced as if in pain.

Laura got up and went over to her. 'Are you okay?'

Louise nodded as she closed one eye and put her hand to her temple. 'Jesus, that hurts.'

'I'll get the nurse.'

'It's fine.' Louise grimaced.

Laura dashed to the door and waved to a nurse. 'I think we need some help in here.'

The nurse came just as the oscilloscope started to beep urgently. Louise's heart rate was rising rapidly. Her eyes were now closed and she wasn't moving.

The nurse checked her hurriedly and then hit the red call button by the bed.

'I'm going to need you to leave the room, please,' the nurse stated quietly.

'Is she going to be okay?'

A doctor came in and Laura made her way outside into the corridor. The door closed behind her.

Briefing had been going for about ten minutes, but Laura was barely listening. She'd spoken to the ICU at Llandudno and been informed that Louise had been placed in an induced coma until they could do more tests on her brain injury. She was still processing Louise's comment that Sam had been on to Butterfield. Even though she'd suspected Sam's death was linked to something like that, it was the first confirmation that she and Pete were on the right lines. She'd spoken to the local police and arranged for a uniformed officer to be stationed outside Louise's room. Whoever had run her down might even now be trying to track down her whereabouts and try to finish the job.

Gareth took a swig from his water bottle and then looked out at the team with a serious expression. 'Listen up, everyone. A word of caution. DI Hart had a brick thrown through her window last night.'

Several CID officers gave Laura concerned looks.

'Whoever our killer is, they're brazen enough to attempt to intimidate a police officer, so I want us to be vigilant out there and watch each other's backs. It's likely that this person has now committed three murders and that they're incredibly dangerous. We have to find them before that becomes four.' Gareth perched himself on a table. 'As most of you know, Declan and I chased the suspect from the scene of Rhys Hughes' murder yesterday. The biggest clue we have is the Harley Davidson motorbike and distinctive helmet that our killer was wearing. Declan?'

Declan looked over. 'The DVLA have five Harleys registered on the island. I've got the addresses here.'

'Good,' Gareth said.

'Boss,' Ben said. 'We now have a DNA sample from the bone marrow of our victim. We just don't have John's DNA to match it to.'

'Maybe Jenny has something of John's. Like a keepsake,' Laura suggested. 'A shirt or an old comb. It's worth asking.'

'Good point,' Gareth said. 'Can someone chase up the carbon dating of the remains? And stress that this is a murder investigation.'

Declan nodded. 'I'll give the university a call, boss.'

Ben looked down at his notes. 'Forensics found no match for Mark Weller's DNA on any of the remains.'

Gareth rubbed his chin for a moment, went over to the board and pointed to a photo. 'Despite the Irish connection and Witness Protection, my mind also keeps coming back to Mark Weller. My instinct is that he and John had some kind of altercation that night. We just don't have any proof.'

'Boss, we've still got to talk to that Peter Bishop,' Ben said. 'Maybe he saw something that night.'

Ben signalled that he had something. 'Boss, forensics have just got back to me about the SOCO evidence from Rhys Hughes' house.'

'Go on,' Gareth said.

'They've got a decent footprint from the garden,' Ben explained. 'And given the rain we had a couple of days ago, they're certain the footprint was made in the last seventy-two hours.'

'What can they tell us?'

'It's a Nike trainer, men's size 10,' Ben said.

'Good. Anything else?' Gareth enquired.

'I pulled all the council CCTV from the seafront, Chapel Street and New Street,' Ben said. 'I think I've found something.'

Gareth gestured to the large HDTV screen that was mounted on the wall. 'Let's take a look, shall we?'

Ben clicked his computer and the screen on the wall lit up with the frozen CCTV footage. Hitting the Play icon, the footage began. There was a caption: *New Street 21.56 p.m.*

'New Street? That's about ten minutes' walk from the Approved Premises building on Rose Street,' Declan said.

Ben nodded. 'It's also ten minutes on from there to Rhys Hughes' house.'

A figure appeared from the left of the screen, hands thrust in pockets and head looking down at the pavement.

Gareth peered at the shadowy figure. 'It's hard to see anything, isn't it?'

'Yeah, it is . . . but then this happens, boss,' Ben said, gesturing to the screen.

A car entered from screen right, its headlights bathing the figure in bright light.

Gareth took a step closer, squinted as he recognised the face on the screen. 'Mark Weller.'

Andrea came through the doors to the CID office and headed straight for where everyone was sitting. Whatever she was going to tell them, it looked urgent.

'Deep dive on Mark Weller,' Andrea explained, gesturing to the print-out she was holding. 'In the early nineties, Weller was a member of Combat 18, a Neo-Nazi group who had an affiliation to football hooligan gangs such as the Chelsea Headhunters. The one and eight refer to the letters A and H in the alphabet, the initials of Adolf Hitler.'

'Nice,' Ben said sardonically.

Gareth frowned. 'I don't see how this helps us very much.'

'Combat 18 also had direct links to loyalist paramilitary groups in Northern Ireland,' Andrea explained. 'In fact, Combat 18 were responsible for desecrating the graves of several members of the IRA, including the hunger striker

252

Bobby Sands. Weller was arrested in 1993 during a UDA march in Belfast.'

Gareth's eyes widened. 'I'll go with Declan to pick up Weller now. Andrea and Laura, talk to Jenny Maldini and see if we can get John's DNA. And check the eyewitness from the pub the night John was killed.'

The Plas Mona care home in Llangefni was tucked away at the end of a well-maintained drive, with a discreet sign on the lawn. To the right of the gravelled driveway was a large pond that had been fenced off. Laura presumed they didn't want any of the residents wandering over there by accident.

Once inside, Laura and Andrea made themselves known to the young ponytailed girl on reception. The air smelled of cleaning products – bleach and pine-fragranced polish. Under that lay the unmistakeable aroma of the residents' lunch being prepared. Reception was a neat and muted medley of olive green and grey. A radio was playing classical music from somewhere, interrupted by the occasional bristle of echoes of laughter from staff members climbing or descending the enormous staircase in their dark green uniforms.

Eventually, Laura and Andrea were led down to the bright and airy day room, where some residents read newspapers or played cards.

'Peter?' the ponytailed girl called over to an elderly man reading a copy of the *Daily Mail*. 'There are a couple of police officers here to see you.'

Putting down his paper, he smiled at them over his thick reading glasses. 'Well, police officers are certainly getting younger and prettier than when I had dealings with *the law*.'

'Sorry, I . . .' Laura frowned.

'Don't worry, dear,' he chortled. 'I used to be a magistrate many years ago. How can I help?'

Laura was relieved that Peter had his wits about him – he

253

might prove to be a valuable witness. They sat down on two nearby chairs, and Andrea took out her notebook and a pen.

'We'd like to ask you a few routine questions about a historic case we're working on, if that's okay?' Andrea said with a polite smile.

'Historic?' Peter grinned. 'It would have to be if you're talking to me.'

'Do you remember a man called John Finn?' Laura enquired. 'He drank in a pub called The Panton Arms.'

Peter thought for a second and then nodded slowly. 'Yes, I do remember him. He was a military man, wasn't he?'

Laura gave him a kind smile. 'That's right, he was. We believe you were in The Panton Arms the night that John disappeared. It was Tuesday, 12 October 1999.'

Peter gave them a wry smile. 'I'm sorry, but I forgot who our prime minister was this morning, so I'm not sure I'm going to be much help.'

Andrea looked over. 'John and some others raised some money for a local hospice. He handed over one of those giant cheques to the manager of the hospice. A local newspaper covered it. And it was also the pub quiz night.'

'Good God, yes.' Peter's face lit up. 'I do remember that evening. John didn't join us for the pub quiz.'

'Do you remember seeing John that night?' Laura enquired.

'Yes. I remember the whole cheque thing,' Peter said thoughtfully. 'Bloody great big thing, it was.'

'Do you remember seeing John at any other point?' Laura asked, fearing that they were now clutching at straws. 'Was he talking or even arguing with someone?'

Peter pulled a face. 'I'm so sorry. It's just such a long time ago.'

Laura looked at him. 'Do you remember a man called Mark Weller?'

His face reacted immediately. 'Oh yes. Horrible man. Drank

too much. Arrogant but stupid with it, if you know what I mean.'

'Yes, I do.' Andrea nodded. 'Did you ever see Weller talking to John?'

'I remember them having cross words on several occasions. But I can't remember when that happened.'

'I know this is a long time ago, but after John presented the cheque, do you remember seeing him after that point?' she asked. 'Before he didn't show for the pub quiz?'

Peter shrugged with a knowing expression. 'I know why John didn't show up for the pub quiz.'

Laura and Andrea exchanged a look.

'Sorry, I'm not with you.' Laura frowned.

'The last time I ever saw John, he was sitting in a car in the pub car park with a woman.'

What?

Laura leaned forwards. 'Are you sure?'

'Yes,' Peter replied matter-of-fact. 'I assumed he got, to put it delicately, *distracted* by this woman. I remember it so well because I thought *you lucky bugger.*'

'Did you tell anyone this?' Andrea enquired.

'I couldn't really.' Peter pulled a face. 'I mean, John was seeing that Jenny girl. I couldn't exactly go round the pub telling everyone John was in a car with some other woman, could I?'

'And you could see that it wasn't Jenny?' Laura asked.

'Yes,' Peter said. 'I'm sure it wasn't her. I remember thinking it was odd.'

'Did you get a clear look at the woman who was in the car with John?'

'Not really. Just the back of her head,' Peter explained.

'What about hair colour?' Laura asked.

Peter shrugged. 'Sorry, it was dark.'

'And you've never told this to anyone before?' Laura enquired.

'No. When John went missing, I just assumed he'd eloped with this woman. But I couldn't exactly go and tell Jenny. I just thought, if he's in love with someone else, good luck to him.'

'Can you remember what car it was?' Andrea enquired.

Peter nodded. 'Yes, it was a Peugeot 406.'

Andrea frowned. 'You seem very certain.'

'Well, only because my wife and I had one. Ours was metallic blue. But I think the one I saw was a dark green. Hard to tell in that light.'

'And you never went to the police and told them what you'd seen?'

'No, of course not,' Peter snorted. 'It's a sort of male code, isn't it? If a man decides to *play away* from home, it's not my business to go gossiping about it.'

Laura looked over at Andrea. Did that put a spanner in the works for their theory that Weller was responsible for all three murders?

CHAPTER 40

Gareth and Declan pushed open the door to the Approved Premises building and looked around for the manager, Steve. He appeared and gave them a nod of recognition.

'Mark's at work, I'm afraid,' Steve said.

'Do you know if Mark has access to a motorbike? Or have you seen him with a motorcycle helmet while he's been here?' Gareth asked.

Steve thought for a moment. 'No, I don't think so.'

Gareth nodded. 'I'm gonna need to see his room.'

Steve shrugged and pointed to his office. 'Right you are. I'll just grab the key and show you the way.'

A few seconds later, he reappeared and gestured to the stairs. 'We're up on the first floor.'

Gareth and Declan followed him up the newly carpeted stairs. Reaching the landing, Steve pointed along the corridor.

'Up here on the left.'

Landscapes and a large photograph of a sunrise were mounted on the walls. Gareth assumed it was to give the place a peaceful, optimistic feel after prison.

Steve arrived at the door marked 18, turned the key and allowed Gareth and Declan to enter.

'Just give me a shout when you've finished, eh?' Steve said as he turned and left.

The room was sparse, basic but clean and tidy. There was a single bed that had been neatly made with a green blanket and pillow covers. There was a book beside the bed: *The Chimp Paradox* by Steve Peters. Gareth remembered hearing about it but couldn't remember what it was about.

He walked over to the window and looked out. About four feet below the window ledge was a small asphalt roof that covered the ground-floor dining room. Gareth opened the sash window about a foot before it hit the locks on the window frame.

'Do you reckon Weller could have squeezed out of that?' Gareth enquired, gesturing to the space.

Declan, who was rummaging in Weller's wardrobe, nodded. 'Bit of a squeeze, but he's not a big fella, is he?'

'No, he's not.'

'Boss,' Declan said, looking up from where he was squatting by the wardrobe.

'Please tell me you found that motorbike helmet.'

'No, sorry, boss.' Declan pointed to something inside the bottom of the wardrobe. 'But we do have Nike trainers.'

'Men's size 10?'

Declan smiled. 'Got it in one.'

Bingo!

'I know this is delicate,' Laura said gently. 'But we wondered if you might still have something with John's DNA on it.'

There was an awkward silence.

Laura and Andrea had been talking to Jenny inside the small living room in her home for about five minutes. Sunlight illuminated bright purple flowers on the cream unlined curtains. The room smelled of furniture polish and dust and of disuse. The sofa was hidden beneath a yellow-and-green gingham

258

cover. Beyond that, a bookcase stood against the wall, its top shelves draped with cobwebs and pitted with woodworm. Pictures, lamps, books, ornaments adorned a large oak table and a dark red rug covered the floor.

'I'm sorry,' Jenny said quietly. 'I don't know what you mean.'

Laura thought for a moment. She needed to put this delicately.

'We can get a trace of DNA from hair or even tiny particles of skin,' she explained. 'So, an old comb or toothbrush? Even an old T-shirt or shoes might help us.'

Jenny shook her head sadly. 'I'm sorry. I've thrown all that stuff away. All I've got are a few old photos packed away in the loft. That's it.'

Laura looked over at Andrea. Jenny had been their one hope of getting a DNA sample for John. It looked like they were going to have to rely on the carbon dating for some kind of confirmation, or try to track down John's relatives in Northern Ireland.

There was a framed photograph of Jenny with the man they'd seen down at the lodges: glasses, bushy grey beard and a long mane of hair pulled back into a ponytail.

Jenny saw Laura looking at the photo. She turned to look at it, too, and for a second her brow and her mouth relaxed and her eyes lightened and widened.

'Me and Duncan,' she said with a twinkle in her eye.

'Does he live here?' Laura enquired.

'God no,' Jenny laughed. 'He's a messy sod.'

Laura now had the unenviable task of broaching what Peter Bishop had told them at the Plas Mona retirement home in Llangefni.

'There have been a couple of developments in the case, so I'd like to ask you a few more questions, if that's okay?' Laura smiled kindly.

Jenny looked confused but nodded. 'Of course.'

'We have an eyewitness who believes they saw John in the car park of The Panton Arms with a woman,' Laura said gently.

The colour drained from Jenny's face. 'What?'

'I'm sorry. I know that must be difficult to hear,' Andrea said.

Jenny looked horrified. 'I don't understand. What would John be doing in the car park with another woman?' she asked, visibly shaken by what they'd told her.

'We hoped that you might have some sort of idea,' Laura said.

'Why?' Jenny snapped.

Laura took a few seconds and then asked, 'Did you ever have any suspicions that John was having an affair around the time he disappeared?'

'No, of course not.' Jenny's eyes were now filled with tears. 'I wouldn't have been with him if I'd thought that, would I?'

'No, I suppose not,' Andrea said gently. 'Do you know if John had any female friends at that time? Possibly someone he knew at The Panton Arms.'

'Christ, no. Not in that place.' Jenny shook her head. 'It was a man's pub. As far as I know, the only women in there were the barmaids.'

'Okay, thank you, Jenny.' Laura got up from the sofa. 'We'll keep you informed of any developments.'

Jenny appeared lost in thought.

'There was someone, actually,' she said eventually.

Laura looked over at Andrea and they sat down again.

'Go on,' Laura said reassuringly.

Jenny shrugged. 'It's just that she wasn't from round here, so I don't know if it's relevant.'

Laura gave her a patient smile. 'Anything, however small, could help.'

'John was in contact with someone from his past,' Jenny explained. She clearly found it difficult to say. 'And I don't even know her name.'

260

'When you say in touch,' Andrea said, 'what exactly do you mean?'

'There were a few times I caught John on the phone to someone. When I asked who it was, he'd just brush it off and say it was an old mate. But I could tell that he was talking to a woman. You know, he just sounded different.'

'How do you know she wasn't from round here?' Laura asked with a puzzled expression.

'I got hold of his phone once and looked at the calls. I knew that she'd called him earlier, so I wrote down the number and the code.'

'Did you ring the number?' Andrea asked.

'No, I never had the guts,' Jenny admitted. 'But I looked up the code. It was a Belfast number.'

Gareth and Declan drew up outside Dobson & Sons garage on the outskirts of Beaumaris. Part of Weller's probation and rehabilitation involved working there while training as a mechanic.

As they got out of the car, Gareth peered up at the miserable grey sky, which was filled with drizzle. The garage itself was ramshackle and the air was filled with the smell of oil, the sound of metallic banging and a tinny radio playing music. They walked along the pathway flanked by an eight-foot corrugated-iron fence.

They came through the iron gates and Gareth saw a couple of cars up on jacks and two large workshops where mechanics were working on a couple of transit vans.

'The problem with places like this,' Declan said, 'is they can spot a copper at a hundred yards. I think it's genetic.'

A thick-set man in his late fifties with a shaved head sauntered over.

'We're looking for Mark Weller,' Gareth stated, getting out his warrant card.

261

The man puffed out his chest. He was holding a spanner in his right hand.

'He's not around, sorry.'

'Really?' Gareth asked dubiously.

'Yeah.'

Gareth frowned. 'He's working here while he's on probation.'

'Is he?' the man scoffed.

This bloke is getting right up my nose, thought Gareth.

Declan took an aggressive step towards the man. 'Don't be a smartarse, pal. Just tell us where he is or I'm gonna nick you and take you instead. Where's Mark Weller?'

Before the man could answer, Gareth caught sight of a man walking quickly from an old portacabin and making his way to the far side of the garage site.

Weller!

Gareth glanced at Declan, gestured and then looked back at the man. 'That's all right. I think we've found who we're looking for.'

As he turned to follow Weller, the man stood directly in front of him.

'Where the fuck do you think you're going?'

'Get out of my way, dickhead,' Gareth growled.

The man smirked. 'You need a search warrant to come in here.'

Gareth pushed him hard in the chest. 'No, we don't.'

Before the man could remonstrate, Gareth began to sprint in the direction he'd seen Weller heading. He scanned the far end of the garage and then spotted him clambering onto some wooden buildings and over the rear fence.

'Shit!' Gareth muttered, stopping in his tracks.

Running at full pelt, he came out of the garage gates and thundered down an alleyway to the end. He soon spotted Weller running towards a mini-roundabout. Several pedestrians jumped out of his way when he yelled at them. There was the sound of an irate driver pumping their horn as Weller darted through the traffic and then disappeared round a corner.

Gareth followed, but by the time he reached the side street that Weller had taken, he'd disappeared. He could have gone anywhere.

Gareth's phone rang. 'Declan?'

'You okay?'

'I lost him.'

'Right. There's something you need to see back here at the garage,' Declan explained.

'What is it?'

'There's a Harley Davidson sitting on the far side of the yard.'

'Is it the one that we chased yesterday?'

'It looks very similar, boss.'

CHAPTER 41

Belfast, August 1998

It was a hot, sunny afternoon and John and Bernie were lying in bed. They'd been drinking beer, making love and listening to music. Even though it had been released for over a year, Bernie was still playing The Verve's *Urban Hymns* on a loop. The bedroom was cluttered and untidy. An ashtray beside the bed was full of cigarette butts and spliffs. A breeze came through the window and rattled the dusty Venetian blinds. From outside, there was the noise of children playing and shouting and the dim hum of the traffic on the Falls Road.

Even though John had drunk four or five beers, he couldn't relax. He was preoccupied and anxious. Having passed the information about the planned bombing at Chelsea Barracks to Military Intelligence, he was waiting for something to appear on the news. He prayed that nothing went wrong and that the car bomb had been found and deactivated. If Military Intelligence were involved, there might also be a media blackout and discovery of the bomb might be buried.

'Where are you, mister?' Bernie asked, running her hand down his face and looking at him.

'Nowhere,' he replied.

He hadn't told her about his conversation with Daly forty-eight hours earlier. He didn't want to complicate things.

'You're definitely not here, are you?' she said with a hint of sadness.

John ran his hand over his stubble and looked at his watch: three p.m.

'Sorry,' he said.

'Is there something going on today that I should know about?'

'What?'

'That's the fourth time you've checked your watch in an hour,' Bernie moaned. 'If you're bored, you can go.'

John looked at her and put his hand to her face. He was falling for her, and he knew that wasn't good. And keeping the information about the car bomb to himself was making him feel uncomfortable.

'They're using my bomb this afternoon,' he told her. 'In London.'

Bernie sat up in bed and looked at him. 'Why didn't you tell me?'

'Because Frank Daly told me not to tell anyone. And I don't want to cross Frank because he's a psychopath.'

Bernie laughed. 'Aye, you're not wrong there. The man's one dark fecker.'

John got off the bed and walked naked over to the small portable television that sat on Bernie's bedroom table. He took the tiny remote control and pressed the On button.

As he clicked through the channels, he saw there was horse racing, an old Ealing comedy film and darts. He clicked over to BBC2 and saw the spinning logo of the BBC News and

265

a word that made him squirm in the pit of his stomach –
NEWSFLASH.

The newsreader, Moira Stuart, looked into the camera with a serious expression.

'*A massive car bomb in Northern Ireland has killed twenty-five people, including children. It exploded on a busy shopping street in Omagh, County Tyrone. About a hundred and fifty people were injured. It's the worst bomb attack in thirty years of terrorism in the province. Police had been evacuating roads around the courthouse after a telephone warning, but the bomb went off several hundred yards away in an area people were being sent towards. Linda Duffin reports from the scene.*'

John felt physically sick as he watched the scenes of devastation from Omagh, which was only seventy miles west of Belfast.

'Are you feckin' kidding me!' he thundered as his shock turned to anger. Daly had fucked him over.

How was he going to explain this to Military Intelligence? He'd built a bomb that had killed more than twenty people. His whole body shuddered at the thought.

Bernie looked at him, her face blank. 'I don't understand?'

John pointed to the screen. 'I do. Daly told me the bomb was intended to attack Irish Guards at Chelsea Barracks so I'd finish it. Now it's killed women and children just down the feckin' road.'

Grabbing his jeans, John hoisted them on as he reached for his T-shirt.

'Where the hell are you going?' Bernie asked.

'McCoy's,' John thundered. He wanted to kill Daly with his bare hands.

'That's not a good idea, John,' Bernie warned as she started to get dressed.

'You're not coming with me,' John snapped as he put on his shoes.

Bernie tried to grab him. 'I don't want you to get yourself killed.'

John threw her off, stormed out of the flat and began to march down the Falls Road. It was less than a ten-minute walk to McCoy's and he knew that Daly was usually drinking in there on a Saturday afternoon.

How could he have been so stupid! Why didn't he insist that Military Intelligence intercept the car bomb before it had left Belfast? He knew that might have blown his cover, but it would have prevented what had just happened.

Spotting the door to McCoy's, John pushed it hard and strode into the dark, smoky interior of the pub. Daly was sitting with Davie, Breslin and another man. They all looked up as John charged towards them.

Daly got up, raising his hands defensively. 'Hey, take it east there, cowboy.'

John wasn't about to stop and talk. He felt completely out of control. Grabbing a bottle by the neck from a table as he went, he smashed it so that it became a lethal weapon of broken glass. Everyone else at the table jumped up, realising John's intention.

As John reached where they were sitting, Daly pulled out a revolver and pointed it straight between John's eyes. He froze.

'I think you need to calm the feck down, boyo,' Daly said calmly.

'Have you seen the feckin' carnage over there?' John yelled. 'Women and kids? That's not okay.'

Daly narrowed his eyes. 'You've just crossed the line, you do know that, Johnny-boy?'

'I don't feckin' care about that,' he thundered. 'I've got to live with that now.'

'Come on,' Daly snorted. 'You knew what you were signing up for.'

John tossed the broken bottle onto the table. 'Yeah, well not anymore. I'm done.'

Daly raised an eyebrow. 'You need to watch your back, John. You understand me? Because this isn't over.'

'Wanna bet?' John snapped as he turned on his heels and left the pub.

CHAPTER 42

Gareth had called an impromptu briefing of all CID officers who were in Beaumaris nick and was bringing everyone up to speed with the day's developments. He looked over to Declan. 'Anything on Weller's whereabouts?'

'Nothing, boss,' Declan replied. 'All units have a photo of Weller, but no one has seen anything.'

'What about matching his trainers to the footprint we found at our crime scene?' Gareth said.

Declan shook his head. 'Still waiting for forensics.'

Gareth nodded as he walked over to the scene board. In his hand, he held the photograph of the charity event in The Panton Arms on the night of John's murder. Forensics had done a good job of enlarging it. He took some drawing pins and stuck the photo on the board then peered at the image of John handing over a cheque.

'Okay, let's move on to John Finn's murder. What have we got?' Gareth asked.

'We have Jenny's allegation that John was in contact with a woman in Belfast,' Laura said. 'And the only woman who we know John knew in Belfast was Bernie Maguire. He'd betrayed the IRA and left her pregnant, so it wouldn't be a stretch to think she wanted him dead.'

'Yeah, but I can't see why he'd have regular conversations with Bernie on the phone while he was in Witness Protection,' Gareth stated.

'Unless there was someone else?' Ben suggested.

'You mean he was seeing someone else in Belfast before he left?' Gareth asked. 'And then he kept in contact with her when he was over here?'

Ben shrugged. 'It's possible. Maybe this woman then leaked his exact whereabouts to the IRA. MI5 thought his safety had been compromised.'

'And she's the woman he was with in the car park?' Laura asked.

Gareth ran his hand over his head as he gazed over at the scene boards and put his hands in his pockets.

'We have a witness who saw John with a woman in the car park of The Panton Arms,' he said. 'We assume this was at some point between seven p.m. and eight p.m. During this hour, someone kills him by hitting him across the back of the head and then buries him. And he remains buried there for over twenty years. So, what the hell happened that night?'

'Boss, aren't we jumping to conclusions here?' Declan suggested. 'We're assuming that this unknown woman and his murder must be connected. What if they're not?'

'Go on,' Gareth said.

'Between seven p.m. and eight p.m., John is with a mystery woman in the pub car park. She could be a local who he's met, we don't know. As John is making his way back across the car park, he sees Mark Weller outside. He goes to confront him about Weller's attack on Jenny. Things get out of hand. Weller finds something heavy like a brick and smashes it across the back of John's head and kills him. He bundles

John's body into the boot of his car and waits for a couple of days to bury him up at Castell Aberlleiniog.'

Declan had a good point, Laura thought. Maybe the mystery woman was a red herring and distracting them from a viable suspect in Mark Weller.

Andrea came over. She was holding a print-out and seemed animated as she approached.

'Boss, I think I've got something,' she said as she got to her desk.

'What is it?' he asked.

Andrea gestured to the print-out she was holding. 'I spoke to the DFA, which is effectively the Irish equivalent of the UK Passport and Immigration Control. According to EU law, all passports are now biometric and contain a microchip. That microchip is a record of the passport holder's criminal record *and* a travel record of all trips made on that passport number. The DFA also hold that information on a central database.'

'Where are you going with all this?' Declan enquired grumpily.

'They've just sent over that information for Bernadette Maguire,' Andrea explained, pointing to the paper. 'She told me and Laura that the last time she saw John Finn, aka John Doyle, was on the Falls Road just before he vanished. However, on the second of October 1999, she took a flight from Dublin to Anglesey. And she stayed at a B & B in Beaumaris.'

Eileen Proby, the owner of The Nook B & B, was a broad-faced woman in her sixties. She adopted a curious smile when Laura and Andrea arrived, showed her their warrant cards and explained that they'd like to ask her a few routine questions to do with their inquiry. Her greying hair was scraped-back to reveal a bulky, rounded brow. Her commanding eyes set wide apart gazed at them as she nodded and beckoned them inside.

'Come and sit in my boudoir,' she said, ushering them into a large living room that was cluttered with a strange assortment of objects.

It was as if they'd wandered into some kind of oriental bazaar. Ornate clusters of brightly coloured feathers hung on the walls next to embroidered wall hangings. Necklaces, shells, crystals and uneven pieces of wood carved with symbols filled sea-green Chinese pottery bowls and shelves. There were scrolls with Japanese writing, decorated with pink chrysanthemums and dark green lotus flowers.

Sitting down on the dusty sofa, Andrea gave Laura an imperceptible look as if to say, *well this is different*.

The curtains were half-drawn and a lamp lit the far end of the room in a dull vanilla hue.

'I'm sorry.' Eileen plonked herself down on a vast sixties-style chair covered in cushions. 'Would you like tea? I don't do coffee, I'm afraid. But I have tea from every corner of the world.'

Which is not a surprise, Laura thought.

'That's fine, thank you.' Laura smiled. 'We wanted to talk to you about someone who we believe stayed here in October 1999.'

'Good God! That is a long time ago,' she laughed. 'I'll do my best.'

'In fact, all we know is that she wrote this down as the address she was staying at when she filled out her boarding card at Anglesey airport,' Andrea said. 'Do you keep records of previous guests?'

'Erm, I think so . . . 1999?' Eileen replied, thinking out loud as she got up. 'I think we started using a computer around then. We have our guest registration book as well.' Eileen pottered over to a shelf, thumbed through some ledgers and then pulled one out. 'Here we go – 1999.' She came back and sat down with a sigh. 'Now, what's the date we're looking for?'

Andrea smiled over at her. 'The second of October.'

'And what name am I looking for?'

'Bernadette or Bernie Maguire.'

Eileen continued to turn the pages. 'Shouldn't be hard to find. October is a pretty quiet month. I have something here. But the person has registered themselves as a Bernadette Doyle.'

Laura looked over at Andrea. Doyle was the false surname that John Finn had used when undercover in Belfast.

'Do you check passports for identification when someone's checking in?' Laura enquired.

'We do now,' Eileen stated. 'But I'm pretty sure we didn't back in 1999.'

'So, you wouldn't have checked that Bernadette Doyle was her real name?' Laura asked.

'No. If I'm honest, we used to get couples coming away for dirty weekends who signed themselves in as Mr and Mrs Smith. It wasn't really our business.'

'Did this Bernadette Doyle give her home address?' Andrea enquired.

Eileen peered down at the ledger. 'Yes – 54 Clooney Street, Belfast.'

'Does it give the date when she checked out?'

Eileen shook her head. 'All we've got written here is TBC. My guess is when she booked in, she told us she didn't know how long she was staying but would tell us when she did. If it's quiet, we don't mind.'

'Is there any other way of finding out how many nights she stayed?' Laura asked. They needed to know if Maguire had been on the island on the night of the twelfth of October. 'What about a credit card payment?'

273

'Sorry. It says that she was going to pay in cash.'

'If I showed you a photograph, do you think you could have a look at it for me?' Laura asked.

Eileen raised an eyebrow. 'Do you know how many people have stayed here in the last twenty years?' She shrugged. 'But I'll have a look.'

Laura scrolled through on her phone until she found the one of Bernie Maguire that had been supplied by MI5. She showed Eileen, who leaned forwards to take a look.

'Oh yes. I do remember her.'

CHAPTER 43

It was early evening as Laura walked down the corridor with Gareth towards the main meeting room on the ground floor of Beaumaris Police Station.

'You okay?' Gareth enquired.

'Yeah,' Laura said quietly. 'I feel better now I know there's a patrol car sitting outside our house for when the kids get home.'

'Of course you do,' he said as they arrived at the half-open door. 'I'm sorry this has happened in your first week back.'

'Perks of the job,' she said dryly.

As they went in, Laura saw that Warlow and Amis were already deep in conversation.

'Evening,' Gareth said as he and Laura sat down.

Warlow looked at his watch. 'You'll be pleased to know that the Garda in Dublin were very helpful, especially when I explained it was a murder case. Maguire was being escorted on a plane out of Dublin at seven p.m. She should be here before midnight.'

Gareth nodded. 'Good to hear.'

Amis looked at them. 'I understand you now have two current murder investigations, plus this one?'

'Yes, that's right.' Gareth nodded.

Amis raised an eyebrow. 'Sounds like you've got your hands full.'

'We'll cope,' Gareth reassured.

'Can you guys bring me up to speed with the John Finn investigation?'

Gareth looked at Laura to show she should speak first.

'We know that Bernie Maguire flew from Dublin to Anglesey on the second of October 1999. She stayed at The Nook B & B, which is just down the road from here. She used the name Bernadette Doyle when she checked in. I guess that was her idea of a little joke.'

'When did she leave the island?' Amis asked.

'We're not sure yet,' Gareth admitted.

'What about the B & B?' Warlow frowned.

Laura shook her head. 'No. There's no record of the actual date she left the B & B, either. She paid cash, so there's no credit card or bank paper trail to follow.'

Amis pulled a face. 'The CPS are going to love that.'

'I'm hoping the shock of being arrested and flown out of Dublin tonight will be enough to get her talking,' Warlow said.

Laura wasn't so convinced. They were talking about a woman who was a cold-blooded killer in her twenties and who had been interrogated countless times by Special Branch and MI5 in the nineties. Maguire would not be easily rattled. Gareth was clearly right when he'd told her in the past that Warlow was out of touch to the point of naive.

Gareth moved forwards in his seat and looked over at Warlow and Amis. 'We believe that John was murdered on the night of the twelfth of October. We now have an eyewitness who saw John in the car park between seven p.m. and eight p.m. with a woman.'

'Do you have a description?' Amis enquired.

'No,' Gareth replied. 'Nothing except the woman was of average build and height.'

'That could match Maguire,' Warlow pointed out.

'But it's not enough for any kind of conviction though, is it, sir?' Gareth said.

'No, of course not.'

'Our witness saw John in a car with this woman,' Laura explained.

Warlow pulled a face. 'How does that work? I thought we were working on the assumption that Maguire hated John and that she'd come to Anglesey to assassinate him?'

It was a fair point, Laura thought.

Amis looked at them. 'My understanding is that Maguire was skilled at using her feminine charm as a tactic to ensnare others. In 1993, she flirted with a British soldier in a bar in Dortmund. She suggested they go round the back of the bar, where she put a bullet in his head.'

'So, she pretended she wanted some kind of reconciliation with John to put him off-guard.' Laura thought through Amis' hypothesis. 'They meet in the pub car park. She drives him somewhere and then murders and buries him.'

Gareth shrugged. 'That would tally with what our eyewitness saw.'

Laura nodded. 'It also tallies with what Jenny Maldini told me. When I asked her if she thought John was having an affair, at first she completely rejected the idea. Then she admitted she'd caught John talking to someone, whom she was convinced was a woman. He denied it. However, when she checked the number, it was a Belfast area code.'

Gareth sat back, taking this in. 'Maybe she tracked him down and contacted him to say that she forgave him. Over a series of phone calls, Maguire convinced John that they could rekindle what they had in Belfast. She flew over and then killed him instead.'

Laura looked at them with a dark expression. 'That's a perfectly plausible theory. Maguire had motive, means and opportunity. But how would we ever persuade the CPS to go to trial without a lot more evidence? And twenty years later, I don't even know how we're ever going to get that.'

'Interview conducted with Bernie Maguire, Thursday, seventh October, 11.20 p.m., Beaumaris Police Station. Present are Bernadette Maguire, Detective Inspector Gareth Williams, Duty Solicitor Patrick Clifford and myself, Detective Inspector Laura Hart.' Laura glanced over at Bernie. 'Bernie, do you understand you are still under caution?'

Bernie was staring down at the table as if she hadn't heard her.

'Bernie?' Laura said.

Bernie slowly looked up and met her eyes with an icy glare that was more than unsettling.

'Bernie, do you understand you are still under caution?' Laura asked again slowly.

The duty solicitor leaned in and whispered something in her ear.

'Yes, of course.' Bernie nodded. 'This is utterly ridiculous.'

'Okay.' Laura moved the files so that they were in front of her. 'I'd like to ask you about your whereabouts on Tuesday, 12 October 1999.'

Bernie narrowed her eyes. 'Are you feckin' kiddin' me?'

'No,' Laura said calmly, shaking her head. She took out a photograph and turned it to show her. 'For the purposes of the tape, I'm showing the suspect item reference 4RTF. As you can see, this is a photograph of a man you knew as John Doyle, is that correct?'

Bernie shrugged angrily. 'Yes. I told you that when you talked to me in Dublin.'

Laura turned over a page of notes. 'And in the conversation that you had with me and DC Jones in Dublin, you informed us you hadn't left the Republic of Ireland since 1993. And that you hadn't seen John Doyle since you saw him on the Falls Road in 1998, just before he left Belfast.'

Bernie looked over at the duty solicitor and then back at her. 'What's your point?' she snorted.

Laura fished out another document. 'For the purposes of the tape, I am showing the suspect item reference 3EGF.' Laura turned the document for Bernie to look at, but instead, Bernie sat back in her seat defiantly. 'As you can see, this document shows you made a flight from Dublin to Anglesey on the second of October 1999. Can you tell us the purpose of your journey, Bernie?'

'Tourism,' Bernie said with a raised eyebrow. 'I'd never been to Anglesey.'

Gareth looked over at her. 'Then why lie to us about never leaving Ireland after 1993?'

'I didn't lie,' Bernie stated. 'I just forgot. Christ, it's only a thirty-minute flight!'

Laura waited for a few seconds and then asked, 'Can you tell us how you felt about John Doyle?'

Bernie ran her hands through her thick, red hair and pushed it away from her face. 'I didn't think very much of him.'

'But you admit you had some kind of relationship with him?' Laura asked.

'I told you this already. It was casual. We were young.' Bernie then gave them a quizzical look. 'Am I right in thinking you've found John's remains here on Anglesey? And because I happen to have visited here, now I'm some kind of suspect?'

Neither Gareth nor Laura answered.

'You must have been angry when you found out that John was working undercover for British Intelligence?' Gareth said.

'Can you tell me why you've dragged me all the way from Dublin when the only evidence against me you seem to have is that I visited Anglesey in 1999?' Bernie snapped.

'You were a highly respected member of the IRA,' Laura stated. 'You must have felt pretty stupid having an affair with a British agent?'

Bernie looked at her duty solicitor. 'Are you going to let her get away with that line of questioning?'

The duty solicitor didn't reply.

Gareth shrugged. 'You can answer our questions or we can sit here all night. It's up to you.'

Bernie laughed. 'Jesus, you two haven't got a clue. I was a regular at the Castlereagh interrogation centre in East Belfast. And you should have seen what they did to IRA suspects in there. Even in the nineties.'

She is really pissing me off, Laura thought.

Bernie shrugged. 'I'm not saying anything more until you tell me what this is about.'

Gareth shrugged. 'Okay. Well, we'll pick this up again in the morning.'

'I'm not staying here overnight,' Bernie snapped.

'You're under arrest, Bernie,' Laura said. 'We're not going to put you up in a hotel.'

CHAPTER 44

It was early evening and Llandudno General was bustling as it was visiting time. Laura weaved her way along the corridor and entered the ICU. The noise diminished as she nodded to the nurses at the workstation. The ward sister came over.

'I understand that Louise has been put in an induced coma?' Laura said quietly.

The ward sister nodded. 'We use it to stabilise her heart and other vital organs.'

'Okay if I go and see her for two minutes?' Laura enquired.

'Of course,' the ward sister replied with a kind expression. 'She's in the same room. Just that there's a ventilator in there now.'

'Thank you,' Laura said with a benign smile. 'I assume the police officer is outside her room?'

'Sorry.' The ward sister looked perplexed. 'What police officer?'

Laura frowned. 'I arranged for a uniformed police officer to be stationed outside her room. She's a vulnerable witness.'

'No, sorry,' she said. 'No one's arrived and I've been here all day.'

Laura took a few seconds and then began to feel uneasy.

At that moment, someone brushed past her. She thought nothing of it until she saw the back of him. A man in his twenties, black Puffa jacket, grey trackies and trainers. His head was shaved close all over. She couldn't see his face.

Trying to sound calm, Laura gave a half-smile. 'Someone's got their wires crossed somewhere along the line.'

Out of the corner of her eye, she watched the young man like a hawk. He had the gait and swagger of a member of an OCG. Maybe she was being paranoid, but she wasn't taking any chances.

Her pulse racing, Laura glanced over at the whiteboard behind the nurses' workstation. Each ward and room had a number and a name written beside it in blue marker. Scanning her eyes down it quickly, she saw ICU – Room 21 – Louise McDonald.

Shit!

The young man did a half-turn. His face had a deep scar from the corner of his mouth down to his jawline. It had used to be called a Chelsea smile. Was it her imagination, or did she recognise him from when she worked in Manchester? His face was familiar but she didn't remember the scar. It could have happened in the three intervening years.

Then something in her memory recalled exactly who he was.

Sean Barnes.

He was the younger brother of Chris Barnes, a well-known member of the Fallowfield Hill Gang. And they were the OCG that Laura and Pete suspected were paying off Butterfield.

She took a deep breath. Barnes had clearly come to murder Louise before she came out of the coma and decided to give evidence about the Fallowfield Hill Gang and their relationship with corrupt police officers in the Manchester Met.

Barnes looked around but didn't spot Laura. He headed

over to the nurses' station and looked over at the whiteboard. It would only be a matter of seconds before he located Louise.

Laura reached out and touched the ward sister's arm, gave her a grave look and whispered, 'I need you to remain very calm. And I need you to come with me right now.'

The ward sister sensed the tone of Laura's voice and nodded.

Turning quickly, they set off down the corridor.

'We need to get Louise out of that room fast,' Laura said under her breath.

'Okay.' The ward sister looked terrified. 'Is there someone dangerous here?'

'I think so,' Laura said as they broke into a jog.

A few seconds later, they arrived at Louise's room.

The ward sister opened the door and marched over to Louise's bed, unlocking the wheels with her foot. She raced to the wall and unplugged the oscilloscope and the ventilator, and then lifted them onto the bed. Laura ran round to the top of the bed, pulling it away from the wall.

The ward sister gestured to the equipment. 'In case of power cuts, they've got an emergency back-up battery.'

Laura gave the bed a shove while the ward sister pulled the other end and within seconds, they'd manoeuvred it through the open doorway and into the corridor. Sick with nerves, Laura glanced nervously back up the corridor, expecting to see Barnes at any second.

'This way,' the ward sister said as she dragged the bed down the corridor in the opposite direction from the nurses' station.

Come on, come on, Laura thought.

Building up a head of speed, they turned a corner and the ward sister gestured to some double doors. 'In here!'

Hitting the doors open with her back, they pulled the bed

through into a large stockroom. The doors closed behind them.

'Jesus,' the ward sister gasped.

Laura pointed to the doors. 'Can you lock them from inside here?'

She nodded. 'Yeah.'

'Once I'm gone, lock yourself in and don't come out again until you hear my voice,' Laura instructed.

Pushing open the doors, Laura raced out into the corridor and looked up.

Where the hell is Barnes?

A few seconds later, she arrived back at what had been Louise's room and closed the door. She stood outside with her back to the door and looked up the corridor.

Nothing.

Then a figure appeared, sauntering along, looking casually at all the numbers of the rooms.

It was Barnes.

Shit! Here we go.

Standing straight, Laura turned to face Barnes, who was about twenty yards away. She hoped he'd recognise her or at least realise she was a copper.

They locked eyes for a moment.

If he's got a gun, I'm dead.

Reaching inside her jacket, Louise pretended she was about to take a gun from a shoulder holster. Barnes stopped, frowned and looked at her. Laura thought her heart was going to burst through her chest, but she had to keep up the pretence that she was armed.

If he calls my bluff here, I'm toast.

Barnes smirked and cocked his head to one side.

Laura held her breath. She had no idea if he had a gun or a knife, or if he was going to attack her to get to Louise.

The tension rose for a few seconds.

God, I feel sick.

Then Barnes gave her a wink, turned on his heels and wandered casually away.

Laura let out her breath. *Jesus Christ.*

Resting against the wall, she put her hands on her knees and tried to get her breath back. As she looked up, a figure came wandering back up the corridor. She froze. It was Pete.

'You okay?' he asked, looking concerned.

She shook her head. 'They sent someone to kill Louise.' She gestured to the room. 'But we got her out just in time.'

An hour later, Pete and Laura were sitting in the ground-floor café at Llandudno General. Pete had spoken to the police in Llandudno to get an explanation of why no officer had been sent over to guard Louise McDonald's room. After several more phone calls, it seemed there just wasn't a record of Laura ever making a phone call to make that request. They didn't know if this was human error or something darker and more suspicious. A uniformed officer had now arrived and was stationed outside Louise's room until she was transferred.

Pete ended his phone call and looked over at Laura. 'You okay now?'

'Yeah,' she replied, nursing a mug of tea. 'Can we get Louise transferred?'

Pete nodded. 'I've got officers coming from the PPS. They're going to transfer Louise up to Glan Clwyd Hospital under a fake name so no one can trace when she's up there.'

Laura nodded. 'Good. That makes sense.'

Pete delved into his coat, took out an envelope and gave her a dark look. 'I know why Louise has been doing what she's doing.'

'What is it?' Laura gestured to the envelope.

'Take a look.'

She picked it up. Inside were a series of photographs. The

first few showed Louise at a party, drinking and then snorting lines of cocaine. The last few were explicit photographs of her having sex with a man and then with two men.

'Jesus.' Laura shook her head.

Pete raised an eyebrow. 'I'm guessing that you'd do anything for those not to appear on your boss' desk or be plastered all over social media.'

CHAPTER 45

Belfast 1998

It was midnight when John sat in the back of a black Astra speeding through the backstreets of Belfast. He'd been picked up by two officers from British Army Intelligence twenty minutes earlier. He knew that after the Omagh bombing, he'd have to break cover, even if was just to explain what had happened – and how everything had gone so monumentally wrong.

As they reached the outskirts of the city, they began to head for Gilnahirk in Ulster. Any other time, John might have taken comfort in the clear blue skies that rolled out like a beautiful canvas awning above them. The winding roads, the rocky fields and the little houses, all felt familiar, much like where he grew up only fifty miles to the south. But the car was uncomfortably silent. He wondered if the two officers knew why he'd been called and the gravity of what had happened. Was their silence a damning judgement, or was he being paranoid? Months alone and undercover hadn't been good for his mental health. He'd lived on his nerves, which now felt frayed and worn like the unravelling of disintegrating rope.

Eventually, the car drew up outside a remote farmhouse and John was ushered inside. He was led down a corridor and into a large, sparsely furnished living room. Immediately, he spotted Captain Palmer and Detective Chief Inspector Wood, the men he'd met six months earlier when he first arrived in Northern Ireland.

Before John had had a chance to say anything, Palmer had stood up from the table where he was sitting. 'Jesus Christ, sergeant, what the bloody hell happened?'

John wasn't sure where to start. He could see Wood giving him a thunderous look.

'It was in my report. I built them a car bomb,' John said, wondering if anyone was going to tell him to sit down. Maybe they'd just leave him standing, to signal their anger.

'A car bomb that you told us was being taken over to the British mainland, driven to London and exploded outside Chelsea Barracks!' Palmer roared.

'Frank Daly lied to me,' John explained.

'Bloody hell!' Wood muttered under his breath. 'What a shitshow.'

'You've seen what it did in Omagh?' Palmer growled.

'Of course I did,' John stated as calmly as he could. 'And I've got to live with that, sir.'

'We all have to live with it, sergeant,' Palmer reminded him sharply. 'It was my idea to put someone undercover into the Real IRA. Ultimately, I'm responsible for what happened.'

Wood looked at John. 'You can't stay out there.'

John felt deflated. 'You can't pull me in now.'

'After Omagh, we can do what we want,' Wood barked.

'We heard a rumour that Frank Daly wants you dead,' Palmer said.

John shrugged. 'Probably. I made it very clear that I wasn't happy about what happened in Omagh. It wasn't something I could just shrug off, because that would have been suspicious.'

'What if he kills you?' Palmer asked.

'Don't worry. I can get you Frank Daly before he gets to me. And maybe some of the others,' John pleaded. 'Otherwise, all these months will have been for nothing.'

Wood looked over at Palmer. 'It's your call, Captain. Technically, he's your man. But I think he's a liability out there.'

John looked over at Palmer. 'Frank Daly planned and executed the Omagh bombing but you know my testimony on its own isn't going to be enough. You've got to give me a chance to find the evidence to convict him. And I can do that.'

'I don't know,' Palmer muttered as he pulled out a packet of cigarettes.

'The people of Omagh deserve justice, don't they, sir?' John asked. 'I can hand you Daly. I just need some time.'

Palmer looked at him. 'You've got two weeks, sergeant, and then you're done.'

CHAPTER 46

It was 7.15 a.m. and the sun was just rising over Beaumaris beach. Laura had managed five hours' sleep, which was just about enough to keep her going. As a copper, she'd grown used to functioning on minimal sleep – it was just part of the job.

Her sleep had been fitful and disturbed, full of dreams about Louise McDonald. The race to get her to safety. The look on Barnes' face as he stared at her. And the images of her that Pete had found in her flat. There was part of her that felt a strange relief that Louise hadn't been corrupted by the offer of money. She had no idea how she'd allowed herself to be photographed in such compromising situations – maybe she'd been drugged and didn't even know what she was doing. And now that she and Pete knew Louise was being blackmailed, it did make her partly a victim in the whole scenario.

Come on, Laura. Clear your mind. It's a new day.

She stretched out her arms, allowing the cold early morning wind to blow against her. This is why she came here. To clear her mind and find some kind of temporary peace.

Elvis had been in a deep sleep when she left. He hadn't even stirred when she passed him on the way out, so she'd left him to it.

The sea extended before her in a swirling mixture of blues and greens. It was timeless and unending. Generous and brutal at the same time. The tide was coming in and the sea was clearer and calmer than usual. The icy water slipped gently over her feet and toes, icing the sand with a damp velvety coating. As she peered into the sea in front of her, tall dark trees of seaweed waved gently and tiny silver fish swam in between.

Before she'd even decided to get in, she'd hit the water. This was the feeling she wanted. To possess the ocean and be possessed at the same time. Embracing the sea, it felt more like an old friend this morning than it had ever done. It was a glassy, heaving, reassuring presence that embraced and held her. As if the sea itself were a protective force for peace and life. She lay back, the freezing water numbing her mind as she let herself relax and be borne tenderly by its buoyancy. A gentle hand that constantly lifted her up and set her down like a baby in its mother's arms.

From somewhere, she heard the soft splashing of water and turned to look.

It was Gareth.

'Hey, stranger,' she smiled.

'I'm going to have to find another place to swim if you keep stealing my spot,' he joked.

'Ha, ha.' She gave him a sarcastic grin.

'Where's Elvis?'

'Having a lie-in,' she joked. She gestured to the water. 'I'm trying to numb my brain before the day kicks in again.'

'I know the feeling.' Gareth nodded then sank under the water, reappearing with a gasp.

They looked at each other for a moment.

'Do you think Bernie Maguire killed John?' she asked.

'Yes.'

'What about Frank Daly and Rhys Hughes, then?'

'Weller killed them.'

'Can we prove Maguire killed John?'

'God knows.' Gareth lay back in the water and kicked his feet gently. 'I guess we keep digging away. Historic cases are a major ball-ache.'

'Talking of which,' Laura grinned, 'the sea seems a bit colder this morning, doesn't it?'

Gareth laughed and then looked at her. 'I've booked us a night away at the Lake Vyrnwy Hotel and Spa.'

'Have you now?' she replied with a delighted smile.

'I can move it if something crops up,' Gareth said. 'But I was feeling spontaneous, so I just gave them a ring.'

'No, I like that.' Laura moved to a shallower part of the sea and put her feet down on the ridges of sand. 'Spontaneous is romantic.'

'Oh, good.' Gareth swam a little closer. He had a strange, serious look on his face. 'I . . .'

'Is everything all right?' There was something unsettling about his expression.

'I'm not sure,' he replied quietly. 'I need to tell you something.'

The six words that a woman never wants to hear come out of the mouth of the man she's seeing.

'That doesn't sound good, Gareth,' she said, moving ahead of him with what he was going to tell her.

She saw him take a deep breath. Whatever he was about to tell her, it wasn't going to be pleasant.

'I slept with Nell the other night.' He winced.

The thought of it made her stomach drop like a lead weight.

'What?' she said and then waited for a few seconds as she processed what he'd told her. 'Why?'

'Because I'm a fucking idiot, that's why,' he said, now unable to look at her properly. 'I'm really sorry.'

She took a breath and closed her eyes.

For fuck's sake!

Then she glared at him. 'So, your ex-wife turns up with a black eye and you shag her out of pity? I don't understand!'

'Neither do I,' he said, squirming. 'And I wish it hadn't happened. But I also don't want to lie to you.'

'You did bloody lie to me, Gareth!' she snapped. 'You told me she stayed over. And you categorically told me that you didn't sleep with her. That is a fucking lie, Gareth.'

'I'm s-sorry,' he stammered. 'I . . . I just panicked. I thought if I told you that you'd just finish with me.'

'But you've told me now!' she seethed.

'I know. I'm an idiot.'

Laura's pain had been replaced by fury. She looked at him. 'I don't trust you. So, that means nothing can happen between us. You've screwed it up for some five-minute revenge fuck with your ex-wife. I hope she was worth it.'

Laura splashed angrily out of the water and marched down the beach to where her clothes were.

Laura rounded the corner of her road ten minutes later, still full of hurt and anger. Spotting a car she didn't recognise parked directly outside, her stomach immediately tightened.

Who's that?

The uniformed police car that had been stationed outside was pulled up on the other side of the road exactly where she'd seen it when she left. As she broke into a run, she spotted that the two officers she'd waved to on her way out were no longer in the car.

Oh my God, what's happened? The kids!

She sprinted towards the house, sick with terror.

Thundering up the drive, her mind went through an array of chilling scenarios. She crashed through the side door and immediately saw Rosie looking at her. She was crying.

'Are you all right?' Laura gasped as she went to her. 'Where's Jake?'

293

'It's Elvis,' Rosie sobbed.

'What?'

'It's Elvis,' Rosie whispered. 'I think he's dead.'

It took a second to process what she'd said.

'I couldn't wake him up,' Rosie explained. 'I went to the policemen out in the car and they called an emergency vet.'

'Where is he?' Laura asked anxiously.

'I found him in the kitchen, just lying there.'

Laura rushed down the hallway. In the kitchen, a man was kneeling on the floor, checking him with a stethoscope. The two police officers were standing over by the cooker with Jake.

'Mum!' Jake cried, running over to her and wrapping his arms around her waist.

Laura looked over at her beloved dog. He wasn't moving.

The vet glanced up at her with an expression she couldn't read.

'It's okay,' he said reassuringly. 'My guess is that he's been heavily sedated. But his heart and breathing seem to be fine now.'

'Sedated?' Laura asked.

The vet nodded as he got to his feet. 'Something as simple as diazepam would do it.'

'How the hell did someone tranquillise him?' Laura said to no one in particular. Then she looked at Jake and Rosie, who were hovering by the door. 'He's going to be fine. Don't worry.'

Rosie handed her a blank white envelope. 'This was lying on the mat.'

Laura already knew who it was from as she opened it, fury and fear causing her hands to shake. Inside was the same type of printed page of A4.

NEXT TIME IT WILL BE POISON.
LEAVE THE JOHN FINN CASE ALONE.

CHAPTER 47

Taking a wooden stirrer, Gareth tipped some brown sugar into his coffee and looked around the canteen. He was still rattled by what had happened between him and Laura at Beaumaris beach two hours earlier. He was pretty sure she wasn't going to forgive him and quite apart from the emotional pain that it caused him, it was going to make working together difficult – at least for the next few months.

He'd been such an idiot! Had telling her been the right thing to do? They were getting on so well and the night away to Lake Vyrnwy would have been incredible. However, he knew that the fact that he'd slept with Nell and not told her would have weighed on his conscience. He wondered if Laura would see it differently when the dust settled. A moment of stupidity and weakness on his part, but possibly understandable.

'You okay, boss?' asked a voice.

It was Andrea.

'Sorry. Miles away.' Gareth shook his head.

'I thought you vowed never to come to this place the last time you sampled their coffee?'

'Yeah, I did,' he said with a half-smile. 'I just needed a walk and a few minutes to myself.'

'Trying to avoid someone?'

'Not really,' Gareth lied. He looked at his watch and gestured to the doors. 'Better get back for briefing. Any news on Mark Weller?'

'No, boss. It sounds like he's vanished off the face of the earth,' Andrea said as they walked across the canteen.

It was noisy with the chatter of mainly uniformed officers eating breakfast or drinking tea. The clatter of cutlery and china came from the kitchen beyond.

'After you,' Gareth said, opening the door for her.

'I take it Bernie Maguire is our prime suspect for John's murder?' Andrea asked.

'Looks that way,' Gareth stated as they took the stairs up to the first floor where the CID office was located.

'Do we know how she knew John Finn was in Anglesey?'

'No. But in my experience, if people like the IRA want to find someone,' Gareth said with a dark expression, 'they usually find a way. Bribery, intimidation, you name it.'

They got to the doors of CID and went inside.

'Okay, everyone, listen up,' Gareth announced, marching to the front of the room. His eyes met Laura's for a moment, but he looked away. 'Lots to get through.' He had to put Laura out of his mind and concentrate on the job at hand. He went over to the scene board. 'Our search for Mark Weller is still ongoing. As far as I'm concerned, Weller is our prime suspect for Frank Daly and Rhys Hughes' murders.' He pointed to another photo. 'In terms of John's murder, I believe this is our prime suspect. Bernie Maguire. We think she was having a sexual relationship with John Finn when he was pulled out of Ireland by MI5. Daly claimed she was pregnant with his child.'

Declan looked over. 'What about Mark Weller as a suspect for John's murder too, boss?'

'Weller is definitely someone we need to keep looking at.

But my instinct is that the woman in the car with John that night at The Panton Arms was Bernie Maguire. Her trip to Anglesey from Ireland coincides with John's disappearance. And my theory in police work, for what it's worth, is that there are no such things as coincidences.'

Laura sat forwards in her chair. 'Someone tranquillised my dog this morning. He's going to be fine, but I had another threatening note telling me to leave the John Finn case alone. Bernie Maguire was in Dublin the day someone put a brick through my window. And she was in a cell this morning.'

'Sounds like she's got someone on the island doing her dirty work for her,' Declan said.

Ben, who had just put down the phone, signalled to Gareth. 'Boss, Bernie Maguire's solicitor from Dublin has just arrived.'

Gareth glanced over at Laura, with all the awkwardness that went with that look. 'Looks like we'd better get downstairs and interview her again.'

Laura settled herself at the table in the interview room. Gareth was sitting next to her, which made her feel uncomfortable. She'd tried to process what he'd told her three hours ago and had come to no conclusion. It was best for her to 'park it' as best she could and wait until she'd calmed down and had time to process it.

Bernie sat next to her own solicitor, John Flanaghan, who had flown in from Dublin that morning. Laura thought Bernie must be doing well for such an extravagance. Flanaghan was stout, with a puggy face but quick, astute eyes that roamed over the paperwork in front of him with intense concentration.

Laura pressed the button on the recorder and waited for the long electronic beep to stop.

'Interview conducted with Bernadette Maguire, Friday,

eighth October, 10.05 a.m., Beaumaris Police Station. Present are Bernadette Maguire, Detective Inspector Gareth Williams, the suspect's solicitor John Flanaghan and myself, Detective Inspector Laura Hart.' Laura glanced over at Bernie. 'Bernie, do you understand that you are still under caution?'

Laura looked over at Bernie, who was wearing an annoying smirk.

'Oh yes, I understand,' she said. 'I've now had a chance to have a long conversation with Mr Flanaghan and he's advised me to answer *all* of your questions to the best of my knowledge.'

Gareth nodded. 'I'm glad to hear it.'

Laura could sense something was wrong. Bernie wasn't acting like someone who was about to confess to coming to Anglesey to murder someone. In fact, quite the opposite. She was supremely relaxed and confident, as if she had something up her sleeve.

'If we can establish a few things to start off with.' Gareth reached over for one of the folders. 'You admit that you and a man you knew as John Doyle were in a sexual relationship while in Belfast, and that you were both members of the Belfast Brigade of the Real IRA?'

Bernie looked over to Flanaghan, who gave her a nod. 'Yes, that's right.'

'And you were aware that when John disappeared in 1999, he'd been working undercover for the British military, gaining intelligence about the Real IRA and their operations?'

'Not really.' Bernie pulled an amused face. 'I was aware that was what MI5 and Special Branch thought he was doing.'

What the hell is she talking about? Laura wondered.

'Sorry, I'm lost,' Gareth said, sitting forwards in his seat with a deep frown.

'Don't you get it?' Bernie laughed.

Laura was now seriously confused. What was John Doyle

298

doing in the Real IRA if he wasn't collecting intelligence for the British military?

'You seem to imply that wasn't what John was doing,' Laura said. 'Which, from our point of view, is confusing.'

Bernie looked over at Flanaghan then leaned in, exchanging a whispered conversation.

'John Doyle, aka John Kelly, aka John Finn, *was* a member of the IRA,' Bernie stated triumphantly.

There were a few seconds of silence as Bernie's last statement seemed to hang in the air.

Gareth shrugged. 'I don't understand.'

Bernie looked at them both. 'John joined the IRA when he was twenty. His uncle was in the Newry Brigade of the IRA. It was the one thing the IRA never had. An undercover member within the British military.'

Jesus Christ!

Laura looked at Gareth in utter shock.

CHAPTER 48

Belfast 1998

It had been thirty minutes since John and Bernie had left Belfast. They'd been sleeping together for nearly a month, but Bernie refused to let John refer to her as his *girlfriend*. She said it was sexist and a construct of the patriarchal society that they lived in. John had no idea what she'd been talking about.

Slipping the battered VW Golf Mk1 into fourth gear, John rounded a long bend as they headed out towards Black Mountain, which was, in fact, a large grassy hill that overlooked Belfast. It was covered in grassland heath, with paths and views over to the Mourne Mountains and Strangford Lough. Ireland was in the middle of a heatwave. Bernie had packed sandwiches, snacks and a few beers, insisting that it was the perfect place to spend the afternoon.

He looked over at her as she slept in the passenger seat. The shadows of the roadside trees moved rhythmically over her body and face. She looked so peaceful and young, John thought. It was hard to think of her as someone who had shot a British soldier in cold blood in Germany. He knew he had feelings for her, but he also knew that she was dangerous. Having a relationship with Bernie might give him what he needed to get Daly. It's just that there was also a nagging sense that he was getting too close to her.

John was living on borrowed time. Once word got out what had happened in McCoy's, Daly would have to kill him to save face. John needed to keep out of his way until he collected enough evidence to convict Daly of the Omagh bombing. His testimony wouldn't be sufficient. The Director of Public Prosecutions would require hard evidence too if they were to secure a conviction.

The previous evening, John and Bernie had been up to an open-air Sinn Fein rally smack bang in the middle of the Falls Road. A lorry was used as a platform where local members of Sinn Fein made speeches about a new Ireland. John knew he was safe there. Daly wouldn't give Sinn Fein the time of day after the Good Friday agreement. As far as Daly and Magan were concerned, the political wing of the IRA had sold them out. Bernie admitted she had mixed feelings about the ceasefire but agreed it was a relief not to walk the streets of Belfast in continual fear.

John found a decent parking space and woke Bernie. They made their way along the dusty footpath that led to the top of Black Mountain. He put his arm around her shoulder as they walked. She bowed her head and rolled her brow against his arm. He felt the warmth of her against his skin.

'You need a shave,' she said to him as she ran the back of her hand over his face.

'I'm going for that rugged look.'

'Are you now?' she teased, raising an eyebrow. 'I like it. It suits you. Maybe it's because you've got a wee bit of a baby-face.'

John laughed. 'Hey.'

The footpath was getting crowded, as half of Belfast seemed

to have headed out of the city for the cool breeze of the nearby hills. Reaching the top, they looked around for a suitable place to sit, eat and drink for the next few hours. They walked for another ten minutes before finding a flat piece of heathland beside a tree with a panoramic view across the city. The sun was blazing and even though they were high up, the heat was stifling.

John grabbed two beers from the bag and handed her one. 'Get this down you.'

'Trying to get me drunk, Mr Doyle?' she enquired with a sexy grin.

'Definitely.'

Bernie pointed out to the view. 'They reckon on a clear day you can see Scotland. That's why I love it up here.'

'I thought it was the Isle of Man?'

'Maybe.' Bernie knocked her can of beer against his. 'Slainte.'

'Slainte,' he smiled. 'Thanks for bringing me up here.'

The wind picked up and she pointed to a peregrine falcon that was gliding on air currents below. John watched as it seamlessly adjusted its wings to account for every change in direction and speed of the wind. Suddenly, it swooped down towards a field below in a blur.

'Beautiful, aren't they?' Bernie commented. 'The ultimate killing machine.'

'I love it when you're all romantic.'

'If you want me to be romantic,' she said with a smile, 'you're with the wrong woman, boyo.'

Her red hair was tousled in the wind and he leaned over and swept it from her face. Then he moved in and they kissed. As he adjusted his arm to sit up, John knocked against the virtually full can of beer that Bernie was holding. It tipped over the front of his shirt, soaking it.

'Shit, sorry,' she said, putting the beer down on the ground.

'It's fine, don't worry.' John shook his head.

'Hey, give that here.' Bernie grabbed hold of his shirt. 'Lay it in the sun and it'll be dry before you know it.'

'It's fine,' John said anxiously.

He had good reason not to take off his shirt and expose his naked torso. It was the same reason why he wore a T-shirt in bed.

Before he could stop her, she yanked the shirt. 'Come on, fella, no need to be shy.'

For a moment, he tried to grab the shirt back, but she pulled it up and over his head.

'What's the matter with you?' She frowned. 'It's not as if you're some fat fecker.'

Then she spotted what he'd been trying to hide. A large circular scar on the top of his left arm from where he'd been shot while attacking the personnel carrier in the Iraqi desert.

'What the feck is that?' Bernie asked as she laid the shirt out in the sun.

'Motorbike accident,' John replied far too quickly.

Bernie moved across, ran her finger over it and then glared suspiciously at him. 'Bullshit. That's from a bullet. I've seen scars like that before.'

John looked at her and shrugged. 'Okay.'

He needed to buy himself some time to think. The chances of someone seeing the scar from the bullet were so rare that he hadn't prepared a plausible story.

'Except you didn't want me to see it, did you?' she said, angry. 'Why not? How the feck does a merchant seaman get a bullet wound like that, John?'

John was panicking but trying not to show it. 'It's a long story. I got shot in a bar fight in Canada, that's all.' He gave her a forced smile. 'You should see the other fella. They had to feed him through a straw for a month.'

She pointed to his ear, where he was missing a chunk of cartilage. 'Do I take it this wasn't from a dog attack, then?'

'No, that really was a dog attack,' he replied, getting a flash of the young Iraqi soldier shooting at him before he plunged a knife into his throat. But he could tell that Bernie was suspicious. She sensed his uneasiness, and she wasn't about to let it go.

'You're lying to me.' She looked him right in the eyes, and he saw in them the moment it dawned on her. 'I knew I'd seen you before. It was ages ago. Fifteen years maybe.'

She's getting far too close for comfort.

John shook his head. 'Sorry, I don't know what you're talking about.'

'Yeah, I knew it when I saw you in that place.' Bernie's eyes were wild. 'There was a room at the back of O'Neil's pub on North Street in Crossmaglen.'

'You're getting me mixed up with someone else,' John protested as his carefully balanced double life began to unravel.

'Bullshit, John. It was you,' Bernie snapped. 'The South Armagh Brigade. You were sat with Jimmy Murphy. Younger, skinnier, but it was you.'

'I swear to you, it wasn't me.'

There were a few tense seconds when her eyes widened and her mouth opened a little. 'You're the one, aren't you, John?' she whispered.

His pulse quickened.

'The one?' He gave her a smile as if to say that she was being ridiculous. 'I really have no idea what you're talking about, Bernie. Come on now, you're being a wee bit dramatic here.'

'Oh my God, it is you,' she said under her breath in astonishment.

John looked at her for a few seconds. 'I'm lost.'

'Jesus,' she gasped, shaking her head. 'The boys from South Armagh always bragged that they'd managed to get a man into the British Army. They called him Lazarus. And legend had it that he'd fought in the Gulf War and joined the SAS.'

'Bloody hell, Bernie!' John snorted with laughter. 'Do I look like a fella who's been to the Gulf War and in the bloody SAS? I'm virtually feckin' illiterate, for starters.'

'Yeah, you are,' she agreed, still looking at him suspiciously. 'You might not be Lazarus, but you're definitely lying to me about how you got shot. Was it over a woman?'

'That would be telling.' John gave her a cheeky grin and then leaned over and kissed her hard on the mouth. 'Stop your jabbering and kiss me properly.'

But then John stopped kissing her for a moment. The desire to tell someone who he really was and what he'd been doing was overwhelming.

'You're right,' he said quietly.

Bernie looked concerned. 'What do you mean?'

'It is me,' he nodded. 'I'm Lazarus.'

Bernie gave him a playful hit. 'Very funny. Stop takin' the piss, will ya?'

John gave her a dark look. 'My real name is John Kelly. I'm a member of the Newry Brigade of the IRA. And I've been in the British Army for the past fourteen years. The SAS sent me to work undercover in Belfast. And I am Lazarus.'

Bernie looked at him aghast. 'Are you feckin' kiddin' me?'

John got up and grabbed her by the hand. 'Come on. We'll go somewhere, get really drunk and I'll tell you all about it.'

'I'm not going anywhere with you!' she snapped.

'I couldn't tell you, could I?'

'Why not?'

'There are only four people in the world who know who I am and where I'm from. I wanted to tell you so many times . . . I'm sorry, okay?'

She looked at him and took his hand uncertainly as he pulled her to her feet. They began to walk down the pathway towards the car. John couldn't tell if she was still angry or in shock.

'That makes no sense,' Bernie said after a few seconds.

'What?'

'If you're working for the Newry Brigade, why are you dicking around in West Belfast?'

'The boys in Newry are pro the ceasefire and the peace agreement,' John explained. 'They wanted me to report back on Magan, Daly and the rest of the Real IRA.'

'What for?'

'So they can stop them causing bloody mayhem like in Omagh and wrecking the peace agreement.'

'With force?'

'If needs be.'

'Then there'll be a civil war in the IRA,' Bernie said, thinking out loud.

'Maybe.' John shrugged as they arrived at the car park, which had emptied a little. 'If that's what it takes.'

Bernie was seething. 'They sold us out, John. All those boys died for nothing.'

'You don't believe that,' John said as they reached the car. 'I know you don't.'

Before they could continue, John heard a shout from across the car park.

CRACK!

A bullet hammered into the car door, leaving a hole in the metal.

There were screams as people scattered from the gunfire. John instinctively flinched, ducked and looked around for the gunman. A figure walked towards him with a revolver stretched out before him.

Fuck! It's Daly.

CRACK!

The car windscreen dissolved in a shower of glass.

'Get in!' John shouted to Bernie.

For a moment, she looked at him. She had a curious expression on her face. Then the penny dropped.

Shit! She's set me up. She told Daly we were coming here today. It was her idea.

CRACK!

A bullet whistled past his ear and hit the ground with a cloud of dirt.

After grappling with the car door, John scrambled into the car and jammed the key into the ignition.

'Stay there, Doyle, you fecker!' Daly shouted as he jogged towards him.

Turning the key, John kept his head down below the dashboard. The engine spluttered.

Come on! Come on!

Bernie had run to the other side of the car park. Glancing up, John could see that Daly was only twenty yards away.

Shit, I'm a sitting duck. I'm a dead man.

The car engine burst into life.

Thank God!

John crunched the gear stick into first and stamped on the accelerator.

CRACK!

The rear window exploded with a deluge of glass.

If Daly had been a decent shot, John knew he'd be dead by now.

With the tyres skidding on the dirt of the car park, John pulled the car left, clipping a van before straightening. For a second, he caught Bernie's eye as he sped out onto the main road and escaped.

CHAPTER 49

Two minutes since Bernie had dropped the bombshell about John, Gareth peered across the interview table, trying not to look completely shocked. 'You mean to tell me that John Kelly joined the Irish Guards, was recruited into the SAS and won a Victoria Cross in the Gulf War given to him at Buckingham Palace, *while* he was a member of the IRA?'

'I know.' Bernie cackled. 'It was a stroke of genius on our part, don't you think? His codename was Lazarus. It's a biblical reference. He became this mystical figure . . . The only problem was that his SAS unit weren't posted to Ireland, so it took John twelve years to get to Belfast.'

Laura couldn't get her head around it. *John, a sleeper agent inside the British Army?*

Gareth shook his head. 'And they asked him to go under-cover in the IRA?'

Bernie nodded. 'There's a beautiful symmetry to it, don't you think?'

'Not really,' Laura said coldly. Bernie's smugness was getting right up her nose. 'But from what I understand, John Doyle didn't make himself known to the Belfast Brigade immediately.'

Bernie raised an eyebrow. 'John didn't reveal to anyone

308

that he was, in fact, Lazarus, except me. He worked specifically for the Newry Brigade. They were suspicious of what was going on with the Real IRA in Belfast. They wanted John to report back to them and not reveal who he was.'

Laura shook her head. 'He was spying for the Newry Brigade on the Real IRA?'

'Exactly.'

'But he told you that?' Gareth asked.

'Yeah, he told me the day that Frank Daly tried to assassinate him. And a few days before Military Intelligence came and took him out of Ireland.'

Laura looked over at her. 'And you didn't tell anyone inside the Belfast Brigade who he actually was?'

'God, no,' Bernie snorted. 'All hell would have broken loose. That would have started a civil war in the IRA. And I didn't want some fella coming up from Newry and putting a bullet in my head.'

There were a few seconds of silence as Laura and Gareth took in all that she'd told them.

'So, what were you doing in Anglesey?' Gareth enquired.

'I came to warn John that his life was in danger,' Bernie replied.

'From members of the Belfast Brigade?' Laura asked.

'What?' Bernie looked at them as if they were mad. 'No, from your lot. MI5 and Special Branch.'

Gareth frowned. 'Why would he be in danger from them?'

'I don't understand how you don't know any of this,' Bernie said with a withering sigh. 'In September 1998, John's identity as Lazarus became compromised. Someone somewhere let it slip who John Doyle actually was. That meant Military Intelligence knew the man now called John Finn, living under UK Witness Protection on Anglesey, was a double agent working for the IRA.'

Laura suddenly had a dark thought. 'Are you trying to tell

us that John was murdered by British Military Intelligence because they'd found out he was a member of the IRA?'

'It's taken you a while, but yes, that's exactly what I'm telling you,' Bernie said sarcastically. 'I spoke to John several times in September while he was living with Jenny. I told him he needed to leave Anglesey before they sent someone to assassinate him. When he refused, I jumped on a plane to persuade him face to face.'

'You arrived on Anglesey on the second of October,' Laura stated, looking down at one of the documents in front of her. 'When did you leave?'

'I got a ferry back to Dublin on the fourth – two days later,' Bernie explained confidently.

'Can you prove it?' Gareth asked dubiously.

'Yes.'

Bernie pulled over a folder that was in front of Flanaghan. She reached inside, extracted a photograph and turned it to show them. It was an image of Bernie, wind in her hair, sitting by the railings of what looked like a ferry with the sea stretched out behind her.

Gareth peered at it and shrugged. 'Yeah, that just proves you were on a ferry once.'

Bernie turned over the photograph. It had a small date stamp on it as all photographs did before the digital age: 04.10.99

'It was taken by a lovely old American couple who were on their way to Ireland to research their ancestry. I never thought I'd have to use it in a police interview.'

Laura looked at Gareth. The photo effectively proved that Bernie didn't murder John.

Bernie looked at them. 'Listen, I loved John. And I'm really sad that his life ended so horribly. But you need to be looking far closer to home as to who killed him.'

*   *   *

310

Gareth had called in the whole CID team to get them up to speed. He was convinced that Weller was guilty of Frank Daly and Rhys Hughes' murders. However, the focus of the John Finn investigation had changed again.

Laura was sitting close to the scene boards, looking up at the growing array of photographs, maps and information. The investigations had shifted track numerous times. Three murders, with changing prime suspects – it wasn't like anything she'd worked on before.

'I'm confused,' Ben stated with a frown as he pointed to the scene board. 'So, MI5 and Military Intelligence sent that man, John Finn, or whatever we now call him, to work undercover in the IRA? Except he was already in the IRA and had been for over ten years.'

'Exactly,' Gareth said. 'John was a double agent.'

Declan looked over. 'What was he doing for the twelve years before he was sent to Ireland?'

'He fought with the SAS in the Gulf War,' Gareth said. 'Then Bosnia in the mid-nineties.'

Laura looked up at some of the photos. Close to where she was sitting was the enlarged photograph that had been taken at The Panton Arms on the night John had disappeared. At the centre of the photograph was John holding an enormous cheque, handing it to another man, whom she assumed worked for the local hospice they'd raised money for. Now that she looked at the image, it was clear that John had deliberately tilted his face away from the camera so that it wasn't clear at all. Given that he was in a Witness Protection Scheme, that wasn't a huge surprise.

Andrea sat forwards in her chair. 'And if we believe Bernie Maguire, MI5, Special Branch or whoever sent someone to Anglesey to assassinate John. And we think that happened on the night he disappeared?'

'This is sounding bloody ridiculous,' Declan groaned as he shook his head.

Gareth shrugged. 'That's only if we believe what Bernie told us.'

'Maybe Laura and I should pay Jenny Maldini another visit and see if she was aware of any of this,' Andrea suggested.

Gareth looked at her and nodded. 'Good idea.'

Ben shook his head. 'Do we really think some MI5 assassin arrived secretly on the island to assassinate John?'

Gareth shrugged. 'I know it sounds like some terrible movie and very far-fetched, but we do have to pursue it as a line of enquiry nonetheless. At least until we run it past the appropriate authorities.'

Andrea gave him a withering look. 'No one is ever going to let us poke about in that, are they? It's probably protected by the Official Secrets Act, for starters.'

Although Laura agreed with what Andrea had said, something in the photograph had caught her eye. A face in the background, over by the pub door.

'I know who killed him,' Laura blurted as she got up from her seat and went over to the photo.

Everyone stopped talking and looked her way.

Laura peered closely at the photograph to confirm her suspicions.

'This is going to sound mad, but I'm 99 per cent certain that's DI Amis standing by the door,' Laura said.

'What?' Gareth headed over to take a look. 'Jesus, you're right.'

Laura frowned. 'Amis told us the last time he saw John was when he dropped him here in November 1998.'

Gareth perched himself on a nearby table and rubbed his hand over his scalp. 'Why would he lie to us unless he had something to hide?'

Declan narrowed his eyes. 'Why would DI Amis be in that

pub on the night we believe John was murdered unless he had something to do with it? There's no way it's coincidental.'

Gareth gave the CID team a dark look. 'This is way above my pay grade, I'm afraid. But a British police officer being involved in the murder of an IRA double agent is going to cause one hell of a shitstorm.'

'Don't we need to interview Amis?' Ben enquired.

'We do,' Gareth said. 'But not before I go upstairs and run it past Warlow.'

Laura frowned as something occurred to her. 'Aren't we forgetting something?'

'Go on,' Gareth said.

'What about the woman who was seen in the car park with John?' Laura asked. 'We know she's not Bernie Maguire, because she wasn't in the country.'

Andrea looked at her. 'Jenny Maldini?'

CHAPTER 50

Andrea and Laura were sitting in Jenny Maldini's kitchen. It was cluttered but clean, and smelled of burned toast and coffee. Jenny grabbed two mugs from the cupboard and poured coffee for Andrea and Laura before bringing them over to the table.

'Thanks,' Laura said with a kind smile.

Jenny looked tired and drawn.

'Do you have any idea when I might get John's remains back?' Jenny enquired tentatively. 'I'd like to have them cremated and scatter his ashes somewhere nice.'

'We're not sure,' Laura explained. 'We're running some tests over at Bangor University and then it's down to the coroner to decide when his remains can be released. But we'll let you know as soon as we hear anything.'

Jenny nodded sadly. 'Thank you.'

'There are a few more questions we'd like to ask you.' Andrea fished her notebook from her jacket pocket. 'If that's okay?'

'Yeah,' Jenny said quietly.

Laura took a sip of her coffee. It was hot and strong and just what she needed after the emotional turmoil of the morning so far.

'We'd like to ask you what John told you about his life before he came to Anglesey,' Andrea said.

Jenny shrugged. 'He didn't tell me much. He told me he'd been in the Irish Guards, then the SAS. He'd won a medal in the Gulf War.'

'Anything else?' Laura enquired.

'Not really,' Jenny replied. 'I don't think he liked to talk about it much.'

'What about Ireland?' Laura enquired. 'Did he talk about his family or his childhood?'

'A little. He said that his family hadn't wanted him to go into the British Army. I think he lost touch with them after he left.'

Either Jenny was an incredibly good liar, or John had kept up the story he'd told Military Intelligence and Witness Protection.

Laura looked at her. 'I think this is going to come as a bit of a shock, then. Did you know John was part of the UK Protected Persons Service?'

Jenny frowned. She had no idea what Laura was talking about. 'What's that?'

'It means that he was in Witness Protection,' Andrea explained.

'No, he wasn't.' Jenny pulled a face. 'He'd have told me if he'd been in some kind of Witness Protection.'

Laura and Andrea looked at each other. They were about to open a whole can of worms, which would turn everything Jenny knew about John upside down. It was difficult to know how much they needed to tell her. There was certainly no reason to tell her that John had been a double agent who had actually been working for the IRA. At the moment, that information was politically explosive and there was nothing to gain from Jenny knowing.

'John never mentioned anything about that at all?' Laura enquired.

'No.' Jenny looked upset. 'I don't understand. If John had been in the army, why would he need to go into Witness Protection?'

'We can't discuss the full details with you at the moment, as they're protected under the Official Secrets Act,' Laura said. 'But what I can tell you is that John worked in Northern Ireland. And the work he did there meant that his life was in danger.'

'Jesus.' Jenny sighed as she shook her head. 'I didn't know any of that. I feel so stupid.'

Laura shrugged and gave her a comforting look. 'I guess he just wanted to start a new life here without all the baggage of what he'd done before.'

Jenny took some comfort in what Laura had said. 'Yeah, I suppose that makes sense.' Then something occurred to her. 'Is that why he was talking to that woman in Belfast?'

'I'm really sorry, but we can't discuss that with you at the moment,' Laura replied.

Jenny stared into space. Even though she'd spent less than a year with John, she was still shocked by what they'd told her.

'And you think that all this stuff in Ireland and the Witness Protection is why John was killed?' Jenny enquired.

'I'm afraid so,' Laura said.

Jenny looked at them. 'I always thought it was something to do with Mark Weller. After John had threatened to sort him out. You know, because Mark attacked me.'

Laura nodded. 'We're not ruling anything out at the moment, Jenny. But at present, we're working on the theory that John was killed by someone who was connected to his past rather than someone he'd met here on the island.'

Andrea shifted forwards. 'We also have an eyewitness who saw John in a car with a woman in the pub car park. Is there anyone you think that can be?'

Jenny shook her head slowly. 'I've told you before – I don't have any idea.'

Laura waited for a second. 'And there's no way it could have been you that night?'

'I told you – I was at home.' Jenny looked upset at the suggestion. 'I don't understand why you don't believe me.'

Warlow had been completely rattled by what Gareth had told him about John's work as a double agent and their suspicions about DI Amis.

'I'll need to run this past the chief constable, for starters,' Warlow explained, scratching his head. 'What do we know about DI Amis?'

'He works for the UKPPS and is based in Manchester,' Gareth stated. 'Their office deals with the North West and Wales.'

Warlow went to his computer and tapped at the keys. 'I should be able to access his personnel file from here.'

'The fact that he lied to us about being on Anglesey the night John was killed is incredibly suspicious, sir,' Gareth said.

'I agree.' Warlow peered at the screen as he read from Amis' personnel file. 'Detective Inspector Roger Amis. Born in Harrogate in 1962. He's been working at the PPS since 1997. Before that he worked as a detective sergeant in Cumbria.' Warlow stopped and glanced at Gareth. 'Amis was a detective constable attached to Special Branch in Northern Ireland from 1992 to 1995.'

'I don't think there's any crossover with John's time in Belfast,' Gareth said, wondering if there was a connection. 'But I'm guessing that his experience in Ireland would have coloured his view of the IRA.'

'Especially if he thought he'd just helped a member set up a new life, with a new identity on Anglesey, courtesy of Her Majesty's Government,' Warlow pointed out.

317

Gareth took a breath. 'I'm wondering if he was working off his own bat. There is no way that a DI working with the UKPPS would be instructed to carry out a murder. That's the stuff of fiction.'

'I agree with you there,' Warlow said.

Gareth was thinking out loud as he began to speculate. 'But if he felt that he'd been tricked into helping a member of the IRA, especially one who had infiltrated the British Army and British Intelligence, escaped justice and had a nice new life, then maybe he'd have travelled to Anglesey to put things right.'

'We have to go and talk to him for starters.' Warlow was using the royal *we*. 'And we have to treat Amis with kid gloves at this stage.'

'What about the IOPC?' Gareth enquired, referring to the Independent Office for Police Conduct.

They conducted independent investigations into serious allegations of misconduct or criminal offences by police officers and were effectively the force's Internal Affairs Unit.

Warlow shook his head. 'I think we should wait until we've spoken to Amis and let him tell us his side of the story. Once we hand over to the IOPC, all hell will break loose and I think this needs to be managed very carefully to start with.'

'Can you arrange for us to talk to Amis as a matter of urgency?' Gareth asked.

Warlow nodded. 'I'll ring the PPC now.'

CHAPTER 51

As Laura and Gareth joined the M53 towards Liverpool, she checked her watch. It was 9.23 a.m. Warlow had spoken to the chief constables of both North Wales Police and Merseyside Police. At this stage, there was no disciplinary action being taken against Amis until he'd been interviewed by Laura and Gareth.

Laura gazed over at the Cheshire Oaks Retail Park in Ellesmere Port. She and Gareth had exchanged pleasantries at Beaumaris Police Station, but since then they'd driven in an awkward silence.

'I'm sorry to hear about Elvis,' Gareth said eventually. 'Is he going to be okay?'

'Yes,' Laura replied, her voice tight.

'Rosie and Jake must have been very upset?'

Given what he'd done, Laura didn't want Gareth talking about her children, but it felt churlish not to respond.

'They were. They've gone to stay with a family friend on the mainland,' she said quietly.

There was a frosty silence.

Gareth looked over at her. 'Don't we need to talk?'

Laura continued to look out of the window. The fact that

319

Gareth had slept with Nell had hurt her pride and damaged her self-esteem. Why hadn't she been enough? Why hadn't his feelings for her been strong enough for him to resist his ex-wife?

'I don't know what there is to talk about,' she said.

'Really?'

There were a few more seconds of tense silence.

'What do you want me to say? Hey, you know what, Gareth. I think it's completely fine that you slept with your ex-wife while we were meant to be having some kind of relationship. I know your fragile male ego took a bit of a battering when she left you for another man, so shagging her probably made you feel a lot better about that. You must have got rid of all that anger, jealousy and self-loathing when you fucked her, so I'm really glad you feel a lot better. Let's just carry on as we were.'

Silence.

'I don't think you know how much I regret what I did,' Gareth said quietly.

'Regret doing it, or regret telling me?' she snapped.

'I told you because I wanted us to have a clean slate, with no lies or secrets.'

'Us? There is no *us*!' She sighed in a withering tone. 'How am I meant to trust you ever again? How do I know that the next time you're feeling needy or vulnerable and Nell turns up on your doorstep, you're not going to take her straight upstairs?'

'I won't. I'm so sorry. It was a moment of madness.' Gareth sounded desperate.

'Yeah, well I don't trust you. I've got a very vulnerable little boy at home to look after. And a daughter who's about to leave home and needs all my help doing that, after all she's been through. I can't allow you to come into my life and fuck with my head. I won't allow it.'

'I really do understand that. And if you need time, that's okay.'

'I don't need time. I allowed myself to be vulnerable, and that was stupid. And I have no intention of doing that again.'

'But we're so good together.'

She sighed. 'That's not enough. And we've got a long day ahead of us, so I'd really prefer it if we stopped talking about this right now.'

'Okay.' Gareth looked at the road ahead. His phone rang and he answered.

'Ben?' he said. After a few seconds, he said solemnly, 'Okay, thanks for letting me know.'

'Problem?'

'A body found hanging in the woods at Baron Hill Golf Club has been confirmed as Mark Weller,' Gareth said. 'Declan went down there. There's no suggestion of foul play.'

It was eleven a.m. by the time Laura and Gareth arrived at Merseyside Police Headquarters in Grosvenor Street, Liverpool. They'd been shown into a modern interview room with large glass doors and a long table. Laura thought it looked like a conference room in a business hotel.

The doors opened, and Amis and his Police Federation rep came in and sat down opposite them. Amis avoided looking at them and instead talked to his rep in a hushed voice.

'Okay.' Gareth looked over at them. 'I'm going to start.' He leaned forwards and pressed the red recording button. There was a long electronic beep. 'Interview with Detective Inspector Roger Amis. Present are Detective Inspector Laura Hart, Detective Inspector Gareth Williams, and DI Amis' Police Federation representative, Detective Chief Inspector Charles Moffat. Please identify yourselves for the DIR.'

The four officers said their names in turn.

Laura looked over at Amis. 'DI Amis, you do not have to say anything, but it may harm your defence if you do not mention, when questioned, something you later rely on in court. Anything you do say may be used in evidence. Do you understand?'

'Yes,' Amis said confidently.

'Could you tell us the last time you were on Anglesey?' Gareth asked.

'Yes, of course. October 1999.'

Laura glanced at Gareth. *Looks like he's not going to deny it, then.*

Gareth leaned forwards, opened a folder and took out a photograph. 'For the purposes of the tape, I'm showing DI Amis a photograph, item reference E232.'

Gareth turned the photograph to show Amis. 'This photograph was taken on the night of the twelfth of October 1999 at The Panton Arms pub on Anglesey. At the centre of this photograph is a man we know as John Finn, who we believe was murdered that evening. On this side of the photograph, at the back, is a man who we believe is you, DI Amis. Can you confirm that?'

Amis leaned over towards Moffat and they talked for a few seconds before Amis replied. 'Yes. I can confirm that's me.'

'DI Amis, you work for the UK Protected Persons Service, don't you?' Gareth asked.

'Yes, I do,' he said.

If Amis was feeling under pressure, he certainly wasn't showing it.

'Can you tell us what your relationship was to John Finn?'

'John Finn's real name was Sergeant John Kelly,' Amis explained. 'He was an SAS officer who was recruited by Military Intelligence to infiltrate the Real IRA, in particular the West Belfast Brigade. John was successful in this but was

322

unable to forewarn Military Intelligence or the British Army about the Omagh bombing that took place in August 1998.

'Both John and members of MI5 and Special Branch believed that his identity had somehow been compromised and that his life was in danger. It was my job to create a new identity and to relocate him. In September 1998, I brought the man you have identified as John Finn to Anglesey. We set him up with a job and a home.'

'And you kept in regular contact with John after that?' Laura enquired.

'Yes. At first we spoke on a weekly basis and then more sporadically,' Amis stated. 'John reported he'd settled into the local community and was happy.'

Gareth pointed to the photograph. 'You told us when we spoke to you previously that the last time you saw John or visited Anglesey was in September 1998.'

Amis looked over and nodded confidently. 'Yes, I did.'

Laura was confused by Amis' unwavering confidence in the interview. He wasn't trying to hide the fact that he was in The Panton Arms the night that John had been murdered. Why?

'Can you tell us why?' Gareth asked.

'At the end of August 1999, a rumour began that the IRA had placed someone undercover who worked undercover within the British Army for over twelve years. MI5 investigated the allegations and found that this agent had not only been a member of the SAS, but they'd also been posted to Belfast to infiltrate the IRA. He'd effectively been working as a double agent,' Amis said, sitting forwards in his seat. 'When we learned this individual was now in UK Witness Protection, we knew that it was John Kelly.'

Laura raised an eyebrow. 'That must have come as quite a shock.'

Amis narrowed his eyes. 'The potential ramifications of this were politically explosive. If the media ever got hold of the fact that the IRA had a man in the British Army . . . Jesus.'

'You still haven't told us what you were doing in The Panton Arms that night,' Laura said with a frown.

'I'd come to take John back to the British mainland,' Amis explained. 'And I hoped he'd come with me quietly, and without any fuss.'

'As far as I know, there's no record of that with the police on Anglesey,' Gareth said.

'There wouldn't be. I've explained how sensitive the situation was. There were only a handful of people within Witness Protection and MI5 who knew who John really was and we needed to keep it that way.'

'So, what happened?' Laura asked. 'How did John end up disappearing that night?'

Amis shook his head. 'I have no idea. I was in The Panton Arms for around fifteen minutes. That photograph was taken just as I entered the pub. Before I could make contact with John, he'd disappeared towards the bar. The pub was incredibly crowded that night, so it was difficult to move around. I spent the next fifteen minutes searching for him, but as far as I could see, he'd vanished.'

Laura wasn't sure that she was buying what Amis was telling them. Would they really go to Anglesey to try to persuade John to hand himself over? What then? If he was later tried for criminal offences, his story would become public. Wouldn't it be better for everyone if John just disappeared?

'Is there anyone who can verify any of this?' Laura asked.

'Yes.' Amis reached into a folder and pulled out two pieces of paper. 'I had two detective constables from the PPS sitting outside in a car in case John decided to do a runner. These are their sworn and signed affidavits as to the events of that night. And of course you're more than welcome to interview them, too.'

Laura exchanged a frustrated look with Gareth. It certainly looked as if Amis was telling the truth and had been as mystified about John's disappearance as everyone else. They were back to square one – again.

CHAPTER 52

Belfast 1998

John parked on a narrow lane that bordered the slender
Lagan Canal, built in the 1700s to link Belfast to Lisburn.
He was due to meet a man named Jack Hills who had stolen
the Vauxhall Cavalier that was used in the Omagh bombing.
Hills had confirmed that it had been Frank Daly who had
tasked him with stealing the car. Daly had made it clear it
was going to be used as a car bomb.

Hills was on the fringes of the West Belfast Brigade, but
to all intents and purposes, he was a civilian. More impor-
tantly, Daly had shagged Hills' wife the previous year – a
fact that had only just come out the previous week during
an almighty matrimonial row. Hills had confided in John
when he was drunk in a local pub a few nights earlier.

Hills had told John he had it in for Daly and was looking
for revenge. It was just the break that John was looking for.
If he could persuade Hills to go on record that Daly had
directly ordered him to steal the car that was going to be
used as a bomb, it would go a long way to convicting Daly.
The boys over in Newry had made it clear that Daly was a

loose cannon who they wanted off the streets. Either dead or in prison – they didn't care.

John stared over the sullen water of the canal. In the distance, a forklift truck on a building site moved concrete slabs. He glanced at his watch. It was 2.05 p.m. Hills was only five minutes late.

Stepping off the kerb, John glanced down the road.

Suddenly, a car screeched to a halt beside him, its back doors opening as it stopped. Before he could react, two strapping men had virtually lifted him off the ground and bundled him into the back of a car.

Shit! Daly.

John knew how this was going to go. He'd be hooded, driven out of Belfast, shot and left by the side of the road or in a ditch. He'd taken a massive risk by staying on the streets of Belfast and it had backfired.

He struggled, but the men pinned him down. They pulled him up so that he sat on the back seat between them.

That's weird. No punches, kicks, hood or ties?

Glancing at the two men, he immediately knew they weren't IRA. And they weren't Provo terrorists, either.

'We've been told to bring you in, sergeant,' one of the men said.

They were British Military Intelligence officers.

'You can't do that!' John thundered. 'I've got an agreement with Captain Palmer.'

There was a sudden explosion and flash of light.

Turning round, John saw that his car had been ripped to pieces by a bomb and was now engulfed in huge orange flames. It had all the hallmarks of Frank Daly. John knew his time in Belfast was over.

CHAPTER 53

It was mid-afternoon and the CID team was assembled. Gareth felt deflated. There had been more lines of enquiry than he could ever remember in any case he'd ever worked. And at the moment, all of them had either proved to be wrong or there wasn't sufficient evidence to take them further. On top of that, he'd managed to bugger up the best relationship he'd had in over a decade.

'Right, guys.' Gareth perched on his usual table at the front of the office. 'Let's start with our mystery woman who John was embracing in the car park before sitting in her car. Where does she come into this?'

Laura frowned. 'We've established that it can't be Bernie Maguire, so who was she?'

Declan, who was gazing at his computer screen, looked up at them all. 'I know exactly who she was.'

Laura raised an eyebrow. 'What? How?'

Declan pointed to his screen. 'Pete Bishop remembered that the car that he saw our mystery woman and John in that night was a dark green Peugeot 406. And according to the DVLA, Jenny Maldini's mother had a dark green Peugeot 406 registered to her in 1999.'

Gareth narrowed his eyes. 'Eh? How does that work? It makes sense that they were seen embracing in the car park. It also makes sense that they were in her car together. But John was murdered that night. Are we saying that Jenny Maldini murdered John?'

Declan shrugged. 'Why would she murder him?'

'Mark Weller told us that Jenny was all over him like a rash the night she claimed that he sexually assaulted her,' Andrea stated. 'We didn't believe Weller because he's a scumbag. But what if Weller and Jenny actually had an affair? She lured him into her car, where Weller is lying in wait. They kill John and bury him a few days later.'

Laura looked puzzled. 'That works as a hypothesis. But I wonder if the motive was different and whether or not there was something going on between John and Bernie Maguire. We know they spoke on the phone regularly. And then she travelled from Dublin to Anglesey to persuade him that his life was in real danger. What if something happened between them when she was over? Maybe Jenny was worried John was going to leave her for Bernie. She lured him into her car that night and killed him.'

Gareth thrust his hands deep into his pockets. 'Clearly, the first thing we have to do right now is see what Jenny has to say for herself.'

Laura looked over at Andrea. 'We've established a rapport with her. I think me and Andrea should go and talk to her.'

Gareth nodded in agreement.

Laura and Andrea got out of their car. The island was covered by ominous low black cloud that hid the sun. Looking around, Laura got her bearings. Beaumaris was about three to four miles directly to the east. The Menai Strait and the Menai Bridge only two or three miles due south. Even though she'd left Anglesey for a period of time, that internal map of her childhood had stayed with her. People from the mainland saw Anglesey as one community. But it wasn't like that at all. She'd grown up in Beaumaris and felt no more affinity to those in Holyhead or Rhosneigr, as she did to the communities just over the strait in Bangor or Llanfairfechan.

Traipsing across the car park, Laura and Andrea made their way towards reception, where they'd encountered Duncan, the bearded man with the ponytail, a few days ago. The barking noise of a speeding Canada goose drew Laura's attention over the lake. She recognised its distinctive black neck and head, its grey-brown back and white cheek patches as it skittered along the surface of the water, its feet skimming it with tiny splashes. A moment later, it was joined by three more geese. They flew in formation like RAF Spitfires at a display, moving with total synchronicity. And she was taken back to her taid, who had taken her and her sister to a small lake close to their farmhouse to sail a wooden boat that he'd built during the winter months. It had sailed perfectly across the water. And then she had a thought.

That's who Gareth reminds me of. It's my taid. His quiet strength.

She hadn't really allowed herself to process Gareth's confession about the night he'd spent with Nell. There was part of her that wondered if she'd reacted with such anger and indignation because her pride and ego had been wounded. Why wasn't she enough in that moment for him to reject Nell? But if she really examined it with some objectivity, she could see the damage that Nell had done to him when she left him for another man. Laura had listened to Gareth blaming himself, his job, his failure to give her the attention and time she required. But she wondered where all his anger and seething resentment was. Maybe he was just too scared to reveal that side of himself to her. And however wrong, sleeping with her must have lessened the self-loathing, fury and emotional pain. Nell had come back to him, even if it was for a fleeting moment.

'After you, boss,' Andrea said, opening the door to the reception area and breaking Laura's train of thought.

'Thanks.'

A man and woman sat behind the desk. They were oblivious as they busied themselves with some kind of paperwork. The man was thin and gangly, with a face that tapered severely into an apology of a chin. The woman had tiny round eyes set like buttons, a short kink of a nose, skin speckled with moles and long, lank hair. They were what Sam would have once described as 'hard on the eye'.

Laura got out her warrant card. 'Hi there. DI Hart and DC Jones from Beaumaris CID. We're looking for Jenny Maldini.'

The woman looked at her. 'She is gone. Finish.' She had an Eastern European accent, probably Polish, given North Wales' large Polish community.

'Oh, okay,' Laura said, looking at her watch, not entirely certain what she meant. 'Finished her shift for the day, then?'

That was fine. They'd drive down to Jenny's house to talk to her.

The woman shook her head to show they'd misunderstood. 'No, no. I mean Jenny not work here anymore. She finish today.'

Laura and Andrea looked at each other. *Really?*

The man looked over and scratched his stubbly chin. 'Bit of a bolt from the blue, if I'm honest.'

'She quit her job today?' Andrea asked to clarify.

'Yeah,' the man said. 'I thought she'd have given us a bit of notice. She's worked here for donkey's years.'

Laura frowned. 'Did she say why?'

The woman nodded. 'She say she has to go away.'

'Did she say where she was going?' Andrea enquired.

The man shook his head. 'She was in a bit of a rush.'

'Okay, thanks,' Laura said. 'Is there anywhere you can think where she might have gone?'

The man shook his head. 'Jenny keeps herself to herself.'

The woman frowned. 'She say she always wanted to visit Ireland. But she told me that months ago.'

Laura looked over at Andrea and saw her own shock reflected back at her.

CHAPTER 54

Laura and Andrea sped through the driving rain, covering the three miles over to Jenny Maldini's home in a matter of minutes. They got out of the car. Thick black clouds were rolling in from the west and there had been the first sounds of thunder.

'Her car's here.' Andrea pointed to an old red Ford Focus on the driveway.

Jogging up the garden path, Laura knocked authoritatively on the door.

Nothing.

Andrea moved over to a downstairs window, cupped her hands and looked inside.

'Anything?'

Andrea shook her head. 'Nothing, boss.'

Laura knocked again, and this time listened for any tell-tale signs of movement from inside.

Still nothing.

'If you're looking for Jenny, I think she said she was going away,' a neighbour called over as he went over to a parked car.

'Did she say where?' Laura asked in a raised voice.

The man shrugged as he got into his car. 'Sorry. No.'

Andrea pointed to the side of the house, where there was a gate and passageway. 'What about down here, boss?'

Laura nodded and followed. She could feel that her hair was now matting to her head and forehead.

Andrea opened the gate and they proceeded down the side of the house towards the back garden. Water was streaming from above where a gutter was blocked. Emerging onto a small patio, Laura could see the garden had a neat lawn and tidy flowerbeds. She moved across to the patio doors and peered inside. The living room was empty except for a sofa. No other furniture, no television, nothing on the walls – it was bare.

'Looks to me like she's moved out,' Laura stated.

Andrea frowned. 'She's left her job, and it looks like she's moving somewhere. But she didn't inform us, which you'd expect her to do, seeing as she claimed to be concerned about John's remains.'

'Yeah, you would.' Laura raised a suspicious eyebrow.

Then she heard a noise. The deep sound of a car engine. And it was close. She glanced at Andrea.

'Shit!' they said in unison.

Clearly, they'd both had the same thought. It was the sound of the engine of the Ford Focus on Jenny's drive.

Are you kidding me?

'Come on!' Laura yelled as they turned and sprinted back down the passageway, only to see Jenny's Ford Focus speed off the drive and then zoom away with a screech of tyres.

They bolted towards their car and Andrea clicked her radio.

'Control from Yankee six-three, over.'

'Yankee six-three from Control. Go ahead, over.'

'We are in pursuit of possible suspect, Jenny Maldini. Red Ford Focus, registration unknown, heading north towards Pentraeth on the B5109. Over.'

334

'Received. Stand by, over.'

They jumped into the car. Andrea turned the ignition and hit the accelerator, spinning the wheels as they set off in pursuit.

'What the hell is she doing?' Laura asked rhetorically as Andrea built up speed.

Jenny's Ford Focus was still nowhere to be seen.

'Whatever it is, she's scared enough to run from us.'

They hit 70 mph in less than a minute. Laura gripped the door handle with one hand and the dashboard with the other as the car screamed round a bend.

Andrea sat forwards a little, peering through the windscreen. 'Where the hell is she?'

Jenny's Focus came into view, speeding up a hill ahead of them. Laura felt the Astra's back tyres losing grip and slipping as they cornered another bend.

Andrea took a quick look at her. 'You okay, boss?'

'Brilliant,' she replied dryly.

High-speed pursuits had never been her favourite part of the job. She knew plenty of officers who thought the opposite and loved the adrenaline rush.

Andrea went hammering up the hill and over the crest. Jenny's Focus was now only about half a mile ahead, and they were gaining. Andrea pulled out to overtake a car towing a caravan and shot past it.

'The fact that Jenny quit her job, packed up her stuff and is now trying to escape is an admission of guilt, isn't it?' Laura said.

'It has to be. Why do all that if you have nothing to hide and you're innocent?'

'She must have met John in the car park at The Panton Arms,' Laura said. 'And for some reason, they then decided to leave there together.'

Laura suspected Jenny wouldn't stop now and would be driven on by fear. She grabbed the radio.

'Control from Yankee six-three, received. Suspect still heading west on the B5109. One mile south of Talwrn. Over.'

A moment later, they careered through the tiny village of Talwrn and screeched round a bend beyond. They were going so fast that Laura felt the houses and stone walls were only inches from the passenger door.

Ahead, a transit van pulled out of a turning in front of them. Andrea swung the car onto the opposite side of the road, missing it by a few feet, throwing Laura hard against the passenger door.

'You bloody idiot!' Andrea bellowed at the driver.

Laura closed her eyes for a second as they careered around another bend.

Jenny's Focus was now only 500 yards away. It pulled out to overtake and whizzed past two cars. As Andrea pulled out to do the same, an enormous tractor was coming the other way.

Laura's eyes widened.

Oh shit. We're never going to make it!

Andrea slammed the car down into third gear and gunned the engine. Laura felt herself being pushed back into her chair as they zipped through the gap with inches to spare.

'Sorry,' Andrea said, still looking at the road ahead with determination.

Laura gave her a wry smile. 'That was an impressive piece of driving.'

'Thanks.'

'Impressive and terrifying.'

Just as Laura's gaze returned to the road, an old blue Land Rover pulled out in front of them.

'Jesus!' she gasped through gritted teeth as Andrea slammed on the brakes.

Laura felt the Astra's tyres skidding as the car went sideways. Laura felt like everything in her body was contracting as the Astra continued to skid at speed towards the Land Rover. She instinctively pulled her knees up and screwed her eyes closed.

A thunderous metallic smash threw her forwards. The sound of glass. The sensation of spinning. Now they were travelling backwards. After a few more seconds, they came to a stop.

Laura blinked and immediately looked over at Andrea. She looked back at her and blew out her cheeks.

'You all right?' Andrea asked.

'Yeah, I think so,' Laura gasped, getting her breath back.

They both looked at the road ahead – Jenny Maldini was out of sight.

'Shit!' Laura growled.

It was twenty minutes later by the time Laura and Andrea arrived at Holyhead, where the ferries travelled over to Dublin. With the mention of Ireland, it was the only lead they had. Gareth had put out a request for all units to be on the lookout for Jenny's car, but so far they'd drawn a blank. The rain had stopped and the black clouds seemed to have retreated to the east.

Pulling into the enormous Holyhead Port, they scoured the area to see if they could see Jenny or her car. There were cars and lorries everywhere – they were essentially looking for a needle in a haystack.

Getting out of the car, Laura looked over at a rotund security guard who was wearing an orange hi-vis vest and carrying a clipboard.

She pulled out her warrant card. 'Afternoon. We're over from Beaumaris CID.'

'Right you are.' The security guard nodded – he was eager to help.

'Can you tell us when the next ferry leaves for Dublin?' she asked.

He pointed further along the port side. 'It hasn't even moved into dock yet. It goes in just over two hours.'

Andrea looked at him. 'If I was a passenger waiting for that ferry, is there somewhere I could go to get food and drink?'

The security guard pointed to an extensive building down on the right. 'Yeah. The terminal centre down there has got fast-food places, coffee, bookshops and toilets. I'd try there.'

'Thanks,' Andrea said as she and Laura made their way past the lines of articulated lorries that waited in vast lines for docks marked 'Freight'. The air was thick with diesel fumes and a hint of the Irish Sea. Gulls swooped and cawed incessantly.

A huge concourse greeted them that accommodated various food and drink outlets. Chairs and tables were spread out in little groupings outside each place and the entire area was busy with passengers walking to and fro.

For the next ten minutes, Laura and Andrea spread out to opposite sides of the concourse and scoured every shop and seating area. Eventually, they met back at the far end.

'Nothing.' Laura sighed.

'Maybe we got it wrong. It was a bit of a long shot.'

Laura nodded slowly. 'She could just as easily have headed over the Menai Bridge and escaped into England.'

Out of the corner of her eye, Laura spotted a man leaning with his back against a wall beside a coffee bar. For a moment, she wondered where she'd seen him before until she saw him move and a grey ponytail appeared.

Then it clicked.

It was the man who had been on reception at Lakeside Lodges. It was also the same one whom they'd seen in a photograph at Jenny's home and with whom they'd assumed she was having some kind of relationship.

Bloody hell. That's Duncan.

The man moved out of sight.

Am I seeing things?

'You okay, boss?' Andrea asked.

'Up there,' Laura said, pointing.

'What am I looking at?'

'Duncan, the guy with a ponytail.' Laura beckoned for Andrea to follow her. 'The one from the Lakeside place.'

Then suddenly, in the same place where the man had been standing, a woman appeared. She was wearing sunglasses, but even from a distance, Laura recognised her.

Shit! That's Jenny!

'They're over there. Come on!' Laura grabbed Andrea by the arm and they both broke into a run.

'Did they see you?'

'I don't think so.'

'And you're sure it was them?'

'Yes.' Laura gave her a scornful look. 'Come on. If we keep circling, we'll find them.'

They ran, zig-zagging their way through queues of passengers and seated areas, eyes scanning left and right.

Eventually, they arrived back at the entrance. Laura was hot and out of breath.

'Bloody hell!' Andrea gasped. 'We've been everywhere.'

By now, Laura was starting to doubt what she'd seen.

'Where would you go if you wanted to keep out of sight until your ferry arrived?' Laura asked, putting herself in Jenny's shoes.

Suddenly, two figures rose from their seats on the other side of the concourse. They headed towards the green light of the nearest fire exit.

Laura nudged Andrea and pointed.

'Over there!'

They broke into a run and, a few seconds later, Laura

smashed through the exit doors with Andrea just behind her.

They looked left and then right.

Nothing.

'Where are they?' Andrea shrieked.

Laura could hear the sound of running above them on the fire escape staircase. 'Up this way!'

Leaping up the steps, two by two, Laura felt the muscles in her thighs burn.

Jesus, it hurts.

Reaching the next floor, she glanced both ways. Nothing. The sound of running came again from above.

'Come on,' Andrea urged, as she took over the lead.

Dragging in air, they arrived at a doorway that led out onto the roof of the passenger centre. It gave them a bird's eye view of Holyhead Port, which stretched out before them. The wind whipped around their faces as they spotted Jenny and Duncan racing for the other side of the roof, where there appeared to be another doorway.

'*Stay there! Police!*' Laura yelled.

The fugitives had now reached another door with a FIRE EXIT sign. As Laura and Andrea sprinted after them, they could see the door was locked as Duncan frantically pulled at the door handle.

Right! Now they're trapped! Laura thought.

Her phone rang. It was Gareth.

Jenny and Duncan had now climbed awkwardly over the safety rail and onto the perimeter wall. Nothing now protected them from a hundred-foot drop onto the concrete below. Laura and Andrea stopped at the rail, panting.

Laura's phone rang. It was Gareth – again!

She hung up, took a deep breath and shouted at them, 'What are you doing?' before climbing over the rail herself.

'Stay where you are!' Jenny shouted at Laura before backing towards the edge.

Oh, God. If she slips now, she's going to die.

'You need to tell us what happened that night, Jenny!' Andrea yelled, raising her voice over the noise of the wind.

Duncan hadn't moved a muscle.

Jenny shook her head. 'You don't understand. I can't tell you that, can I?'

'You can't throw yourself off there, though, can you?' Laura asked, moving an inch closer.

Jenny glanced backwards. The heels of her shoes were now only a foot from the edge. The battering wind made it feel even more precarious.

'I don't understand why you can't just leave us alone,' Duncan said. 'We haven't done anything.'

Laura was now sure that his accent wasn't Glaswegian, as she'd thought before. In fact, she was certain that it wasn't Scottish.

Her phone rang again. It was Gareth.

She clicked Answer and snapped. 'I'm kind of in the middle of something here! So unless it's really bloody urgent . . .'

'The remains at Castell Aberlleiniog aren't John Finn,' Gareth said.

For a second, Laura thought she'd misheard. Then she processed what he'd just said.

'What are you talking about? Are you sure?' she blurted. Her adrenaline was running high.

'Not unless John Kelly is about three hundred and fifty years old,' Gareth explained. 'The carbon dating came back from Bangor University. The remains date from the late 1600s.'

'Okay,' Laura mumbled. 'I'm going to need to call you back.'

If the remains in that grave weren't John Finn, then where the hell were his remains?

As her mind whirled, she saw Duncan grab Jenny by the arm and pull her away from the edge.

'Come on now, Jenny. I'm not going to let you do this. We have to talk to the police.'

His accent isn't Glaswegian. It's Irish, she thought.

And then she looked at him. He was about five foot nine, of medium build. And then her eyes went to his right ear. There was a small chunk missing at the top of the cartilage.

CHAPTER 55

Newry, Northern Ireland 1986

John grabbed a couple of Penguin chocolate bars from the cupboard, shoved them into his rucksack and looked around at the kitchen. He'd lived in this house for twenty-two years, but he had no idea when or if he'd ever see it again. There were two plates up on the wall – Pope John Paul II and John F. Kennedy. Catholic heroes of the twentieth century.

When John was little, his favourite saints had been the martyrs. Men and women who had suffered torture and even death for their religion. It fascinated him. The nuns at catechism at Sunday school would smile and say, *Here he goes again, wee John Kelly and his love of the martyrs.* His favourite was Edmund Campion, a Jesuit priest who had worked secretly in London in the sixteenth century when the Catholic faith had been banned in England. Campion took a false identity, calling himself Mr Perkins and claiming that he was a jewel merchant while he secretly administered the holy sacraments and preached to Catholics. It was John's aunt Theresa, a staunch Catholic, who had often told him of Campion's bravery. She used to tell him that he needed to remember that everything he did was 'for God and for Ireland'.

Making his way down the hallway, John went into the sitting room, where members of his family were gathered to say their goodbyes. His mother had cried twice already and now dabbed at her eyes with a screwed-up tissue. He looked around at the room. Where other families might adorn their mantelpieces with happy photos from their family holidays, the Kellys displayed, with enormous pride, photos of relatives in prison or at court. Their shared commitment to the cause of Irish republicanism was unwavering. Their island was being occupied by an enemy and they needed to be exterminated by any means necessary.

'Have you got everything?' his mam asked with a forced smile.

'He's a grown man,' his father laughed, getting up from the armchair and stubbing out a cigarette.

There was a knock at the door.

John's stomach tightened. This was it.

'That'll be Jimmy.' His mam sounded flustered as she scuttled out to answer the front door.

Jimmy Murphy was her older brother. He was a commander in the South Armagh Brigade of the IRA.

John's father came over to him and placed both palms on John's shoulders.

'Do you know how proud I am of you, son?' His voice broke.

John nodded as a lump came to his throat. 'It's fine, Da. I'm gonna be fine.'

His da put his warm hand to John's face and winked. 'Of course you are. You're gonna be grand.'

Jimmy popped his head round the door and looked at John. 'You ready, sunshine?'

344

Jimmy was lithe, with a broken nose from when he used to box as a middleweight.

'Yeah.' John turned and hugged his mam, who was now sobbing. 'Hey, less of that, Mam. I'm gonna be fine.'

'I know.' She blinked away the tears.

Following Jimmy down the garden path, John threw his rucksack onto the back seat of the Ford Cortina and got into the passenger seat. As Jimmy pulled away, he looked back to see that his parents had pulled back the net curtains and were waving.

'You're gonna be fine, son,' Jimmy assured.

'Where are we going?'

'O'Neil's.' Jimmy winked.

John had been to O'Neil's pub on North Street in Crossmaglen dozens of times since he was old enough to drink. There was a back room there that was effectively the headquarters of the South Armagh Brigade of the IRA. It was also the place where six months ago, a plan had been hatched with wee John Kelly at its centre.

O'Neil's was where John had heard all the stories. Pat Gallagher, who had joined the Irish Republican Army when he was only a boy in the 1930s and gone to England to help with a bombing raid on Coventry city centre in August 1939. Five people had been killed and seventy were injured. It had been designed to show Nazi Germany how strong the IRA were in the lead-up to the Second World War.

Michael Brennan, a tall man with tobacco-stained fingertips and thick-lensed glasses, had recounted his escape from prison in Portadown, along with ten other IRA prisoners, through a tunnel they'd spent nearly six months constructing. To cover the noise of their escape, three other prisoners had played the bagpipes within the prison.

John looked wistfully out at the countryside that lay between Newry and Crossmaglen, which was about fifteen miles to the south. The skies were rolling out a dark metal canvas. Purple heather and white cotton lay on top of the peaty bogs that stretched into the distance. It was a flat, uncompromising landscape that soon turned to rocky fields and outcrops. A soft, misty rain began to fall onto the windscreen.

He glanced to the left and saw a sign for Warrenpoint, which was a small port in County Down, overlooked by the Cooley Mountains and separated from the Republic of Ireland by a narrow strait of water. It was also the place where the IRA ambushed a British Army convoy in 1979 and killed eighteen soldiers. It was still the IRA's greatest victory over the British Army during the Troubles.

'How are you feeling about tomorrow, then?' Jimmy asked.

'Fine.' John shrugged. He wasn't. He was terrified by what he was about to do.

'When do you fly?'

'Flight goes from Belfast at one p.m. tomorrow. Gets into Manchester at two,' John explained. 'Then it's two hours on the train to the barracks in Catterick.'

John had signed up to the Irish Guards in the British Army and he was about to embark on the gruelling fourteen-week Infantry Combat Training. The IRA had provided him with false papers and a false birth certificate so he could pass the British Army's background check. He was going to be the first member of the IRA to become an undercover agent in the British Army.

By the time they got to O'Neil's, John was looking forward to having a few beers to settle his nerves. He didn't like the black stuff. But a cold pint of lager would be just fine.

As he sat next to Jimmy in the back room, the older men teased John about the operation, but he knew they were kidding. It wasn't long before they toasted his good health and success.

As John finished his pint, he spotted a girl in her early twenties coming into the pub with Brendan O'Brien, a senior member of the Armagh Brigade. She was attractive and wore her fiery red hair in a ponytail. For a moment, their eyes met before she moved away to the bar and then she was gone.

CHAPTER 56

The doors opened to Interview Room 1 at Beaumaris Police Station and John Kelly was brought in wearing handcuffs. Gareth had requested that two AFOs – Authorised Firearms Officers – be stationed close to the interview room. As far as they knew, Kelly was still a member of the IRA – whether or not he was still active – and they weren't about to take any chances.

It was the first time that Gareth had got a proper look at Kelly. He spotted the missing chunk of cartilage at the top of his right ear. It was incredible to think that Kelly had done such a convincing job of faking his own death while remaining on the island.

Laura settled in the chair next to him and pulled over some papers and folders so they were in front of her. They'd chatted briefly when she returned from Holyhead as she brought him up to speed on what had happened.

'Okay.' Gareth looked over at them. 'I'm going to start.' He leaned forwards and pressed the red recording button. There was a long electronic beep. 'Interview with John Kelly. Present are Detective Inspector Laura Hart, Detective Inspector Gareth Williams and Duty Solicitor Will Newman.'

Laura looked over at him. 'John Kelly, you do not have to say anything, but it may harm your defence if you do not mention, when questioned, something you later rely on in court. Anything you do say may be used in evidence. Do you understand that?'

'Yes,' John said confidently as he sat back in his seat and crossed his legs.

Gareth leaned forwards, opened a folder and took out a photograph. 'For the purposes of the tape, I'm showing John Kelly a photograph, item reference E232.' Gareth turned the photograph, which was an image of Kelly as a soldier. 'Can you confirm that you are John Kelly, born first of October 1964 in Newry, Northern Ireland?'

'Yes, I can confirm that.' John's expression was open and relaxed.

'And you are the same John Kelly who joined the Irish Guards in 1986 and fought with the SAS in the Gulf War in 1991,' Gareth enquired.

John took a breath. 'Listen, fella, I'm going to make this very easy for everyone in here. You know exactly who I am. I came here in 1999 as part of the UK's Witness Protection Scheme. I was set up with a new identity as John Finn. We all know this and I'm not going to deny any of that.'

Well that's a refreshing relief, Gareth thought. Most interviews were a series of lies that police officers then had to pick through to discover the truth.

'However, what I do want to make clear is that Jenny had nothing to do with any of this,' John said. 'It was my idea to fake my own death. And it was my idea to remain on the island and pose as someone else.'

Gareth nodded. 'Okay, I thank you for your frankness. I can't, however, promise that Jenny won't face a charge of perverting the course of justice. She's continually lied to us in recent days, prolonging a serious police investigation. In fact, Jenny led us to believe that you'd been murdered over twenty years ago.'

John thought for a few seconds and then looked at Gareth. 'Will she go to prison?'

'That's not really a decision I can make. All I can promise is that if you and Jenny are fully cooperative with us, then we can ask that to be taken into account at sentencing.'

'I'm not sure I can do that, then.' John glared hard across the table.

'It's the best you're going to get, John,' Gareth explained.

Laura looked over at him. 'Look, it's likely that Jenny will receive a custodial sentence. She was harbouring a criminal, and she lied to police officers.'

'Jenny never knew much about my past,' John explained. 'I made sure that I didn't go into details.'

'Did she know you'd been a member of the IRA?' Gareth enquired.

'No, no way,' John said emphatically. 'I never told her about that. She knew I was in the army, the SAS, and that I'd worked in Northern Ireland. I told her that after working in Ireland, I was sent over to Anglesey for my own safety. That was it. I told her I couldn't tell her any more for her own protection.'

'Okay, so talk us through the events leading up to the twelfth of October 1999,' Laura said.

'As you know, a few months before, I got a tip-off from Belfast that British Military Intelligence had been asking a lot of questions about me and who I was to various inform-ants. It was clear that someone had let it slip that I'd been a member of the IRA since I joined the Irish Guards in 1986.' John uncrossed his legs. 'And that meant either I was going to serve a long prison sentence or worse.'

Laura frowned. 'When you say *or worse*, do you mean you thought your life could be in danger from MI5 agents or officers from Special Branch?'

350

'I had no idea.' John shrugged. 'We all know what happened in Gibraltar in 1988, though.'

Laura vaguely remembered the case – three plain-clothes SAS officers had gunned down and killed three members of the IRA in a petrol station in the British territory of Gibraltar, off the Spanish mainland. The controversy surrounding the case was that eyewitnesses claimed the three IRA suspects either had their hands raised or were lying on the ground when they were shot dead. There were no weapons or explosives found in the car they'd been travelling in. There were many who believed the men had simply been assassinated, with no evidence and no trial.

'And if it wasn't one of them directly,' John continued, 'we all know that the UVF, the UDA and the British colluded on the assassinations of IRA men. I half expected to see some Proddy scumbag popping up on my doorstep with a gun.'

Laura raised an eyebrow. 'Why didn't you just run?'

'Run and hide?' John pulled a face and let out a sigh. 'I haven't been able to live as John Kelly since I was twenty-two years old. And I'm now fifty-seven. That's thirty-five years of living as someone else. I was too tired.'

'Is that why Bernie Maguire came to Anglesey to talk to you?' Laura asked.

John couldn't hide his surprise. 'You know about that?'

'We've spoken to her,' Laura said.

'Yeah. We'd spoken on the phone and she warned me to leave. When I told her I wasn't going to do that, she flew over to see if I could be persuaded.'

'Did you know that Detective Inspector Amis was going to be at The Panton Arms on the night of the twelfth of October?' Gareth asked.

'No, of course not.' John shook his head. 'When I saw him, I panicked.'

'What happened then?' Laura enquired.

351

'I rang Jenny and told her I needed her to come and pick me up. And that I needed to find somewhere to disappear to.'

Laura looked over at Gareth. 'Yeah, we have two eyewitnesses who saw you with a woman in the car park that night.'

'Where did you go?' Gareth asked.

'Jenny's grandmother lived in a bungalow on the other side of the island. She was getting on a bit and had dementia, so she needed looking after. Jenny convinced her I worked for the local council's social care unit.'

'I assume this was Jenny's father's mother?' Laura asked.

'Oh yeah.'

'So, you stayed hidden there?' Gareth asked.

'Yeah, I stayed over there for a year. And then she died. By that time, the missing case file on me had gone cold. Everyone assumed that I'd run off somewhere.' John patted his stomach. 'I'd put on a lot of timber, wore glasses and grown a beard. My hair was going grey and it was long. Even I didn't recognise myself in the mirror sometimes. So I moved back closer to Jenny.'

'Explain the remains that we found up at Castell Aberlleiniog,' Laura said.

'Yeah, that didn't go according to plan.' John shook his head. 'The day after I went missing, Jenny and I went up to St Peter's Church and we dug up an old grave and removed the bones. Then we drove up to Castell Aberlleiniog and buried them there, making sure we dropped in the bank card and an Irish Guards pin badge, which I assumed you found?'

Gareth nodded. 'Yes, we found those.'

'I took a hammer to the back of the person's skull and their teeth just for good measure. You know, make it seem that someone had killed me. I guessed that within a year, someone would stumble on those remains. They'd find the bank card and the pin badge, put two and two together and I'd be declared dead.' John gave them a wry smile. 'Didn't think it would take over twenty bloody years for that to happen.'

Gareth looked at him. 'It wasn't until we got the carbon dating back that we realised the remains weren't you.'

'Christ, I never even thought about bloody carbon dating.' John sighed. 'The luck of the Irish, eh?'

'And you killed Frank Daly?' Laura asked.

'Yeah.'

'How did he find you?'

'I went back to Belfast. About a month ago.'

'After all this time?' Laura frowned. 'Why?'

'There's been over twenty years of peace in Northern Ireland. I believed in the Good Friday agreement. And now those arseholes in Westminster are going to undermine it with their bloody protocol. The DUP are threatening all sorts. I couldn't watch the agreement be destroyed, so I went home to see what was going on.'

'And someone spotted you?' Gareth asked, putting the pieces together.

'Yeah.' John snorted. 'Bloody Tommy Breslin did a double-take at me as I walked up Broadway. He didn't say anything, but he knew it was me. The next thing I know, Frank Daly turns up on the island asking questions. It was always going to be me or him in the end.'

'And Rhys Hughes?' Laura asked.

'He knew I wasn't dead all along. He discovered I was still alive a month after I disappeared. He pretty much black-mailed me into clearing his debts in return for his silence. Just after you questioned him, he got in contact with me, threatening to tell you what he knew unless I paid him more cash.'

'So you killed him?' Gareth asked.

'Yeah. I didn't have much choice.' John looked over at

Laura. 'For what it's worth, I'd never have harmed your dog. I love animals. In fact, I prefer animals to most human beings I've ever met.'

Laura and Gareth had been interviewing Jenny for ten minutes. She was emotional and frightened.

'I don't understand,' she said, her voice breaking. 'I don't understand how he could have been a terrorist and kept it from me.'

Laura looked over at her. 'Jenny, there are a few things in John's statement that we need to verify with you.'

Jenny nodded and wiped a tear away.

'Can you tell us why you drove to pick up John from The Panton Arms on the evening of the twelfth of October 1999?'

'John rang to say that he'd seen someone from his past. From Ireland,' she said. 'He was scared, and he wanted me to pick him up in case there was anyone else waiting outside the pub for him.'

'Can you tell us where you took him?'

'My nain lived over on Cemaes Bay. She had a bungalow over there,' Jenny explained. 'John stayed there and kept out of the way. And he cared for my nain while he was there.'

Gareth nodded. 'How long did he stay there?'

Jenny thought for a few seconds. 'It must have been over a year. We wanted to make sure that no one was looking for him anymore. He'd started wearing glasses, put on a few stone, grew a beard and wore his hair long. He was virtually unrecognisable after a while.'

'Where did you get the remains that you buried at Castell Aberlleiniog?' Laura asked.

'The graveyard at St Peter's over in Cefniwrch,' she said.

'Whose idea was it to take remains from there and bury them elsewhere and make them look as if they were John's remains?' Gareth asked.

Jenny looked at them and hesitated.

'If you're concerned, I should tell you that John claimed the idea was his and that it had nothing to do with you,' Laura said.

Jenny nodded slowly, with no expression. Then she looked at them. 'What's going to happen to John?'

'It's not something we can really discuss with you,' Gareth stated.

Jenny put her head in her hands for a moment. 'I keep going over it in my head. How could I have been so stupid not to have realised who John was?'

'He had the British Army fooled for nearly fifteen years,' Laura said. 'He was clearly good at living a lie.'

Jenny glanced over at Laura with a desperate expression. 'After all he's done, they're going to lock him away forever, aren't they?'

Laura looked at her with a kind expression. Jenny might have broken the law, but she was in a lot of emotional pain. 'We can't tell you if John will be convicted or how long he'll serve if he is.'

'What if they put him in prison in Ireland?' Jenny asked as the thought suddenly occurred to her. 'What will I do then?' Her face twisted in anguish. 'What the hell am I going to do without him?'

It was late afternoon, and the wind was whipping up an eerie melody as Laura and Gareth made their way out into the rear car park at Beaumaris Police Station. Laura was enjoying its coldness pressing against her face. She was bone-tired. The day had a luminous gauzy blandness, where everything had been rendered colourless by the opaqueness of the sky. She longed for the sun and long evenings. A couple of gannets flew low overhead before disappearing behind the building.

What a first week it had been. She thought about teasing Gareth about his use of *the Q-word* a few days earlier and her warning of what that would bring. But she and Gareth weren't in that place.

They stood in an uncomfortable silence as a white high-security prison transport vehicle – informally known as 'The Sweat Box' by prisoners – from HMP Rhoswen drew up at the rear staircase that led down from the custody suite and the holding cells. John Kelly was being transferred to the Welsh mainland and would be on remand under tight security until his trial.

DI Amis came out of the custody suite with John hand-cuffed to his wrist. A black BMW X5 approached at speed and stopped close by. A couple of Armed Response Officers – AROs – carrying Glock 9mm pistols and dressed in their black Nomex boots, gloves with Kevlar helmets over bala-clavas – moved purposefully in to protect Amis and the prison guards as they took John towards the door at the back of the large prison vehicle.

Laura could hear a rhythmic mechanical sound in the sky above. She glanced up to see a black-and-yellow police heli-copter hovering several hundred feet above them. John was an IRA hero. And with the coming trial, he was about to become world-famous as the IRA agent who tricked the British Army into allowing him into the SAS and to work undercover in Belfast. They didn't want an armed IRA unit arriving and trying to rescue him, so no one was taking any chances.

As John mounted the steel steps that led into the holding cell inside the vehicle, he glanced over at Laura and Gareth before disappearing inside. He had a curious look on his face. As if he knew something they didn't. Laura couldn't work it out.

Amis looked their way, too, and gave them a nod as he

went in behind John to make sure that he was secured properly. Laura thought it was decent of him, given they'd interviewed him under caution the day before.

Gareth and Laura watched as the prison vehicle pulled away, followed closely by the BMW X5, with four AROs inside. From above, the helicopter swooped away and then circled back.

'Guess we can go back inside,' Laura said as she turned.

Gareth put his hand gently on her arm. 'Listen, there must be a way back for us. Let me take you for a drink after work. It's been a hell of a week.'

Laura pulled her arm away. She couldn't help herself. She was still angry and hurt. 'What's the point?'

Gareth looked directly at her. 'Please. I know I messed things up. But I think what we have, or had, was special.'

Laura shook her head. 'But it wasn't *special* enough, was it?'

'Come on – ten minutes.'

'Gareth,' she sighed, 'I've said everything I wanted to say on the way to Liverpool yesterday. I've got nothing to add. You hurt me.'

'And I swear I'll never hurt you again,' Gareth pleaded.

'I don't trust that you won't. Maybe if we were younger, we could try to make it work. But I have two damaged kids. I don't have time for the kind of crap you've put me through. So, no. And if that means I have to find another DI job on Anglesey or even over on the mainland, then so be it.'

Gareth came out of his office and looked at his watch. It was six p.m. He glanced over at the scene boards with the photo of John Kelly at their centre. A clean-shaven, handsome soldier in the Irish Guards. He wondered how he'd got away without detection for so long. He assumed it would all come out at trial.

'Right, guys,' he announced loudly with a clap of his hands to get the CID team's attention. 'John Kelly is arriving at HMP Rhoswen as we speak.' He pointed over to the scene board. 'I know how much hard work you all put into this investigation and I want to thank you all. You've made me incredibly proud. And even though we ended up with a surprising outcome, we still got an important result. A dangerous IRA terrorist is now in prison, and that's down to you.' He looked at his watch again. 'So, I want you to pack up your stuff and get yourselves home right now.'

'Hang on, boss,' Declan said with a grin as he pointed over to the doors.

At that moment, Ben walked in with a crate of lager, followed by Andrea, who cracked open a bottle of Prosecco. There were shouts of 'Yay!' and 'Get in!'

Declan went over, grabbed a can of lager and tossed it over to Gareth. 'Here you go, boss. We need a bit of a celebration before we go home.'

Gareth caught Laura's eye and then looked away.

Declan sidled over to Gareth as he took a huge gulp of beer. 'Think I owe you an apology, boss.'

'Why's that?'

Declan gestured to Laura, who was laughing with Ben and Andrea.

'DI Hart. She's a bloody good copper. I shouldn't have doubted your judgement.'

'Don't worry about it. Cheers,' Gareth laughed as he tapped his can of lager against Declan's.

'You reckon she's got a fella?'

Gareth frowned. 'DI Hart?'

'Yeah. I mean, I heard about her husband. It sounds like she's been through a lot. But I just wondered.'

Gareth raised his eyebrow. 'I thought you were a happily married man, Declan?'

'I wouldn't go that far, boss,' Declan laughed. 'But yeah, I am married. I was thinking about you. Now you're divorced, eh?'

'Probably not a good idea.' Gareth spotted Laura grabbing her coat from her chair.

'Yeah, don't shit on your own doorstep, they say, don't they?' Declan chortled.

'Nicely put, Declan,' Gareth said with a wry smile and he went towards Laura to intercept her before she reached the doors to the CID office. 'You going already?' he asked.

'Yeah. After the last few days, I need to spend some time at home with the kids.'

'Of course.'

'I'll see you tomorrow, then.'

Gareth looked at her. 'Laura?'

'Yes?'

'For what it's worth, you're an incredible copper. And you're going to be a massive asset to the team here.'

'Thank you,' Laura said as she opened the door. 'Have a good evening, then.'

CHAPTER 57

Laura marched up the stairs at Llandudno General and looked at her watch: nine p.m. She'd spoken to Pete and the PPS officers and Louise was being transferred from the ICU over to the critical care unit at Glan Clwyd. It was a fifteen-mile journey east along the A55 coastal road.

Taking a deep breath, she strolled along the corridor towards the ICU, trying to process all that had happened in her first week back at work. It had been a rollercoaster of an investigation. She hoped that things might calm down a bit in Beaumaris CID. She was feeling guilty about the lack of time she'd spent with the kids.

The spectre of Gareth also loomed large in her mind. It was too much for her to deal with at the moment. He'd cheated on her and lied, and that was that. If she couldn't trust him, how was she going to be in any kind of relationship with him?

Pushing those thoughts to one side, Laura arrived at the ICU. She squirted some hand sanitiser on her palms and made her way into the main part of the ward. She spotted Pete standing talking seriously to a man and woman, who were both smartly dressed. *They must be the officers from the PPS,* she thought.

'Pete,' she said quietly as she approached.

He turned but had a dark expression.

'Everything all right?' she asked.

'She's gone,' Pete said.

For a second, she didn't quite know what he meant, but his expression said it all.

'Oh, God, no.'

Louise was dead.

'What happened?' A wave of sadness and frustration came over her.

'Brain haemorrhage. There was nothing anyone could do.'

CHAPTER 58

Midnight. The sea seemed to whisper on the sand, rather than crashing or whooshing against the rocks. Even the gulls were relaxed as they sat bobbing on the water's surface.

Laura loved this place and loved this feeling. All the stress, worry and anxiety was dissolving. It felt miraculous. Tonight, the sea appeared still as it murmured comfortingly to her. It was as if the sea itself knew just what she needed at that very moment. Sometimes it was a cold, sharp hit of a crashing wave. Tonight, it was a whispered welcome. The intangible embrace of an old friend. Being held gently in its silky darkness with no thought of future or past – just now, this very moment.

And then a shadowy movement about twenty yards away. An inaudible splash on the surface. And then a face.

Sam.

'Come to spoil my serenity?' she asked as she floated and bobbed towards him.

'The cold water is good for my circulation.'

Laura wasn't in the mood for jokes. She looked at him with a sad expression. 'I wish I didn't have to be out here alone. Don't get me wrong, I do love the solitude and stillness.

But I wish me and you could walk down to the beach with Elvis together. And swim together.'

'I know.' Sam sighed. 'But that can't happen.'

'It doesn't seem fair.'

A swell in the water lifted her and then dropped her.

'You know about Louise?' she asked.

Sam nodded sadly.

Laura shook her head. 'What a waste. She used to be so full of life.'

There were a few seconds of silence.

Sam gave her a meaningful look. 'Anyway, you have got someone you can come to the beach with. And swim with.'

Laura frowned and then smiled. 'Yeah, I'm talking about someone real. You know, with a pulse. That kind of thing.'

'I'll pretend you didn't say that.' Sam grinned. 'I'm not talking about me, you idiot.'

'Gareth?'

'Of course.' Sam rolled his eyes.

'You can't stand Gareth.' Laura frowned.

'I'm only joking when I call him names. He's all right. In fact, he's more than all right. He's a decent bloke.'

Laura looked at him across the water. His face was bathed in moonlight, his wet hair tousled and his eyes full of compassion.

Laura felt a lump in her throat. 'Why are you saying this?'

'If you'd died three years ago, would you want me to stay single, mourn you and be lonely for the rest of my life?' he asked.

'Yes, of course,' Laura joked. 'How could you ever get over me?'

Sam rolled his eyes. 'You know what I mean. He's a good man. And he's crazy about you.'

'And he slept with his ex-wife at the beginning of the week,' Laura said sardonically.

'I know.'

'How do you know that?'

'I think you're being a hypocrite, aren't you?'

Laura frowned. She didn't know what Sam was talking about. 'Why am I being a hypocrite, Sam?'

'When we got together, you were seeing some terribly pretentious bloke called James. He liked The Lemonheads and lit loads of candles the night Kurt Cobain died.'

'Oh yeah, don't remind me.' Laura hadn't thought of James in over twenty years. *What the hell was I thinking?*

'I'm pretty sure there were a couple of weeks where there was some kind of crossing over going on. Me and James?'

'Was there?' Laura knew exactly what Sam was talking about. 'That's different. We were in our twenties.'

'I'm just saying, we all make mistakes. And if you put yourself in Gareth's shoes, you might see how it might have happened. His ex-wife had done a real number on him.'

Laura narrowed her eyes. 'You know how weird it is, you trying to convince me to have a relationship with another man?'

'Yeah, well, this whole thing is pretty weird. But I want you to be happy. And it wouldn't be a bad thing if eventually there was a man around the house when Jake grows up.'

'Sam Hart, I never knew you possessed such selflessness and humility,' Laura said in a mocking tone – but she meant it. It took courage to say that having another male role model would be good for Jake.

Sam grinned. 'I also know that Gareth is a United fan. And if you ever hooked up with a Liverpool fan and brought him home, I'd be physically sick.'

Laura laughed and then splashed water at him. 'I knew there was a bloody ulterior motive.'

Sam moved closer to Laura in the water as they looked at each other. He put his arms around her.

'I just want you and the kids to be happy, that's all,' he whispered. 'And as hard as it is to think about, I believe this would make you all happy in the long run.'

Laura closed her eyes and held him tightly.

Gareth sat in his living room sipping a cold beer and listening to jazz. It was that kind of evening. Even though his mind had replayed the dramatic events of the last few days, his thoughts kept returning to Laura. He couldn't help but dwell on what might have been.

His eye was drawn to the photo of his brother, Rob, with his family. There hadn't been many times when Gareth had felt jealous, but tonight was one of them. How had Rob managed to get his life so incredibly right and Gareth had screwed his life up so monumentally? He knew that he was going down a dark alley of self-pity, but he didn't care.

He finished his beer and wondered if he should just get drunk. Or watch a film that might distract him from how he was feeling.

His phone buzzed. When he saw who it was, he nearly choked on his beer.

Taking a deep breath, he answered it. 'Hi, Laura.'

'Hi.' Her voice sounded uncertain. 'What are you doing?'

'I'm drinking green tea, doing some yogic meditation and feeling grateful for all that I have in life,' Gareth joked.

'Really?' Laura laughed.

'No. I'm drinking beer, listening to Miles Davis and feeling very sorry for myself.'

'Yeah, unfortunately, that does sound more likely.'

'Thanks.'

There was an awkward silence. *Why is she ringing me for a chat?* He could feel his pulse quicken.

'Erm, what are you up to?' he asked.

'Well, actually, I'm standing on your doorstep.'

Gareth resisted the urge to jump up and sprint to his front door. 'Okay . . . Do you want to come in?'

'I'm not sure.'

Gareth got up from the sofa and walked calmly down the hallway. 'It seems a bit weird if you don't come in. Even if it's only for five minutes, doesn't it?'

He opened the door and looked at her. She was standing with the phone to her ear.

Laura smiled at him and gestured to her phone. 'We should probably stop doing this.'

'Yeah.' Gareth nodded as he hung up and then looked at her. 'It's really nice to see you.'

Laura looked flustered. 'There are a few things I need to say to you.'

'Okay.'

'So . . . I want us to give this, us, a go.'

'Great, I—'

'I haven't finished talking yet.'

'Sorry.'

'But if you even look at another woman while you're with me, I'll cut your bollocks off.'

'Okay. Seems fair.'

'And I have no intention of sleeping with you tonight.'

'Okay.' Gareth had a bemused look on his face.

'But I would like to go away to Lake Vyrnwy with you in a few weeks' time.'

Gareth felt his whole being light up. 'Great. That would be really nice.' He looked at her, uncertain if she'd finished or if there was more.

Laura shrugged. 'I think that's it.'

'Do you want to come in?'

'No . . . I have to go.'

'Can I kiss you?'

'Yes.'

'That was probably the strangest conversation I've ever had in my life.'

Laura laughed. 'Me too. But I just had to get it all out.'

Gareth moved towards her, put his arms around her waist and leaned in and kissed her.

CHAPTER 59

Taking a swig of white wine, Laura refilled the glass and wandered into the living room. She knew she should be tired, but adrenaline was keeping her awake and alert. Making her way over to the sofa, she could see that the kids had left all the curtains and blinds open. She clicked on the TV and sat back to relax.

Suddenly, out of the corner of her eye, she saw something move in the garden. They had motion sensors on the security lights, so she didn't know why they hadn't been triggered. After the week she'd had, maybe she was just seeing things.

Maybe I should go and have a look . . .

Pushing herself up off the sofa, she saw Elvis trot into the room and immediately go over to the patio doors to look outside. He made a noise that sounded like the beginnings of a growl.

Okay, he never does that unless he's seen something, she thought, uneasy.

'What's wrong, Elvis? Who's out there?'

Taking a breath, she moved slowly towards the patio doors, when she was blinded by a sudden explosion of light from outside.

She squinted through the large glass doors, but she could see the garden was empty.

I'm just being paranoid.

Maybe the wind or a cat had triggered the security lights. Sitting in this house in the middle of nowhere had never bothered her before. Maybe she needed another glass of wine.

Elvis was still trotting up and down. He was clearly agitated.

Just to be on the safe side, Laura moved forwards towards the glass. She peered cautiously outside, but there was definitely nothing or nobody there.

Nope. I can't see anything.

The light dropped again as the motion sensor switched off. The garden was plunged into darkness.

But not a moment later, the garden was flooded with light again, and where previously was just an empty lawn, a shadowy figure stood.

Laura shrieked and jumped away from the window.

'Jesus Christ!'

The figure was backlit.

Laura couldn't see anything but the outline of a person standing there. Although she couldn't see their eyes, she could feel their stare boring into her. She took another step back from the door in panic.

Elvis barked loudly. She was about to turn and run, when the figure stepped into the light. It was Ian Butterfield.

Jesus Christ! What the hell is he doing here?

Louise moved forwards and looked at Butterfield through the glass. His face was gaunt, his eyes sunken. He looked desperate and broken as he pointed to indicate that he wanted to come in.

Laura reached for some scissors on a nearby table. Her pulse was rocketing as she grabbed Elvis' collar and then unlocked the patio doors.

Should I be scared here? Is he going to attack me?

They looked at each other.

'I'm sorry.' Butterfield looked lost and pitiful. 'I need to talk to you, Laura. I need to tell you everything that happened.'

Laura beckoned him in and closed the patio doors.

Acknowledgements

Thank you to everyone who has worked so hard to make this book happen. The incredible team at Avon who are an absolute dream to work with. Thorne Ryan and Helen Huthwaite for their patience, guidance and superb notes that brought a complicated book to life. We got there guys! The 'heaving lifting' was worth it.

The other lovely people at Avon – Becci Mansell, Ellie Pilcher, Elisha Lundin, Molly Walker-Sharp, Gabriella Drinkald and Maddie Dunne-Kirby. Cover designer, Claire Ward, whose work is such a joy. The publicity and sales team who work so incredibly hard.

To my superb agent, Millie Hoskins, at United Agents. Emma and Emma, my fantastic publicists at EDPR. Dave Gaughran and Nick Erick for their ongoing advice and working their magic behind the scenes.

Finally, my mum, Pam, and dad, Dave, for their overwhelming enthusiasm.

And, of course, my stronger, better half, Nicola, whose initial reaction and notes on my work I trust implicitly.

DCI Laura Hart returns for the third thrilling instalment
in Simon McCleave's Anglesey Series . . .

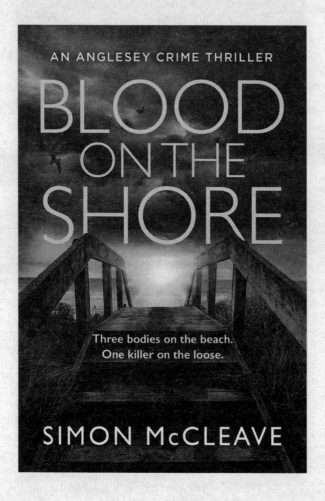

AN ANGLESEY CRIME THRILLER

BLOOD
ON THE
SHORE

Three bodies on the beach.
One killer on the loose.

SIMON McCLEAVE

Available to pre-order now

Your FREE book is waiting for you now!

Get your FREE copy of the prequel to
the DI Ruth Hunter Series NOW!

Visit:
http://www.simonmccleave.com/vip-email-club
and join Simon's VIP Email Club.

Will there be blood in the water?

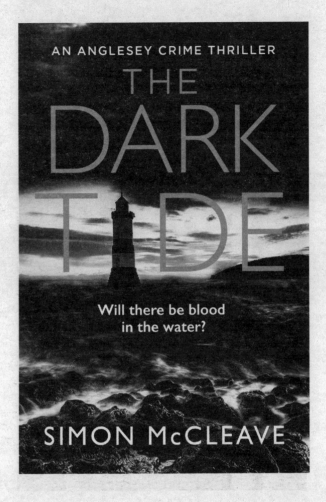

AN ANGLESEY CRIME THRILLER

THE DARK TIDE

Will there be blood
in the water?

SIMON McCLEAVE

The first book in Simon McCleave's gripping, atmospheric
crime thriller series.

Available in all good bookshops now.